P9-CME-133

SANDRA BROWN

CHARADE

WARNER
VISION
BOOKS

A Time Warner Company

WARNER BOOKS EDITION

Copyright © 1994 by Sandra Brown
All rights reserved.

Cover design and illustration by Andrew Newman

Warner Books, Inc.
1271 Avenue of the Americas
New York, NY 10020

Ⓦ A Time Warner Company

Printed in the United States of America

Originally published in hardcover by Warner Books
First Printed in Paperback: July, 1995

10 9 8 7 6 5 4 3 2 1

Acknowledgments

During the research and writing of this novel, I relied on the assistance of professionals, all of whom were gracious and giving despite their demanding schedules.

Many thanks go to Anne Wagner, Public Relations/Public Education Coordinator, Southwest Organ Bank; to Nancy Johnson, RN, Chief Transplant Coordinator, University of Texas Southwestern/St. Paul Medical Center; and to John Criswell, KDFW-TV, Dallas, Texas.

And a special thank you to Louann, whose candor is surpassed only by her courage.

—SANDRA BROWN

Chapter One

October 10, 1990

"*C*at, wake up! We have a heart!"

Cat Delaney slogged through the mire of drug-induced sleep toward the shore of consciousness. Opening her eyes, she attempted to focus on Dean. His image blurred at the edges, but his smile was wide, bright, and distinct.

"We have a heart for you," he repeated.

"For real?" she asked, her voice raspy, weakened. She'd entered the hospital with the understanding that she would leave either with a transplanted heart or in a hearse.

"The retrieval team is winging it here as we speak."

Dr. Dean Spicer turned away from her to address other hospital personnel who'd accompanied him into the ICU. She could hear his voice, but his words seemed meaningless.

Was she dreaming? No, Dean had clearly stated that a donor heart was on its way. A new heart—for her! A life!

Suddenly she experienced a greater burst of energy than she'd felt in months. She sat bolt upright in the hospital bed

1

and jabbered to the nurses and technicians who swarmed around her, brandishing needles and catheters with which to poke and probe her.

The medical violation of tissue and orifice had become such an everyday occurrence that she barely noticed it. Over the past few months, enough body fluids had been withdrawn from her to fill an Olympic-size swimming pool. She'd lost a significant amount of weight, and very little flesh remained on her petite skeleton.

"Dean? Where'd he go?"

"Here I am." Her cardiologist shouldered his way to her bedside and clasped her hand. "I told you we'd get you a heart in time. Didn't I?"

"Don't be smug. You doctors are all alike. Cocky asses."

"I resent that." Dr. Jeffries, the cardiac surgeon who would perform the transplant, ambled into the room as though he were taking a casual evening stroll—on water. He perfectly fit the stereotype to which Cat had referred. She acknowledged his talent, trusted his ability, but despised him personally.

"What are you doing *here*?" she asked. "Shouldn't you be in the OR sterilizing your instrument?"

"Is that a double entendre?"

"You're supposed to be the genius. You figure it out."

"As disagreeable as ever. Who do you think you are, a TV star?"

"Precisely."

Unflappable, the surgeon turned to the senior ICU nurse. "Does this patient have a fever?"

"No."

"Head cold? Virus? Infection of any kind?"

"What is this?" Cat demanded in annoyance. "Are you trying to back out of it? Want the night off, Doctor? Made other plans?"

"Just checking to make sure you're okay."

"I'm okay. Get the heart, cut me open, and make the switch. Anesthesia is optional."

He turned and sauntered out.

"Arrogant ass," she muttered.

"Better not call him names," Dean said, chuckling. "He'll come in handy later on tonight."

"How long do we have to wait?"

"A while."

She hounded him to be more specific, but that was all he would say. Encouraged to rest but charged by adrenaline, she remained wide awake, watching the clock as the hours slowly passed. She wasn't as nervous as she was excited.

News of the impending transplant made its way through the hospital grapevine. Organ transplants were fairly commonplace, but they still inspired awe. Especially heart transplants. During the night, well-wishers popped in to her room.

She was given a bath in iodine, which was sticky and nasty and turned her skin an obnoxious gold. She choked down her first dose of cyclosporine, the vital antirejection drug. The liquid had been mixed with chocolate milk in a vain attempt to cover its olive oil taste. She was still complaining about it when Dean rushed in with the news she'd been waiting to hear.

"They're en route to the hospital with your new heart. Ready?"

"Is the pope Catholic?"

He leaned down and kissed her forehead. "I'm going down now to scrub. I'll be there with Jeffries the whole time, watching over his shoulder." He paused. "I'll be with you every step of the way."

She grabbed his sleeve. "When I wake up, I want to know immediately if I've got a new heart."

"Of course."

She'd heard of other transplant patients who had been

informed that a suitable heart had been harvested. A man she knew had even been prepped for surgery and put under anesthesia. Upon the heart's arrival, Dr. Jeffries had inspected it and declined to transplant it, saying it wasn't good enough. The patient still hadn't recovered from the emotional setback, which was worsening his critical heart condition.

Now, with surprising strength, Cat clutched the sleeve of Dean's Armani jacket. "The second I come out of it, I want to know if I have a new heart. Okay?"

He covered her hand with his and nodded. "You have my word."

"Dr. Spicer. Please," a nurse beckoned.

"See you in the OR, darling."

After his departure, everything moved with remarkable swiftness. Cat gripped the side rails of the gurney as she was whisked along the corridors. When the gurney burst through the double doors, she wasn't prepared for the blinding glare of the operating theater, where the masked personnel moved about with speed and purpose, everyone intent on his or her duty.

Looking beyond the lights suspended over the operating table, Cat saw faces peering down through the glass that enclosed the observation gallery.

"I see I've drawn quite a crowd. Do those people up there have tickets and printed programs? Who *are* they all? Hey, somebody say something. Am I the only one here who speaks English? What's that you're doing over there?"

One of the figures wearing scrubs and a mask groaned. "Where's Dr. Ashford?"

"Coming," the anesthesiologist said as he breezed in.

"Thank God you're here. Knock her out so we can get some work done, will you?"

"She's a blabbermouth, a real pain in the butt."

Cat took no offense, knowing none was intended. The eyes

above the masks were smiling. The mood in the OR was upbeat; she preferred it that way.

"If you guys are always insulting the patients, it's no wonder you wear masks to conceal your identities. Cowards."

The anesthesiologist moved into place beside the table. "I understand that you're a little hyper and causing quite a ruckus, Miss Delaney."

"This is my big scene. I'll play it the way I want to."

"You're gonna be great."

"Have you seen my new heart?"

"I'm not in on all the good stuff. I just pass gas. Relax now." He swabbed the back of her hand in preparation for an IV needle. "You'll feel a little prick."

"I'm used to little pricks."

Everyone laughed.

Dr. Jeffries approached with Dean and Dr. Sholden, the cardiologist to whom Dean had referred her when he withdrew as her physician for personal reasons.

"How are we doing?" Dr. Jeffries asked.

"Your script needs work, Doctor," Cat said scornfully. " 'How are we doing?' should be my line."

"We've examined the heart," he replied calmly.

She caught her breath expectantly, then frowned up at him. "We use these pregnant pauses in the soaps all the time to build suspense. It's a cheap shot. Tell me about the heart."

"It's beautiful," Dr. Sholden said. "It looks terrific. Has your name on it."

From the corner of her eye, she noticed a group of OR technicians fussing over a cooler.

"When you wake up, it'll be beating inside your chest," Dean said.

"Ready?" Dr. Jeffries asked.

Was she ready?

Naturally she'd had some misgivings when the idea of

transplantation had first been broached. But she'd thought all her doubts had been allayed by now.

She'd gone into a slow decline shortly after Dean had first diagnosed her heart problem. Medication had been a temporary remedy for her profound fatigue and lack of energy, but, as he'd told her, ultimately there was no cure for her condition. Even then, she'd refused to accept the severity of her illness.

Only when she began to feel truly sick, when taking a shower became an ordeal and eating a plate of food was strenuous exercise, had she acknowledged that her heart condition might be terminal.

"I need a new heart."

Until she made that bold announcement to the television network executives, they had been unaware of her illness. The cast and crew of the daytime soap opera *Passages*, with whom she worked every day, had never seen the telltale pallor beneath her makeup.

They, along with the network hierarchy, went into a predictable state of denial. None wanted to believe that Cat Delaney, winner of three Emmy awards, their star, whose Laura Madison character was pivotal to the story line of *Passages*, was that sick. With their unstinting support, and using her acting skills and ebullient personality, she continued to work.

But it had finally reached a point where, no matter how determined she was, she could no longer keep pace with her demanding schedule, and so she had taken a leave of absence from the show.

As her health continued to deteriorate, she lost so much weight that her legion of fans wouldn't have recognized her. Dark circles ringed her eyes because she couldn't sleep, even though she was perpetually exhausted. Her fingers and lips turned blue.

The tabloids reported that she was afflicted with diseases

ranging from German measles to AIDS. Ordinarily that kind of cruel media exploitation would have angered and upset her, but she had lacked the energy to let it. Instead, she ignored it and concentrated on surviving.

Her condition became so perilous, her depression so abject, that one afternoon she said to Dean, "I'm so tired of being this weak and useless, I'd just as soon the credits roll."

Dean rarely honored her comments on death, even her joking ones, but on that particular day he sensed her need to speak her haunting thoughts aloud. "What's on your mind?"

"I have daily conversations with Death," she admitted softly. "I bargain with it. Every day at sunrise, I say, 'Let me have one more day. Please. Just one more.' I mark everything I do as possibly being for the last time. Is this the last time I'll see rain, eat pineapple, hear a Beatles song?"

She looked up at him. "I've made my peace with God. I'm not afraid of dying, but I'd rather it not be painful and frightening. When I do check out, what will it be like?"

He didn't glibly dismiss her concerns, but rather answered her honestly. "Your heart will simply stop beating, Cat."

"No fanfare? No drum roll?"

"Nothing. It won't be traumatic like a heart attack. There'll be no preliminary tingle in your arm. Your heart will simply—"

"Quit."

"Yes."

That conversation had taken place only a few days ago. Now, by a quirk of fate, her future had reversed direction and was moving toward life.

But it suddenly occurred to her that in order for her doctors to install her new heart, they had to cut out the old one. It was a chilling thought. While she deeply resented the malfunctioning organ that for the past two years had assumed control of her life, she also had an inexplicable fondness for it. True, she was eager to be rid of her sick heart, but she thought that everyone seemed obscenely cheerful about removing it.

Of course it was too late to start entertaining qualms. Besides, this surgery was relatively simple compared to other open-heart procedures. Clip. Remove. Replace. Suture.

During her wait for a donor, the transplant team had invited her questions. She'd engaged them in extensive discussions and had soaked up volumes of information gleaned on her own. Her support group, comprised of other heart patients awaiting transplant, had exposed and shared their fears during the meetings. Their exchanges were interesting and thought-provoking because organ transplant was a multifaceted issue riddled with controversy. Opinions varied according to the individual, and took into account 'emotions, spiritual convictions, moral issues, and legal implications.

During the months of waiting, Cat had sorted through all the ambiguities and was comfortable with her decision. She was well acquainted with the risks involved and was prepared for the horrors awaiting her in the recovery ICU. She accepted the possibility that her body might reject the heart.

But her only alternative to the transplant was certain death—and soon. Given that, there really wasn't any choice.

"I'm ready," she said confidently. "Oh wait, one more thing. While I'm under, if I begin composing odes to my personal vibrator, everything I say is a lie."

Their laughter was muffled by their masks.

Seconds later the fluid warmth of anesthesia began stealing through her, spreading a silky lassitude. She looked at Dean, smiled, and closed her eyes for what might be the last time.

And just before unconsciousness seized her, she had a final thought that flared once, brilliantly, like an exploding star an instant before disintegration.

Who was my donor?

Chapter Two

October 10, 1990

*H*ow can divorce be more sinful than this?'' he asked.

They were lying on the bed she normally shared with her husband, who was presently working his shift at the meat-packing plant. Because of a leak in the gas line, their office building had been evacuated for the remainder of the day. They were taking advantage of the unexpected holiday.

The small, cluttered bedroom was redolent with the steamy essence of sex. Sweat was drying on their skin, assisted by the ceiling fan that slowly circled overhead. The sheets were damp and tangled. The window shades were drawn against the afternoon sun. Scented candles burned on the nightstand, casting flickering light over the crucifix hanging against faded, floral wallpaper.

The somnolent atmosphere was deceiving. They were on a deadline; their time was limited, and they were frantic to wring from it every ounce of pleasure. Her two daughters would be returning home from school shortly. She hated to waste the precious moments they had remaining on this recurring and painful disagreement.

This wasn't the first time he'd implored her to divorce her husband and marry him. But she was Catholic. Divorce was not an option.

"I'm committing adultery, yes," she said softly. "But my sin affects only the two of us. We're the only ones who know about it. Besides my priest."

"You've confessed our affair to your priest?"

"Until my confessions became repetitious. I no longer go to confession. I'm too ashamed."

She sat up and moved to the edge of the bed, facing away from him. Her heavy dark hair clung damply to her neck. The cheval glass in the corner mirrored his view of her. Her unblemished back tapered at her waistline before gracefully flaring into her hips. She had twin dimples in the small of her back.

She was critical of her body, believing that her hips were too wide, her thighs too heavy. But he seemed to like the lushness of her form and the duskiness of her skin. It even tasted dusky, he'd told her once. Pillow talk whispered in the heat of passion meant nothing, of course. Nevertheless, she had cherished his praise.

He stretched out his hand and stroked her back. "Don't be ashamed of what we do. It destroys me when you say you're ashamed of our love."

The actual affair had begun four months ago. Prior to that they'd spent several agonizing months wrestling with their consciences. They worked on separate floors but had seen each other in the elevators of the office skyscraper. They had first met in the basement commissary when he accidentally backed into her, causing her to spill her coffee. They'd smiled at each other with chagrin while exchanging apologies and names.

Soon, they coordinated their lunch hours and coffee breaks. Meeting in the commissary became a habit, which then evolved into a necessity. Their well-being depended on seeing each other. Weekends seemed torturously long, eternities to be endured until Mondays, when they could meet once more. They both began working overtime so they could capture a few moments alone before departing for home.

One evening as they were leaving together, it began to rain. He offered to drive her home.

She shook her head. "I'll take the bus like always. But thank you anyway."

Gazing at each other with regret and longing, they said good night and parted. Clutching her handbag against her chest with one hand and holding an insufficient umbrella with the other, she dashed through the downpour to the corner bus stop.

She was still huddled there in her thin coat when his car pulled to a stop at the curb. He rolled down the passenger window. "Get in. Please."

"The bus will be here soon."

"You're getting soaked. Get in."

"It's only a few minutes late."

"Please."

He was pleading for more than the privilege of driving her home, and they both knew that. Unable to resist the temptation, she slipped inside when he pushed the car door open for her. Without another word, he drove to a remote spot in the municipal park a short distance from downtown.

No sooner had he cut the motor and turned to her than they began kissing hungrily. With the first touch of his lips, she mentally abandoned her husband, her children, and her religious convictions. She was governed by carnal demands, not the mores she had been espousing since she was old enough to discern right from wrong.

Impatiently they grappled with buttons and zippers and

hooks until they had loosened their damp clothes and were touching skin to skin. First his hands and then his mouth did things to her she found both thrilling and shocking. When he entered her, her conscience couldn't be heard above his ardent professions of love.

That initial passion hadn't abated. If anything it had escalated during their stolen hours together. Now, she turned her head and looked at him over her shoulder. Her full lips fashioned a shy smile.

"I'm not ashamed enough to end our affair. Even though I know it's a sin, I'd die if I thought I'd never make love to you again."

With a groan of renewed desire, he pulled her back against him. She twisted her body around until she lay on top of him, her open thighs straddling his hips.

He thrust himself deep inside her, then raised his head off the pillow to nuzzle her breasts. She pressed her large nipple against his lips. He caressed it with his tongue, then greedily drew it into his mouth.

This position was still a novel and exhilarating experience for her. She rode him hard until they enjoyed another explosive and simultaneous climax, which left them weak and panting for breath.

"Leave him," he rasped urgently. "Today. Now. Don't spend another night with him."

"I can't."

"You can. Thinking of you with him is driving me crazy. I love you. I *love* you."

"I love you, too," she said tearfully. "But I can't just walk away from my home. I can't desert my children."

"Your home is with me now. I don't expect you to desert your children. Bring them. I'll be their father."

"He's their father. They love him. He's my husband. In the eyes of God, I belong to him. I can't leave him."

"You don't love him."

"No," she admitted. "Not the way I love you. But he's a good man. He provides for me and the girls."

"That's not love. He's merely fulfilling his responsibilities."

"To him they're more or less the same." She rested her head against his shoulder, willing him to understand. "We grew up in the same neighborhood. We were sweethearts in high school. Our lives are entwined. He's a part of me, and I'm a part of him. If I left him, he'd never understand why. It would destroy him."

"It'll destroy me if you don't."

"That's not so," she said. "You're smarter than he is. More self-confident and strong. You'll survive no matter what. I'm not sure he would."

"He doesn't love you the way I do."

"He doesn't *make* love to me the way you do. He would never think of . . ." Embarrassed, she ducked her head.

Sexuality was still a secretive subject, closed to candid discussion. It had never been openly acknowledged, either in her family when she was a girl or in her marriage. It was done in the dark, a necessary evil tolerated and forgiven by God in order to perpetuate the human race.

"He's not sensitive to my desires," she said, blushing. "He'd be shocked to know I even have desires. You encourage me to touch you in ways I would never touch him because it would offend him. He'd think your sensuality is wimpy. He wasn't taught to be giving and tender in bed."

"Machismo," he said bitterly. "Do you want to settle for that the rest of your life?"

She looked at him with sorrow. "I love you more than my life, but he is my husband. We have children together. We have a heritage in common."

"We could have children."

She touched his cheek, feeling both affection and regret. Sometimes he was like a child, unreasonably demanding something he couldn't have.

"Marriage is a holy sacrament. Before God, I pledged my life to him until death—and only death—parts us." Tears formed in her eyes. "I've broken the vow of faithfulness for you. I won't break the others."

"Don't. Don't cry. The last thing I want to do is make you unhappy."

"Hold me." She snuggled down next to him.

He stroked her hair. "I know that being with me violates your religious convictions. But that gauges the depth of your love, doesn't it? Your sense of morality wouldn't allow you to sleep with me unless you loved me with all your heart."

"I do."

"I know." He wiped the tears from her cheeks. "Please don't cry, Judy. We'll work it out. We will. Just lie with me for the time we have left today."

They clung to each other, their misery over the situation as absolute as their joy in their love, their naked bodies joined seamlessly.

That's the way her husband found them a few minutes later.

She was the first to notice him standing in the doorway of the bedroom, quivering with righteous indignation. She sprang up and groped for the sheet to cover herself. She tried to speak his name, but her mouth was arid with fear and shame.

Muttering vicious deprecations, lavishing them with lewd epithets, he lurched across the room toward the bed, raised a baseball bat above his head, and swung it down in a deadly arc.

Later, even the paramedics, who were accustomed to seeing gory crime scenes, had difficulty keeping down their lunches. There was an unspeakable mess splattered on the floral wallpaper behind the bed.

Meaning no disrespect to the blood-spattered crucifix on the wall, one whispered, "Jesus Christ."

His partner knelt down. "I'll be damned, I feel a pulse!"

The other gazed doubtfully at the lumpy matter oozing from the split cranium. "You think there's a chance?"

"No, but let's haul anyway. We might have an organ donor here."

Chapter Three

October 10, 1990

*I*s there something wrong with the pancakes?''

He raised his head and gave her a blank look. ''What?''

''The batter mix promises lighter-than-air pancakes every time. I must've done something wrong.''

He'd been toying with his breakfast for five minutes without taking a bite. He poked his fork into the syrupy mush on his plate and smiled apologetically. ''There's nothing wrong with your cooking.''

He was being kind. Amanda was a terrible cook. ''How's my coffee?''

''Great. I'll take another cup, please.''

She glanced at the kitchen clock. ''Do you have time?''

''I'll make time.''

He rarely allowed himself the luxury of being late for work. Whatever had been preoccupying him for the last several days must be vitally important, she thought.

Awkwardly, she rose and moved to the Mr. Coffee on the

counter. Bringing the carafe with her, she returned to the table and refilled his cup.

"We need to talk."

"Conversation will be a welcome change," she said, resettling into her chair. "You've been in another world."

"I know. I'm sorry." A frown formed between his brows as he stared at the steaming mug of coffee, which she knew he really didn't want. He'd been stalling.

"You're scaring me," she said gently. "Whatever it is that's troubling you, why don't you just tell me and get it over with? What is it?" she probed. "Another woman?"

He shot her a retiring glance, clearly conveying that she knew better than even to suggest such a thing.

"That's it," she said, slapping the tabletop. "You're disgusted with me because I look like Dumbo's mother. My water-retentive ankles are a turn-off, right? You miss the small, pert tits you used to tease me about. My inny is nothing but a fond memory, and you find my outy repugnant. Pregnancy has robbed me of all sex appeal, so you've got the hots for a sweet, young, slim babe and dread telling me about her. Am I warm?"

"You're crazy." He reached across the small round table and pulled her to her feet. When she was standing before him, he splayed his hands over her distended abdomen. "I love your belly button, inny or outy."

He kissed it through her loose cotton nightgown. Some of the coarser whiskers of his mustache penetrated the sheer fabric and tickled her skin. "I love the baby. I love you. There's no other woman in my life and never could be."

"Bull."

"Fact."

"Michelle Pfeiffer?"

He grinned at her while pretending to ponder it. "Gee, that's a tough one. How're her pancakes?"

"Would it matter?"

Laughing, he pulled her down onto his lap and wrapped his arms around her.

"Careful," she warned. "I'll crush your privates."

"I'll take my chances."

They kissed deeply. When he finally released her mouth, she gazed into his worried face. Despite the early hour and his recent shower and shave, he looked haggard, as if he'd already put in a full day.

"If it's not my cooking, not another woman, and you're not disgusted by my bloated figure, what is it?"

"I hate like hell that you had to put your career on hold."

Fearing that it would be something much more serious, she felt a deep sense of relief. "Is that what's been eating you?"

"It's unfair," he said stubbornly.

"To whom?"

"To you, of course."

Amanda peered at him suspiciously. "Or were you planning to take early retirement, become a couch potato, and let me support you?"

"Not a bad idea," he said with a half-smile. "But honestly, I'm thinking only of you. Because biology strongly favors the male—"

"Damn right," she grumbled.

"You're having to make all the sacrifices."

"How many times have I told you that I'm doing exactly what I want to do? I'm having a baby, *our* baby. That makes me very happy."

He'd greeted the news of her pregnancy with mixed emotions. First, he'd been shocked. She'd gone off the pill without discussing it with him. But once the shock had worn off and he'd become accustomed to the idea of parenthood, he liked it.

After the first trimester, she had alerted the partners in the law firm of which she was an associate that she would be taking a leave of absence to stay at home with her child during the critical bonding months. At the time, he hadn't questioned her decision. Now it surprised her that he'd been harboring misgivings.

"You've been away from the office only two weeks and already you're antsy," he said. "I recognize the signs. I can tell when you're restless."

With a gentle touch she swept errant strands of hair off his forehead. "Well, it's only because I've run out of things to do around here. I've washed the baseboards, alphabetized the canned goods, sorted both our sock drawers. I've completed my list of prebaby projects. But once the baby arrives, I'll have more to do than I can handle."

His remorseful expression didn't change. "While you're playing Happy Homemaker, the other associates are getting the jump on you."

"So what if they do?" she asked, laughing. "Having our baby is the most important thing I've ever done or ever will do. I believe that with all my heart."

She took his hand and laid it on her belly. The baby was moving. "Feel that? How can a lawsuit possibly be more awe-inspiring than that? I made a decision, and I'm at peace with it. I want you to be peaceful, too."

"That may be asking too much."

Silently, she agreed. He would never be totally at peace. But he did find surcease in his love for her and in knowing that his child was soon to be born. He rubbed the spot where the baby had just landed a healthy kick.

"I thought the masculine ideal was to keep the little woman at home, barefoot and pregnant," she teased. "What's wrong with you?"

"I just don't want the day to come when you regret putting your career on hold."

She reassured him with a smile. "That'll never happen."

"So why do I feel like there's an ax hanging over my head?"

"Because you always look at the glass like it's half-empty."

"And you see it half-full."

"I see it full to the point of brimming over." She made an elaborate gesture with her hands, which made him smile, tilting his mustache in the way she loved.

"Yeah, yeah, I'm the eternal pessimist."

"So you admit it?"

"No. It's just that we've covered this ground before."

"Ad nauseam," she said.

They smiled at each other, and he drew her close again. "You've already sacrificed so much for me. I don't deserve you."

"Keep that in mind if Michelle Pfeiffer ever crooks her finger at you."

She settled into the crook of his arm as he leaned down and kissed her with increasing passion. His hand waded through the fabric of her nightgown and found her breasts. They were taut and heavy, ready to lactate. He fondled her, gently pinching her nipples.

Then, pushing down her nightgown, he caressed her breasts with his lips and tongue. When he nuzzled their stiff centers with his mustache, she moaned and said, "You're not playing fair."

"How long do we have to wait?"

"Minimum six weeks after the birth."

He groaned.

"We'd better not start something we can't stop."

"Too late," he said, wincing.

Laughing, she readjusted her nightgown and slid off his lap. "You'd better get going."

"Yeah, I'd better." He stood, pulled on his jacket, and moved toward the door. "Are you feeling okay?"

She cradled her large belly between her arms. "We're fine."

"You didn't sleep well."

"You try sleeping while someone plays soccer with all your internal organs."

At the door they kissed goodbye. "What would you like for dinner tonight?"

"I'll take you out," he offered.

"Chinese?"

"You bet."

Most mornings, she waved him off at the door. Today, however, she walked with him arm in arm to the car. When it came time to release him, she felt unaccountably reluctant to let him go. It was as though his pessimism were contagious. His sense of foreboding must have rubbed off on her, because she had an urge to cling to him and ask him to call in sick and stay home with her that day.

To cover what was probably nothing more than a temporary, pregnancy-related emotional imbalance, she teased him. "Don't think I'm going to martyr myself to motherhood. Once the little one gets here, you're going to change your share of dirty diapers."

"I look forward to it," he said, grinning. Then he sobered, placed his hands on her shoulders, and drew her close. "You make it so easy for me to love you. Will you ever know how much?"

She tilted her head and smiled up at him. "I know." The sunlight was blinding. Maybe that was why tears suddenly formed in her eyes. "I love you, too."

Before kissing her, he held her face cupped between his hands and gazed into it for a long time. His voice was gruff with emotion when he said, "I'll try and be home early."

As he got behind the steering wheel, he added, "If you need me, call."

"I will." When he reached the corner, she raised her hand and waved.

Her lower back began to ache while she was washing the breakfast dishes. She rested before making the bed, but the dull ache persisted.

By noon, she was experiencing abdominal twinges that couldn't be ignored. She thought then of calling him, but held off. Contractions could occur weeks before actual labor began. The baby wasn't due for another fourteen days. This could be a false alarm. His work was demanding and difficult, and she didn't want to distract him unless it was absolutely necessary.

Shortly after four o'clock her water broke and labor began in earnest. She phoned her obstetrician. He assured her that there was no need to rush, that first children sometimes took hours to be born, but advised her to check in at the hospital.

She could no longer delay alerting him. She called his office but was told he was currently unavailable. That was okay. There were still things she needed to do before leaving for the hospital.

She took a shower, shaved her legs, and shampooed her hair, not knowing when she'd have another opportunity. Her suitcase was already packed with nightgowns, a new robe and slippers, and a unisex sacque in which to dress the baby for its homecoming. She added her toiletries and last-minute items, then latched the suitcase and placed it near the front door.

The pains began coming harder and closer together. She called again and asked for him. "He's out," she was told. "But I can track him down for you. Is this an emergency?"

Was it an emergency? Not really. Women had babies in every conceivable circumstance. Surely she was capable of getting herself to the hospital. Besides, it would be out of his way to drive home and then backtrack to the hospital.

She desperately wanted to speak with him. Hearing his voice would bolster her. Instead, she had to settle for leaving word that he should meet her at the hospital as soon as possible.

She realized that there was no sense in being noble and driving herself, but no friends or family were available. She called 911. "I'm in labor and need a ride to the hospital."

The ambulance arrived within minutes. The paramedic checked her over. "Tricky blood pressure," he said as he removed the cuff from her upper arm. "How long've you been in labor?"

"A few hours."

The pains were severe now. The breathing and concentration exercises learned in the childbirth classes they'd attended were less effective when done alone. She tried them, but they did nothing to lessen her pain.

"How much farther?" she asked, gasping.

"Not far. Hang on. You're doing fine."

But she wasn't. She knew that when she saw her doctor's frown after his preliminary pelvic examination. "The baby is in a breech position."

"Oh God," she whimpered.

"Now don't get excited. Happens all the time. We'll try to turn it. If that doesn't work, we'll do a c-section."

"I called the number you gave me," the obstetric nurse told her, sensing her panic. "He's on his way."

"Thank God." Amanda sighed, relaxing somewhat. He would be here soon. "Thank God."

"He's your coach?"

"He's my everything."

The nurse squeezed her hand and talked her through the next dark tunnel of pain while the doctor tried to turn the baby into the correct position. Its heartbeat was being monitored continuously. The nurse took her blood pressure at increasingly short intervals.

Finally the doctor said, "Prepare her for a c-section."

The next several minutes passed in a blurred kaleidoscope of light and sound and motion. She was rushed into the delivery room.

Where was he? She called out for him in a plaintive, hushed voice, then ground her teeth in an effort to ward off the pain that knifed through her midsection.

Then she overheard an exchange between two of the obstetric nurses. "There's been a terrible pileup on the Loop."

"I'll say. I just came through the ER on my way up. It's a zoo down there. There've been a few fatalities, mostly head injuries. So several organ and tissue retrieval teams are standing by to talk to next of kin as soon as they arrive."

Amanda felt a needle prick in the back of her hand. Her belly was being swabbed with cold liquid. They were draping her legs with sterile blue sheets.

A pileup on the Loop?

He'd be coming by way of the Loop.

He'd be in a hurry to reach her before the baby was born.

Driving too fast.

Taking chances he wouldn't ordinarily take.

"No!" She groaned.

"Hold on. In just a few minutes you'll be holding your baby." It was a kindly voice. Not his, though. Not the one she yearned to hear.

And suddenly she knew that she wouldn't be hearing his voice anymore. In an instant of cruelly sharp ESP, she knew, inexplicably but unarguably, that she would never see him again.

That morning when her eyes had stung with unshed tears, she'd had a premonition that their goodbye kiss was to be their last. Somehow she'd known she would never touch him again.

That's why she had been so reluctant to let him go. She recalled how intently he'd looked at her, as though memorizing the nuances of her face. Had he also sensed that it was their final goodbye?

"No," she sobbed, "no." But their fate was sealed, and her realization of that was profound and unequivocal. "I love you. I love you."

Her hoarse cry echoed off the tile walls of the delivery room. But he wasn't there to hear. He was gone.

Forever.

Chapter Four

October 10, 1990

"Cyc is one ugly sumbitch." Petey pared a sliver of oily dirt from beneath his fingernail, then wiped the blade of his knife on his jeans. "And he's meaner than he is ugly. If I was you, I'd give her back to him. That'd make life a whole lot more comfortable for you, Sparky."

"Well, you're not me." He hacked and spat a glob of phlegm near his friend's scuffed black boot. "And I won't be giving Cyclops anything but grief if he comes sniffing around her again."

"Kismet was his old lady first, remember. Long before you came into the picture. He ain't likely to forget that."

"He treated her like shit."

Petey shrugged philosophically.

"If he as much as lays a hand on her . . . if he as much as looks like he's thinking about laying a hand on her, I'll nail his balls to a stump."

"You're crazy, man," Petey exclaimed. "A good piece

of ass is a right fine thing, but it's fairly easy to come by, you know. It sure as hell ain't worth dying for." He shook the tip of his knife like a remonstrating finger. "Watch your back. Cyc's used to having his way. That's how he got to be leader."

Sparky muttered an expletive. "Leader my ass. He's a goddamn bully."

"Same as."

"Well, I'm not scared of him. I won't take any of his shit, and from now on neither will she."

He looked toward the group of women who had mellowed out on a joint they'd passed around as they lounged on the rickety porch of the roadhouse. The tavern was located in the foothills above town on a state highway that was rarely traveled now that there was an interstate nearby.

It was an out-of-the-way place. In bygone days it would have drawn bootleggers, whores, gamblers, and gangsters on the lam. Now it attracted bikers, petty criminals, and others who lived on the fringes of society. A brawl broke out at least once nightly, but even disputes that drew blood were settled without the interference of police.

Among the women clustered on the porch, Kismet stood out like a jewel among ashes. Her hair was dark, dense, and curly. She had sultry dark eyes and a lush figure, which she proudly displayed in skin-tight jeans. Her waist was cinched by a wide black leather belt with silver studs. Tonight she had on a tank top with a scooped neckline so low it revealed the crescent moon tatoo above her heart. He was pleased to notice that around her biceps she wore the brass bracelet he'd brought her from Mexico a few weeks ago. Several glittering loops and charms dangled from her ears.

She felt his glance and met it with a challenging toss of her head. Her lips parted enticingly. She laughed at something one of her friends said, but her dark eyes remained steadily on him.

"You're pussy-whipped, all right," Petey said with resignation.

He resented Petey's remarked but let it pass. This mental zero wasn't worth the energy it took to argue with him. Besides, Sparky wasn't certain he could put into words what he felt for Kismet, but it was beyond anything he'd felt for any other woman.

He was reticent about his past and reluctant to divulge his real name. The other bikers in the gang would be surprised to know that he'd earned a degree in literature from an Ivy League college. Among this crowd, intelligence and knowledge gleaned from books tended to be scorned. The less they knew about him, the better.

Evidently Kismet was equally as disinclined to talk about her life before linking up with Cyclops, because she'd never broached the subject of her past. He'd never pried.

Like kindred spirits, they had recognized in each other a common restlessness, a wanderlust, which was more an escape than a pursuit. Each was running away from a situation no longer tolerable.

Perhaps without knowing it they'd been searching for each other. Perhaps their search was over. He rather liked that metaphysical scenario and entertained it in his daydreams.

The first time he'd seen her, she was sporting a swollen, discolored eye and a busted lip. "What the fuck are you lookin' at?" she asked him belligerently when she noticed his stare.

"Just wondering who worked you over."

"What's it to you?"

"Thought maybe you'd like me to stamp the shit out of him for you."

She looked him over and snorted contemptuously. "You?"

"I'm tougher than I look."

"And I'm the Queen of fuckin' Sheba. Anyway, I can take care of myself."

But it appeared that she couldn't. A few days later, she bore fresh bruises on her face and upper body. By then he'd learned that she belonged to Cyclops, so called because he had a glass eye.

The handicap didn't lessen his sinister demeanor. His good eye was as cold and lifeless as the one made of glass. When he fixed his ominous, solitary stare on someone who'd fallen out of favor, it more than compensated for the poor prosthesis, which was slightly askew.

Behind his back everybody referred to Cyclops as "the breed." Along with the Anglo blood that flowed in his veins he had either Mexican or Indian, no one was sure. Probably Cyc himself didn't know his origins. It was doubtful that he cared.

He was swarthy and lean and as tough as whipcord. A knife was his weapon of choice. If it hadn't been for Kismet, Sparky would have avoided tangling with him.

Unfortunately, fate had intervened. He'd been instantly attracted to Kismet's voluptuous body, her sloe eyes, her untamed hair. On a deeper level, he'd responded to the fear and vulnerability he saw lurking behind her defiant eyes and hostile expression. Miraculously, she'd been likewise drawn to him.

He had never made an overt move, never vocalized an invitation for her to ride with him. Nevertheless, she must have read the silent signals. One morning as they were pairing off and mounting their bikes, she climbed on behind him and placed her bare, sleek arms tightly around his waist.

An expectant hush fell over the gang as Cyc sauntered toward his bike. He glanced around, obviously looking for her. When he spotted her seated behind Sparky, Cyc's good eye narrowed menacingly. He peeled back his thin lips in a feral snarl. Then he tromped on the petal of his bike and roared off.

That night Kismet joined him. He had planned on treating

her gently because of the recent beatings she'd taken from Cyclops. Surprisingly, she'd been the aggressor, attacking him with her nails and teeth and seemingly insatiable sexual appetite, which he was more than capable of satisfying.

They'd been lovers ever since; they were now regarded as a pair. But those who'd been with the gang longer than he, those who knew Cyc well and had witnessed the vengeance he'd taken on real or imagined slights, feared that their ring leader's temper was merely simmering and might suddenly reach the boiling point.

No one took something belonging to Cyc and got away with it.

Petey's words of caution were unnecessary. Sparky was already wary of Cyc, whose indifference to Kismet's jilting was probably a pose, an attempt to save face with other members of the gang. He was distrustful of Cyc's nonchalance and remained constantly on alert for a surprise attack.

That's why the hairs on the back of his neck rose when Cyc stumbled through the doors of the bar onto the porch. He placed one hand on the door jamb to regain his balance while raising a bottle of vodka to his mouth with the other. Even from a distance, peering through the tricky shadows of twilight, he saw the brute's good eye single out Kismet.

Cyc staggered toward her and reached out to stroke her neck. She swatted his hand away. Bending from his narrow waist, he leaned down and said something to her. Her lewd comeback made the other women laugh.

Cyc wasn't amused. He dropped the bottle of vodka and whipped a knife from the leather sheath at the small of his back. The other women scattered. Kismet stood her ground even when he tauntingly waved the tip of the blade directly in front of her face. She didn't flinch, not until he made a quick, jabbing motion with it. He laughed at her spontaneous recoil.

Heedless of the warnings being whispered to him by Petey and others loitering about, Sparky stormed toward the porch. Cyc sensed his approach, whirled around, and assumed a crouching, attack pose. He tossed the knife from hand to hand and goaded him.

"Come and get it."

Sparky deftly parried several vicious swipes of the knife blade, any of which could have sliced him in half. Cyc was physically superior. Relying strictly on his sobriety, speed, and dexterity, Sparky carefully timed his counterattack.

He waited until the moment was right, then kicked Cyc in the wrist. His boot solidly connected with bone. The knife sailed from Cyc's hand as he howled in pain. Then Sparky's well-placed fist against Cyc's chin sent him reeling backward. He landed hard against the wall and sank to the porch in an ignominious, drunken heap.

Sparky retrieved Cyc's knife from the dusty ground and threw it as far as he could. Everyone watched, transfixed, as it turned end over end, the honed steel blade glinting in the light from the roadhouse's neon sign, until it landed in a patch of shrubs.

His breathing was labored, but, with quiet dignity, he held out his hand to Kismet. She took it without hesitation. Together they moved away and climbed onto his bike. He didn't look back. She did. Cyc was coming around, shaking his head groggily. She gave him the finger before the bike shot off into the gathering darkness.

The wind shrieked in their ears, making conversation impossible, so they communicated by other means. She clasped his hips tightly between her thighs and rubbed her breasts against his back while fondling his crotch with eager hands. Her teeth sank into the meaty part of his shoulder. He grunted in pleasure, pain, and anticipation.

She was his now. No question. If she'd had any feelings left for the vanquished Cyclops, she would have chosen to stay behind. Instead, she was his prize. As the victor, he'd earned the right to claim her. As soon as they had put a few more miles between them and Cyc—

"Shit. He's coming after us, Sparky."

A split second before she spoke, he had noticed the headlight piercing the darkness behind them, glowing like the single eye of a monster, a simile he thought particularly appropriate but disturbing.

The headlight grew larger in his rearview mirror as Cyc gained on them at an alarming speed. Already taking the steep curves at a dangerous pace, Sparky accelerated to maintain a relatively safe distance ahead.

Knowing that Cyc was maddened by vodka and fury, he reconciled himself to the death-defying chase down the hairpin curves into town, where, he hoped, he could lose him. It was an unrelenting challenge to keep his bike under control.

He shouted for Kismet to hang on tightly and took a curve at a terrifying angle, laying the bike nearly on its side. Once they'd straightened out, he glanced in his rearview mirror and saw that the curve hadn't slowed Cyc down.

"Hurry!" she shouted. "He's getting closer. If he catches us, he'll kill us."

He pushed the bike to go even faster. The landscape was a blur. He dared not think about oncoming traffic. There'd been none so far, but—

"Look out!"

Cyc had pulled almost even with them. Sparky whipped his bike into the opposing lane ahead of Cyc so that they could maintain their lead. If he let Cyc get even with them or ahead of them, they were as good as dead.

The road wasn't as steep now, but it still ribboned its way around the foothills. Not much farther to go. They'd lose the maniacal bastard once they reached town.

He was mentally laying out his strategy when he took

another curve. When they came out of it, it was like being hurled into another landscape. Suddenly the foothills were gone. Open road stretched out before them like a silver ribbon pulled taut, leading straight to the center of town. If fate had favored them, it would have been a welcome sight.

Instead, Kismet screamed. He cursed. They were barreling headlong into an intersection. A cattle truck pulled directly into their path. They were going too fast to turn. Cyc was riding their exhaust pipe. The cattle truck lacked the speed to clear the intersection before they reached it.

There was no time to think.

A half-hour later, a fresh-faced resident raced down the hospital corridor to the emergency room waiting area, where a motley group of bikers awaited word on the condition of their friends. Even the roughest among them blanched when they saw the amount of blood staining the doctor's scrubs.

Breathlessly, he said, "I'm sorry. We did everything we could. Now we need to speak with next of kin—about organ donation. And quick."

Chapter Five

May 1991

*H*ey, Pierce. This is a public building. As such, it deserves some respect. Get your goddamn foot off the wall."

That voice could have awakened the dead. It certainly snapped Alex Pierce to attention. His gaunt face broke into a smile as the bailiff approached him. Contrite and obedient, he slid the sole of his cowboy boot off the wall.

"Hey, Linda."

"That's all you've got to say? 'Hey, Linda.' After all we've meant to each other?" She planted her meaty fists on her wide hips and glared at him, then dropped the pose and walloped him affectionately on the shoulder. "How's it going, handsome?"

"Can't complain. How're things with you?"

"Same as always." She frowned toward the crowded jury room where hundreds of prospective jurors hoped desperately to be excused from fulfilling their civic obligation.

"Nothing 'round here changes except the faces. Always the same lame excuses, the bitching and moaning and bellyaching about being called to jury duty."

Her gaze swung back to him. "Where've you been keeping yourself these days? Heard you'd left Houston."

Before the preceding Fourth of July, he'd frequently been in the Harris County courthouse to testify as a witness in court trials involving criminals he'd helped to apprehend.

"I still get my mail here," he replied indifferently. "Been traveling, mostly. Went to Mexico and did some fishing."

"Catch anything?"

"Nothing to tell about."

"Not the clap, I hope."

He smiled wryly. "These days you'd better hope the clap is all you catch."

"Ain't it the truth?" The husky bailiff sadly shook her helmet of burgundy hair. "I read in yesterday's newspaper that my deodorant's poking holes in the ozone. My tampons can give me toxic shock. Everything I eat is either clogging my arteries or giving me colon cancer. Now they've even taken the fun out of screwing around."

Alex laughed, taking no offense at her vulgarity. They'd known each other since he was a rookie cop on the Houston police force, riding shotgun in a squad car. Linda was a courthouse institution, known to everyone. She could be counted on to know the latest gossip and to tell the dirtiest joke circulating at any given time. Her profane gruffness was a cover for a tender spot that she revealed only to a privileged few. Alex was among them.

She gazed at him meaningfully. "So, how are you really, sweetheart?"

"Really, I'm fine."

"Miss the job?"

"Hell no."

"I know you don't miss the politics and the bullshit. What about the action?"

"These days I let my characters dodge bullets."

"Characters?"

"Yeah," he said with embarrassment. "I've been doing some writing."

"No shit?" She seemed impressed. "Going to write a tell-all book about the inner workings of a big city police department?"

"Fiction, actually. But based on my experiences."

"Having any luck?"

"Publishing you mean?" He shook his head. "That's a long way off. If ever."

"You'll make it."

"I don't know. My career track record's not so good."

"I have every confidence in you." Then she asked, "You seeing anybody?"

"You mean a woman?"

"Unless you've switched gears," she said dryly. "Of course a woman."

"No, I haven't switched gears, and no, I'm not seeing anybody. Nobody special."

She gave him a critical once-over. "Maybe you should. Your wardrobe leaves a lot to be desired. It could stand a woman's touch."

"What's wrong with my clothes?" He glanced down and could find no fault with the manner in which he was dressed.

"To begin with, that shirt hasn't seen the hot side of an iron."

"It's clean. So are my jeans."

"Looks to me like when you left the force, you got lazy and sloppy."

"That's what comes with being my own boss. I dress for comfort, and if I don't feel like shaving, I don't."

"You're scrawny as a scarecrow," she observed.

"I'm trim."

Skeptical, she raised her eyebrows.

"Okay. One of those Mexican bugs got hold of me while I was down there. Puked till there was no tomorrow. Haven't regained my weight yet."

Her baleful stare said she wasn't buying it.

"Look, I'm fine," he insisted. "Sometimes I forget to eat, that's all. I start writing at dusk, and it's dawn before I realize I didn't have supper. Opting for sleep over food is a hazard of my new profession."

"So's alcoholism, I hear."

Alex quickly averted his head and said testily, "I've got it under control."

"That's not what I hear. Maybe you ought to back off some."

"Yes, Mother."

"Look, asshole, I think of myself as your friend. And you ain't got all that many to brag about." She sounded both annoyed and concerned. "Honey, I hear you're having blackouts."

The goddamn courthouse grapevine. He wasn't even one of the players anymore, yet his name still caused juicy gossip. "Not in a while," he lied.

"I only mentioned your love affair with Johnny Walker because I'm worried about you."

"Then you're the only one around here who is." Hearing what sounded like self-pity in his voice, he let down his guard a notch and softened his expression. "I appreciate your concern, Linda. I know I went a little crazy after all that shit came down, but I'm okay now. Honest. Squelch any rumors you hear to the contrary."

The bailiff regarded him skeptically but let the subject drop. "So what brings you here today?"

"Just trying to scare up an idea for a book. The upcoming Reyes trial might have possibilities."

The bailiff's eyes narrowed with suspicion. "Any particular reason why you picked the Reyes trial when you've got all these others to choose from?"

Alex had been closely following the intriguing case for several months. "It's got all the ingredients for a titillating novel," he said. "Illicit sex. Religious overtones. Lovers caught in the act by an enraged husband. A baseball bat for a weapon—much more dramatic than a bullet from a Saturday night special. Blood and brains on the wallpaper. A body on its way to the morgue."

"A body not quite dead."

"Brain dead," he argued.

"That's a medical call, not a legal one," she reminded him.

"Reyes's lawyer contends that he didn't actually kill the victim because the heart was being kept alive for harvesting."

"Harvesting," Linda said scornfully. "Leave it to the doctors to make it sound more like a goddamn cotton crop than a human heart." Alex nodded. "Anyway, a whole legal can of worms has been opened up. If the stiff wasn't really a stiff when they harvested the heart, is Reyes really guilty of murder?"

"Fortunately you or I don't have to decide," Alex said. "It'll be up to the jury."

"If you were on the jury, which way would you go?"

"I don't know because I haven't heard all the evidence yet. But I intend to. Do you know which courtroom has been assigned?"

"Yeah, I know." She grinned, revealing extensive gold bridgework. "What's it worth to you?"

Any courthouse employee could have given him the number of the courtroom, but he played her game. "A few beers at quitting time?"

She smiled. "I was thinking more along the lines of dinner at my place. And then . . . Who knows what?"

"Yeah?"

"Steak, potatoes, and sex. Not necessarily in that order. Admit it, Alex my boy. That's the best offer you've had today."

He laughed, not taking her invitation seriously and knowing that she hadn't intended him to. "Sorry, Linda. Can't tonight. Previous plans."

"I'm no beauty queen, but don't let my looks deceive you. I know my way around the male anatomy. I could bring tears of gratitude to your eyes. Swear. You don't know what you're missing."

"I'm certain that's true," he said solemnly. "You've got enormous sex appeal, Linda. I've always thought so."

Her smile widened. "That's pure bullshit, but you were always good at slinging it. Sometimes you even make me believe it. That's why I think you'll succeed as a writer. You've got a real knack for making people believe anything you tell them."

She nudged his arm. "Come on, handsome. I'll escort you to the courtroom. They'll start jury selection soon. Try not to make a nuisance of yourself, okay? If you get drunk and disorderly and they kick you out, I won't take responsibility for you."

"I promise to be on my best behavior." He drew an imaginary *X* over his heart.

The bailiff snorted. "Just like I said, pure bullshit."

The murder trial of Paul Reyes had generated much public awareness and curiosity. Alex had to arrive at court earlier each day to get a seat. Reyes's family and friends took up much of the available seating.

The prosecutor heavily relied on the testimonies of the first policemen on the scene, which was described in lurid detail. When the jury members were shown the 8 × 10 glossy photos, they shivered.

Defense counsel had organized a phalanx of co-workers and friends, including a priest who testified to Reyes's good character. Only his beloved wife's adultery could have driven him to commit such a violent act.

The jury heard the testimonies of paramedics, called to the scene by Reyes himself. The victim had a pulse when they arrived, they said. The emergency room doctor determined that there was no brain activity but kept the heart and lungs alive with machinery until permission could be obtained to harvest organs and tissue. The surgeon who performed the retrieval procedure testified that the heart was still beating when he extracted it.

This testimony caused a furor in the courtroom. The judge rapped his gavel. The assistant D.A. tried, but failed, to look unconcerned. In Alex's opinion he should have gone for a manslaughter charge instead of murder. Murder implied premeditation, which in this case couldn't be proved. Most damaging to Reyes's case was that the survivor of the attack was unavailable to testify.

Despite these setbacks, the D.A. delivered a brilliant summation speech, urging the jury to bring in a guilty verdict. Whether or not the victim died at the moment of impact, Paul Reyes was responsible for another human being's death and should therefore be found guilty.

The defense attorney had only to remind the members of the jury, again and again, that Paul Reyes was in jail when the victim had actually died.

The case was turned over to the jury after three days of testimony. Four hours and eighteen minutes later it was announced that the jury had reached a verdict, and Alex was one of the first to return to the courtroom.

He tried to gauge the jurors' moods as they filed in, but it was impossible to guess their decision by their blank expressions.

The courtroom fell silent as the accused was commissioned to stand.

Not guilty.

Reyes's knees buckled, but he was bolstered by his jubilant attorney. Relatives and friends surged forward to embrace him. The judge thanked the jury and dismissed them.

Reporters were eager to get statements, but Reyes's attorney ignored them and ushered him up the center aisle toward the exit. When Reyes reached the end of Alex's row, he must have sensed Alex's stare.

He stopped suddenly, turned his head, and, for a split second, their eyes connected.

Chapter Six

May 1991

*E*at. Sleep. Breathe. These life-sustaining functions were now done by rote. Why bother? Life no longer had purpose.

There was no solace to be found—not in religion, meditation, work, exhausting physical exercise, or raging fits. All had been tried as a means of easing the wrenching pain of loss. Yet, it prevailed.

Peace was unattainable. Each breath was laden with sorrow. The world had been reduced to a tiny sphere of abject misery. Very little stimuli penetrated the encapsulating grief. To one so steeped in bereavement, the world seemed monochromatic, soundless, flavorless. The grief was so severe, it was paralyzing.

The untimely death had been unjust and infuriating.

Why had this happened to them? No two people had ever loved as deeply. Their love had been rare and pure and should have endured for years, then extended beyond death.

They'd talked about it, pledged everlasting love to each other.

Now, the immortality of their love was impossible because the cache where it was stored had been extracted and given to someone else.

Ghastly, that postmortem vandalism. First robbed of life, then robbed of the core of existence, robbed of the chamber where that sweet spirit had dwelled.

Now somewhere, inside a stranger, that beloved heart was still beating.

Moans echoed softly in the small room. "I can't bear it another day. I can't."

Although the loved one lay dead in a cemetery plot, the heart lived on. The heart lived on. That was a haunting preoccupation, tenacious in its grip, shackling and inescapable.

The surgeon's scalpel had been swift and sure. Painful as it was to accept, what had been done was irreversible. The heart continued to live while the spirit was unfairly doomed to eternal incompleteness. The soul would search endlessly and in vain for its home, while the still-beating heart continued to mock the sanctity of death. Unless . . .

There *was* a way!

Suddenly the keening ceased.

Breathing became agitated and choppy with excitement.

The mourner listened to the rioting, fleeting, galvanizing thoughts suddenly unfurling.

The idea came alive, took shape, divided, expanded, rapidly, like an ovum just fertilized. Once born, it frolicked inside a brain that for months had been stagnant with despair.

There was a way to achieve release from this unbearable torment. Only one way. One solution that swiftly evolved from that single cell of an idea and suddenly was fully formed. It was converted into words that were whispered precisely,

with the reverence of a disciple to whom a divine mission
has been revealed.

"Yes. Of course, of course. I'll find that dearest of hearts.
And when I do, mercifully and with love, to reunite our
spirits and give us peace, I'll stop it."

Chapter Seven

October 10, 1991

Cat Delaney circulated through the ballroom like a bright butterfly, lighting briefly to chat with one group of party-goers before flitting off to the next. Everyone with whom she spoke was dazzled by her verve and vivacity.

"She's incredible."

Dr. Dean Spicer, who'd been proudly observing Cat from the sidelines, turned toward the man who had extended the compliment. Dean had been Cat's date to countless social affairs, and he knew many of the people with whom she worked. However, this tall, distinguished gentleman was a stranger to him.

"Yes, she is rather incredible," he replied conversationally.

"My name's Bill Webster." Dean introduced himself as they shook hands. "Weren't you Ms. Delaney's cardiologist?"

"Initially," Dean said, pleased that his name had been

recognized. "Before our personal relationship got in the way."

Webster smiled with understanding, then returned his gaze to Cat. "She's a charming young woman."

Dean wondered who Webster was and why he'd been invited to this network-sponsored, black-tie gala to commemorate the one-year anniversary of Cat's transplant.

Executives from network affiliate stations were there, along with commercial sponsors, members of the news media, talent agents, actors, and others who had a vested interest in the success of *Passages*.

Curious about Webster, Dean asked, "How'd you recognize my name?"

"Don't underestimate your notoriety, Dr. Spicer. You've become almost as famous as your companion."

"Fan magazines," Dean said with a self-effacement he didn't truly feel. He enjoyed the public recognition he received for being Cat Delaney's "significant other," as a Hollywood gossip columnist had recently labeled him.

"The publicity generated by the tabloids hasn't detracted from your renown as a cardiologist," Webster told him.

"Thank you." He paused. "I only wish I could give all my patients as good a prognosis as Cat's. Her recovery has been remarkable."

"Are you surprised?"

"Not at all. I expected it of her. She's not only an exceptional patient but an exceptional individual. Once she made it through the first difficult weeks of recovery," Dean continued, "she resolved to live to a ripe old age. She'll make it, too. Her greatest asset is her optimism. She's the pride of the entire transplant program at our hospital."

"I understand she's a very vocal proponent of organ transplants."

"She speaks on behalf of donor awareness and frequently

visits the transplant patients who are waiting for organs. When they get down, she encourages them not to give up hope. They look upon her as an angel.'' He chuckled and smiled affectionately. ''They don't know her as well as I do. She has the fiery temper redheads are noted for.''

''In spite of her temper, you're obviously an admirer.''

''Very much so. In fact, we plan to marry soon.''

That wasn't entirely the truth. He planned to marry Cat. She continued to hedge. He'd asked her many times to move into his Beverly Hills home, but she still resided in her beach house in Malibu, claiming that the ocean was therapeutic, vital to her spiritual and physical health. ''I draw strength just from gazing at it.'' She also maintained that her independence was essential to her well-being.

The independence issue was a flimsy excuse for them not to marry. Dean certainly didn't intend to shackle her to the kitchen stove once she became his wife. In fact, he *wanted* her to continue her career. The last thing he needed was a hausfrau.

They dated each other exclusively. No ghosts from past relationships haunted either of them. Upon her full recovery, he'd been delighted to discover that they were sexually compatible. Each was financially secure, so it wasn't a matter of unbalanced earning capacity. He could see no viable reason for her continued refusal of his proposals.

He'd patiently deferred to her wishes, but now that her transplant was considered a total success and her stardom was firmly reestablished on *Passages*, he intended to apply more pressure for a commitment.

He had resolved not to give up until Cat Delaney was wholly his.

''Then congratulations are in order,'' Webster said, raising his glass of champagne.

Dean returned Bill Webster's smile and clinked glasses.

* * *

While listening to an advertising executive wax poetic about her incredible courage—he'd never before actually *touched* someone who'd had a heart transplant—Cat was looking beyond his shoulder at Dean and the man to whom he'd been talking for the last several minutes. She didn't recognize him; her curiosity was aroused.

"Thank you so much for all the cards you sent during my convalescence." As unobtrusively as possible, she pulled her hand from the ad exec's clasp. "Please excuse me now. I just spotted a friend I haven't seen in a while."

With the practiced ease of a diplomat, she negotiated her way through the crowd. Several people tried to engage her in conversation, but she paused only long enough to exchange pleasantries and respond to congratulations and compliments.

Because she had looked so bad for so long before her transplant, she felt quite justified in her conceit over how fantastic she looked tonight. Her hair had regained its luster, although the steroids she'd had to take immediately following the surgery had turned it a darker, but no less vibrant, shade of red. For tonight's festivities, she'd swept it into a topknot designed to appear haphazard.

Her eyes, described as "laser beam blue" almost every time her name appeared in print, had been artfully enhanced with makeup. Her skin had never glowed so healthily. She was showing it off in a snug-fitting black sequined minidress that left her arms and back bare.

Of course, the dress had a high neckline that fastened halter-style at the back of her neck. She hadn't wanted to expose her "zipper," the scar that ran vertically from the hollow of her throat to the center of her breastbone, where the ribs separated. Every item in her wardrobe had been chosen to conceal that scar. Dean insisted that it was hardly detectable and fading more each day, but she could still see it clearly.

She knew that the scar was a small price to pay for her

new heart. Her self-consciousness about it was undoubtedly a holdover from childhood, when she'd often been wounded by thoughtless or cruel comments by her classmates. Illness had made her an object of curiosity then, just as being a heart transplantee did now. She had never wanted to spark pity or awe in other people, so now she hid her scar carefully.

Although she felt fabulous tonight, she would never take good health for granted. Her recollections of her illness were still too vivid. She was grateful to be alive and able to work. Her resumption of the Laura Madison role, and all the physical demands it placed on her, had caused no health problems. Now, a year after her transplant, she'd never felt better.

Grinning, she moved up behind Dean and slid her arm through his. "Why is it that the two most attractive men in the room are monopolizing each other and depriving the rest of us?"

Dean smiled down at her. "Thank you."

"Likewise," the other man said. "The compliment is especially welcome coming from the belle of the ball."

She executed a mock curtsy, then smiled and extended her hand. "I'm Cat Delaney."

"Bill Webster."

"From . . . ?"

"San Antonio, Texas."

"Ah, WWSA! You're that Webster." She turned to Dean and said in a stage whisper, "Top dog. Owner and CEO. In other words, kiss up."

Webster chuckled modestly.

His name was known and respected industry-wide. He appeared to be in his midfifties. There was an attractive feathering of gray at his temples, and his suntanned face had accommodated maturity very well. Cat liked him instantly.

"You're not a native Texan, are you?" she asked. "Either that or you conceal your accent."

"You have a good ear."

"And great legs," she said, winking.

"I concur," Dean said.

Webster laughed again. "I'm originally from the Midwest. I've been in Texas almost fifteen years. It's become home."

"Thank you for tearing yourself away long enough to attend the party," she said sincerely.

"I wouldn't have missed it." He nodded toward Dean. "Dr. Spicer and I have been talking about your remarkable recovery."

"He deserves all the credit," she said, smiling up at Dean. "He—and all the doctors and nurses in the transplant program—did all the work. I was just their dummy."

Dean placed his arm around her slender waist and said proudly, "She's been an ideal patient, first for me and then for Dr. Sholden, who took over her case when our relationship progressed to the point where medical considerations could have become clouded. As you can see, it turned out all right."

Cat sighed theatrically. "It's been all right since I got those blasted steroids adjusted. Of course, I had to give up my mustache and chipmunk cheeks, but one can't have everything."

The unpleasant side effects of the steroids had disappeared once her dosage had been lowered. She'd regained the pounds she'd lost and now held steady at her ideal, pretransplant weight.

Even before the "zipper" became part of her body, her slight figure had never had centerfold potential. She'd been a gangly, skinny child. Adolescence hadn't paid off for her as it had for many girls; the fervently desired curves had never developed. The angular bone structure of her face and her vibrant coloring were her best assets. She'd learned to maximize them. Cameras loved them.

"I'm an unabashed fan, Ms. Delaney," Bill Webster was saying.

"Please, call me Cat. And unabashed fans are my favorite kind."

"Only a very important luncheon appointment can keep me from tuning in *Passages* every day."

"I'm flattered."

"I attribute the show's enormous success to you and the character of Laura Madison."

"Thank you, but you're far too generous. *Passages* was successful before Laura Madison was written into it. And it held its own in the ratings during my absence. I share the show's success with everyone involved, the scriptwriters, the whole cast and crew."

Webster looked at Dean. "Is she always this modest?"

"To a fault, I'm afraid."

"You're a very fortunate man."

"Hey, guys," she said, "I think it only fair to warn you that one of my pet peeves is being talked about as though I'm invisible."

"Sorry," Webster said. "I was just picking up the conversation where we left off when you joined us. I had just congratulated Dr. Spicer on your impending marriage."

Cat's smile faltered. Angry heat rushed to her head. This wasn't the first time Dean had fabricated their engagement. His self-esteem wouldn't allow him to take seriously her declinations to his repeated marriage proposals.

In the beginning, their developing friendship had jeopardized his objectivity as her cardiologist. Throughout her illness and following her transplant she'd relied on that friendship. During the past year, it had advanced to a deeper, more mature level. He *was* important to her, but he continued to misread the nature of her love for him.

"Thank you, Bill, but Dean and I haven't set a definite date."

Despite her attempt to hide her irritation with Dean, Webster must have sensed it. Self-consciously he cleared his

throat and said, ''Well, there are a lot of people here wanting
your attention, Cat, so I'll say good night.''

She extended her hand. ''It was a pleasure to meet you. I
hope our paths will cross again.''

He squeezed her hand. ''You can count on it.''

She believed him.

Chapter Eight

October 10, 1991

The day was only minutes old when they decided they'd had enough of the video games.

After the darkness of the arcade, where one individual's features were more or less indistinguishable from another's, the fluorescent light in the empty shopping mall seemed unnaturally harsh and bright. They laughed at having to give their eyes time to adjust.

The mall's stores and cafes had been closed for hours. Their voices echoed in the cavernous atrium, but it was a relief to carry on a conversation without having to shout above the electronic cacophony inside the arcade.

"You're sure it'll be okay?"

Jerry Ward shot his new companion the cocky, confident grin that belongs exclusively to happy, well adjusted, sixteen-year-old boys. "My folks'll be asleep by now. They don't wait up for me."

"I don't know. It seems strange for you to invite me home with you just like that. I mean, we hardly know each other."

"What better way to get to know each other?" Jerry saw that he still had some convincing to do. "Look, you just got laid off and need a job, right? My dad's got a business. He's always hiring new people. He'll find something for you.

"And tonight you need a place to crash. It'll save you some bucks to stay at my house. We've got a guest room. If you're nervous about what my mom and dad will think about you spending the night, I'll sneak you out first thing in the morning and introduce you to them later. They never have to know you slept over. So, relax." He laughed and spread his arms wide. "Okay? You cool?"

Jerry's amiability was contagious and earned him an uncertain smile. "I'm cool."

"Good. Wow! Look at those blades!" Jerry jogged to a sporting goods store. In the window were displayed in-line skates and all the safety paraphernalia. "See that pair there, the ones with the green wheels. They're *bad*. That's what I want for Christmas. And the helmet, too. The whole outfit."

"I've never tried roller blading. It looks dangerous."

"That's what my mom says, but I think by Christmas she'll come around. She's so glad I can finally do normal stuff that she's a real soft touch." Jerry gave the display one last covetous glance before moving on.

"What do you mean, 'do normal stuff'?"

"What? Oh, never mind."

"Sorry. I didn't mean to butt into private matters."

Jerry hadn't intended to give offense. But he'd been a geek for so many years, and was so glad no longer to be one, that he hated reminders of his infirmity.

"It's just that, see, I was sick when I was a kid. I mean, real sick. From age five until last year. In fact, it'll be a year tomorrow. Mom's having a big party to celebrate it."

"Celebrate what? If you don't mind my asking."

They'd reached the exit doors. The guard on duty was slumped on a bench, sound asleep. Jerry faced his new friend, his face filled with doubt. "If I tell you, promise you won't think I'm a dork."

"I won't think you're a dork."

"Well, some people get really weird about it." Jerry took a quick breath. "I had a heart transplant."

The declaration was met with a guffaw of disbelief. "Yeah. Right."

"Swear. I almost died. They got a heart for me just in time."

"You're serious? No shit? Jesus Christ."

Jerry laughed. "Yeah. My folks firmly believe He had something to do with it. Come on." He pushed the door open and was confronted by a cold, damp wind. "Aw, hell. It's raining again. Every time it rains this hard, the creek out by our place floods. Where's your car?"

"That way."

"Mine's in that area, too. Want me to walk with you?"

"No. Just pull up in front of Sears. I'll follow you from there."

Jerry gave a thumbs-up sign, pulled his windbreaker up over his head, and charged into the downpour. He didn't see his companion glance back at the sleeping guard.

Following the successful surgery, the Wards had bought Jerry a brand-new compact pickup. He proudly swung it into the lane in front of Sears, tooted the horn twice, and watched in his rearview mirror as the other car pulled up behind him.

He sang along with the radio and added a few bass percussion sounds as he negotiated the familiar streets that led from the Memphis suburbs to a rural area. He kept his speed moderate so as not to outdistance the car following him. If one didn't know his way around in this neck of the woods, it was easy to get lost after dark.

As he neared a narrow bridge, Jerry reduced his speed.

Just as he'd predicted, the creek below was running swift and high. He'd almost reached the middle of the bridge when his pickup was rammed from behind.

"What the—"

Jerry was pitched forward by the impact, but his seatbelt restrained him. Then he was slammed backward by the recoil, and it felt like someone had driven a hot spike through the back of his neck.

He cried out in pain and reflexively reached for his neck. Just as he let go of the steering wheel, the other vehicle gave his rear bumper another vicious nudge. Wood splintered and snapped as the pickup crashed through the rickety barricade. For only an instant the small truck was airborne, then the grille splashed into the swirling, dark waters. Within seconds the swift current was slapping against the windshield.

Screaming hoarsely, Jerry groped for the seatbelt release. It sprang open and he was free. In the darkness he searched for the door handle and tugged on it, frantically, before remembering that the doors were automatically locked while the engine was running. Shit.

He felt water closing over his knees. He raised his legs and kicked at the driver's window, kicked with all his might, until the glass cracked. But it was the force of the water that finally broke the glass.

Gallons of creek water gushed in, instantly filling the cab of the truck.

Jerry held his breath, although he realized that his life was over. Death, which he'd miraculously cheated so many times during his youth, was finally claiming him.

He was on his way to meet Jesus. More accurately, a virtual stranger had *sent* him to meet Jesus.

And Jerry Ward's last thought was one of anger and perplexity.

Why?

Chapter Nine

Summer 1992

You're angry." Clearly, Dean was not asking a question.

Cat continued to stare through the windshield of his Jag. "What was your first clue?"

"You haven't spoken a word in twenty minutes."

"Because I have you to speak for me. Once again, you practically posted banns."

"Cat, I was merely carrying on a conversation during dinner with the woman seated beside me."

"Who later cornered me in the powder room and begged to know the details of our forthcoming wedding." She turned to him. "You must have led her to believe it was imminent. The real irony is that we *don't* have plans to marry."

"Of course we do."

Cat would have argued, but he swung the Jag into the semicircular driveway of his house. On cue, his housekeeper opened the front door to greet them. Cat smiled at her and said hello as she entered the domed foyer. Being waited on by servants made her uncomfortable. Dean took dealing with hired help in stride.

Cat now wished she hadn't agreed to spend the night at his house. She had done so only because it promised to be a long evening, making it too late to drive to Malibu and then return early tomorrow morning for her studio call.

She decided that if their brewing argument developed as she feared it might, she would call the Bel-Air and ask them to send a car for her. She went into his study, preferring it to the other rooms in the house because it was the coziest and least formal.

"What something to drink?" he asked, following her.

"No, thank you."

"A snack? I noticed you didn't eat much dinner. You were too busy chatting with Bill Webster."

She ignored that. Since their first meeting, she and the TV executive from Texas had crossed paths several times at network functions. Dean mistook the nature of her attraction to him. "No, thanks. I'm not hungry."

"I can have Celesta fix something for you."

"No need to bother her."

"She's paid well to be bothered. What would you like?"

"Nothing!" She regretted her sharp tone and drew in a deep breath to subdue her temper. "Don't coddle me, Dean. If I were hungry, I'd ask for something to eat."

He left the study only long enough to dismiss the housekeeper for the night. When he rejoined Cat, she was standing at the window with her back to the room, gazing out over the formal garden. She heard his approach but didn't turn around.

He placed his hands gently on her shoulders. "I'm sorry. I didn't realize that a casual comment would create such a fuss. Why don't we just get married and spare ourselves this recurring argument?"

"Hardly a good reason to get married."

"Cat." He grasped her shoulders more firmly and turned her to face him. "That's not the reason I want to marry you."

They could be talking about anything—the weather, their favorite sundae topping, the national debt—but the subject always came back to this. She squeezed her eyes shut. "I don't want to rehash this tonight, Dean."

"I've been patient, Cat."

"I know."

"Our wedding doesn't have to be a media event. We can fly to Mexico or Vegas and have it over and done with before a single reporter gets wind of it."

"It's not that."

"Then what?" he pressed. "Don't give me that crap about not wanting to give up your house in Malibu, or your fear that you'll sacrifice your independence. Those are stale arguments. If you continue to turn me down, you'll have to come up with more valid objections."

"It's only been a year and a half since my transplant," she said quietly.

"So?"

"So you might saddle yourself with a wife who'll spend a good portion of her life, and yours, in a cardiac ward."

"You didn't experience a single rejection event." He raised his index finger. "Not one, Cat."

"But there's no guarantee that I won't. Some transplantees live with their heart for years, then *wham*! For no apparent reason they reject."

"And some die from causes totally unrelated to their hearts. In fact, there's a one-in-a-million chance you'll get struck by lightning."

"I'm serious."

"So am I." He softened his tone. "Many transplantees have lived for twenty or more years without any signs of rejection, Cat. Those patients received hearts when the procedure was still experimental. The technology has improved considerably. You stand an excellent chance of living out your normal life expectancy.''

''And every day of that 'normal life,' you'll be monitoring my vital signs.''

He looked puzzled.

''I was your patient first, Dean, before I became your friend and lover. I think you'll always look upon me as your patient.''

''Not so,'' he said firmly.

But she knew better. He hovered over her protectively, a continual reminder that she had once been very fragile. He still treated her with utmost care. Even when they made love, he handled her as though she might break. His nerve-racking, irritating restraint made her feel cheated rather than cherished and severely curtailed her passion.

For fear of damaging his ego, she'd borne her frustration in silence, while yearning to be treated like a woman, without being qualified as a heart transplantee. With Dean, she doubted that would ever be possible.

Still, she knew that his overprotectiveness was only a symptom; the real problem was that she wasn't in love with him. Not in the way she should be before entertaining marriage. Life would be much simpler if she were in love with him. At times she fervently wished she could be.

She'd always tried to spare his feelings, but now she felt that a more straightforward approach was in order.

''I don't want to marry you, Dean. I care about you deeply. If it weren't for you, I'd never have made it.'' Smiling at him tenderly, she said, ''But I'm not head over heels.''

''I realize that. I don't expect you to be. That's for kids. We're beyond that romantic silliness. On the other hand, we make a good team.''

''A team,'' she repeated. ''That doesn't really appeal to

me, either. I haven't *belonged* to anyone since I was eight years old, when my parents . . . died."

"All the more reason to let me take care of you."

"I don't want to be taken care of! I want to be Cat. The new Cat. The well, strong Cat. Every day since my transplant has been a discovery into the new me. I'm still becoming acquainted with this woman who can take the stairs instead of the elevator. Who can shampoo her hair in three minutes when it used to take thirty."

She pressed her fists against her chest where her heart was beating strongly. "Time has a new dimension for me, Dean. It's precious. I jealously guard the time I spend with myself. Until I know completely this new Cat Delaney, I'm unwilling to share her with anyone."

"I see," he said stiffly, sounding more peeved than heartbroken.

She laughed. "Stop sulking. I don't buy it. You won't suffer unduly if we don't marry. What you love most about me is my celebrity. You enjoy sharing the limelight, attending Hollywood premieres, being seen at Spago in the company of a TV star." She struck a starlet's pose, one hand on her hip, the other behind her head.

He laughed, his sheepish grin as good as a signed confession. But she pressed on. "Admit it, Dean. If I clerked at a supermarket, would you still be pleading for my hand in marriage?" She had him pegged, and they both knew it.

"You're a cold woman, Cat Delaney."

"I speak the truth."

If the nature of Dean's love for her were different, she would have ended their relationship long ago in order to spare him real heartache. As it was, he admitted to loving her only as much as he was capable of loving.

He took her in his arms and kissed her forehead. "In my way, Cat, I do love you, and I still intend to marry you, but I'll relent for now. Fair enough?"

They hadn't solved anything, but at least she'd been granted another reprieve. "Fair enough."

"Good." He hugged her close. "Ready for bed?"

"I thought I'd take a swim first."

"Want company?"

He wasn't particularly fond of swimming, which was a shame since he had a gorgeous pool surrounded by more lush greenery than a tropical lagoon.

"You go on up. I'll be there shortly."

He climbed the sweeping staircase to the second floor. Cat went out through the terrace doors and followed the flagstone path through the manicured garden to the pool. Unselfconsciously, she unfastened her dress and stepped out of it, then peeled off her stockings and panties and slid naked into the deliciously cool water. It felt cleansing. Perhaps it would wash away the nagging dissatisfaction that had plagued her for months, not just with Dean but with everything in her life.

She swam three laps before turning onto her back to float. She still marveled that she could swim without having to gasp for breath or be afraid that her heart would come to a screeching halt. A year and a half ago she couldn't have believed that such a feat was possible. She'd been prepared to die. And she would have died, if someone else hadn't died first.

That thought was never far from her consciousness, but whenever it thrust itself forward, it was jolting. Now, it brought her out of the pool. Shivering, she tiptoed to the cabana and wrapped herself in a large towel.

But the thought stalked her: Someone's death had given her the gift of life.

She'd made it clear to Dean, and to everyone on the transplant team, that she wanted to know nothing about the donor of her heart.

Rarely did she allow herself to think of that anonymous

person as an individual, with a family who had made a tremendous sacrifice so that she might live. When she did permit herself to think about that unnamed someone, her ambiguous discontent seemed the Mt. Everest of selfishness and self-pity. One life had been cut short; she'd been granted a second one.

She lay down on one of the chaise lounges, closed her eyes tightly, and concentrated on counting her blessings. She'd conquered the overwhelming odds of her unfortunate childhood, pursued her dream, and achieved it. She was at the peak of her career and worked with talented people who liked and admired her. She had more than enough money and wanted for nothing. She was adored and desired by a handsome, cultured, highly respected cardiologist who lived the lifestyle of a prince.

So why this vague restlessness, this disquiet that she could neither explain nor dispel? Her life, so hard-won, now seemed without purpose or direction. She yearned for something she couldn't describe or identify, something beyond her reckoning and her grasp.

What could she possibly want that she didn't have? What more could she ask, when she had already received the gift of life?

Cat sat up abruptly, sudden insight infusing her with energy.

Self-doubt could be a positive motivator, and there was nothing wrong with self-examination. It was the focus of her self-analysis that was misdirected.

Instead of asking what more she could *want*, perhaps she should be asking what she could *give*.

Chapter Ten

October 10, 1992

*H*er house always smelled like something just out of the oven. This morning it was teacakes. Golden and sugar-dusted, they were cooling on a wire rack on the kitchen table, next to a chocolate layer cake and two fruit pies.

Ruffled curtains fluttered in the open screened windows. On the refrigerator, magnets held in place Valentines made of red construction paper and white paper doilies, Thanksgiving turkeys drawn around small handprints, and Christmas angels that bore an unsettling resemblance to Halloween bats. All was the artwork of numerous grandchildren.

She answered the knock on her back screen door with a glance, a smile, and wave to come on in.

"You've got every mouth in the neighborhood watering. I could smell the cookies as soon as I stepped outside my door."

Her plump face was flushed with heat from the oven. When she smiled, her animated, guileless eyes crinkled at the corners. "Have one while they're still warm." She gestured at the teacakes.

"No. They're for your party."

"Just one. I need an opinion. Be honest now." She picked up one of the teacakes and extended it expectantly.

Knowing it would be rude to refuse, the guest acquiesced. "Hmm. Melt-in-your-mouth delicious. Just like Grandmother used to make."

"You've never told me about your family. Not in the three months you've lived next door." Turning her back, she began washing the mixing bowls and measuring cups that had been soaking in the sink.

"Not much to tell. Dad was in the military. We moved around a lot when I was a kid. Twelve grades, twelve schools."

"That can be so hard on a child." Her usually cheerful smile became a frown of sympathy.

"This is a royal proclamation! No sad thoughts today! I decree this a day of celebration. *Your* day."

She giggled like a girl, although she was well into her fifties. "I've got so much to do before this afternoon. Fred's taking off early. Said he'd be home by two. The children should be arriving with their families around five."

"You can't possibly make all the preparations yourself. Put me to work. I took the day off so I could help."

"Oh, you shouldn't have done that!" she exclaimed. "Won't your boss get mad?"

"If he does, that's tough. I told him how fortunate I am to be living next door to a very special lady and that, whether he liked it or not, I was going to help her celebrate her second year with a new heart."

She was touched. Tears glistened in her eyes. "I've been so blessed. When I think how close . . ."

"Hey, none of that, now. Remember the royal proclamation. Where should we start?"

She blotted her eyes with an embroidered handkerchief, then returned it to her apron pocket. "Well, you could start setting up the extra folding chairs while I water my plants."

"Lead the way."

They moved into the family room. It was homey and bright. On one wall was a glass sliding door that opened onto the patio. In order to catch the morning sun, a Boston fern had been hung on a hook in the ceiling, directly in front of the large glass pane.

"I guess Fred waters that fern for you. You'd never be able to reach it."

"Oh, it's not hard to reach, dear," she said. "I use a stepladder."

It had been a year since the Ward boy had met with that unfortunate accident in Memphis. Twelve months of careful planning had passed. Although it was anxiety-producing, the protraction was necessary. The methodology was essential to the mission. Without order and discipline, the mission would be madness.

The longest part of the year had been the hours since midnight last night. They had seemed as long as all the hours that had gone before. Each second had been counted in eager anticipation. Now, the long wait was almost over, the anticipation was minutes away from being gratified.

"Watch, love. I'm doing this for you. It's a demonstration of love that even death cannot vanquish."

"A stepladder. How convenient."

Chapter Eleven

November 1993

I didn't even ring the doorbell."

"I heard your car." Cat moved aside, silently inviting Dean to come in, then turned and led him into the living room of her house in Malibu.

Three Emmy awards were displayed on a shelf built especially for them. The stark white walls were decorated with framed magazine covers on which she had appeared. It was a personal room and gave the impression of warmth and coziness despite its high cathedral ceiling and tall windows. The house was a contemporary structure perched on a precipice, connected to the beach by wooden steps that zigzagged down the steep, rocky slope.

The fire in the fireplace relieved the chill of the overcast day. Beyond the wall of windows overlooking the Pacific, the view was monochromatic, the horizon undetectable. The water was the same dull gray as the low-hanging clouds.

Even during the most inclement weather, Cat loved the

seascape her house afforded. The ocean never failed to amaze her. Each time she looked at it, she felt as if she were seeing it for the first time. Its incessant rhythm filled her with awe, mystified her, and made her feel insignificant compared to such elemental impetus.

Recently, she'd taken many long walks along the shore. She'd spent hours gazing out over the waves, weighing her options, searching for answers in the surging surf.

"Would you like something to drink?" she asked.

"Nothing, thanks."

She returned to the deep easy chair where she'd cast off an afghan when she'd heard the approach of his car. On the end table beside her were a cup of herbal tea and a high-intensity reading lamp focused on her lap.

Dean sat across from her. "What's that?"

"Rough drafts for scripts. Each writer on staff submitted an idea as to the fate of Laura Madison. They're all very good, and very sad. Rather than knocking her off, I urged them to hire another actress to continue the part." She sighed and ran her fingers through her unruly curls. "But they're adamant about writing her out."

"There isn't another actress alive who could play that role," Dean said. "You've ruined it for anybody else. Meryl Streep couldn't handle it. You *are* Laura Madison."

She recognized in his features signs of frustration and anxiety that would be invisible to anyone who didn't know him well. She was responsible for his unhappiness, and that bothered her tremendously.

"Well, it's official, isn't it?" he said. "*Entertainment Tonight* broke the story yesterday. You're leaving *Passages*. Effective when your contract runs out, shortly after the first of the year, I understand."

She nodded, but said nothing. The wind buffeted the glass walls as though trying to snuff out the candles on the mantel. She threaded the fringe of the afghan through her fingers.

When she looked up, Dean was gazing out the window, his expression as turbulent as the surf.

"How much did Bill Webster factor in to your decision?"

She was slow to respond. "WWSA is his television station."

"That's not what I'm asking."

"If you're implying that our relationship is anything other than professional, you couldn't be more wrong. I have flaws, Dean, but lying isn't one of them. If anything, I'm too honest for my own good. Furthermore, Bill is very happily married to a woman who is as attractive and charming as he."

His features remained taut. "In a desperate attempt to understand why you're turning your back on your career, everything you've worked for, I've looked at your decision from every angle. Naturally it occurred to me that a romance might factor in."

"It doesn't," she said emphatically. "The Websters have six children. They also had a daughter who died several years ago. She was their firstborn. They took her death very hard.

"I haven't been entirely happy with my life for a long while. But it wasn't until Bill told me about his daughter—this was about six months ago—that I knew I had to make a fresh start. Life's too precious to waste a single day.

"That evening, Bill and I had a very earnest and honest talk about the loss of their daughter, and before I realized it, I was telling him about my childhood. I told him how it felt to be orphaned, to become a ward of the state, to be shunted between foster homes, never quite fitting in.

"That turned the conversation to an enormously successful program that he'd seen implemented in several major cities, where children who need adoptive parents are featured during the news broadcasts. He expressed an interest in beginning one at WWSA as a community service. That's when I began to see a new start for myself.

"I didn't mean to shut you out, Dean. Countless times, I

wanted to bounce the idea off you, but I knew you couldn't be objective. Nor could you grasp my reasons for wanting—*needing*—to do this."

She laughed softly. "I'm not sure I grasp them myself. But I feel them. Intensely. I wrestled with them, tried to evade them, but they got their hooks in me and wouldn't let go. The more I thought about the outreach this program could have, the more excited I became.

"I thought back to all the times I was rejected for adoption because of my age, my sex, my medical history. Even my red hair was a deterrent, it seems.

"There are so many children with special problems who don't have loving parents. They began to haunt me, Dean. I couldn't sleep for hearing them crying in the darkness, lonely and afraid and feeling unloved." She gave him a sad smile. "I've got to do something for those kids. It's that simple."

"I admire your philanthropic spirit, Cat. If you want to adopt a kid, more than one, I'm perfectly willing."

She laughed outright. "Oh, I can just see that! Dean, get real, okay? You're a brilliant physician, but you lack the flexibility necessary to parenting."

"If it meant the difference between having you and not—"

"It doesn't. Believe me, if I thought a judge would award me—a single heart transplantee—a child, I'd already have one. But this isn't about my adopting. *Cat's Kids* is about convincing other people to adopt."

"*Cat's Kids?*"

"Nancy Webster's idea. Like it?"

"It's real . . . catchy."

She wished he could share her enthusiasm, but he considered the whole idea preposterous.

"Cat, do you really want to . . . *demote* yourself this way? Leave your career and move to Texas?"

"It'll be different," she conceded with a chuckle.

"Couldn't you just sponsor the program, be the official

spokesperson, without having to become personally involved?''

"Be a figurehead, you mean?''

"Something like that.''

"That would be counterfeit. If my name's attached, it's my baby. It'll be a hands-on project all the way.''

She regarded him sadly. "Besides, I don't view this as a 'demotion.' To my mind, I'm not taking a step backward, but several steps forward. I expect overwhelming rewards.''

Restless with excitement, she tossed aside the afghan and left the chair. "This is the part that you won't get.'' Turning to face him, she splayed her hand over her chest. "I'm doing this because I can't live with myself if I don't.''

"You're right,'' he said, also coming to his feet. "I don't get it. You had a tough childhood. But who the hell didn't? *Ozzie and Harriet* was a fairy tale, Cat. In real life, every damn one of us grows up feeling unloved.''

"Yes! Especially if your mom and dad choose death over living with you!''

His angry retort was held in check. He looked at her with puzzlement. "Suicide? You told me your parents were killed in an accident.''

"Well, they weren't.'' She now regretted blurting out the nasty truth of her parents' demise because he was looking at her with the same mix of fascination and horror as the social workers had always regarded skinny, redheaded, recalcitrant little Catherine Delaney.

"That's when I learned to crack jokes instead of cry. I had to become either a wit or a basket case. So don't pity me, Dean. It was a bad scene when it happened, but it made me strong, gave me enough grit to survive a heart transplant. I hope you can understand why I must do this.

"I know firsthand what it's like to be set apart from other children. If your parents are dead, or you're disabled, or poor, you're discriminated against. Those disadvantages make a kid an oddball. And you know as well as I do that if you're different, you're out. Period.

"Hundreds of thousands of kids are hurting, Dean. They have problems we can't imagine. Just getting through the day represents a challenge. They can't play, learn, or interact with other children because they're too burdened with being abused or orphaned or sick or any combination of the above.

"There are families that are capable and willing to even the odds for these children, if only they knew how to go about it. I'm going to help match the two. It's a challenge I welcome. It's given me purpose. I believe this is why I was given a second life."

He groaned. "Don't go philosophical on me, Cat. You were given a second life because medical technology made it possible."

"You've got your interpretation, I've got mine," she said. "All I know is that there should be some payback for my good fortune. Being a TV star, making lots of money, always being surrounded by the beautiful people—that's not what life's about. Not *my* life anyway. I want more. And by more, I don't mean more money and fame. I want something real."

She reached for his hands and clasped them. "You're invaluable to me. You were a stalwart friend during the most difficult period of my life. I love and admire you. I'm going to miss you like crazy. But you can't continue being my safety net."

"I'd rather be your husband."

"Romance and marriage don't fit into the picture right now. What I'm going to do deserves my full-time attention. Please give me your blessing and wish me well."

He stared into her pleading eyes for several long moments. Eventually he smiled regretfully. "I'm certain that you'll make *Cat's Kids* an overnight success. You've got the talent, the ambition, and the know-how to achieve anything you want."

"I appreciate your vote of confidence."

"However," he added sternly, "I'm a sore loser. I still think Bill Webster has dazzled you with his rhetoric about public service programming. It's too bad about his daughter, but I think he took advantage of your sympathy to lure you to his TV station.

"With you there, his ratings will soar, and he damn well knows it. I doubt his interest in this project is entirely altruistic. My guess is that you'll learn he's fallible, as human and self-serving as the rest of us."

"Bill has given me an opportunity," she said. "But he's not the reason for my decision. His motives have nothing to do with mine. I wanted to make a change in my life. If it wasn't *Cat's Kids* it would be something else."

Dean declined to comment. Instead, he said, "My guess is that you'll come to miss me and your life here so much that you'll soon return." He stroked her cheek. "When you do, I'll be waiting for you."

"Please don't hold out for that."

"One of these days, you'll come around. In the meantime, I'll do as you ask and wish you well."

Chapter Twelve

January 1994

The clock on the desk was old-fashioned, with a round, white face and large, black, Arabic numbers. It had a red second hand that ticked off every second with a rhythmic click, remindful of a heartbeat.

The cover of the scrapbook was made of imitation leather, but it was a good imitation, with a realistic grain. Heavy and solid, the volume felt good against the palms that caressed it as one would a pet.

In a way it was just that—a pet. A friend who could be trusted to keep secrets. Something to coddle, to play with during idle moments, or when one felt the need for comfort and companionship. And unqualified approval.

The pages of the volume were filled with newspaper clippings. Many gave an account of young Jerry Ward's life, his valiant struggle with a congenital heart defect, his transplant and recovery, and finally his untimely accidental death by drowning. Such a tragedy, after all the teen had been through.

Then there was the grandmother in Florida. She'd been eulogized by friends and family who were devastated by her unexpected death. The woman seemingly had not had a single enemy in her life. Everyone loved her. Following her transplant, her cardiologist said that her prognosis was good. She would likely have lived for many more years if not for that shard of glass that had pierced her lung when she fell through the patio door while watering a Boston fern. And of all days for such a hideous accident to occur—the second anniversary of her transplant.

A page in the volume was turned. Memory lane led to October 10, 1993. Three months ago. Another state. Another city. Another heart recipient. Another ghastly accident.

Messy, that business with the chain saw. Bad idea. But he'd been an outdoors type, so . . .

The mission had one glaring flaw—there was no way of knowing exactly when it was accomplished. It might have been already, with Jerry Ward's death, or with one of the other two. But the mission couldn't be assumed completed until all the possible recipients had been eliminated. Only then would it be certain that the heart and the spirit of the loved one had been reunited.

The scrapbook was closed reverently. The back cover received a loving pat before the volume was gently laid in the desk drawer and locked away from prying eyes. Not that there would be any. No one was ever invited here.

Before the drawer was locked, a thick, bulging manila envelope was removed. The metal clasp was worked open and the contents spread across the desk. Each article, photograph, and clipping had been carefully labeled to facilitate study. Every fact contained in this treasure trove of information had been memorized and analyzed.

Known were her height, weight, dress size, likes and dislikes, religious preference, favorite fragrance, pet peeves, California driver's license number, Social Security number, political affiliations, ring size, and the telephone number of the maid service that cleaned her house in Malibu.

It had taken months to compile the information, but it was amazing how much could be learned about a person when one's time was devoted solely to that undertaking. Of course, because she was a celebrity, there was much to be learned from the media, although the reliability of that information was sometimes questionable. Tabloids weren't always accurate, so "facts" garnered from them had to be verified.

Interesting, this change of heart she'd had recently. She was leaving her fabulous life in Hollywood for what appeared to be charity work in San Antonio, Texas.

Cat Delaney would be an intriguing person to get to know. And a real challenge to kill.

Chapter Thirteen

May 1994

Say, this might sound crazy, but, well, I've been sitting in that booth over there, looking at you and thinking I know you from somewhere. All of a sudden it hit me like a ton of bricks. Aren't you Alex Pearson?"

"No."

"You sure?"

"Positive."

"Damn. I could've sworn you were him. You look just like him. The writer, you know? Wrote that crime novel that everybody's reading? You're a dead ringer."

This had gone on long enough. Alex stuck out his right hand. "Alex *Pierce*."

"Hot damn! I knew it was you! Recognized you from the picture on the back of your book. Lester Dobbs is the name." The friendly stranger pumped his hand enthusiastically. "Pleased to meet you, Alex. Is it all right for me to call you Alex?"

"Of course."

Without invitation, Dobbs slid into the booth across from Alex. It was breakfast time at Denny's. The coffee shop was crowded with people on their way to work and those who'd just gotten off night shift.

Dobbs signaled the harried waitress for a fresh cup of coffee. "Don't know why she's acting so pissed," he muttered after he got the refill. "By moving over here, I freed up a booth."

Alex folded his morning newspaper and laid it on the seat beside him. It appeared he wouldn't be returning to it anytime soon.

Dobbs said, "Read that you were a Texan. Didn't know you still lived here in Houston."

"I don't. Not on a permanent basis anyway. I move from place to place."

"Guess your line of work gives you the freedom to do that."

"I can plug in my computer anywhere there's a post office and a telephone."

"Wouldn't do me any good to get the wanderlust," Dobbs said with regret. "I work in a refinery. Been there twenty-two years. It ain't going nowhere and neither am I. The job keeps bread on the table, but that's about all I can say for it. Got me a bastard of a supervisor. A real tight-ass when it comes to that time clock, know what I mean?"

"Yeah, I know the type," Alex replied sympathetically.

"Used to be a cop, didn't you?"

"That's right."

"Traded in your handgun for a hard disk."

Alex looked at him with surprise.

"Clever, huh? Didn't make it up myself. Read it in an article about you in the Sunday supplement a few months back. Sorta stuck in my mind. Is this the nonsmoking section? Shit. Anyway, me and the wife are real fans."

"I'm glad to hear that."

"I don't read much, you understand. She's always got her nose stuck in a book. Buys 'em at the secondhand place a dozen or more at a time. Me, I only like the kind of stuff you write. The bloodier the better."

Alex nodded and took a sip of his coffee.

Dobbs leaned forward and lowered his voice to a man-to-man pitch. "The dirtier the better, too, know what I mean? Jesus, the things you came up with in that book of yours. I got a hard-on 'bout every twenty pages. The wife thanks you, too." He added a broad wink.

Alex struggled to keep a straight face. "I'm glad you became so involved in the story."

"Do you, uh, actually know broads like the one in your book? You ever had one pull that kinky feather trick on you like that gal did to your hero?"

The Lester Dobbses of the world wanted to believe that he wrote from experience. "I write fiction, remember?"

"Yeah, but you gotta know a little bit about what you're puttin' down on paper, right?"

Alex wanted neither to exaggerate his lone life nor to disappoint his fan, so he remained silent and let Dobbs draw his own conclusion. He reached the one that pleased him and chuckled, shaking loose smokers' phlegm from his throat.

"Some sumbitches have all the luck. Ain't no woman gonna do that for me, and that's for damn sure. Guess it's just as well," he added philosophically. "I'd probably die of a heart attack, spread-eagle there in the bed, mother naked, my dick standing up straight as a flagpole, and—"

"More coffee, Mr. Pierce?" The waitress had the carafe poised over his cup.

"Oh, no thanks. You can bring my check. And add Mr. Dobbs's tab to it."

"Now that's right decent of you. Thanks."

"You're welcome."

"The wife'll pee her pants when I tell her I met you. When's your next book coming out?"

"In about a month."

"Great! Is it as good as the first?"

"I think it's better, although the writer is rarely a good judge of his own work."

"Well, you can't write 'em fast enough for me."

"Thank you." Alex picked up the check and his newspaper. "Sorry, I've gotta run. I enjoyed meeting you."

Alex paid at the cash register and left the bustling coffee shop, although he would have enjoyed lingering over another cup of coffee. In a very real sense he'd been working when Dobbs joined him. His mind had been busy soaking up atmosphere, studying people, their unique mannerisms and distinctive facial features, making mental notes for future reference. He did all this unobstrusively, not wanting to call attention to himself. He was surprised that Dobbs had even noticed him.

He was still startled when he was recognized by his readers. It didn't happen very often, though. His first novel, published a year ago in hardcover, had enjoyed only mediocre commercial success.

But when the paperback had come out, word-of-mouth endorsements and extra publicity from his publisher kicked in. Now it was on several bestseller lists and making the rounds in Hollywood for consideration as a TV movie. The reading public was eager for novel number two, due out next month.

For his third novel, his agent had demanded an enormous advance, which the publisher had paid. The book had been enthusiastically accepted by his editor and had generated much excitement within the publishing house. A knockout cover had been designed, and plans were being made for extensive prepublication promotion.

But for all his recent success in the publishing world, Alex Pierce was far from being a household name. He was still an unknown among nonreaders and those whose tastes lay outside his genre.

His crime novels were about men and women caught up in dangerous, sometimes brutal situations. His characters were drug lords, slum lords, pimps, whores, gang members, assassins, loan sharks, arsonists, rapists, thieves, extortionists, informers—the worst of society. The heroes were the cops who dealt with them inside or outside the law. In his stories the lines between right and wrong, good and evil, were so faintly drawn as to be virtually invisible.

His stories had a tough veneer and an even tougher core. He wrote with a jaundiced eye and a cast-iron stomach, sparing his readers' sensibilities nothing, packing his narrative and dialogue with as much realism as possible.

Although no words in the English language could adequately describe a grisly homicide, he tried to capture on paper the sights, sounds, and smells of the atrocities that one human being was capable of inflicting on another and the psychology behind the commission of such crimes.

Using the vernacular of the streets, he wrote the sexual passages as graphically as those detailing autopsies. His books had impact. They weren't for the squeamish, the fastidious, or the prudish.

In spite of its crudity, one critic had said that his writing had ". . . heart. [Pierce] has uncanny insight into the human experience. He cuts to the bone in order to expose the soul."

Alex was skeptical of the praise. He feared that these first three books were a fluke. He questioned his talent daily. He wasn't as good as he wanted to be and had come to the dismal conclusion that writing and success—insofar as how successful the writer perceives his work—were incompatible.

Despite these self-doubts, he was cultivating an expanding

and loyal reading audience. His publisher had deemed him a rising star, but he hadn't let the praise go to his head. He mistrusted fame. His previous experience in the media spotlight had been the most turbulent period of his life. Much as he wanted to succeed as a novelist, he was content living in anonymity. He'd had more than his share of notoriety.

He climbed into his sports car and within minutes was speeding along the freeway, one of the most fearless of the fearsome shark-drivers. He kept the windows open, listening to the whiz of traffic, liking the feel of the wind in his hair, even enjoying the pervasive smell of auto exhaust.

He reveled in such simple sensations. He'd been amazed at how sensually stimulating the world was, once his senses were no longer dulled by alcohol.

He'd kicked his drinking habit by checking himself into a dry-out hospital. After weeks of pure hell, he'd emerged, pale, skeletal, and shaking, but stone cold sober. He'd been sober for more than two years now.

No matter what kind of pressure he came under in the future, he was determined not to fall back on that crutch. Those blackouts had scared the shit out of him.

He arrived at his apartment, but it wasn't like coming home. The Spartan rooms were filled with packing crates. His research required frequent travel and periodic stays in a variety of locales. There was no point in nesting. In fact, he'd already made arrangements for his next move.

He weaved through the boxes, making his way toward the bedroom, which also served as his office. This was the only room in the apartment that looked lived in—an unmade bed in one corner, a desk and worktable taking up most of the floor space.

And there was paper everywhere. Reams of printed material were stacked on every conceivable surface and tacked to the walls. This chaotic, haphazard library was a grim reminder of his deadline. He glanced at the wall calendar. May. Time was passing quickly. Too quickly.

And he had an awful lot to do.

Chapter Fourteen

What's it going to take to get this kid on TV and into a permanent home?"

Exasperated, Cat thumbed through the case file. At four years old, Danny had already received more hard knocks than most people experienced in a lifetime.

She scanned the reports, paraphrasing aloud as she went. "His mother's boyfriend beats him repeatedly, so he's removed from her custody and placed in a foster home where there are already several other children."

She glanced up and addressed the rest of her remarks to Sherry Parks, a child protection specialist with the Texas Department of Human Services.

"Thank God he's no longer serving as a punching bag for the boyfriend, but Danny needs full-time, one-on-one attention. He needs to be adopted, Sherry."

"His mother's more than willing to give him up."

"So what's the problem? Let's do a segment on him and get some families interested in adopting him."

"The glitch is the judge, Cat. If you like, I can plead Danny's case with him again, but I can't promise that his decision will be any different the second time around. Danny's abuse caseworker is arguing just as strenuously that he belongs in a foster home. So far the judge has ruled in favor of that."

Since the inception of *Cat's Kids*, Sherry Parks, who was middle-aged and motherly, had been Cat's liaison with the state agency. She strived to get abused or special children out of the foster care system and into permanent adoptive homes.

It wasn't an easy undertaking. There were miles of red tape involved. Sherry frequently butted heads with abuse caseworkers and judges who, like everyone else, had biases and opinions that governed their decisions. Once a victim at home, the child sometimes became a victim of the sluggish system.

Cat said, "I'm certain the caseworker's heart is in the right place, but I strongly believe that Danny needs to be placed in a permanent home. He lacks security and needs parents he can count on to be around for a long time."

"The caseworker insists that he needs more therapy before he's ready for adoption," Sherry Parks argued, playing devil's advocate. "He was neglected from the day he was brought home from the hospital. He needs to learn to live within a family structure. Recommending him for adoption now is premature and doomed to failure, she says. We'd be moving him through the system too quickly."

Cat's auburn eyebrows pulled into a frown above the bridge of her nose. "Meanwhile, the message to him is coming through loud and clear—*nobody wants you*. 'Your foster parents are only housing you until you prove yourself worthy enough to be adopted.'

"Don't they realize that they're placing the burden of responsibility on Danny? And because he can't cut it, his feelings of failure and alienation are only reinforced. It's a vicious cycle from which he can't escape."

"In fairness, Cat," Sherry said, "he's provoking as hell. He bites indiscriminately. He throws tantrums. He destroys everything he lays his hands on."

Cat shook back her hair and raised her hands in surrender. "I know, I know. I read the report. But the bad behavior is symptomatic. It's an attempt to get attention. I remember some of the stunts I pulled just to prove how undesirable and unadoptable I was. That was after several good prospects that ultimately resulted in rejections.

"I know where he's coming from. He'll be impossible to live with until somebody sits him down and says, 'Throw tantrums, Danny. I'm going to love you anyway. Nothing you do is going to keep me from loving you. *Nothing!* And I'm never going to beat you or leave you or give you away. You're mine. I'm yours.'

"Then that someone should hug him until the message penetrates all the crap that's collected around his little heart and mind to make him socially and emotionally dysfunctional."

Jeff Doyle applauded. "That was a stirring speech, Cat. We ought to use it in a promo."

She smiled at the young man on her staff. In the short time they'd worked together, he'd become an able assistant. No job was too large for him, yet he didn't mind being asked to do menial tasks. He was so instrumental to the success of *Cat's Kids* that she'd recently invited him to sit in on her meetings with Sherry. He had taken an interest not only in the broadcast quality of each segment but in the welfare of the children featured in those segments.

"Thanks, Jeff," she said. "But I wasn't composing

promotional copy. I meant every word." Turning back to Sherry, she asked, "Do you feel comfortable pleading Danny's case with the judge again?"

"Comfortable, yes. Confident, no," Sherry replied. "But I'll do it anyway." She reached for the file and wedged it into her overstuffed briefcase. "I'll let you know when they schedule the hearing."

Cat nodded. "If I'm unavailable, leave word with either Jeff or Melia."

"Leave word with *me*," Jeff countered. "Otherwise Cat might not get the message."

Sherry divided a curious glance between Cat and him, but Cat ignored it. Jeff had spoken out of turn. She would chastise him later, in private. Their inner-office disputes were not open for discussion with outsiders.

The social worker gathered her things. "I guess that's everything for now. I'll be in touch." At the door to Cat's office she stopped to add, "By the way, that was a brilliant piece that aired last night."

"Thanks. I'll share your compliment with the crew. The video photographer got some beautiful shots of Sally."

The five-year-old was afflicted with a speech impediment resulting from repeated physical abuse. The disability, as well as her retarded social skills, could be reversed by loving care and attention.

"Of course, her eyes said it all. All we really had to do was get close-ups of them. They told her story and made a script almost superfluous. She has so much potential, such a capacity for love," Cat said sadly. "I hope the phone lines in your office melt this morning with incoming calls."

"So do I," Sherry said. "Once again, are you sure you don't mind filling in for me this morning?"

"I volunteered."

After making an appointment with a couple who had

applied to adopt, Sherry had discovered a conflict in her schedule. Cat had prevailed upon her to let her take the interview.

"Thanks again. I'll call you this afternoon to see how it went."

After Sherry's goodbye, Jeff refilled their coffee cups. "What's on the agenda today?"

"See if Melia has come in, please. And in the future, Jeff, keep your opinions of her or anyone else here at WWSA to yourself. Okay?"

"I'm sorry," he said contritely. "I know I was out of place to say what I did in front of Ms. Parks, but it just slipped out. It's true, though. Any messages left with Melia have a good chance of getting lost before reaching your desk."

"That's my problem, not yours."

"But—"

"*My* problem. And I'll handle it. Agreed?"

"Agreed."

He went out and returned moments later with Melia King. The two formed a contrast that went beyond gender. Jeff was fair-haired and blue-eyed. His clothing was inspired by Ivy League prep schools.

Melia had heavy-lidded, Latin eyes that she skillfully accented with kohl eyeliner. Her lips were full and sensual. She was partial to vibrant colors that set off her olive complexion and dark hair.

"Good morning, Melia."

"Hi."

This morning she was wearing a tight-fitting knit dress the color of poppies. She sat down and crossed her long, shapely legs. Her smile was smug, arrogant, affected, and as irritating to Cat as a torn cuticle. The chip on her shoulder had become a source of malcontent within the office. Unfortunately, bad chemistry wasn't grounds for dismissal, otherwise Cat would have fired her months ago.

Besides, she didn't feel she could make that decision independently. Bill Webster had handpicked her staff before her arrival at WWSA. The "candidates" had been introduced to her for approval.

Jeff Doyle had applied for a job to produce news, but he had jumped at the chance to work on *Cat's Kids*, which he knew would provide a more creative challenge.

Melia King had been recruited from the newsroom staff. She too had expressed a desire for more variety, more challenge, and more money. *Cat's Kids* had provided her an opportunity.

Cat had felt it would be churlish to reject Bill's recommendations, although she'd sensed Melia's antipathy to her the moment they shook hands. Since she had no other explanation for the young woman's hostility, she had figured that Melia was nervous about meeting her new boss and would soon warm up. However, after six months of working together, their relationship was still chilly.

Melia was never late. She hadn't been grossly derelict in her duties. Whenever a minor mistake was committed, she was ready with a viable excuse. Her apologies were lukewarm and lacked sincerity, but they qualified as apologies.

In other words, Cat thought sourly, *she covers her ass.*

"What appointments do I have scheduled for today?" she asked.

With a negligent flick of her hand, Melia opened her spiral steno pad. "You're interviewing Mr. and Mrs. Charlie Walters for Ms. Parks."

"Right. What time?" Cat asked, glancing at her desk clock.

"Eleven. She left their file on my desk."

"I'll get it from you on my way out."

"They live on a rural route out toward Kerrville. Do you know where that is?"

"No."

Melia rolled her eyes as though Cat's ignorance of Texas geography was the height of stupidity. "I'll have to give you directions."

"That would be helpful," Cat said tightly. "Anything else?"

"You have an edit session at three this afternoon."

"I'll be back long before then."

"And Mr. Webster wants to see you sometime today. At your convenience, he said."

"Call upstairs and see if he's in. I'd like to see him before leaving for my appointment."

Without acknowledging the request, Melia stood and moved toward the door. She had the gliding gait of a jungle cat. It was obvious that Jeff wasn't impressed by it. His lips were thin with disapproval as she went out.

Cat pretended not to notice. She wouldn't play one of her staff members against another. Nor did she want to show partiality. Getting down to business, she asked, "Have we confirmed where we'll shoot the segment on Tony?"

She always called the featured children by their first names, remembering how she'd hated being referred to as "the child" or "the girl," as though being a ward of the state had made her a nonperson.

"How about Brackenridge Park?" Jeff suggested. "You could take Tony on the miniature train ride. That would be good visually."

"More important, I think Tony would enjoy it. What six-year-old boy doesn't like trains?"

Melia stuck her head through the door. "Mr. Webster's in his office. He said for you to come on up." She popped out of sight again.

Cat stepped around her desk. "While I'm away, go to the

park and check everything out," she told Jeff. "Tell whoever is in charge that we'd like to do the shoot on Wednesday morning. Make sure the train will be running then, et cetera. Also, call Sherry's office so they'll know when to have Tony there. Double-check the time of the shoot with the newsroom assignments editor so a video crew will be available."

Jeff was taking rapid notes. "Anything else?"

"Yes. Lighten up. Life's too short to be taken so seriously."

He raised his head from his frantic scribbling and looked at her with puzzlement.

"Trust me, I know."

Cat's office was connected to the bustling newsroom via a short corridor. Bill Webster had offered her a larger and better-appointed office on the executive floor of the building, but she'd declined it. *Cat's Kids* was under the auspices of the news department, as was all locally originated programming. Integrating her staff with video photographers, editors, directors, and the studio crew was important to her.

She had told Webster, "I depend on them to make me look and sound good on camera. I can't afford to alienate them by setting myself apart."

There had been some built-in resentment toward her from newsroom personnel. Cat Delaney hadn't worked her way up through the ranks as they had. She was an actress, not a journalist.

Cat admitted to having no journalistic skills, and she knew she'd been foisted on the news department. The news team had no doubt expected her to condescend to them since she'd come from Hollywood, to be a Miss Know-it-all from Tinsel Town.

Instead, she was constantly asking their advice. Although she'd spent years in front of studio cameras, the news format was foreign to her. By asking questions, flubbing her lines, requiring retakes, and cracking self-deprecating jokes, she was gaining acceptance.

The CEO's secretary greeted her warmly. "Mr. Webster is expecting you, Ms. Delaney. Go right in."

"I couldn't be more pleased with the way things are going," Bill said once Cat was seated.

"So you've said on numerous occasions." She smiled at him across the surface of his black lacquered desk, which was so glossy it could have been used as a makeup mirror. "If you lavish me with any more praise, I'm liable to blush."

"They're not empty compliments," he said, chuckling. "I've got the increase in market shares to back them up. *Cat's Kids* is an overwhelming success."

Her smile reversed itself; her eyes turned stormy. "Not according to Mr. Truitt." A reporter for *The San Antonio Light*, Ron Truitt had been panning *Cat's Kids* since its debut.

"He was particularly scathing in his latest article," Cat said. "Let's see, how'd he put it? 'These segments are sappy and sentimental and have no more place in a newscast than a soft-shoe dance routine.' That hack can really turn a clever phrase, can't he?"

Webster took the reporter's criticism in stride. "Unfortunately, San Antonio is known in TV circles as a 'bloody market.' Like any other city, we have our share of violence. Among the TV news departments, the credo has been: the more gore the better.

"WWSA's policy on explicitness is no exception, I'm afraid. We've had to follow the trend in order to remain competitive. I don't like it. That's just the way it is," he said, spreading his hands in a submissive gesture.

"When compared to our lead news stories, which almost always relate to a violent crime, your segments are like a breath of fresh air. They remind viewers that there is still some good in the world. So forget Mr. Truitt's criticism. Consider it free publicity."

She didn't share Webster's lack of concern for the articles. A bad rap was a bad rap. It wouldn't have been nearly as upsetting if Truitt had criticized her performance; she would have sloughed that off. But he was attacking her "baby," and, like a mama bear, she was savagely protective.

"If they want to see violence and bloodshed, we ought to show the situations most of these kids come from," she said bitterly.

"All the more reason for you to blow off any criticism. Thumb your nose at Mr. Truitt."

"I tried, but the coward never returns my calls." She shrugged. "It's just as well, I suppose. I wouldn't want to give him the satisfaction of knowing that his slanted articles disturb me."

Webster offered her something to drink, but she declined, explaining her appointment with the couple who had applied to be adoptive parents.

"Interviewing the applicants isn't your responsibility."

"Not ordinarily. But Sherry made an appointment she can't keep. Rather than disappoint them, I offered to stand in for her. Besides, they sound like good prospects.

"The fact is, Bill, I would welcome meeting personally with all the applicants. It would give me an opportunity to describe exactly what they're letting themselves in for, which I could do from a unique perspective."

"That of a former foster child."

"Right. They're required to take the Positive Parenting course, but even after ten weeks of training they're not prepared for every eventuality that arises when dealing with a special child. It would also give them an opportunity to see that I and the program are strictly legit."

"You've assumed enough responsibility as it is."

"I thrive on work."

"And you're a control freak. You want to oversee everything."

"Guilty," she said with a smile.

"Just go easy on yourself."

She bristled. One thing she didn't tolerate was deferential treatment because of her transplant. "Don't mollycoddle me, Bill."

"Cat," he said reproachfully. "I caution the salesmen and midmanagement personnel—all type A's like you—not to work to the detriment of their health. None of them has had a heart transplant. It's good advice for anyone."

"I'll concede that."

"Is everything working out well with your staff?" When she hesitated, Webster's eyebrows arched inquiringly. "Problems?"

"Anytime more than one person works on a project, there's bound to be some friction," she answered diplomatically.

He leaned back in his chair. "Friction can often lead to beneficial brainstorming. I think your staff was well chosen."

She decided to approach her problems with Melia by going through the back door. "Jeff's a workaholic. He's superefficient. But he can be high-strung."

"Is he gay?"

"Does it matter?"

"Not at all," he replied, unruffled by her sharp tone. "Just curious. That's the gossip. Either way, I think his personality is much more suited to *Cat's Kids* than to the hard news format. Do you get along with Melia?"

"She has her mood swings," Cat said, hedging.

"Don't we all?"

"Of course. It's just that sometimes her moods and mine are on a collision course."

She wanted to avoid suggesting that all the blame belonged to Melia. Perhaps it didn't. Their dislike had been mutual, although Cat had done her best to give Melia the benefit of the doubt. She'd cut her more slack than she thought was deserved.

Webster didn't pick up her hint of disharmony. "As you said, Cat, when more than one person is involved, there are bound to be some differences of opinion."

Bill had bent over backward to make her transition to WWSA easy and enjoyable. She didn't want to appear to be a whiner. So, for the time being, she shelved her grievances. "I'm sure that in time we'll smooth out all the wrinkles."

"I'm sure you will, too. Anything else on your mind?"

She consulted her watch and found that she still had a few minutes. "I'd like you to start thinking about the possibility of a fund-raiser."

"Fund-raiser?"

"For the kids, those still in foster homes and the ones already adopted. Foster parents get two hundred dollars a month per child from the state. Medicaid pays for their health care. But that doesn't cover everything.

"Wouldn't it be good PR for the station, as well as enormously beneficial for the kids, if WWSA sponsored a concert, or a celebrity golf tournament, something like that, to raise money for the extras? Extras like orthodontia and eyeglasses and summer camp."

"Great idea. Do whatever you like."

"Thanks. But I need help. I'm still the new kid on the block and don't know very many people. Do you think Nancy would consider helping?"

"Consider it?" He laughed. "It'd be right down her alley. She loves nothing better than rolling up her shirtsleeves and plowing into a project. Fund-raisers are her forte."

"Great. I'll call her." Cat stood. "If that's all, I've gotta run."

He came around his desk to walk her to the door. "You're doing a terrific job, Cat. We're so fortunate to have you. You've given the station credibility and an aura of class. But have we been equally good for you? Do you have any regrets over leaving California? Are you happy?"

"Regrets? None, Bill. I love the kids. I'm doing something worthwhile, and it feels good."

He waited, but when she said nothing more, he probed. "That answers only half of my question."

"Am I happy? Of course. Why wouldn't I be?"

"What about Dr. Spicer?"

Cat was chummy with her new co-workers but hadn't had time to cultivate any close friendships. Furthermore, it was her policy to keep professional matters separate from her personal affairs. Her long, demanding workdays didn't leave much time for meeting people outside the industry. Consequently, Dean was still her best friend, and that's the way she answered Bill's question.

"We talk every few days."

He looked worried. "Any chance of his talking you into returning to California?"

"None. I've got too much work to do here." She glanced at her wristwatch. "Beginning with my eleven o'clock appointment."

Chapter Fifteen

The doorbell echoed through the ranch house. Through the screened front door, Cat saw a wide hallway extending to the rear of the house. Several rooms opened off this central foyer, but, from her viewpoint, she couldn't tell what they were.

Somewhere nearby a dog barked, a large dog, she guessed by the gruffness of his bark. Thankfully, it sounded more curious than ferocious.

She rang the bell again and glanced over her shoulder in the direction from which she'd come. The house was situated behind a low hill, out of sight of the state highway. A white rail fence formed a neat boundary around the property and divided it into several pastures where horses and beef cattle grazed.

The single-story house was constructed of native limestone. Shading the deep veranda was a wooden grid covered with leafy wisteria. Scarlet geraniums bloomed in clay pots.

Everything had a well-tended, well-kept appearance, including the golden retriever that loped around the corner of the house and up the stone steps.

"Hi, pooch." The dog sniffed the hand she offered, then gave it a friendly lick. "Are you the only one at home? I thought they were expecting me—or Sherry."

She rang the bell again. Mr. and Mrs. Walters must be somewhere in the house, she reasoned. It was unlikely that they would leave without closing and locking the front door.

Cupping her hands around her eyes, she peered through the screen and called out, "Hello? Anybody here?"

Toward the back of the house, a door squeaked open and a man stepped out into the hallway. Cat dropped her hands and jumped back, embarrassed at having been caught peeking through the screen.

He was tall, rangy, and barefoot. His jaw was shaded by a dark scruffy beard at least two days old. As he was ambling toward the door, he unhurriedly buttoned the fly of his Levi's, but gave up after securing only two of the buttons. He tried to smooth out his tousled hair, yawned broadly, then idly scratched his bare chest. "Something I can do for you?" He scowled at her through the screen.

Cat was bewildered. Had Melia given her the wrong directions? Had Sherry made an error on the house number or mistaken the time of her appointment?

Mr. Walters obviously wasn't expecting company. He'd come straight from bed. Had Mrs. Walters been in bed with him? If so, exactly what had she interrupted? *Sleep*, she hoped.

"Uh, I . . . I'm Cat Delaney."

He stared at her for several moments, then abruptly pushed open the screen door and looked at her even more intently through narrowed, suspicious eyes. "Yeah?"

Her name usually evoked a response. When salesclerks

realized who had passed them a credit card, they typically became either speechless or gabby. Headwaiters stammered effusively while leading her to choice tables. When sighted in public, she drew double takes.

Mr. Walters hadn't even blinked. Apparently her name meant nothing to him. "Actually I'm filling in for Ms. Parks. Sherry Parks? She couldn't make it this morning, so I—"

"Git!" he shouted, slapping his thigh.

Cat flinched, then realized that he wasn't addressing her. He was speaking to the dog, which was still laving her hand with his long, pink tongue.

"Lie down, Bandit," he ordered brusquely.

She watched sympathetically as the dog slunk to the edge of the porch and did as he was told, settling his head on his front paws but keeping his woeful eyes on her.

She turned back to the man. He was holding open the screen door with a taut, straight arm, providing her an unobstructed, intimate view of his armpit. A single drop of sweat rolled down the corrugated surface of his ribs toward his waistline, which tapered into the unfastened blue jeans.

She swallowed dryly. "I'm afraid there's been a mistake."

"I need some coffee. Come on in."

He turned and disappeared down the hall. She caught the screen door before it slammed shut, then hesitated, deliberating the wisdom of following him inside. He seemed in no frame of mind to entertain a guest. His wife had yet to make an appearance.

On the other hand, it went against her grain to retreat in the face of adversity. She'd invested over an hour of her valuable time in the long drive out here. If she left now, the trip would be a total washout. Besides, Sherry expected a full report. She couldn't leave without getting to the bottom of this.

She was piqued by Mr. Walters's incredible rudeness but

curious as well. She'd read the couple's application, and it had excited her. Both were college graduates; forty-something, but, after fifteen years of marriage, still childless.

Mrs. Walters was willing to end her career as a librarian to become a full-time mother to a special child. Her retirement and thus the suspension of her income would place no financial burden on them because Mr. Walters was a successful cement contractor.

They had seemed ideal to parent one of Cat's Kids. Why would they take the time and trouble to apply for adoption, then go to no effort whatsoever to prepare for their first interview? It was too intriguing a question to leave unanswered.

"Curiosity killed the Cat," she reminded herself as she pulled open the door and went inside. The adage would make a clever headline if she didn't come out alive, she thought wryly.

The arched opening through which Mr. Walters had disappeared led into a spacious living area. Wide windows allowed for plenty of sunlight and brought the breathtaking Hill Country landscape indoors. The furniture had been chosen for comfort and coziness. It would have been a lovely room, if not for the mess.

A man's shirt dangled from the arm of the sofa. A pair of cowboy boots and a pair of socks lay in the middle of the floor. The TV was on, but it had been muted, which spared Cat from having to listen to the sound of one cartoon character chasing another and whacking him over the head with a tennis racquet.

Newspapers were scattered everywhere. A pillow had been wadded into one corner of the sofa and bore the imprint of a head. There were two soda cans on the coffee table, along with an empty, crumpled potato chip bag and what looked like the remains of a bologna sandwich.

Cat stood just inside the arch, disgusted by what she saw.

Beyond a dividing bar was the kitchen, where Mr. Walters was taking mugs from a cabinet. He blew dust out of them.

"Is Mrs. Walters here?" she asked haltingly.

"No."

"When do you expect her?"

"Can't say. In a few days I guess. Coffee's ready. I set the timer to come on at seven. It's been sitting here for a few hours, but the stronger the better, right? Cream or sugar?"

"Really I don't—"

"Whew! Forget the cream." He'd taken a carton of half-and-half from the refrigerator and opened it. Cat could smell it from where she stood. "There's a sugar bowl around here somewhere," he muttered as he went searching. "I remember seeing it a day or two ago."

"I don't need any sugar."

"Good. 'Cause I can't find it."

She wasn't surprised. The kitchen was in a worse mess than the living room. The sink was full of dirty dishes that overflowed onto every available inch of counter space. There were crusty pans on the stove. The dining table was littered with more dirty dishes, unopened mail, books and magazines, stacks of paper, and a greasy cardboard box with **Carlotta's Homemade Tamales** stenciled across the top of it. Something yellow and gelatinous had dripped onto the floor.

The neat exterior of the house had been deceiving. Its inhabitants were slobs.

"Here you go." He slid a mug of coffee across the bar toward her. It sloshed onto the tiles, but he seemed not to notice. He was already sipping from his mug. After several swallows, he sighed. "Better. Now, what is it you're peddling?"

She gave a small, incredulous laugh. "I'm not peddling anything. Sherry Parks was under the impression you had an appointment this morning."

"Huh. What'd you say your name is?"

"Cat Delaney."

"Cat—" He squinted at her through the steam rising out of his coffee mug. His eyes took her in, head to feet and back again. "Well I'll be damned. You're the soap opera queen, right?"

"In a manner of speaking," she replied coldly. "I'm standing in for Ms. Parks, who had an appointment with you at eleven o'clock this morning."

"An appointment? This morning?" He shook his head in befuddlement.

Cat waved her hand in dismissal. "Never mind. The signals got crossed somewhere, but it makes no difference." She looked at the clutter surrounding her, then faced him squarely. "I'm terribly sorry, but I don't think you'll do."

He slurped his coffee. "Won't do what?"

He was either dense or extremely clever. She couldn't tell if he was playing with her or if he was indeed clueless as to what had brought her to his house.

Mrs. Walters might have submitted the application and arranged this meeting without her husband's knowledge, in a covert attempt to win him over to the idea of adopting. That happened sometimes. One partner, usually the wife, wanted to become a parent, while the husband did not. Sometimes the husband was even bitterly opposed to the idea.

That could be the case here. Cat certainly didn't want to get caught in the cross fire of a marital dispute. "Have you and Mrs. Walters discussed every aspect of this?"

He turned to pour himself a second cup of coffee, asking over his shoulder, "Every aspect of what?"

"Adopting a child," she answered impatiently.

He gave her a sharp, hard glance, then bowed his head, closed his eyes, and pinched the bridge of his nose. "I must've been up later than I thought," he mumbled, then raised his head and looked at her again. "You're here to talk about adopting a kid?"

"Of course. What did you think?"

"I don't know," he said, matching her vexed tone. "For all I know, you're selling Girl Scout cookies."

"Well I'm not."

"So what—" He broke off when a light of realization went on behind his eyes. He slammed his mug down on the counter. "Oh *shit*! What day is this?"

"Monday."

He consulted the calendar hanging beside the refrigerator, then slapped the wall with his palm. "Damn." He came back around, raking his fingers through his dark hair and looking chagrined.

"I was supposed to call you—or this Ms. Parks—on Friday and cancel the appointment. Entirely my fault. Forgot to check the calendar every day like she told me to. She'll be good and pissed," he said, almost to himself. "Look, I'm sorry. I could've saved you the trip. The interview will have to be rescheduled."

"I don't believe that will be necessary," she said crisply. "Tell your wife—"

"My wife?"

"You mean you aren't married?"

"No."

"But she goes by Mrs. Walters."

"Of course she does." The suggestion of a grin pulled at his lips. "Irene Walters is married to Charlie Walters. They'll get a real kick out of you mistaking me for him."

In answer to her puzzled look, he shook his head and said, "I'm housesitting for them. They were called away unexpectedly last week when one of Charlie's relatives took sick in Georgia. I needed a peaceful place to work while my apartment's being painted. So it was a good trade-off."

"They left you in charge of their house?" She looked pointedly toward the sink filled with food-encrusted dishes.

He followed her gaze and registered surprise, as though noticing the mess for the first time. "Guess I should tidy up before they get back. A lady came the day before yesterday— I think it was—to clean, but I ran her out. She was dusting around me and running the vacuum while I was trying to write. Drove me freaking nuts. I think I yelled at her. Anyway, she left in a huff. Irene will have to smooth her feathers. Irene'll be pissed about that, too." He gave a tsk of remorse.

"Write?"

His eyes swung back to Cat. "Pardon?"

"You said you were trying to write."

He sidestepped her and moved to a built-in bookcase in the living room. Taking a book from it, he thrust it at her. "Alex Pierce."

She read the title of the book, then turned it over to look at the photograph on the back of the sleek dust jacket. The man in the picture was well groomed and fully dressed. But his eyes were the same—gray and incisive beneath heavy eyebrows, one of which was halved by a vertical scar. Attractive squint lines. Straight nose. Unsmiling yet sensual mouth. Square jaw. It was an extremely masculine face. Hard and handsome.

She kept her head down, finding it easier to look into the eyes in the photograph than to meet the real thing. She was unaccountably warm and felt the need to clear her throat. "I've heard of you. But I wouldn't have recognized you."

"I cleaned up for the picture. My agent Arnie insisted."

"How many books have you had published, Mr. Pierce?"

"Two. Third one's due out early next year."

"Crime fiction, isn't it? Something like that?"

"Something like that."

"I'm sorry. I haven't read them."

"You wouldn't like them."

That brought her head up with a defensive snap. "Why not?"

"You just don't look the type." He shrugged. "My stories are about guts and guns. Blood and brains. Murder and mayhem. Not nice novels."

"Although alliterative."

Impressed, he arched his jagged eyebrow.

"Why don't you think I'd like your books?"

He gave her another insolent once-over, then reached out and fingered a strand of her hair. "Because the redheads in them are always easy."

Her stomach quickened, which made her angry, because she suspected that that was the reaction he wanted. She knocked his hand aside.

"And short-tempered," he added with an arrogant smile.

She shoved the book back at him. "You're right. I wouldn't like your writing." Struggling with her temper, she succeeded only in holding it in because she didn't want to live up to the stereotype. "When do you expect Mr. and Mrs. Walters to return?"

He set the book on the end table and took another sip of coffee. "They said they'd call before leaving Georgia. Until I hear from them, it's anyone's guess."

"Tell them to contact Ms. Parks's office when they get back. She'll reschedule an appointment."

"Irene and Charlie are great. They'd make wonderful parents for one of those kids."

"That'll be for a judge to decide."

"But your endorsement goes a long way, doesn't it? I'll bet you influence Ms. Parks and others in authority, don't you? Don't they value your opinion?"

"What's your point, Mr. Pierce?"

"My point is," he said succinctly, "don't screw it up for Irene and Charlie because of a few dirty dishes. Don't pass judgment on them because of me."

"I resent your implication. I didn't come out here to pass judgment."

"Like hell. You already said I wouldn't do."

"*You* wouldn't."

"See what I mean? You think highly of your opinion and like to throw your weight around. Why else would a soap queen like you be slumming in San Antonio?"

Cat was seething, but in a war of words she feared she would lose. "Goodbye, Mr. Pierce."

He followed her to the front door. She knew that the middle of her back was a target for his piercing eyes as she strode across the veranda.

"Goodbye, Bandit."

The dog came to his feet and whined as she stamped past. He was probably unhappy because his owners had left him in the care of a creep who could curdle cream.

Lord. More alliteration.

Alex Pierce was more abrasive than sandpaper. He had grated on her, unnerved her, and insulted her. However, she was more angry with herself than with him. Why had she let him get the upper hand? Instead of becoming embarrassed over her blunder, why hadn't she laughed it off? Humor was her antidote for most awkward situations.

But this time her supply of wisecracks had dried up. She had blushed and stammered like a nervous schoolgirl and now was left with only shreds of her pride and a prevailing resentment toward an author of sleazy cop stories who lived like a pig and drank scalding black coffee as though it were tap water.

Doubly galling was that she thought everyone should look as good as he when they got out of bed.

The subject of her scorn sauntered out onto the veranda

and dropped into the porch swing, which squeaked pleasantly beneath his weight. He patted the space beside him. Bandit, deliriously happy over the unspoken invitation, jumped onto the seat and laid his chin on the author's thigh.

Cat left with the vision of Alex Pierce gently rocking in the swing, sipping coffee, and idly scratching Bandit behind the ears.

Chapter Sixteen

Y ou two look beat."

Melia, looking as fresh as an exotic blossom in a florist's refrigerator, greeted Cat and Jeff from behind her desk as they trudged in.

"We've been to a steam bath. Also known as Brackenridge Park." Cat eased her heavy bag off her shoulder. "There wasn't a breath of breeze. Remind me never to wear silk again in the summertime in San Antonio." She plucked the fabric away from her clammy skin.

"Otherwise how'd it go?"

"Very well."

"We got some great video of Tony," Jeff told Melia as he wilted into an armchair. "He wasn't the least bit camera shy."

Melia passed Cat a handful of telephone messages. "Sherry Parks wants to speak to you right away. She believes the judge is going to approve Danny for adoption."

"That's great!" she said, her fatigue vanishing. "See if you can get her for me, please."

Retrieving her bag, she went to her private office, kicked off her shoes, and sat down at her desk. Out of habit, she checked the clock, then reached for her bottom desk drawer.

The telephone beeped. She depressed the speaker button as she opened the desk drawer. "Yes, Melia?"

"Ms. Parks on line one."

The drawer was empty.

"Want me to put her through?"

The drawer was empty.

"Cat? You there?"

"Yes, but my . . . Melia, where is my medication?"

"What?"

"My pills. My medication. Where is it?"

"Don't you keep it in your desk drawer?" Melia asked, sounding puzzled.

"Of course, but it's not here."

She slammed the drawer shut, then immediately yanked it open again, as though the empty drawer had been an optical illusion that would reverse itself.

But the drawer was empty. Her pills were indisputably gone.

Melia appeared in the doorway. "I told Ms. Parks you'd call her back. What's happened?"

"Exactly what I said." Unintentionally shouting, she quickly brought her voice under control. "My medication is missing," she stated calmly. "I keep all my pills here in the bottom drawer. Always. But they're not here now. Somebody's taken them."

"Who'd want your pills?"

Cat glared at her. "That's what I'd like to know."

Jeff came in. "What's the matter?"

"Somebody's taken my medication from my drawer."

"What?"

"Have both of you gone deaf?" she cried. "Must I repeat everything? Somebody waltzed in here and stole my medication!"

She knew she was being unreasonable, but the drugs were her lifeline.

Jeff stepped around the desk and looked into the empty drawer. "Who would have stolen your pills?"

Cat shoved her hand through her hair.

"I already asked her that," Melia said in an undertone. "It pissed her off."

"Couldn't you have misplaced them yourself?" Jeff ventured.

His soft-spoken, earnest attempt to help only heightened Cat's exasperation. "You can misplace a tin of aspirin and find it six weeks later in a coat pocket. It'd be hard to lose fourteen bottles of pills."

"Maybe you took them home with you last night?"

"I wouldn't do that." She was shouting again. "I have duplicates of every prescription. One for home. One for work. That way I can take my midday dose here. Sometimes the evening dose, too, if I'm working late."

Three of the fourteen medications were crucial antirejection pills. The other eleven prevented side-effects from those. She religiously stuck to the prescribed schedule of three doses per day.

"If I had toted all fourteen bottles home last night—which I didn't—I would remember it," she told her assistants. "Somebody's been in my desk. Somebody moved them. Who's been in here this morning?"

"Just myself and Mr. Webster," Melia replied. "He brought down a videotape he wanted you to see." She pointed at the cassette lying on the desk. "At least he's the only one I saw."

"Were you away from your desk for any length of time?" Jeff asked.

Melia resented his question, and she showed it by answering defensively, "What'd you expect me to do, pee in my chair? Sure, I went to the ladies' room a couple of times, and I went out for lunch. Since when is that a crime?"

Cat hated suspecting that Melia had played this malicious trick. She thought of outright accusing her, but what purpose would that serve? If Melia was guilty, she'd just deny it. If she was innocent, the accusation would cause a wider breach between them.

More important, however, was that in the wrong hands, the drugs could be dangerous.

"Melia, please get Dr. Sullivan on the line." The local cardiologist to whom Dean had referred her had an office nearby. "Track him down if he's not available. I don't care where he is, find him. Tell him to call the pharmacy and have them send over my prescriptions as soon as possible."

Melia turned and left the office without a word.

"I could drive to your house and bring back your pills," Jeff suggested.

"Thanks. But for that matter, I could go home myself."

"You're too upset to drive."

She hated to admit it, but she was very upset. The medication could be replaced soon enough; it wasn't as though her desk had contained the last supply on earth. Rather, she was shaken because someone had stolen something far more valuable than jewelry, furs, or money. Her life depended on that medication.

"I appreciate the offer, Jeff," she said with more composure than she felt. "But once the pharmacist gets a call from Dr. Sullivan, he'll take care of it."

"Where are you going?" Jeff fell into step behind her as she left her office.

"I'm holding for Dr. Sullivan," Melia told Cat as she walked past her desk. "He's with a patient, but his receptionist said she'd interrupt."

"Thank you."

She turned to Jeff, who was still behind her. "If some son of a bitch thinks this is funny, I want to set the record straight. Now."

The newsroom was a practical joker's paradise. The staff was always playing one-upmanship to see who could devise the best—or worst, depending on your point of view—practical joke.

The pranks ranged from putting plastic vomit in the communal refrigerator to reporting that the President of the United States had been assassinated while taking a leak in the men's room at a Texaco station on Interstate 35.

Cat approached the assignment editor's desk. He was a grizzled, crotchety chain-smoker with emphysema who resented that the newsroom was now a smoke-free environment. He wore a habitual scowl and was friends with no one. Yet, his instinct for news had earned everyone's utmost respect. When he said "jump," even the most egotistical reporters asked how high.

He nearly had a seizure when Cat depressed the intercom button on his telephone.

"Hey, you guys." Her voice boomed through the speakers in the vast room, which was honeycombed with partitions separating individual desks. "Hey, y'all," she corrected herself. She'd learned that Texans hated "you guys." "I want to tell the sick person who thought it might be funny to take my antirejection drugs that it isn't."

"What the fuck're you talking about?" the assignment editor asked, wheezing.

Ignoring him, Cat said into the intercom speaker, "It was a real hoot when my sanitary napkins were used to soundproof the lunch room. I even got a laugh out of the poster of me with a handlebar mustache and an extra tit. But this isn't funny, okay? I don't expect the culprit to fess up. Just don't do it again."

"Get away from that thing." The assignment editor reclaimed his telephone, which no one had ever had the temerity to touch before. "What got you riled?"

"Somebody snatched my pills." Newsroom personnel had stepped from their cubicles and were looking at her curiously.

The news director approached, a frown creasing his forehead. "What the hell's going on?"

She repeated her statement. "I'm sure that whoever sneaked into my office and took them from my desk drawer didn't mean any harm. However, it was a stupid and dangerous thing to do."

"How do you know it was someone from the newsroom?" the news director asked.

"I don't," she admitted. "But someone working on this floor would have had the best opportunity to wander into my office without attracting attention. And everyone in here loves a good joke. The sicker it is, the more hilarious. Those drugs are nothing to joke about."

"And I'm sure that everybody in the news department is well aware of that, Ms. Delaney."

His confidence in his staff caused Cat to reassess her knee-jerk reaction. Perhaps she'd been too hasty in issuing the blanket accusation.

"I apologize for the disruption," she said, feeling small. "If you hear anything, please let me know." Before there could be any further discussion, she retreated to her private office.

"The delivery is on its way," Melia told her, still looking sulky. "It'll take about twenty minutes they said. Is that soon enough?"

"That'll be fine. Thank you. Give me a minute and then get Sherry back on the phone. Jeff, bring Danny's file to my office, please."

Needing a moment's privacy, she closed the door between herself and her subdued staff. She leaned against the door and took several deep breaths. Her silk blouse clung to her more now than it had when she'd come in from the sweltering heat. She was bathed in damp, nervous perspiration. Her knees were shaking.

For three years she had tried to convince herself that she was just an ordinary person like everyone else, that there was nothing special about her.

But the fact was that she was a heart transplantee.

That meant she was extraordinary, with needs very few others shared, whether or not she wanted it that way. And that's the way it would be every day for the rest of her life.

Today's crisis had been short-lived and it hadn't resulted in a life-threatening situation. Nevertheless, it had been a rude reminder of just how fragile she was.

Chapter Seventeen

❧

Cat was getting her first taste of Bill Webster's infamous, controlled rage. She'd heard he seldom lost his temper, but that when he did, it caused fear throughout the building. This morning it was directed at her.

"They were positively irate, Cat."

Her reply was subdued. "They had every right to be."

"They felt that the little girl had been misrepresented to them."

"She had. But not intentionally."

Webster expelled a gust of breath. He tempered his anger, but his face was still flushed. "*Cat's Kids* is an asset to the community. It already has an impressive string of successes to its credit. The program has become a significant attribute of WWSA."

"But *Cat's Kids* also has the potential of being an Achilles' heel," she said, guessing his train of thought.

"Precisely. My commitment to the feature is as strong as

ever. I don't want you to think I'm getting cold feet. But the show leaves us vulnerable to lawsuits. We're a target for litigation from the state, the applicants to adopt, the birth parents—in fact, everybody who nurses a grudge over a slight, either real or imagined. This television station is in a precarious middle-of-the-road position."

"Where we can get hit by trucks going both ways."

He nodded brusquely. "When we initiated this program, we acknowledged the risks involved. As CEO, I'm still willing to accept the risks because the benefits far outweigh them. But extreme precautions must be taken to avoid another incident like this."

Cat rubbed her forehead. The day before, a couple named O'Connor had called Sherry Parks and revoked their recent adoption. Their little girl, whom they'd adopted through *Cat's Kids*, had attempted sexual foreplay with Mr. O'Connor.

"They're claiming that her sexual sophistication was deliberately omitted from her records to facilitate her adoption."

"That's simply not true, Bill. She was analyzed by several child psychologists. She concealed her advanced sexuality from all the doctors, from the social workers, from us, from everyone who had any dealings with her."

"I don't understand how she slipped through the cracks."

"She's seven years old!" Cat cried. "She has pigtails and dimples, not horns and a forked tail. Who would expect her to have sexual problems? But she was abused from the time she was in a crib. Her stepfather taught her how to please him. He taught her how to tease and—"

"Christ," Bill said, turning pale. "I don't need to hear the details."

"Everyone needs to hear them," she said crisply. "If everyone would acknowledge the dirty details, this outrage might not be so prevalent in our society."

"Point taken. Go on."

"Considering her background, the psychologists were initially amazed that she'd survived with so few scars. Now we know how troubled she actually is. She uses her sexuality to manipulate her environment—specifically to get her way with men, any man.

"You're absolutely right, Bill. We can't imagine a child who looks so innocent actually being a femme fatale. Neither can we imagine what was done to create her."

"But we can't blame the O'Connors for wanting to nullify the adoption."

"Of course not. Naturally, they were told that she'd been sexually abused. They were willing to deal with it when nobody knew the extent of the damage. None of us had any idea how cleverly she'd manipulated the experts.

"She knew the right answers for all their questions. She played them like a fiddle because she wanted to live in the O'Connors' house. She wanted to sleep in the pretty pink bed they'd put in her bedroom. She's admitted as much to Sherry now."

Bill shook his head in disbelief.

"This isn't the first time I've heard of cases this severe," Cat said. "They're tragic for everyone involved."

"True. And for that reason alone we don't need to be associated with them. An error like this must never happen again, Cat," he said sternly.

"I can't give you a guarantee. But I accept full responsibility for the selection of the children who appear on *Cat's Kids*. If there's any doubt in my mind—"

"Pass on them."

She disapproved of his terminology. They weren't talking about melons. She resented being told to hand-pick only the children with the fewest bruises. But she nodded in concession.

"I mailed the O'Connors a personal letter of apology this morning. I feel desperately sorry for them. Naturally, they were horrified by what she did; but they'd had just enough time to come to love her. It's a devastating conflict for them."

"Hope they don't sue us for millions," Webster said, speaking now as a businessman.

"I'm sorry that the station has to take this one on the chin."

Mollified, he waved off her apology. "You're the one in the front trenches. But we're all in this together, Cat. Whatever happens, I'll back you one hundred percent. You'll have our attorneys in your corner, and they're as vicious as wolverines."

She disliked the image of legal wolverines being turned loose on the couple who'd already suffered untold distress. "I hope it doesn't come to that."

"So do I." He assumed the posture of a judge ready to hand down a ruling. "However, after this, you might reconsider becoming so personally involved with these children. You take their problems onto yourself. You lose your objectivity."

"Thank God I do," she said heatedly. "I don't want to be objective. They're *children*, Bill, not numbers, not statistics. They're human beings who have hearts and souls and minds, and they've been hurt in one way or another.

"You might regard them as a publicity ploy, a way to increase ratings. Everyone else who works on *Cat's Kids* might see them only as the topic of a story, something to focus a camera on."

She leaned across his desk, bracing herself on her arms. "But the kids themselves are my focus. The rest of it is only a means to an end. If all I wanted was fortune and fame, I would have stayed on *Passages*.

"Instead, I came here to serve a purpose that I'll never lose sight of. To achieve that purpose, I *must* remain personally involved."

"I disapprove, but I trust you know what you're doing."

"I won't betray your trust."

He slid the morning newspaper across his desk toward her, but she'd already read the article he had circled in red. "Now that we've discussed the O'Connor matter, I'd like to hear how you propose we handle this."

Immediately upon returning to her office, Cat summoned Jeff and Melia. "For the sake of time and energy, I'm going to cut through the management handbook b.s. and get right to the point. Yesterday afternoon, you both became aware of the O'Connor situation. Did either of you leak the story to the media?"

Neither said anything.

She flicked her hand at the newspaper, which she'd brought with her from Bill's office. "Ron Truitt strikes again. But this time he had viable ammunition. He couldn't have accidentally run across this story. Somebody fed it to him.

"It's for certain that no one over at Human Services wanted this incident publicized. The O'Connors are almost as upset over having their privacy violated as they are over the incident itself. He didn't hear it from them. All fingers are pointing to WWSA, specifically this office.

"So, which of you is responsible? And, along with your confession, I'd like an explanation. If *Cat's Kids* is taken off the air, we're all unemployed, so what did you hope to gain by undermining it?"

Still, both remained silent, eyes averted.

"Jeff," Cat said after a long moment, "will you please excuse us?"

He cleared his throat and glanced at Melia. "Sure."

He slipped through the office door, pulling it closed. Cat let a heavy silence descend. One thing could be said for Melia King—she had nerve. Her sloe eyes never flinched. They remained steadily on Cat.

"Melia, I'm giving you one last opportunity to admit that you gave Ron Truitt that story. You'll be reprimanded. But as long as you pledge never again to breech our policy on privacy, that'll be the end of it."

"I didn't call that reporter or anybody else. That's the truth."

Cat opened her bottom desk drawer, removed a McDonald's carryout sack, and set it on her desk. It elicited from the stoic young woman a reaction that Cat had long awaited. Melia gaped at the sack, her lips parting in stunned surprise.

"Following the mysterious disappearance of my medication, one of the newsroom interns approached me," Cat said. "He'd seen you cross the parking lot at lunchtime and throw this into the Dumpster. He remembered thinking it was strange that you'd leave an air-conditioned building at noon and go out onto the hot asphalt parking lot to throw away your lunch trash.

"I waded through the Dumpster myself and found this sack. In it were four stale french fries, an unopened packet of ketchup, and fourteen bottles of pills."

Realizing that she was trapped, Melia defiantly tossed back her hair. "You'd really pissed me off that morning. You'd been on my case about writing a telephone number down wrong."

"That's your excuse for this?" Cat said, flicking the sack and making it crackle.

"You weren't going to croak. You got those prescriptions refilled in plenty of time."

"That's not the point. It was a mean, malicious thing to do."

"You had it coming," Melia shouted. "You're always bawling me out in front of that little faggot, making me feel stupid. I'm not stupid!"

Cat stood up. "No, I don't believe for a moment that you're stupid, Melia. I think you're extremely clever. Just not clever enough to keep from getting caught."

She squared her shoulders. "Please clear out your desk immediately."

"You're firing me?" she gasped, incredulous.

"I'll arrange for accounting to pay you what you've earned, plus the standard severance pay, which I think under these circumstances is more than fair."

Melia's eyes narrowed malevolently, but Cat stood her ground. Finally, Melia turned and headed for the door. On her way out, she said, "You're going to regret this." By noon she'd removed her personal items from her desk and left the building.

Cat asked the news director if she could borrow a secretary until she could hire someone to replace Melia. She was relieved to have Melia out of her life, but the entire episode, beginning with the O'Connor incident the day before, had left her feeling drained. She was in a truculent mood, certainly not up to having a guest waiting for her when she arrived home at dusk.

She certainly was not up to facing Alex Pierce.

"What are you doing here?" she asked through the driver's window of her car. "How'd you know where I live?"

He sat astride a motorcycle parked at the curb. "A simple, 'Hello, how are you?' would do."

Cat wheeled into the driveway. As she alighted, he met her and tried to take her heavy briefcase. "I can manage, thanks," she said crossly.

She climbed the front steps of her house and collected her mail, which was mostly throw-away ads. "Why do I get all this crap? Dozens of trees have sacrificed their lives to line my trash can."

Her foul mood seemed to amuse him. "Tough day at the office?"

"A bitch."

"Yeah. I saw your name in the newspaper."

"Not the most flattering write-up I've ever had."

"Tough break about that kid."

"Real tough."

She had to juggle her mail, handbag, briefcase, and keys in order to get the front door open. A third hand would have come in handy, but she stubbornly refused to ask for his assistance. She dumped the mail onto the foyer table, set her briefcase and handbag on the floor, then turned to face him, barring his entrance.

He was gazing beyond her shoulder into the house. "Nice place."

"Nice try."

"Nice comeback." Leaning forward, he added in a whisper, "Two can play that game. And I'm good at games."

"I'll bet you are." She planted a hand on her hip as though to fortify her blockade. "What are you doing here, Mr. Pierce?"

"Now that you've read my book, why don't you call me Alex?"

"How did you know—" Cat broke off, realizing she'd stepped right into his trap. "Okay, you caught me. I read them."

"Them? You read both?"

"I was curious, okay? But I'd still like to know how you found me and why you went to the trouble."

"Hungry?"

"What?"

"Want to go out for a burger?"

"With you?"

He held up his hands, palms out. "I washed my hands. Even under the fingernails. With Lava."

In spite of her determination to resist his roguish charm, she ducked her head and laughed. He relaxed his stance and settled his shoulder against the door jamb. "We sort of got off on the wrong foot the other day, didn't we?"

"Not 'sort of.' We did."

"I'm not at my best in the morning. Especially after a marathon night."

"Of writing?" The question popped out before she could contain it. She wasn't certain she wanted to know what activity he'd taken to marathon proportions.

He must have read her thoughts because he smiled knowingly. "Research, actually. Which isn't nearly as much fun as writing."

"How come?"

"Because it's fact, not fiction."

"You prefer make-believe to reality?"

"From what I've experienced of reality, yeah, I think I do." After a short pause, he said, "Anyway, I can't be held responsible for anything I say or do before my first cup of coffee. It was early—"

"It was eleven o'clock."

"And you had a burr up your ass."

She opened her mouth to protest, but changed her mind. "I was being rather prissy and judgmental, wasn't I?"

"Uh-huh."

"I'm sorry. You rubbed me the wrong way, and I overreacted."

He accepted her apology with a shrug. "I seem to have a knack for pissing people off." His words were tinged with bitterness. "Anyway, what do you say? Do we give each other a second chance?"

She hadn't had a social life since moving to San Antonio. No one at WWSA interested her, but even if there had been an eligible, attractive man, she wouldn't have encouraged him. She was dead set against dating co-workers. If the romance soured, everything began to stink.

But did she want to see Alex Pierce socially?

He was articulate and seemed intelligent. At the Walterses'

place she'd seen his irascibility, but now she was catching glimpses of a sense of humor that wasn't slapstick but witty. She could enjoy the challenge of such verbal sparring.

He was significantly better groomed than he'd been the last time she saw him, but he still bore a greater resemblance to the antagonists in his books than to the protagonists. There was an element of danger about him. His charm obscured a dark side that was both intriguing and frightening.

He was very good-looking. He'd certainly displayed no self-consciousness over meeting a stranger, a woman, wearing nothing but a pair of half-buttoned-up blue jeans. He'd probably known how good he'd looked in them, just as he'd known how unsettling his dishabille had been for her.

Cat weighed the pros and cons and decided that he was definitely the kind of man she would best avoid.

But she said, "Do you mind waiting while I change?"

Chapter Eighteen

~⤜⤛~

The restaurant wasn't a place she would have chosen, nor would she ever have gone into it alone. The parking lot was filled with pickup trucks. Inside, billiard balls clacked in the background; two-stepping music blared from the jukebox. It was a joint that boasted the best burgers and the coldest beer in Texas.

The double-fisted burger was indeed thick and juicy. After taking a few prim nibbles, she said to heck with manners and gorged on each oozing bite.

She dipped a french fry into a glob of ketchup before popping it into her mouth. "You're not off the hook yet for the insulting crack you made about redheads the other day."

"I don't remember."

She gave him a dirty look. "Of course you do. You said the redheads in your books are always easy."

"It was a cheap shot," he conceded, but failed miserably at looking contrite.

"Unfortunately it was also true," Cat said. "In your books, the redheads *are* easy. So are the blondes, the brunettes, and every woman in between. On every other page a female character is . . ."

"Putting out."

"Yes. The heroes never ask permission. And the women never say no."

"There's a large dose of fantasy in every work of fiction."

"In this case, sexist fantasy."

"It worked for Ian Fleming. Did James Bond ever ask 'May I?' Was he ever turned down?"

He wadded up the paper in which his cheeseburger had been wrapped, wiped his mouth on a paper napkin, and rested his forearms on the small round table as though getting down to serious conversation.

"Aside from the blatant sexism, and disregarding that all the female characters get naked and lie down on command, what did you think of the books?"

She resented having to tell him how good they were, but she felt compelled to be truthful. Since her opinion seemed important to him, her conscience wouldn't let her equivocate.

"They're good, Alex. Tough. Gritty. Brutally realistic. I had to scan some of the most violent scenes. But they're damn good. And, hard as it is for me to say so, it was in character every time a woman got naked and lay down."

"Thanks."

"But—"

"Uh-oh, the *but*. You should have been a literary critic. They throw flowers, then kick you in the nuts."

She laughed. "I wasn't going to say anything critical. Truly, I think your writing is brilliant."

"Then what's the but?"

She hesitated. "It's sad."

"Sad?"

"Your writing has a . . . a . . ." She groped for the right word. "A hopelessness about it. Its orientation is fatalistic."

He thought about it for a moment. "I guess that comes from seeing a lot of violence firsthand."

"When you were a cop?" He looked surprised that she knew. "It's in your bio on the dust jacket."

"Right." He sipped his drink. "Too often crime does pay, you know. The bad guys win. These days they seem to be winning more often than not. So if my writing seems fatalistic, I suppose that's why."

"It hit home with me because that's how I felt . . ." Again she hesitated. This was only their first date. How much did she want to tell him?

"How you felt when?"

She cast her eyes down and fiddled with the red plastic basket that held the remains of her meal. "I don't know if you're aware of this. It was publicized, but I don't make an issue of it because some people act really weird when they find out. It's no big deal, really, but . . ."

She raised her head and looked him in the eye, wanting to gauge his initial reaction. "I had a heart transplant."

He blinked once, twice. That was the extent of it. Of course, it was impossible to guess what was going on behind his steady, gray gaze.

After a moment, his eyes dropped to her chest. She saw him swallow. Then he lifted his eyes back to hers. "How long ago?"

"Almost four years."

"And you're okay?"

She laughed to ease her tension. "Of course I'm okay. What'd you think, that I'm going to keel over and stiff you with the check?"

How an individual would react to an organ transplantee was unpredictable. Some were repulsed. They shivered and shook and didn't want to talk about it. Others were filled with awe. They reached out and touched her as though she were vested with spiritual powers; they approached her as they would healing waters or a statue of the Virgin Mary that had been known to cry tears of blood. What magic they expected from her, she couldn't imagine. Still others were rabidly curious, bombarding her with personal and often embarrassing questions.

"Are you restricted in any way?" he asked.

"Yes," she said somberly. "I can't write more than twenty checks a month without a service charge from my bank."

He gave her a retiring look. "You know what I mean."

Yes, she knew what he meant, but this was the part she hated: qualifying herself. "I have to take a double handful of pills three times every day. I'm supposed to exercise and eat healthy foods just like everybody else. Low fat, low cholesterol."

He raised his crooked eyebrow and nodded toward the damage she'd done to the burger and fries.

"But I passed on the coldest beer in Texas," she said self-righteously.

"Alcohol's a no-no?"

"Booze messes with my medication. What about you? It hasn't escaped my notice that you drank a soda while every other testosterone-pumping person in the joint is guzzling suds."

The question made him fidgety, but Cat propped her cheek on the heel of her hand and continued staring at him until he relented. "Booze messes with my mind. We slugged it out a few years ago. I went down for the count, but managed to wobble to my feet."

"You're still wobbling?"

"I don't know. I don't trust myself to get back into the ring."

He seemed to be waiting for her response, to see if knowing

about his former drinking problem would color her opinion of him. She wanted to ask if it had started after he'd left police work or if it had been the reason behind his leaving. The dust jacket bio hadn't been that detailed.

She decided not to pry. It really was none of her business, although she was reasonably sure that alcohol had played a part in developing the dark, secret side of his personality she had detected.

" 'Get back into the ring,' " she repeated, changing the tone of the conversation. "I think I like talking to an author. The dialogue is riddled with metaphors and analogies. Not to mention the similes, segues, and such."

He groaned. "Don't start that again."

As he dropped enough cash on the table to cover their bill and a generous tip, Cat offered to pay her half. "No," he said, standing and signaling her to her feet. "I invited you. Besides, I need the tax deduction."

"This wasn't a business dinner."

"Yes, it was. I just haven't approached you with the business aspects yet."

Once they were outside, he ushered her to his motorcycle and helped her on with the helmet. She swung her leg over the seat, he jumped the starter, and the bike roared to life.

As they sped from the parking lot, Cat gripped the sides of his waist. He drove fast but carefully. Nevertheless, she couldn't help but recall that Dean always referred to motorcycles as "donor-cycles."

That was her only thought of Dean, and it was as fleeting as the cycle's progress through traffic.

When they reached her house, she experienced a pang of regret that the trip had been so short. He must have sensed her reluctance to get off the bike. "What?" he asked curiously as he removed his helmet and pushed his hand through his hair.

"Nothing," she replied, returning the helmet to him.

"Something."

"I want to thank you for not making a big deal out of it." He looked at her quizzically. "My transplant. You didn't blanch at the thought of my riding on the motorcycle with you. You drove just as fast as you did before you knew that I was a transplantee."

"Shouldn't I have?"

"Most people defer to me because of it. They think I'm fragile. They don't take chances with me for fear I might break. All that careful consideration gets tiresome. I appreciate that you didn't treat me with kid gloves. Thanks."

"You're welcome."

Their eyes locked; she knew something important was happening. Her attraction to him was too strong to be ignored. And it hadn't just begun tonight.

She had felt an inner tug the instant he'd pushed open the screen door of the Walters home and their eyes met for the first time. It had been tempting then to gaze her fill, but she'd resisted. Not now. Now she let her eyes explore his face.

There'd been looks like this in scenes she'd played on *Passages*. They communicated that this was a life-changing event, a "wake up and pay attention, this is important" moment. From this time forward nothing would ever be the same. To the delight of home viewers, she'd emoted that impetus, but she'd never experienced it herself. Not like this.

Alex was the first to break the stare by taking her elbow and turning her toward the house. "I have a favor to ask," he said as they went up the front walk.

"Is this the business part of the evening?"

"Yes. Would you consider helping me with some of the research for my next book?"

"How could I help?"

When they reached the front door, he turned to face her. "By putting out on the first date."

"*What?*"

"Will you go to bed with me tonight?"

"No!"

"There. We've completed our business. I asked you to help with my research. You said no, of course, but it was a legitimate and heartfelt request for assistance."

She tried to maintain the frown that her laughter was nudging aside. "Do you think the IRS will consider that a legitimate business transaction?"

"They rarely ask me to be that specific." A car drove past, calling his attention to it. "This is a great street. Not at all like where I pictured you'd live."

"What did you expect?"

"Something more glitzy."

"I have glitzy in Malibu. This is just what I was looking for when I moved here. A tree-lined street in a quiet neighborhood. A thirty-year-old house with hardwood floors and a deep front porch. Something roomy and homey."

"A home your mother would feel comfortable in."

"Yes. Probably."

He immediately picked up on her wistfulness. "I stuck my foot in it, didn't I? Bad scene?"

"No scene. Both my parents died when I was eight."

"Jesus. What happened?"

She avoided answering by pretending not to understand his meaning. "I was absorbed into the system."

"Foster care?"

"Hmm. I never was adopted because I'd been sick."

"All kids get sick."

"Not this sick. I had Hodgkin's disease. It was detected early, and I was completely cured, but people felt it was risky to adopt a skinny redheaded kid with a history of health problems." She glanced up at him. "It's gets really ugly from here. Are you sure you want to hear this?"

"I haven't bolted yet."

"You're free to at any time." She paused; he stayed. She

took a deep breath and plunged on. "I was moved from one foster home to another. Because of repeated rejections, I developed quite an attitude. I misbehaved to get attention. In short, I was a holy terror."

"I can believe it."

"I was always different from other kids, first because I was terribly ill, then because I didn't have a real mother and father. Thankfully, I survived it all without developing too many psychological hangups."

"I can believe that, too. You have the look of a fierce fighter." She flexed her thin biceps, and he laughed. "What caused your heart problem?"

"The chemotherapy I received to combat the Hodgkin's. It killed the cancer, but did massive damage to my heart. It had been slowly dying for years."

"Without your being aware of it?"

"Totally unaware. I lived a perfectly normal, healthy life. Meanwhile, my heart was petrifying. When there was very little workable muscle left, I began to notice a lack of energy. I blamed it on working too hard, but no amount of rest or vitamins alleviated the fatigue.

"I went in for a routine checkup and wound up in a cardiologist's office. To my dismay, he found that a large portion of my heart muscle had become so hard and inflexible, it might just as well have been stone. It couldn't pump sufficient amounts of blood. It was working at less than a third capacity, which qualified me for a transplant. Or else, I was doomed."

"Were you frightened?"

"Not so frightened as angry. I hadn't been dealt the best hand when I was a kid, but I'd overcome all the hardships. I was a TV star. Millions of people loved me. Their schedules revolved around watching me. My life was terrific, then *this*. I wanted to grab God by the collar and say, 'Hey, I hate to be a complainer, but enough is enough!' I guess He got the message because He let me live.''

''Ergo *Cat's Kids*.''

''Ergo *Cat's Kids*,'' she repeated in a whisper, smiling, gratified that he was intuitive enough to make the connection.

They continued smiling at each other. Gradually the smiles relaxed, but the stare endured. Shadows were deep on the porch. So was the silence. Another car drove past, but this time it went unnoticed. A mosquito lighted on her arm. Absently she brushed it away.

They stood face to face, looking into each other's eyes with mounting intensity, moving imperceptibly but ever closer. Without any warning at all, he raised his hand and slipped it into the opening of her collar. The pads of his fingers moved from the base of her throat down the center of her chest. He followed their progress with his eyes.

''I expected to see a scar.''

His hushed baritone coaxed a purling response deep inside her. ''It faded, although I still see it.''

''You do?''

''Yes. Even though it's no longer there.''

''Hmm. Did it hurt?''

''The scar?''

''Any of it? All of it?''

''Some of it was . . . tricky.''

''God, you're brave.''

''Not in the recovery ICU, I wasn't. Tubes, catheters, that sensation of choking. Even though I'd been told what to expect, I panicked. It was a torture chamber.''

''I can imagine.''

''No, you can't. Not until you've lived through it.''

''I'm sure you're right.''

''The only thing that kept me going was the knowledge

that I had a new heart. I could feel it beating. It felt so strong!''

"Like now?'' He pressed his hand more firmly against her breast.

"No. It's beating even stronger now.''

They spoke in whispers. His fingertips continued to massage the center of her chest. Self-conscious as she was about the scar, it amazed her that she was allowing him to touch it. Yet it seemed right, somehow. His touch was curious but gentle and, whether or not he intended it to be, erotic. She was melting.

A delicious languor stole through her, as smoothly pervasive as anesthesia. Her nerve endings hummed and tingled, their sensitivity magnified.

He'd been watching the point of contact between his fingertips and her skin, but gradually his eyes moved back up to hers. They connected and communicated desire. Need.

"Going to invite me in?'' he asked huskily.

"No. Going to leave mad?''

"No. Just disappointed.''

Then his lips claimed hers in a kiss. He wrapped her in his arms. His tongue sought hers, and when they touched, he groaned a sound that was distinctly masculine. It stirred her. She clutched the back of his head, twining her fingers in the hair that grew over his collar.

They moved together. Their middles bumped, stayed, then nestled intimately. His hand remained inside her blouse, splayed over her heart, which was filling his palm with a rapid pounding.

His other hand moved aggressively over her back and hips. He cupped the seat of her jeans and held her more tightly against him. The passion behind his kisses intensified.

Cat flung her head back and gasped for breath. "Alex?''

"Hmm?'' His open mouth was on her throat, kissing it hungrily.

"I should go in now."

He raised his head and blinked her into focus. "Oh, hell. Right." In one restless motion, he withdrew his hand from her blouse, pushed a lock of hair off his forehead, and turned to leave. He took all three porch steps in one wide stride.

Remorse shot through her like a sharp pain. "Will you call?"

He stopped, turned. "Want me to?"

She felt as though all ten of her toes were lined up along the edge of a high diving board. She would free-fall through the unknown until she made a landing that could be either wonderful or dreadful. She wouldn't know until she took the plunge. Dangerous as it was, she wanted to experience the fall and find out what lay below.

"Yes. I want you to."

"Then I will."

It took her awhile to recover from their kisses. Dazed, she wandered through her house, forgetting why she'd entered a room, unable to focus her thoughts on anything but the feel of Alex's mouth on hers, his hands on her body. She undressed, showered, and drank a cup of herbal tea in an effort to relax and bring herself down from the erotic high.

Finally believing she could sleep, she went through the house turning out lights. As she was bolting the front door, she spotted her unopened mail where she'd left it on the entry table.

"Hell." She wanted to go to bed, hug her pillow, and relive the time she'd spent with Alex Pierce. But if she put off opening the mail now, she'd have twice as much to open tomorrow night.

Compromising, she scooped up the correspondence and took it to bed with her. She sorted through it quickly, tossing the advertisements to the floor and placing the bills on her nightstand.

The last envelope in the pile gave her pause because of its stark white plainness. Her name and address formed three typed lines in the very center of it. There was no letterhead or return address, although it bore a local postmark.

Intrigued, she opened it and found a newspaper clipping, one column wide, four paragraphs long. No note. No explanation.

Hastily she scanned the article, then read it carefully and with mounting interest. Its dateline was Memphis, Tennessee. Jerry Ward, a sixteen-year-old boy, had drowned while trapped inside his pickup. Apparently he'd lost control of the vehicle on a rain-slick bridge and had plunged into a creek near his home. It was hours before the wreckage and his body were discovered.

Cat checked the unremarkable envelope in which the article had been mailed to her. Regardless of the dateline, the story could have been printed in any newspaper in the country. It was filler. Most readers would glance at it, then move on to read Ann Landers or the sports page.

But the anonymous sender knew that Cat Delaney's interest would be aroused because she and the boy in Memphis had something in common.

Jerry Ward had been a heart transplantee. After combatting a heart ailment since early childhood, he'd undergone a successful transplant, only to die in a tragic accident.

The cruel irony of that didn't escape Cat.

Which she suspected was the sender's intent.

Chapter Nineteen

Nancy Webster slipped into bed beside her husband. She placed her hand on his tummy, a habitual gesture that brought their day to an official close. He covered her hand and absently stroked the back of it.

"What's on your mind tonight?" she asked softly.

He smiled. "Lots of things."

"Such as?"

"Nothing specific."

In the early days of their marriage he had discussed with her every aspect of his workday. They'd discussed their hopes and dreams in whispers so as not to awaken the children sleeping in the next room.

Over the years, other obligations had pulled at them, sometimes taking precedence over those quiet pillow talks. Nancy missed them and longed for the days when he had valued her opinion above all others. He still did, she was sure; he just didn't ask for it as frequently as he had before his success was assured.

"The new Neilsen ratings come out tomorrow," he remarked.

"Last time WWSA was far and away the leader in this market," she reminded him. "Your primary competitor was running a distant second place. I predict you'll have an even stronger lead this time."

"I hope you're right."

She scooted closer and laid her head on his shoulder. "What else?"

"Oh, nothing. Everything."

"Cat Delaney?"

She sensed his immediate reaction. It was subtle—a tensing of muscle, a slight withdrawal although they continued to touch—but unmistakable.

"Why would I be thinking about Cat?" he asked testily. "Any more than I'd be thinking about Dirk Preston or Wally Seymour or Jane Jesco?" he said, naming WWSA's other popular on-air personalities.

"That's what I'm asking, Bill," she said softly. "Is there any special reason why you'd be thinking about Cat?"

"She does an excellent job for us. But she got herself in a bit of a bind last week, with that couple rescinding their adoption." He paused. "Thank God they didn't place the blame on us."

He resettled himself. Beneath the covers, his foot made contact with hers, but he pulled it back. "Cat's conscientious. Sometimes too much so, I think. I admire her and I like her."

"So do I." Nancy propped herself on her elbow and looked down at him. "But I don't want to share my husband with her."

"What are you talking about?" he asked brusquely.

"Bill, something's wrong between us."

"Nothing's wrong."

"I can feel it. I've been married to you more than thirty years. I've slept beside you every night of that time. I've seen you happy, sad, frustrated, jubilant, distraught. I know all your moods. I . . . I love you."

Her voice cracked and she hated that because the last thing she wanted to become was a whining wife who would drive her husband straight into the arms of another woman, one who was more understanding and less prone to nag and interrogate.

He touched her hair. "I love you, too. And I swear to God I'm not having an affair with Cat Delaney."

"But you're obsessed with her. You were even before you met her."

"I wanted her for WWSA."

"Don't patronize me," she snapped. "It's more than professional interest. You've gone after anchorpeople before, but not with the singlemindedness that you pursued her. Are you sexually obsessed with her?"

"No!" It came out harsh and loud. Lowering his voice, he repeated, "No, Nancy."

She gazed at him, searching for the truth, but his eyes revealed nothing. That implacability had helped to make him an excellent businessman. If he didn't want to be read, no one could read him.

Continuing the argument would be tantamount to calling him a liar and would only widen the rift. For the time being, she decided to let it rest. "All right."

He pulled her close and placed his arm around her. "You know I love you. You *know* that, Nancy."

She nodded. But, for her peace of mind, she wanted it demonstrated physically. Taking his hand, she placed it against her breast. He responded. They kissed, caressed. When he entered her, she wrapped her legs around him possessively.

Afterward, she snuggled against him, listening to his deep, rhythmic breathing. Although they were touching skin to skin, although their coupling had been sexy and passionate, it had lacked the spiritual intimacy they'd shared for years. Something was interfering.

Cat Delaney didn't seem the type to become entangled with a married man, but she was, after all, an actress. Her open friendliness could be an act. Nancy was never complacent when it came to other women. Bill was handsome, charming, and wealthy—quarry for legions of women whose morality would not deter them from breaking up a marriage.

As good as their relationship had been, it could happen. She and Bill had met and married during college, but many marriages broke up after thirty or more years. She couldn't depend on sentiment to hold them together. Nor did she rely on their six children to bind Bill to her forever.

Nancy depended only on the love that had endured for more than three decades—and on herself. Fighting gravity every step of the way, she kept in top physical form. At fifty-four, her skin was taut and virtually unlined. A honey-colored hair rinse concealed what little gray she had. She worked out in a gym three days a week and played golf and tennis socially, all of which helped to combat middle-age sag. When she looked in a mirror, she immodestly considered herself in better shape than most women half her age.

She'd never had career goals of her own. Instead, she had devoted her energies to the pursuance of Bill's. He had started as a studio camera operator while still in his teens and had worked his way up to the sales department, then moved into management, bouncing from station to station, city to city, state to state.

The first fifteen years of their marriage, they'd had so many addresses that Nancy lost count. She hadn't minded the moves. With each job Bill had elevated his position in the industry, and she knew how vitally important that was to him.

While serving as general manager at a station in Michigan,

he had engineered its sale to a media conglomerate and earned himself a whopping bonus. The new owners had asked him to stay, but he opted to use his bonus as a down payment on his own station. WWSA had become like another child to him and Nancy. He had nurtured it. She had nurtured him.

She planned to remain in her role of confidante, wife, friend, and lover until her last breath. She loved William Webster and would go to any lengths to keep him.

Resting her cheek against her pillow, she watched him sleep. With this man she had experienced levels of love she hadn't known existed. Her love for him was complex and multifaceted, marked by cataclysmic episodes in their lives. Their wedding day. Each step of his career. Each success and setback. The birth of each child. The death of one.

Nancy's breath caught in her throat.

Was it possible that Bill was stating the unmitigated truth? What if his obsession with Cat Delaney wasn't sexual? Could it have something to do with Carla?

That possibility filled Nancy with dread.

"Good morning, Ms. Delaney."

Cat stopped dead in her tracks when she saw Melia King behind the reception desk outside the news director's office.

"Excuse me a moment." Melia answered the chiming, hands-free telephone. "Good morning. WWSA news. How may I direct your call?" She beeped one of the reporters, then gave Cat her most ingratiating smile. "I work *here* now."

Cat reversed her direction. Forsaking the elevator in favor of the stairs, she reached the personnel office in record time and approached the secretary. Without preamble she asked if Melia King was still on the payroll.

"She's the newsroom receptionist now."

"How is that possible?" Cat asked. "I fired her two weeks ago."

"She was rehired."

"When? Why?"

"I'm really not at liberty to discuss another employee's business with you, Ms. Delaney. I was told to reinstate her," she said. "That's all I know."

Cat glanced at the closed door to the personnel manager's office. "I'd like to see her. Please announce me."

"She's not here, Ms. Delaney. But I'll leave a message with her."

"No, thank you. This can't wait." She turned to leave, then looked back at the anxious secretary. "I promise to keep you out of this."

She left the personnel office, marched to the end of the hall, and barged into the CEO's executive suite. "Is he in?"

Webster's assistant looked both affronted and afraid, as though this virago with flaming hair and flashing eyes had demanded her money or her life. "Yes, but he—"

"Thanks."

Bill was on the telephone when she flung open the door. He glanced up querulously, but when he saw that his unannounced guest was Cat, he smiled and motioned her in.

"Yes, yes, I'll get back to you on that next week. Surely. Thank you, yes. Goodbye." He hung up and stood politely, a broad smile in place. "I'm glad you came up, Cat. I was hoping we'd have a chance to chat today."

"I'm not here for a chat."

Her harsh tone surprised him. His smile faded. "I can see that. Sit down."

"I'd rather stand. Are you aware that Melia King is back on the payroll?"

"Ah, that's what this is about."

"The personnel manager reinstated her after I fired her. Why she would do that, I can't fathom, but I want and expect you to intervene and uphold my decision."

"I can't do that, Cat."

"You're the CEO. Of course you can."

"I can't because I authorized Ms. King's reinstatement."

She took a seat then, but not consciously. Shock had weakened her knees, and she plopped down onto the chair. After gazing at him incredulously for several seconds, she laid both palms flat on his desk and leaned toward him. "Why, Bill?"

"These issues are complicated, Cat. On the surface they may seem easy, but I assure you they're very complex."

His condescension infuriated her. "You're not going to say it's nothing for me to worry my pretty little head about, are you?"

He frowned. "I wasn't talking down to you."

"Like hell you weren't. And cut the b.s., okay? Give me the facts. Complex as they might be, I think I can muddle through them. Why did you countermand Melia's dismissal?"

"Two reasons. One, she's Hispanic. We have to handle minority hirings and firings very delicately. You've worked in the industry long enough to know that if you violate in any way, shape, or form the Equal Employment Opportunity Act—even if someone just perceives that you've violated it—the FCC places you under a microscope and dissects your entire operation. For the price of a postage stamp, someone can file a complaint that will shut down a TV station."

"My firing her had nothing to do with ethnic origins and you damn well know that."

"I know it, but if we came under investigation, it wouldn't be my opinion that counted. Look, Cat, I know you had difficulties with this employee, but you didn't document specific incidents."

"Because I didn't want to come across as a complainer."

"I appreciate that," he said. "Unfortunately, your finesse didn't serve you well this time. Had there been written reports on Ms. King's negligence or incompetence, you could have made a sound case for her dismissal. Without these documents, it appears that you fired her out of pique, that it was a personality conflict and nothing more. The FCC could take us to task.

"Ms. King was aware of this and brought it to the attention of the personnel director, who referred it to me. It was all done very professionally, but Ms. King's subtle message was clear."

"She bluffed and you crumpled."

"My decision to rehire her was made in the best interest of WWSA," he replied stiffly.

Melia's reinstatement was a fait accompli. Webster's position was unshakable. Cat knew that nothing would be gained now by telling him about the incident with her medication and Melia's eventual confession.

"Not that it matters, but what was the other reason for her reinstatement? You said there were two."

"She has a handicap."

"A handicap?" Cat repeated with a dry laugh. "If any employee is a flawless physical specimen it's Melia King."

"She's dyslexic."

"Oh God." Cat sighed, remembering all the times she had castigated Melia for getting telephone numbers incorrect. "I had no idea."

"No one did. It wasn't on her employee record. She's learned to work around the impairment, but isn't always successful. Perhaps that's why she made so many mistakes."

"Perhaps." Dyslexia still didn't excuse Melia for throwing the medication in a Dumpster. Cat sympathized with her condition and would be willing to forgive past errors and overlook them in the future if Melia had a more cooperative attitude. "Should she be working in a clerical capacity, where she's constantly challenged to write down names and numbers correctly?"

"She insists that she can handle it. Besides, it was the

only position we could offer her. Even at that, we had to juggle some schedules.''

"My, my, you've been accommodating."

"Sarcasm doesn't flatter you, Cat."

Still angry, she stood and prepared to leave. "I understand the awkward position you were in, Bill. I'll even concede that, for the good of the station, you had little choice in the way you handled it. What really riles me is that I wasn't consulted. You made me look like a fool and robbed me of any authority."

"That's not true, Cat."

"I'm afraid it is. If I, or anyone who's supposedly in an executive position, can have our decisions reversed, what's the point of empowering us? Disregarding her dyslexia, Melia deserved to be fired."

"That may very well be, but such is the nature of our industry."

"Well, that part of the industry's nature sucks!"

He stood and came around his desk. "You're blowing this out of proportion, Cat. Has something else upset you?"

Yes, she thought. *That disturbing piece of mail*.

The article and the envelope it had arrived in were still in her nightstand drawer. She'd tried to dismiss it as crank mail and throw both pieces away, but something had compelled her to keep them. More disturbing than the article itself was that it had been sent to her anonymously. That didn't necessarily suggest malevolence; perhaps it indicated only that the sender was insensitive and had a warped sense of humor.

She hadn't reached any conclusions. It was certainly premature to bring up the matter with Bill, who would no doubt think she was being paranoid. And he would be right.

"Everything's terrific," she said, pasting on a phony smile and switching subjects. "Have I told you about our latest success? Chantal—remember her?"

"The little girl who needed a kidney transplant?"

"Right. Her adoptive parents accepted full responsibility for her medical care. Yesterday they found a donor. They operated last night. So far, so good."

"That's wonderful news, Cat. I think we can milk some good PR out of this."

"I think so too. I've already asked Jeff to compose and distribute a press release. I told him to send it first to Ron Truitt. If he doesn't do a story on this, we can rightfully accuse him of biased reporting."

He placed his hands on her shoulders and gave them a slight squeeze. "Don't dwell on that other business. It's small potatoes compared to the excellent work you're doing. Keep it up and leave the daily operation of WWSA to me."

"I'll do my best to remember that. However, when my temper blows, it obscures my memory."

He laughed and walked her to the door. "You had a right to be angry. Let me make it up to you. Nancy's planning a dinner party. She wants to introduce you to some people who can be instrumental in putting together a celebrity fund-raising event like the one we talked about. How's next Saturday?"

"Wonderful. May I bring my own celebrity?"

"Of course. Who?"

"Alex Pierce."

"The writer?"

"You've heard of him?"

"How could I not? He's being touted as the next Joseph Wambaugh. I didn't know he lived in San Antonio."

"I get the impression he calls no place home, but he's here now working on his next book."

"By all means bring him. Nancy will be thrilled."

Chapter Twenty

❧

"So, do you want to go?"

"What do I have to wear?"

"For a start, shoes and socks."

The telephone amplified Alex's deep chuckle. It tickled Cat's ear and caused goosebumps to break out along her arms. This was getting ridiculous, she thought. She was acting like a schoolgirl in the throes of her first crush.

He was never far from her mind. Thoughts of him distracted her at work, and she became giddy at the sound of his voice. Ridiculous!

"I'll see if I can rake up a matching pair of socks," he said.

"It's not a black tie affair, but I don't want to be embarrassed by my date. Some veddy important people will be theah," she told him, mocking a British accent. "Nancy Webster's organizing a fund-raiser for the kids, so I'll never

147

speak to you again if you commit a faux pas that costs the kids some funds.''

"I promise not to scratch or pick or blow anything that shouldn't be scratched or picked or blown in public.''

"Oh, thanks for the assurance.'' She moaned. "You'll probably humiliate me. Or forget to show up.''

"I'll mark it on my calendar.''

"You'll forget to check the calendar. Remember, that's how we met.''

"Best mistake I ever made.''

She blushed with pleasure and was glad he couldn't see her silly grin. "To be on the safe side, I'll call you a couple of hours ahead of time and pick you up in my car.''

"Good idea.''

"Are you working tonight?''

"Yeah, but lately I've been finding it hard to concentrate. Wonder what could be distracting me?''

Again, a tide of pleasure coursed through her. It was flattering to be a distraction. They'd had two dates since their first one. Once they'd met at a restaurant for supper and had gone their separate ways afterward. The next time he'd picked her up—in a car.

They had gone to The Riverwalk, where they ate bad Mexican food at an outdoor cafe, then went for a stroll along the famed walk that channeled the San Antonio River through downtown. After a while they surrendered the shops and galleries to the tourists and moved up to the street level, where it was cooler, quieter, and less crowded.

They crossed the street, bought pina colada–flavored snow cones from a sleepy vendor, and sat down on a secluded, shadowed bench in Alamo Plaza. The sun had gone down and the buses of tourists had departed, leaving the lighted fortress looking stately and serene, a fitting monument to what had transpired there 150 years earlier.

"Hell of a choice they made, huh?'' Alex said, crunching

the chipped ice between his teeth. "Would you have stayed, fought to the death?"

"Tough question. I guess I would have if I didn't feel that I had anything to lose except my life." She scooped out a clump of ice with the tip of her tongue. "I can relate, in a way."

He looked at her inquisitively.

"Right before my transplant, I suddenly realized that they were about to cut out *my* heart. Don't misunderstand," she said hastily. "I desperately wanted a new one. But just for a heartbeat—pun intended—I experienced a pang of uncertainty. I would have to die in order to live. It was a sobering moment." She looked at him and smiled. "But it passed, and I got a new heart, a second life."

They munched their snow cones in silence. A horse-drawn carriage plodded by. There were no passengers, only a driver who sat with his shoulders slumped forward, his bearded chin resting on his chest, looking as weary as the horse.

"Cat?"

"Hmm?"

"Do you know who your donor was?"

"No."

"Do you know anything about—?"

"No, and I don't want to."

He nodded, but it was obvious that he was dissatisfied with her terse responses. "How come? I mean, is that common among heart transplantees?"

"No. Some want to meet the donor's family and thank them personally. They want them to know they're aware of the sacrifice they made. Some want to learn everything they can about their donor." She shook her head adamantly. "Not me. I couldn't deal with that."

"In what way?"

"What if I were a disappointment to them?"

"I doubt that would happen."

"There are too many gray areas involved. Instead of dwelling on who made it possible, I'd rather make my life count for something. Then their sacrifice wasn't made in vain."

The conversation had ended there. He hadn't pursued the topic, and she was glad. It was a sensitive subject. She had talked about it more freely with him than with anyone besides Dean.

Now, she glanced at her nightstand drawer and considered bringing up another unsettling subject—the mail she'd recently received. Would he think the article with the Memphis dateline held any significance for her? If not, why had it been sent to her? She wanted to know Alex's opinion on the matter, but decided against bringing it up now. She'd kept him from his work long enough.

"I'll let you go now. Sorry if I disturbed you."

"Don't worry about it. I've been at it for hours and needed to take a break anyway. Thanks for asking me to the Websters' dinner party."

"Thanks for accepting."

"I'll try and behave."

"I was teasing you."

"I know."

She heard the smile in his voice. It corresponded with hers. "Good night, Alex. See you Saturday evening."

She wore a sappy grin long after hanging up. No doubt about it, this was getting out of hand. It wasn't like her to be so reckless with her emotions. Because of her childhood, she was gun-shy about developing relationships. She'd had to leave several foster brothers and sisters after forming deep attachments. Relationships had inevitably led to break-ups, which had inevitably brought on heartache.

Nevertheless, she was falling hard and fast for Alex Pierce. How did he feel about her?

He'd like to sleep with her. That much she knew. He had

a healthy libido. One had only to read the sexual passages of his books to know that. And Cat had read them. Several times.

Of course she didn't approve of or care for his male characters' attitudes toward women. To call them sexists would be doing sexists a disservice. With few exceptions, they treated women with less regard than they would a used Kleenex.

But Alex seemed not to share his characters' chauvinism. It appeared he thought highly of her and the work she did. He complimented her often.

He was capable of laughter and joking, but by nature he was serious, sometimes even grave. He had little patience for trivialities. He also had little to say about his former police work, and on those rare occasions when he did mention it, his voice was tinged with bitterness. There'd been some unpleasantness attached to his retirement, which she suspected had not been voluntary.

She had fantasized him as a lover, but she would also welcome him as a friend. Dean was still her friend, but he was far away. She needed someone to confide in, and not by long distance.

Her eyes were drawn again to the nightstand where lay the mysterious, original clipping—along with the one that had been in today's mail.

It had arrived in an envelope identical to the first. Also identical to the first, it contained nothing except a newspaper clipping, this one bearing a dateline from Boca Raton, Florida.

A sixty-two-year-old woman had been found dead from an accidental fall. While at home by herself, she'd attempted to water a plant hanging from a hook in her ceiling. Her stepladder had slipped from beneath her, and she'd fallen through the patio door. Broken glass had pierced her lung.

Like the boy in Memphis, she'd had a heart transplant.

Cat didn't know what to make of these cryptic messages. As a former cop, what would Alex's assessment be? Would he think they were cause for alarm, or would he pass them off as the handiwork of a kook?

She had almost decided that that's exactly what the first one was, but then she'd received the second. It was an odd coincidence that two heart transplantees had died in such bizarre accidents. Even more odd was that someone was making it his business to alert her to these deaths.

"Nuts," she said, impatiently stuffing the clippings back into their envelopes and slamming the nightstand drawer closed. They'd probably been sent just to annoy and perplex her.

She wouldn't let them. If she wasted a moment's concern over them, she was letting a nutcase control her mind. Mail sent by wackos was a hazard of her profession. One took it in stride. Unless the messages became outright threatening, they were nothing to fret over.

Besides, she had more pressing matters to think about—like what to wear to the Websters' dinner party.

"Wow."

Cat arrived at Alex's apartment five minutes ahead of schedule. He was dressed in dark slacks and a dove-gray shirt, which he hadn't yet tucked in. The unfastened cuffs were flapping around his wrists and only two buttons were buttoned. He was barefoot.

His compliment hadn't been so much a word as a soft expulsion of breath. Her knees turned to jelly. "Thank you."

"You look great."

"Thanks again. I'm sorry I'm early. Traffic wasn't as heavy as I expected. Rather than wait outside in the car, I thought I'd see if you were ready yet. But it's fine that you're not. There's no rush. We've got plenty of—"

"What are you so nervous about? I promised to wear shoes and socks, didn't I?"

He was very intuitive. She'd been babbling to cover an outbreak of tummy butterflies. It made her even more nervous to know that he could read her so well. But he had a writer's insight. If he were writing this scene, he would have had the nervous character chattering like a moron.

His insight into human behavior and motivation put her at a disadvantage. She'd have to watch herself in the future, play with a poker face, not give so much away.

He moved aside. "Come in."

"Said the spider to the fly."

"I don't bite." He closed the door and locked it. "Not hard anyway."

Laughing, more at ease now, Cat glanced around the living area of his two-story apartment. It smelled of fresh paint. The vaulted ceiling and tall windows reminded her of her house in Malibu. Above, the second-story gallery encompassed two walls.

"Bedroom's up there," he said. "Kitchen back through there. Those double doors open onto a deck."

"I like it."

"It's okay," he said. "As you know, I'm not much of a housekeeper."

Actually she was impressed by the neatness of the apartment, until she noticed the hem of a shirt peeking beneath the sofa cushions. The magazines on the end table appeared to have been stacked hastily, and a Butterfinger wrapper was stuck to the cover of one. On the coffee table were moisture rings linked together like the Olympics logo.

"No shit, Delaney. You look fantastic tonight."

His compliment brought her around quickly. His gaze was hot and intense. It scorched her like a marshmallow in a bonfire. "Thanks."

"I thought redheads weren't supposed to wear orange."

"It's not orange, it's copper."

"It's orange."

The short, straight slip dress was held up by narrow shoulder straps and was covered with thin metal disks that glittered like new pennies. She hadn't worn anything with a scooped neckline since her transplant. She wouldn't have as recently as a few weeks ago. But Alex had rid her of her self-consciousness over her scar.

"Whatever the hell you call it," he said, "it's the same color as your hair and makes you shimmer like flames."

"Spoken like a writer. You're a poet and didn't know it."

"But you can tell by my feet. They're a coupla Longfellows," he said, completing the banality. He looked down at his bare feet. "Make yourself at home. I'll be right back."

He took the stairs two at a time. By the time he'd reached the gallery, he'd unfastened the fly of his trousers and was stuffing in his shirttail. "There might be something in the fridge to drink. I'm not sure. Help yourself to whatever's there."

"Okay, thanks. Where's your motorcycle? I didn't see it outside."

"I put it in the shop for a complete overhaul."

"Shoot. I'd like to ride it again."

"Yeah. Once you have that much power between your legs, you get addicted."

"Very funny."

"I'm going to miss it. The guy said it might take a few months to do the job right."

"How's the novel going?"

"It sucks."

"I doubt that." Her experience with writers was that they typically held low opinions of their current projects.

She meandered around his living room, searching for clues

into the nature of the man. There were none. The only personal aspect to the room was his hasty attempt to straighten it before her arrival. Otherwise it lacked the stamp of occupancy and ownership. There were no family photos, no memorabilia, no mail or coupons or receipts. The furnishings lacked character and looked rented.

She was vaguely disappointed.

Stashed beneath the stairs she discovered two shipping boxes with the titles of his two novels stenciled on them. They were still sealed. Why hadn't he dispensed copies of his books to family and friends? Maybe he had, and these were extras. Or maybe he didn't have any family and friends.

And maybe her imagination was running away with her.

She glanced through the miniblinds on the French doors. There was nothing remarkable about the deck. It looked unused.

On her way down the short hall to the kitchen, she noticed a closed door he'd failed to point out to her. Closet? Powder room? She stepped back to gauge the dimensions of the space behind the door. The area was larger than a closet or small bathroom.

Her hand was on the doorknob before she even realized she was reaching for it. She paused to reconsider. Why hadn't he mentioned this room? Had the omission been intentional?

She cautiously turned the knob. The door opened soundlessly. There was nothing to see inside but darkness. She widened the crack and poked her head into the room.

Faint light leaked through the drawn blinds. She could barely discern shapes, but she saw what looked like a table, a—

His hand clamped down on her wrist.

"What the hell are you doing?"

Chapter Twenty-one

"**D**amn it, Alex!" She wrenched her hand free and whirled around to face him. "You scared the crap out of me! What's the matter with you?"

He pulled the door shut with a decisive click. "That room is no-man's-land. No visitors allowed."

"Then why didn't you post a No Trespassing sign? What do you do in there, print counterfeit money?"

He took her wrist, loosely this time. "Sorry if I startled you. I didn't mean to. It's just that I'm very protective of my work space."

"To say the least," she said crossly.

"Please understand. What I do in there is extremely personal." He stared at the closed door as if he could see through it. "In that room I'm at my best, and at my worst. It's where I give birth to every goddamn word, and giving birth is painful as hell. It's where I create. Also where I curse the creative process. It's my ultraprivate, masochistic torture chamber."

He smiled wryly. "Sounds crazy to a nonwriter, I know, but having somebody invade my work space would be like having somebody rape my subconscious. It would be violated. It would never again belong exclusively to me and my thoughts."

The chastisement was well deserved. She shouldn't have poked her nose into a room with a closed door. Artists and sculptors kept their current projects under wraps until they were completed. No one ever heard a composer's music until it met with his satisfaction. She should have guessed that Alex would be at least as protective of his writing.

"I didn't realize," she said remorsefully. "I'm sorry."

"Except for this room, you can have the run of the place. I'll allow you access to my pantry and refrigerator, my dirty clothes hamper, even my private collection of erotica, but this room is off limits."

"My curiosity," she said, shaking her head. "One of the child welfare counselors predicted that it would be my undoing. But he also thought that chocolate was poison and cautioned me never to eat it." She glanced at him, her expression only partially repentant. "I'm afraid I didn't heed either warning."

He propped one of his forearms against the wall, trapping her there. "You're forgiven for your curiosity. Forgive me for overreacting?"

He'd draped a tie around his neck, but he hadn't knotted it yet. He smelled of soap—clean, damp, male skin, which to Cat was more appealing than expensive fragrance. His hair was still uncombed and looked only towel-dried. Altogether, he was one gorgeous, incredibly sexy man.

"You have a private stash of erotica?" she asked in a hushed voice.

"Uh-huh."

"How long have you been collecting?"

"Since I was old enough to know it was nasty."

"That long? Hmm. I'd like to see it sometime."

He grinned lazily. "I think you have a wicked streak, Cat Delaney."

"That was another thing that confounded the social workers."

His eyes scanned her face, then moved down her throat. He was standing so close that, in order to take in the rest of her, he had to tilt down his head. The top of his head glanced her cheekbone. She felt his breath on her chest.

He still had hold of her right wrist. He flattened it against the wall a little above her head, the underside facing outward. He kissed that delicate, translucent patch of skin where her pulse was racing. He stroked it with his tongue.

Then his lips grazed hers. "What time does that party get under way?"

"Ten minutes ago."

"Damn." Ducking his head, he nuzzled her neck where it merged with her shoulder.

"But I'd planned for us to be fashionably late."

"How come? Figured I wouldn't be ready in time?"

"No. Just in case . . . Uh . . ." It was difficult to think while he was nibbling her earlobe. "You know, just in case we got . . . tied up."

"You want to get tied up?"

Her stomach rose and fell. There was a catch in her throat. "I meant tied up in traffic or something."

"Oh. Traffic. Right."

He began to pull away, but Cat grabbed his necktie. "We're not missing anything," she whispered. "They'll have an extended cocktail hour."

"And neither of us drinks." He placed his hand beneath her breast and pushed it up, bending his head down to the fullness that swelled above the neckline of her dress. He gently sucked her skin against his teeth.

Cat moaned in pleasure and arched against him.

He raised his head and kissed her mouth, his tongue wily and provocative. When the kiss finally ended, he kept his lips resting against hers. His breath rushed in and out. "So . . . ?"

"What?"

"Wanna fuck?"

The unexpected vulgarity doused her desire like a bucket of cold water in the face. She shoved him away.

He raised his hands at his sides in a gesture of innocence and surrender. "You accused the heroes in my novels of never asking permission. Thought I'd give it a try, that's all."

"You could have phrased it a little more politely!"

"Okay." Looking contrite, he folded his hands beneath his chin. "Wanna fuck, please, ma'am?"

"Cute."

She tried to move past him, but he caught her around the waist and placed her between him and the wall again. There was no doubt as to whether he was teasing when he kissed her this time. More possessive than seductive, he continued to kiss her until her anger evaporated and she was kissing him back with equal ardor.

When he finally released her, Cat's lips throbbed hotly. Her entire body was flushed and tingling.

"I want you," he said. "But not when I have to worry about messing up your hair or makeup." He ran his thumb roughly over her lower lip. "Not when I'm in a hurry and under a deadline. Not when we're expected at a party that might earn you some cash for your kids. Because I doubt that once with you will be enough. Got that?"

Left breathless and aroused by his speech, she could only nod in response.

"I was having some fun with you by being crude, but

the invitation stands. As stated." His eyes went measurably darker. "It's only a matter of you choosing the time and place. Understood?"

Again she nodded.

He held her stare for a ten count, then turned away. "Give me a few more minutes."

"Cat, you're here!" Nancy Webster embraced her. "Everyone's dying to meet you."

A uniformed maid had shown Cat and Alex into the living room of the Websters' impressive home. Tonight it was brimming with the city's affluent and influential. The noise level was indicative of Nancy Webster's ability to make her guests feel at ease.

"I apologize for being late," Cat said. "We—"

"It was my fault," Alex interrupted. "Something came up."

That earned him a dirty look from Cat, but Nancy was so eager to meet him that both the wisecrack and Cat's silent rebuke escaped her notice.

Nancy clasped hands with him. "Mr. Pierce, welcome."

"Alex, please."

"I was so excited when Bill told me that Cat was bringing you tonight. I'm honored and delighted to have you in our home."

"I'm very pleased to be here."

"Come meet my husband. What would you like to drink?"

Nancy was a flawless hostess. With seemingly no effort she soon had a Perrier and lime in Alex's hand, and he and Bill on a first-name basis.

"I read your first novel and thought it very good for a first effort," Bill said.

It was one of those qualified compliments to which there was no appropriate response. Alex wondered if Webster realized that, and decided immediately that he did. The man was trying to discredit him without it being obvious.

He mustered some graciousness. "Thank you for the compliment and the royalty."

"Are you working on another book?"

"I'm hard at it, yes."

"Is the story set in San Antonio?"

"Parts of it."

Cat looped her arm through Alex's. "Save your questions, Bill. You won't squeeze anything out of him. He's very cloak-and-dagger when it comes to his work."

Webster looked at him curiously. "Why's that?"

"Talking about the story before it's written spoils the surprises. Not for the reader, but for me."

"You're writing the book, but you don't know what's going to happen next?"

"Not always, no."

Webster frowned, looking doubtful. "I'm afraid I'm too goaloriented to work like that."

Who gives a fuck? was Alex's thought.

Cat broke the awkward silence. "I hate to brag, but Alex has asked me to help with his research."

"Really?" Webster said.

"He was finding the bedroom scenes difficult to write, so I told him some stories from my sordid Hollywood past and gave him permission to . . ." She gestured as though trying to grasp the right word.

"Elaborate?" Nancy said helpfully.

"No. To tone them down."

Everyone within earshot laughed.

"As much as we'd like to monopolize them, Bill, we can't," Nancy said. "Our other guests would never forgive us. Cat? Alex?" She moved between them and linked her arms with theirs. "First, I want to introduce you to our new mayor and her husband."

She guided them around the room; introductions were made. Alex was pleased by the number of people who claimed to be fans. Cat had an even greater number of admirers. Everyone had something good to say about *Cat's Kids*. She never took full credit but shared it with her crew.

"From Bill Webster on down, everyone at WWSA is committed to the success of the project," she said.

One of the guests mentioned a story that had appeared in the Sunday edition of the *San Antonio Light*. It was about the little girl who'd recently been adopted and then had undergone a kidney transplant.

"Yes, Chantal's story is inspiring," Cat remarked to the woman who'd called attention to it. Then she looked at Webster and, in an undertone, said, "Wonder how Truitt likes the taste of crow?"

For several days the entertainment reporter had pursued the O'Connor story, but to no avail. After the station's public relations department issued a statement, there were no further comments from WWSA. At the advice of their attorney, the O'Connors refused to be interviewed. Then, after counseling made them see how skillfully their adopted little girl had concealed her emotional corruption, the distressed couple had decided to keep her after all.

Both the state agency and *Cat's Kids* had narrowly escaped disaster. Cat hoped this most recent newspaper story would dispel any lingering doubts as to the validity of the program.

She said, "What's happened in Chantal's life is nothing short of a miracle. Unfortunately, there are many other children with special problems who deserve their own miracles.

"They're drifting through the foster care system. Be assured that many foster parents are loving, caring people. But these special children desperately need permanent homes."

Dinner was a seven-course affair that lasted more than two

hours. Alex would have been bored stiff if not for Cat, who, at the urging of the other guests, related stories about some of the children featured on *Cat's Kids*.

Her audience was spellbound by her moving accounts. Some evoked laughter, others tears. Cat's animated delivery was as stirring as the nature of the stories she told. Her voice conveyed her passionate dedication to the program she'd undertaken.

By the time the white chocolate mousse was served, she had everyone at the table fired up and chatting excitedly about a celebrity fund-raiser.

As Alex held her chair for her when dinner was over, he leaned down and whispered, "It's in the bag."

After the other guests had left, the Websters prevailed upon him and Cat to stay for a last cup of coffee to toast the evening's success. "Let's go into Bill's study where we can get comfortable," Nancy suggested, leading the way.

A maid carried in a silver service, but Nancy poured. "Would you care for a brandy, Alex?"

"Just coffee, please."

"I noticed that you skipped wine at dinner," Bill observed as he reached for the cup of brandy-laced coffee that Nancy had poured for him. "Are you a teetotaler?"

"Yes."

Feeling no obligation to explain his abstinence to Webster, Alex left it at that. However, his failure to expound created another chasm of silence. Again, Cat bridged it.

"Is this a family picture album?" She reached for the large leather-bound book on the coffee table. She settled herself on the floor, tucking her legs beneath her. "Mind if I look through it?"

"Of course not," Nancy replied. "We could bore you for hours with pictures of the children."

"How many do you have?" Alex asked.

"Six."

"Six!" He raised his cup of coffee in a silent salute. "No one would ever guess by looking at their mother."

"Thank you."

"She keeps herself in perfect shape," Webster said, smiling proudly.

"Are your children still at home?"

While Nancy gave Alex a rundown of where their various offspring were and what they were doing, Cat continued to turn the pages of the album. Every now and then Alex glanced over her shoulder at the photographs. From what he could tell, the Webster children were much like their parents. They had all-American good looks and seemed to be overachievers, as they were frequently photographed holding a trophy or ribbon.

"So actually," Nancy summarized, "only the youngest still lives with us, although he's rarely at home. He's editor of his high school newspaper and that—"

"My God!"

Cat's startled exclamation cut Nancy off.

In an instant, all eyes were focused on her.

Chapter Twenty-two

Did you know you were a dead ringer for their daughter Carla?"

Fully aware of Alex's heavy stare, Cat concentrated on driving and kept her eyes on the road. "There was some resemblance," she acknowledged.

"That's a prince of an understatement."

"She had brown eyes, not blue."

"But she had curly red hair, and the shape of her face was the same." Tilting his head, he analyzed her profile. "Her bone structure wasn't as pronounced. Not as angular. But the likeness was remarkable."

Her eyes riveted on the road, she kept a white-knuckle grip on the steering wheel.

"You know I'm right," he persisted. "When you saw her picture, you looked ready to faint. Your cheeks turned red."

"You're very observant."

"That's what I do. I observe people and write down what I observe."

"Well, I don't like being observed!"

"That's too bad, because you're a fascinating observation. So's Webster."

"Bill? Why?"

"Well, for one thing, he disliked me on sight. Not that I give a damn, but it's peculiar."

"Why peculiar? Does everyone you meet automatically like you?"

"Don't pretend you didn't notice, because you did. To cover for him, you jumped in with that joke about helping me with research. Then he nearly had apoplexy when you picked up that photo album. He didn't want you to see that picture of his late daughter."

Cat called upon her acting skills to keep her face impassive. She hadn't been watching Bill as Alex had, so she couldn't accurately say what his reaction had been to her interest in the album. However, it hadn't escaped her notice that he'd been virtually silent following the episode, leaving it to Nancy to handle the situation.

Nancy had quietly acknowledged the striking resemblance between their daughter and Cat, saying, "Bill and I noticed it when you first joined the cast of *Passages*. We even teased Carla about it, accusing her of having a double life she hadn't told us about. Remember, dear?"

He had given a gruff, muttered, affirmative reply.

Following that, she and Alex had declined a refill on coffee and insisted that they should call it a night. Cat had profusely thanked the Websters for hosting the party. Nancy felt confident that with the assistance and endorsement of those who'd attended, she could arrange a fund-raiser to top all fund-raisers.

"I enjoyed myself," Alex had said to his hosts. "Thank you for including me."

At the door, Nancy had hugged them in turn. She'd kept

up her composure. Bill, on the other hand, had appeared shaken and . . . what? Guilty?

And why had he been so cool to Alex?

"Did you know about Carla before tonight?" Alex asked now.

"I knew they'd lost their eldest child. She was killed in an auto accident returning to the university in Austin."

"Webster told you that?"

She nodded. "Even before I moved here. Apparently they haven't fully recovered. But who could? Your daughter comes home for the weekend. You do her laundry, listen to her going on about the boy she's seeing, about the professor she hates. You tell her goodbye, instruct her to drive carefully, give her a hug. The next time you see her, you're identifying her body in the morgue."

Cat shuddered and added softly, "I can't imagine anything worse than having to bury your child."

Alex was respectfully silent for a moment, then threw her a curve ball. "Does Webster have the hots for you?"

"No!"

"Yeah. Right."

"He doesn't," she insisted. "That would be really sick, considering my resemblance to his daughter."

"Maybe that's what first interested him. His attraction was innocent enough when you met. Over time, it's evolved into something else."

"It hasn't."

Alex maintained his skeptical silence. Finally, she qualified her answer. "Or if it has, he's never given me any indication of it."

"I doubt he'd chase you around the office or try to cop a feel while no one's looking. He's too proud for that."

"He's never made a pass, sneakily or overtly."

"But you two share more than a routine employer-employee relationship."

"I consider him a friend," Cat said cautiously. "But nothing romantic has ever even been suggested. From all appearances, he and Nancy have a perfect relationship."

"No relationship is perfect."

She gave him an arch look. 'Speaking from experience?"

"Unfortunately yes. Too many."

"So I gathered."

"But back to you and Bill Webster—"

"There is no me and Bill Webster," she argued. "He's given me a wonderful opportunity. I like and respect him. That's it."

"I don't think so, Cat." She was about to protest, but he said, "I'm not calling you a liar. It's him. Something about him bugs me."

"He's a handsome man in a stately, distinguished way. He's extremely successful. He's vested with a lot of power. He emanates an air of authority."

"Wait a minute," he said testily. "Are you implying that I'm jealous of him?"

"You tell me."

"You've got it backward, sweetheart. He was jealous of me tonight because I was your date."

"Bull!"

"Okay, fine. It's bull. But I'm telling you, Webster's got something to hide."

They had reached a Mexican standoff. Cat wouldn't admit what she was thinking—that Bill's behavior this evening had been curious and disturbing. She needed time to make sense of it.

Alex, however, wouldn't leave it alone.

"Why do you suppose he acted so weird when you saw that picture of Carla?"

"Because if the similarity between us was the reason he first noticed me, he was embarrassed. That sentimental trait doesn't fit the image of a tough CEO, an image he's carefully cultivated and stringently maintained.''

"Maybe."

She struck the steering wheel with her fist. "Are you always right? Don't you ever say something like, 'I never looked at it from that angle. I might be wrong'?"

"Not this time," he said stubbornly. "There's something about Webster that doesn't ring true. I feel it in my gut. The picture's too perfect. His life is like an illustration of a contemporary fairy tale. I keep looking for the camouflaged troll.''

"You've slipped into your cop mode, you know."

"Probably. Instinct. It's a hard habit to break. I look at everybody with a certain degree of suspicion.''

"Why?"

"Because people are just naturally suspicious. Everyone has something to hide.''

"You mean like a secret?"

Her mischievous whisper didn't make a dent in his solemn expression. "Exactly like a secret. We all have something we'd rather keep under lock and key.''

"Not me. My life's an open book. I've been poked and probed and X-rayed inside and out. They literally pried open my chest and looked around inside. If I had anything to hide, it would have been discovered long before now.''

He shook his head. "You've got a secret, Cat,'' he insisted. "Maybe it's such a deep, dark secret that it's buried in your subconscious. Even you don't know what it is. You don't want to reveal it to yourself because then you'd have to deal with it. We—meaning all of us—bury the ugly aspects of ourselves because we can't bear to face them.''

"Gee, I'm so glad I asked you to come with me tonight. You're a barrel of laughs.''

"I tried joking with you earlier," he reminded her. "You didn't seem to appreciate my sense of humor.''

She threw him a reproving frown. "I think you're taking your Cop Psychology course far too seriously."

"Maybe. But fiction writers are psychologists too, you know. Hour after hour, day after day, I plot the lives of people. I study their behavior patterns and try to figure out what makes them tick. Think about this," he said, turning toward her. "You hit your thumb with a hammer. What do you do next?"

"Chances are I'll yowl, scream something profane, and hop around holding tight to my thumb."

"Exactly. That's cause and effect. Given that stimulus, we all behave basically the same way. On the other hand, events occur in our lives that are unique to us. They may be accidental or coincidental, but our responses to them are also programmed.

"And each of us is programmed differently depending on our sex, I.Q., economic background, birth order, and so on. Each of us has reasons for reacting and behaving the way we do. That's motivation. As an author, I have to know what motivates a particular character to respond to a particular situation in a particular way."

"You study human nature."

"In all its forms."

"And it's human nature to bury our secrets?"

"Like a dog does a bone. Except we rarely want to dig them up and gnaw on them."

"What's your secret, Sigmund?"

"Can't tell. It's a secret."

She stopped at an intersection and turned to look at him. "I think you probably have more than one."

He didn't take the bait. Instead, he held her gaze with his. "Are we going to sleep together tonight?"

She regarded him thoughtfully until the traffic light changed and the driver behind them tooted his horn. "I don't believe so," she said as she stepped on the accelerator.

"Why not?"

"Because you've talked so much about studying me, I'm self-conscious. Would I be the first television personality you've taken to bed? The first heart transplantee? The first redhead who wears a size seven narrow shoe? Do you want to sleep with me so you can store the experience in your mental encyclopedia on human nature?"

He didn't jump in with a denial, and it bothered her that he didn't. She wanted him to adamantly repudiate the charge. She glanced across at him. He was watching her, saying nothing, revealing nothing. His stony silence reinforced her decision.

"Sorry, Alex. I don't want to see myself in the bedroom-conquest scene of your next book."

He turned from her and stared out through the windshield. His jaw was flexing angrily, and she feared it was because she'd hit the nail squarely on the head. At least he had the decency not to lie about his motives. Nevertheless, she was terribly disappointed.

"You make me sound like a real shit," he said.

"I think more than likely you are."

He whipped his head around, and when he saw that she was smiling, he chuckled softly. "Well, you're right. But even shits are given the benefit of the doubt sometimes."

"Okay. Coffee at my house?"

"Yeah. I'll take a cab home from there."

"Coffee. Nothing else."

"I'm not an animal, you know. I can curb my urges when I must." He was joking, but then he turned serious again. "I really enjoy talking to you, Cat."

"Is this a new tack?"

"No. It's not a line. I mean it. You're quick. Smart. Competitive. A good sport."

"Hmm, quick, smart, and competitive. And a good sport. Maybe I should give up trying to be a sex symbol and audition for *Jeopardy* instead."

For the remainder of the drive they kept the conversation light. They were still laughing over an anecdote from the dinner party when they turned down her street.

Cat braked suddenly. "Who's that?"

A dark sedan was parked at the curb in front of her house. Although it was visible from half a block away, it was partially obscured by the shadows of the overhanging branches of the live oak trees in her yard.

"You don't recognize the car?" Alex asked.

She shook her head.

"Expecting company?"

"No."

She had told herself that the two clippings sent to her anonymously were nothing to worry about, but she knew it would be foolish to dismiss them entirely. Nutcases were known to have committed heinous crimes due to their fixations on celebrities.

She'd been taking extra safety precautions—making certain her doors and windows remained locked, scanning parking lots before leaving buildings, and checking her backseat before getting into her car. She hadn't gone completely paranoid, but exercising common sense couldn't hurt.

"Hey. What's got you so spooked?" Alex asked.

"I'm not spooked. I just—"

"Don't lie to me. You're practically choking the steering wheel. I can see your pulse racing in your carotid. What gives?"

"Nothing."

"Cat!"

"Nothing!"

"Liar. Pull over."

"I—"

"Do it!"

She parked at the curb but left the engine running.

"Cut the lights. Be quiet. Stay put." He opened his door and got out.

"Alex, what are you going to do? *Alex?*"

Ignoring her, he sprinted across the neighbors' front lawns toward her house. Soon he melded with the shadows and she could no longer see him.

Her initial anxiety had abated. She had been spooked, but only for a moment. Her skittishness now seemed silly. For all she knew, the car belonged to someone visiting a neighbor.

Impatiently she tapped her fingers on the steering wheel. "Be quiet. Stay put. Sit, roll over, play dead," she muttered with pique. She didn't need him to rescue her.

In seconds she was out of the car. Following the path Alex had taken, she ran on tiptoe, sticking to the shadows. The closer she got to her house the more ridiculous she felt. Would someone with a grudge against her park in front of her house, announcing his presence?

On the other hand, how could she account for the eerie feeling of being watched that she'd experienced lately? Those damn white envelopes and their cryptic warnings were playing mind games with her. She'd always scorned cowardice. It wasn't like her to be jumpy, to imagine bogeymen lurking in shadows, ready to pounce.

Yet, her nervousness increased the closer she came to her house. Except for the soft glow of the porch light, all was in darkness. There was no sound; nothing moved.

Then, coming from the backyard, she heard raised voices. A shout. A grunt. Scuffling sounds. Shortly, two figures materialized out of the darkness. Alex was struggling with another man as he virtually dragged him into the front yard.

"I found him trying to break in the rear door," he told her.

"You son of a bitch," the other man growled. "Let go of me."

"Not a chance."

Alex threw him facedown onto the ground and crouched over him, planting his knee in the small of the man's back. He shoved his right hand up between his shoulder blades. "If you so much as move, I'll break your frigging arm," he threatened. "Cat, call 911."

Galvanized, she ran up the front walk, but almost tripped on the steps when her name was once again called out, this time by a voice ragged with indignation and pain, but nevertheless familiar.

"Cat, for crissake, call this cocksucker off me."

She whirled around, her eyes wide with astonishment. *"Dean?"*

Chapter Twenty-three

Cat swabbed the scrape on Dean Spicer's cheek with peroxide. The cardiologist winced and cursed beneath his breath. Alex, straddling a chair backward, struggled to contain his smile.

They were gathered around Cat's kitchen table. It was exactly the kind of kitchen Alex would have assigned her if she were one of his fictional characters.

The basic color was white, accented with splashes of color—a Georgia O'Keeffe poppy on one wall, African violets blooming on the windowsill, a whimsical black and white teapot patterned like a Holstein cow.

Spicer brushed aside Cat's hands. "It's fine," he grumbled. "Do you have anything to drink?"

"You mean liquor? No."

"Aspirin?" She shook her head remorsefully. He sighed. "Well, I guess you weren't expecting a guest to be attacked and wrestled to the ground." He glared at Alex. "I think an apology is in order."

"I won't apologize for reacting to what I saw, which was you trying to pick the lock on Cat's back door."

True, he'd roughed Spicer up before discovering that he was friend, not foe, but he hadn't really hurt him. All that was wounded was his pride, and Alex couldn't work up any sympathy for that.

"You shouldn't have been prowling around in the dark trying to break into her house," he said.

"You should have asked for some identification before attacking me."

Alex snickered. "That's a good way to get your head blown off. You don't walk up to a perp and politely ask to see some ID. You contain him, then ask questions. You wouldn't last ten minutes on the streets doing it any other way."

"I wouldn't know. Unlike you, I'm not from the streets."

Alex came out of his chair so fast that it went over backward. "You'd better be glad Cat recognized you when she did. I was about to sew your asshole shut for calling me a cocksucker."

"Guys!" Cat exclaimed. "We're all friends here, right? A mistake was made, but it's the kind of thing that we'll laugh over in a few weeks."

Alex doubted that either he or Spicer would ever think this was funny, but he didn't argue with Cat. She was already as jumpy as her namesake. He righted his chair and sat back down. He and Spicer continued to eye each other with animosity.

As Cat recapped the bottle of peroxide and set it aside, she mildly chided her unexpected guest. "If only you'd called and told me you were coming, this could have been avoided."

"I wanted to surprise you."

"Well you certainly succeeded in doing that!" she said brightly.

Too brightly. Her smile seemed forced. Alex guessed that she wasn't too thrilled to see Dr. Spicer, whom she'd introduced only as her friend. Alex didn't need it spelled out that Spicer had been more to her than that. Her voice sounded thin and strained now as she politely asked about his flight.

"Did you get a meal on the plane? Can I fix you something?"

"I didn't eat the meal they served, but I've had your cooking. Thanks anyway."

"Coffee?"

"None for me."

"Me, either."

"Well then, we should go into the living room." Neither of them moved, so she joined them at the kitchen table. "I can't believe you actually came to San Antonio," she said to Spicer. "I didn't think you'd be caught dead out here in the provinces."

"From what I've seen so far, it lives up to my low expectations."

"Thanks a lot!" Her umbrage was in jest, but he took it seriously.

"I didn't mean that the way it sounded. Your house is nice." He gave the kitchen a critical glance. "Nothing compared to your place in Malibu, of course."

"True. There is a shortage of beachfront property in San Antonio." Cat laughed nervously at her joke. Neither Alex nor Spicer cracked a smile. They left it to her to carry the conversation. "When did you decide to make the trip, Dean?"

"It was a spur-of-the-moment decision. I had only a few appointments over the next several days. It was easy to reschedule them and take a few days off."

"However it came about, I'm awfully glad you're here."

She was lying and Alex knew it. Furthermore, so did Spicer.

"Actually your timing was good," she said with forced gaiety. "We were just returning from a dinner party hosted by the Websters."

Spicer made a noncommittal grunt.

"Nancy's organizing a celebrity fund-raiser for *Cat's Kids*."

"How nice."

"The crème de la crème of San Antonio society were there."

"Which I'm sure isn't saying much."

Alex admired the self-control it must have cost her to ignore Spicer's insulting remark. Even her smile held up. "The women there were all aflutter over meeting Alex."

Spicer turned to him. "You're a cop, right?"

"Formerly."

Another harrumph, rife with disdain.

"Alex writes crime novels now. He's become quite famous. Have you read either of his books?"

Spicer looked at her as though the very idea was unthinkable. "No."

"Maybe you should," Alex said blandly.

"I can't think of a single reason why I'd want to."

"You might learn something useful, like how to defend yourself."

Spicer shot to his feet, then swayed dizzily and had to grab hold of the back of his chair to keep from pitching forward. Alex suppressed another satisfied grin.

Cat had sprung up to assist the cardiologist back into his chair. As soon as he was resettled, she planted both fists on her hips and said angrily, "All right, I've had it with you two. I'm trying to be Emily Post, *and* trying to referee, and neither role suits me. Now cut it out! You're acting like jerks. Over nothing.''

"I wouldn't call this nothing," Spicer said, pointing to the scratch on his cheek.

"Gimme a break," Alex muttered.

"You almost did." Spicer sneered. "In fact, you threatened to break my arm."

"Dean—"

"Because I thought you were a burglar. Turns out you're only a fool for creeping around in the dark and—"

"Alex . . ."

He came to his feet. "Save it, Cat. Doesn't matter. I think I heard my taxi pull up outside."

"You've already called one?"

"While you were getting the first-aid stuff."

"Oh. I thought you'd stay and visit with us."

"No, I wouldn't want to keep you from your guest. It's been an experience. Doctor."

Spicer glowered at him. To cover his rudeness, Cat murmured, "I'll see you out, Alex."

She walked him through her house to the front door. She'd removed her high heels, so her footsteps fell silently on the hardwood floors, although they creaked pleasantly beneath his weight.

The rooms were spacious, illuminated by strategically placed lamps instead of ceiling light fixtures. Their soft light fell on framed photographs, magazines, and bowls of fragrant potpourri. The sofas and chairs were oversized and overstuffed and piled with pillows. The ambience was unpretentious, soft, and friendly.

She opened the front door. "You were right. The taxi's here." It was parked at the curb behind Spicer's rental car.

Turning back, she said softly, "Thanks again for escorting me to the party tonight."

"Thanks for asking me."

If she were smart, she would leave it there and say good night. But she didn't. Laughing weakly, she said, "We had a surprise ending to the evening, didn't we?"

"Yeah."

"More exciting than a quiet cup of coffee."

"Less exciting than a roll in the sack."

She tossed her head. "Must you be so crude?"

"Must you be so coy? You know damn good and well that we were headed for bed."

"I had already said no."

"But did you mean it?"

She lowered her head. He touched her chin and brought it back up. "We're grown-ups. We both know what we're leading up to, so don't try and bullshit me, okay? Since I looked at you through Irene and Charlie's screen door I've wanted you. And you've known it. And you've wanted me, too. Everything we've said and done since then has been foreplay."

She glanced nervously toward the kitchen. That irked him. "I get the message. Good night, Cat."

He slipped through the door and was about halfway down the walk when he glanced back over his shoulder. She was still standing in the doorway, silhouetted against the light behind her. One hand was raised and resting on the jamb, as though it had been arrested in a motion of entreaty.

Whether it was because she looked wistful and a little forlorn, or because he was still pissed because her former lover had shown up at an inopportune time, or because he truly was the shit he'd confessed to being, he disregarded his conscience and his better judgment and reversed his direction. He covered the same distance in a fraction of the time.

Without a word, he cupped the back of her head and slid his fingers up through her hair. His other arm encircled her waist and pulled her against him. He kissed her with lust and anger, his mouth hard. His tongue thrust deeply and possessively.

Then, as abruptly as he'd begun the kiss, he ended it.

She stared up at him, her wet lips parted in astonishment. He left her looking stunned and aroused, kissable, and fuckable; and when he marched down the walk the second time, he was angrier than before. With Spicer, with her, with himself. With everything.

Every goddamn thing.

"How long has this been going on?"

Dean didn't waste any time. No sooner had she cleared the kitchen door than he plunged right into the topic she'd hoped they could avoid.

"What?"

"Don't play dumb, Cat. This thing with that cop cum writer." His interrogative stare demanded an answer.

"There's no *thing* with Alex and me." She told him about the mix-up at the Walterses' house. "Since that bizarre first meeting, we've seen each other a few times. It's friendly. That's all."

Dean snorted skeptically.

Because she had lied with the same lips that still throbbed from Alex's kiss, she went on the offensive. "Look, Dean, I'm glad you came to see me, but who gave you the liberty to break into my house while I wasn't home?"

"I didn't think you'd mind. I already tried to explain it to you and that Neanderthal. When you weren't here, I decided to let myself in and wait. I can't understand why you're so upset. I had a set of keys to your house in Malibu. I fail to see the difference."

"The difference is that I gave you the keys to the Malibu house. I knew you had them." She realized that her voice was rising along with her anger, so she scaled it down. "You should have let me know you were coming. I don't like surprises. I've told you that a million times."

"Then your dislike for surprises is one of the few things about you that hasn't changed since you came here."

Abruptly he stood and began to move around the room without taking his eyes off her. It was as though he wanted to view her from several different perspectives.

"I don't know what's caused the change. Whether it's hanging out with that hoodlum or your job here. But something's had an adverse effect. You're different."

"In what way?"

"You're skittish. Nervous. Like you're about to jump out of your skin."

"I don't know what you're talking about." But she did, and it bothered her that it was so visible.

"The minute I saw you it was apparent to me. Whatever is wrong—" Suddenly his face went slack. "Oh, God. Are you feeling okay? Is there anything wrong with your heart? Have you shown signs of rejecting?"

She held up her hands to ease his alarm. "No, Dean." She shook her head, her expression softening to reassure him. "I feel wonderful. I still marvel over how good I feel. Each day I discover something I can do that was once impossible. Even after all this time, the newness hasn't worn off."

"Just don't get reckless," he said in his stern doctor's voice. "I'm relieved that you're doing well now, but if you ever have any sign of rejection, you know to call me. Immediately."

"I promise."

"I know you get annoyed when I harp on you, but someone has to keep reminding you that you're not like everyone else. You're a heart transplantee."

"I *am* like everyone else. I don't want to be pampered."

He was deaf to her protests. "You work too hard."

"I love to work. I've thrown myself headlong into *Cat's Kids*."

"Is that why you're wound up so tight?"

She wanted to show Dean the mysterious clippings and their envelopes. She would welcome his evaluation. But, knowing Dean, he would probably insist that she notify the police. To do so would be to admit their significance. She was still trying to convince herself that the veiled warnings meant nothing.

"Perhaps I seem uptight because tonight's party was more than just a social gathering. I had to impress a lot of people, and that's exhausting. At any given time I've got a lot on my mind," she told him honestly.

"I love the work and the kids, but a program like this isn't without its headaches, some relating to production and others to dealing with bureaucracy. The red tape is always tangled. By day's end, I feel like a one-armed juggler with ten balls in the air."

"You can give it up."

She smiled and shook her head. "Even with all its difficulties, I love it. It's worth every ounce of effort when we place a child with parents who're going to turn his or her life around, make a dream out of a nightmare. No, Dean, I'm not going to give it up."

"So work's terrific. It must be something else." He probed her eyes. "Is it Pierce who has you on edge?"

"Back to that?"

"How involved are you?"

She could not answer him honestly, for the truth was that she was involved with Alex to the point of wanting their relationship to intensify, to move to the next level.

"He's interesting and intelligent," she said. "Articulate but uncommunicative, if that makes sense. Extremely complex. The better acquainted we become, the less I feel I know him. He intrigues me."

"Cat," he groaned, "listen to yourself. He's a tough-talking, good-looking macho man who intrigues you. Don't you get it?"

"He's the bad boy no woman can resist," she said softly, having thought of that herself before now.

"If you acknowledge that, why are you pursuing it?" He shook his head in bafflement. "What could you possibly see in him? He's a thug. You can tell it at a glance. Have you noticed that scar in his eyebrow? God only knows—"

"A punk hit him with a beer bottle."

"Oh, so you have noticed." He bore down on her, firing questions like bullets. "Does he have any other scars? Have you seen them all? Have you slept with him?"

"That's none of your business!"

"Which means you have."

"Which means that whether I have or have not, it's no concern of yours. I no longer owe you an accounting of whom I see, socially or otherwise." To spare his bruised ego another blow, she downscaled her anger. "I don't want to fight, Dean. Please understand."

"I understand perfectly. You think you want the passion and fire you claimed was lacking in our relationship. You want a tough guy in tight blue jeans who makes your knees go weak."

"Yes," she admitted with a spark of defiance. "The wardrobe is negotiable, but I'd like my knees to go weak."

"Jesus, Cat. That's so . . . juvenile."

"I know you think I'm foolish and idealistic."

"You're right," he said. "I'm a pragmatist. I have no faith in ideals. Life is a series of realities, usually ugly ones."

"No one knows that better than I, Dean," she reminded him. "That's why I'm holding out for something really terrific. In the most important relationship of my life, I refuse to settle for second best. The friendship and camaraderie are essential, but, if and when I fall in love, I want the whole fizzy package. I want romance. I want to tingle.''

"And you think this Alex character can deliver?''

"It's premature to speculate. Besides, he isn't the issue.''

"Like hell. If I weren't here, would he be making you tingle right now?''

For several moments Cat refused to answer. Finally, when it was apparent that he wasn't going to back down, she said, "I honestly don't know. Maybe.'' Then, remembering Alex's departing kiss, she added more quietly, "Probably.''

He yanked his coat off the back of the chair. "Maybe you should call him to come back.''

"Dean, don't go like this,'' she said, reaching for him as he moved to the door. "Don't leave angry. Don't punish me for not being madly in love with you. You're still my best friend. I need you in a very special way. I don't want anything to interfere with our friendship. . . . Dean!''

He never slowed down, just went out the front door and let it slam shut behind him. The tires of his rental car squealed as he sped away.

Chapter Twenty-four

George Murphy was feeling particularly ornery as he strode up the buckled, cracked sidewalk toward the ramshackle rental house. As he stepped onto the sagging porch, the rotting planks threatened to crack. The blue paint on the front door was faded and chipped. When he hauled it open, the hinges squeaked.

The living room stank of old cooking grease and marijuana. Murphy kicked aside a stuffed bunny and cursed when he tripped over a toy truck. In a parody of Ward Cleaver, he sang out, "Honey, I'm home."

She emerged from the single bedroom, her face puffy from sleep. Although it was the middle of the day, she was wearing a light cotton nightgown. She ran her tongue over dry, caked lips. "What are you doing here?"

"What do you mean, what am I doing here? I live here!"

She clasped her hands at her waist. "When did they let you out?"

"Hour or so ago. They had no evidence, so they couldn't hold me."

It had been a pissant possession charge, trumped up by a couple of cops who didn't like his looks and wanted to hassle him. No big deal. But jail time interfered with the things he liked to do. He was thirsty for a beer and horny as hell.

He gave her a calculating look. She seemed unusually nervous. "What's the matter with you?" he demanded. "Aren't you glad to have me back home?"

His eyes narrowed suspiciously, then cut to the bedroom door. "Son of a bitch. If there's a man in there, I'll kill you."

"There's no . . ."

He shoved her aside and barged into the airless bedroom. Lying asleep on his side, amid the dingy sheets, was a child. The little boy had drawn his knees to his chest. His right thumb was in his mouth.

Murphy felt foolish now for revealing his jealousy to her. To save face, he also checked the bathroom, but of course it was empty. As he stepped out of the bathroom, he pointed down at the sleeping boy. "They brought him back?"

She nodded. "This morning. I'd been up crying for two nights. Couldn't work. Couldn't do anything except think about Michael. I was so glad to see him. I thought they'd taken him for good this time." On the brink of tears, she swallowed hard.

"The caseworker said that if . . . if there was any more trouble, they'd take him away permanently. This is our last chance." Tears filled her eyes as she looked at him imploringly. "Please don't do anything that might—"

"Get me a beer." She hesitated and glanced worriedly at the boy. Murphy cuffed her on the side of the head. "I said get me a beer," he repeated, overenunciating each word. "Are you deaf or stupid or what?"

She darted from the room, returning momentarily with a can of Coors. "This is the last one. I'll go get you some more as soon as Michael wakes up. While I'm at the store, I'll buy something for supper, too. What would you like?"

He grunted with satisfaction. This agreeable attitude was more to his liking. Sometimes the bitch got out of line and had to be reminded that he was the man of the household. "I don't want any more of that shit you fixed last week."

"*Pollo guisado*. It's a Mexican stew."

"Couldn't even figure out what the fuck was in it."

"Tonight I'll fix you some fried potatoes."

He belched beer and jail breath. Now, her eagerness to please was getting on his nerves. *Women should be born mute*, he thought.

"And I'll cook hamburger steaks. With onions. Just the way you like them."

No longer listening, Murphy crumpled his empty beer can and tossed it aside, then began rummaging through the junk on top of the dresser. "Wha'd you do with it?"

"Don't, please. You can't. Not here. If the caseworker should come by . . ."

On the dresser was a clear, plastic, compartmentalized box containing dozens of beads in various sizes, shapes, and colors. With a vicious sweep of his arm, he knocked it to the floor. Uttering a soft cry of helplessness, she watched as the spilled beads scattered across the cracked linoleum.

He caught her arms and shook her roughly. "Forget the fucking beads. Where's my stuff?"

Indecision played across her face, but the spark of rebellion in her eyes quickly flickered out. "Bottom drawer."

"Get it."

When she bent down, the nightgown pulled taut across her hips. He fondled her buttocks, squeezing the flesh with his hard, strong fingers. "After a few days in jail, even your fat ass looks good to me."

She straightened up, but he kept his hands in place and began gathering up her nightgown. "Don't. Please," she whimpered to his reflection in the mirror. "Michael could wake up."

"Shut up and cut me a few lines." He saw that she was about to protest, so he pinched her hard on the back of her thigh. "Now."

With trembling hands she opened the plastic bag, dumped out a small mound of cocaine, and, with a playing card, cut two neat lines of it on a chipped mirror. He leaned over and snorted them through a short straw, then rubbed the excess into his gums. The hit was potent.

"Ah, better." He sighed. Splaying his hand in the middle of her back, he bent her forward over the dresser and unfastened his pants.

"Not now!"

"Shut up." He tried to wedge his hand between her legs, but she kept them tightly clamped. He slapped the side of her head again, harder this time, and she cried out. "Open your legs and shut up," he growled.

"I don't want to do it like this."

"All right." His tone was silky, but his face was twisted and ugly. He wound a handful of her hair around his fist and forced her around to face him, pushing her to her knees and cramming his erection into her face.

"If you don't want it like that, we'll do it like this. See how nice I am? You like this better? Huh?" He pulled her hair tighter. "And if you hurt me, I'll tear every frigging hair out of your head by the roots."

"Okay, okay. I'll do it good." Tears of pain and humiliation streamed from her eyes as she looked at the sleeping child. "But in the other room."

"I like this room."

"Not here, please. The baby." She sobbed.

"Jesus, you're ugly when you bawl like that."

"I'll stop crying. I will, I swear. Just please don't make me—"

"The kid's asleep," he whispered. "But I can wake him up. Come to think of it, it might be educational for him." He made a move toward the bed.

She clutched his legs. "No, no." Her pleas were almost soundless.

"Then get to it."

Half his pleasure was derived from watching from above as she avidly went about it, her mouth working hard and fast. In desperation she tried to get him off as quickly as possible and put an end to it.

He was too smart for the bitch. Having caught on to that trick, he held back for as long as he could. When he came, he brayed like a jackass.

Miraculously, Michael slept through it.

After supper, he settled down to watch TV. The news was on every channel. He flipped from one to the other, waiting out the crap until Vanna White came on.

A cute redhead on one of the channels caught his attention. He'd seen her before but hadn't paid much attention. Her face was okay, but she had no tits to speak of. A picture of a kid had been positioned behind her right shoulder. She was speaking earnestly into the camera.

". . . was neglected. Both his parents were drug abusers. He'll have some difficulties bonding, but he has unlimited potential to become a bright, healthy, emotionally stable child. With the right family giving him the affection and guidance he needs, he . . ."

Murphy listened with mounting interest. When the story was over and the redhead turned the newscast back over to the dorky anchorman, Murphy looked hard at the boy playing in the corner of the room with that dirty, stuffed bunny of his.

The kid was a nuisance. He didn't make much noise, and he'd learned the hard way to stay out of Murphy's way. But Michael was always interfering with something he wanted to do—screw, snort, you name it.

He had to watch everything he did in his own house. Because of the kid, she was always nagging him about this or that. Don't do that where Michael can see you; don't say that where Michael can hear you. Don't, don't, don't. *Jesus!* It was enough to drive a man freaking crazy.

And that goddamn caseworker was always poking her long, skinny nose into his business. She was probably the one who'd put the cops onto him the last time he'd had to work over his old lady. So he'd knocked her around a little. She'd needed it. He'd come home and she wasn't there. When she finally showed up, she wouldn't give him a straight answer about where she'd been. What was he supposed to do, let her get away with shit like that? He should never have agreed to let her do that bead stringing, either. It gave her too much independence.

But his major problem was the kid. Almost every time she got out of line, it related to him. If the little fart wasn't around, life would be a lot more pleasurable.

Adoption, the redhead had said. Not for orphans necessarily, but for kids whose parents had grown sick and tired of them and wanted to get rid of them. Garage-sale kids. It sounded good to him.

He glanced at her as she sat working with her beads. She'd go totally apeshit if Michael was taken away permanently. But sooner or later she'd get over it. What choice would she have? Or maybe she wouldn't get that upset if she knew that

Michael had been adopted into a good home. Whatever the hell that was.

Murphy slurped his beer as Vanna turned letters, but his mind was on the redhead. She might have the solution to his problem.

It bore thinking about.

Chapter Twenty-five

C at?"

"Good lord!" She jumped and reflexively flattened her hand over her lurching heart. "I didn't know anybody was in here."

The television studio was dark and, she'd thought, deserted.

"Nobody is. Just me. I've been waiting for you."

Alex eased himself out of the anchorman's chair behind the news desk and sauntered toward her. Fright had rooted her to the floor.

In the dark, the television cameras looked like life forms from an alien environment, with their myriad cables coiling around them and snaking along the concrete floor like electronic umbilicals. The monitor screens were unblinking, sightless eyes. At this late hour, when they were no longer performing their high-tech functions, the studio equipment assumed the shapes of nightmarish creatures.

Until recently, such a silly notion would never have crossed Cat's mind. As it was, she was seeing ghosts and goblins everywhere.

"How'd you know where to find me?" she asked.

"I was told you usually take a short-cut through the studio on your way out."

"Who told you that? How'd you even get in here?"

"I talked my way past the guard."

"They're not supposed to let anyone into the building who isn't authorized."

"Old Bob extended me a professional courtesy."

"Old Bob?"

"We're already on a first-name basis. Once I told him that I was a former policeman, he couldn't have been more accommodating. He served on the San Antonio PD before retiring and becoming a rent-a-cop."

"That former-cop camaraderie must come in handy."

"It opens closed doors," he said with a shrug. "Are you cold?"

Arms folded across her chest, she was hugging her elbows, but she hadn't been aware of it. "A little, I guess. I hadn't really noticed."

"Or are you shivering because of what happened in here this afternoon?"

Her eyes snapped up to his. "How'd you know about it?"

"I was here."

"You were here? Why?"

"I'd come to see you. I arrived just after the fire truck got here. In the confusion, I talked my way past Old Bob, but I didn't make it as far as the studio. It was cordoned off, and they wouldn't let me through.

"I asked one of the cops what was going on, and he told me. I identified myself as a friend and asked to see you, but his orders were to let absolutely no one in."

She wished she'd known that Alex was in the building.

Everyone had been solicitous, but he was a stalwart presence she would have liked to have there following the incident. Keeping her eyes downcast, she murmured, "Accidents happen."

"You're sure it was an accident?"

Her soft, nervous laugh didn't convey much conviction. "Of course it was an accident. I just happened to be seated in that chair when the light fell."

"Show me."

He followed her to the news desk. There were four swivel chairs behind it. Two were for the anchormen, one for the weatherman who chatted with the anchorman before moving to the station's famed "weather center" on the other side of the studio. The fourth chair was for the sportscaster.

"As you know, I'm rarely on the set during a telecast. All my appearances are prerecorded. When I record them, I generally sit here," she said, placing her hands on the back of the sportscaster's chair. "Today, I was about halfway through my opening remarks when it happened."

She pointed upward. The broken studio light had already been replaced with a new one. "Third light from the left," she told Alex.

"It fell from the grid and crashed onto the desk?"

"Here."

The fresh scars in the Formica were clearly visible. A crescent-shaped chunk was missing from the edge of the desk, as though someone had taken a huge bite out of it.

"I'm lucky that didn't happen to my skull," she said, running her finger along the jagged gouge. "The light missed my head by inches and almost fell directly into my lap. Made a heck of a racket. Broken glass. Crushed metal."

She attempted a grin, but it was feeble. "Needless to say, I had to do a second take."

"Did anyone offer an explanation?"

"Within minutes the studio was full of people. Bill left a

sales meeting and rushed down here. Someone called 911. That's why the fire truck was here. Paramedics, too, although neither I nor anyone on the crew was injured, which was a miracle.

"After a while, the police, along with our rent-a-cops, shooed everybody out so the mess could be cleaned up. Bill was on a rampage. He demanded an explanation from the lighting technicians."

"And?"

"They didn't have one. He threatened to fire them all, but I persuaded him not to. It could never be proved whose negligence had caused it to fall, so it would be unfair to punish the entire lighting crew."

"Did they inspect the light?"

"Yes. Apparently the bolt was loose."

"So it *was* negligence."

"Either that or it had worked its way loose."

"Worked its way loose?"

"Something like that," she snapped. She was impatient with his skepticism and frightened because it closely coincided with her own.

"Hmm."

"I hate it when you do that!"

"Do what?"

"That 'hmm.' Implying that whatever I've just said is—"

"Bullshit."

"Well, what do you think happened?"

"I think you had the bejesus scared out of you, and it was no accident."

She folded her arms over her chest again, a subconscious, self-protective gesture. "That's crazy. Who'd want to harm Kurt?"

"Kurt?"

"The sportscaster."

"The light didn't fall when Kurt was on the set. It fell when you were."

"So, you're saying that the light was rigged and timed to fall on me?"

"Yeah. And that's what you think, too."

"Don't presume to know what I think."

"It's an easy guess. Otherwise you wouldn't look like a jigsaw puzzle that's about to come apart."

Knowing it would be useless to deny her jitters, she decided to play devil's advocate. "Assuming you're right, why would anyone want to harm me?"

"You tell me."

"I don't know!"

"But you've got a hunch." He laid his finger against her lips to halt her protest. "I sensed something was wrong the other night when you saw the strange car parked in front of your house."

"I was apprehensive. Anybody would be."

"You were disproportionately apprehensive," he argued. "As though you'd been anticipating trouble. Even before that night, you were acting like a basket case. Any particular reason why?"

"No."

"Liar."

Suddenly drained of energy, she lowered her head and massaged her temples. "You win by default, Alex. I don't feel like sparring tonight."

"Why won't you tell me what's troubling you?"

"Because it . . ." She hesitated. "Because I'm going home to bed."

She turned to go. He fell into step with her. "Is your boyfriend still at your house?"

"He isn't my boyfriend."

He stopped.

She stopped, turned, and looked at him meaningfully. "Not anymore."

"I see."

They tacitly agreed not to pursue her relationship with Dean Spicer and continued on their way out of the building, stopping to say good night to Old Bob.

He beamed at Alex. "Thanks for the autograph." A copy of Alex's book lay open on his desk. "It's my kind of read."

"Enjoy it," Alex said to his new fan as he held open the heavy metal exit door for Cat.

"You bribed him," she accused.

"It was something to fall back on if swapping stories about the good old days didn't do the trick."

"How did you know I'd be here tonight? I usually don't work this late." The parking lot was virtually empty. Even the late news crew had left.

"It was another lucky guess. You weren't at home."

"You went by the house first?"

"And chance bumping into Spicer again? Not on a bet. I called and got no answer."

"What did you want to see me about?"

"I wanted to hear your version of the studio accident."

"Before that. Why'd you come to the studio this afternoon?"

They had reached her car. Propping his elbow on the roof of it, he faced her. "To apologize in person for hurting your . . . uh, Spicer."

"He wasn't badly hurt," she said. "Embarrassed more than anything, I think." Alex seemed on the verge of saying something else. When he didn't, she unlocked and opened her car door. "Apology accepted, Alex. Good night."

"Look, Cat, the guy's a drip. What do you see in him?"

"Well, for one thing he saved my life," she retorted.

"So you feel obligated to him."

"I didn't say—"

"How obligated?"

"Stop it, Alex." She had tried to shout, but her voice cracked. "Just shut up and . . . and leave me alone. I told you I don't feel like fighting with you tonight. I . . . today . . . you . . ."

To her utter mortification, she burst into tears.

"Aw, hell," he said, pulling her against him.

She wanted to resist but hadn't either the physical or emotional strength to do so. His arms held her while she cried. After several minutes of hard weeping, she raised her head, accepted the handkerchief he offered, and blew her nose.

"That incident with the falling light has you more frightened than you know, Cat."

"No, no," she said, shaking her head. "I'm not crying over that. It's something else."

"What?"

"I really don't feel like talking about it."

"Jeez, you're stubborn." He moved her aside and relocked her car door. Then he turned her around and gave her a push in the opposite direction. "Come on."

"Where? I just want to go home."

"I don't mean to be unkind, but I've seen scarecrows who'd put you to shame. I'm going to see that you get something to eat."

"I'm not hungry."

He wouldn't take no for an answer. Within half an hour they arrived at his apartment carting two chicken dinners from KFC. Rather than set the table, they decided to eat off trays in the living room. He sat in the corner of the sofa, Cat on the floor in front of the coffee table.

"I have to admit, this is good," she said around a mouthful. "You're a nutritional saboteur, you know. Burgers and fries. Fried chicken."

"Cops subsist on fast food. I defy you to show me a cop who likes tofu, yogurt, and wheat germ."

She laughed as she saluted him with a plastic spoonful of mashed potatoes and gravy. He wasn't laughing. In fact, he was studying her intently. "What?" she asked uneasily.

He blinked himself out of his momentary trance. "I was just thinking how mercurial your moods are. Not me. My bad moods last for days, weeks, even months if the writing's going badly. You had a crying jag, and you're cleansed. Maybe men should learn to cry."

"Don't let my appetite deceive you. My body was demanding the nourishment I'd denied it the last thirty-six hours or so, but I'm still depressed."

"Why? Spicer leave in a huff?"

"Yes, but Dean's not the reason I'm depressed." She picked at a half-eaten biscuit, pinching off a piece and rolling it between her fingers. "Chantal, the little girl who recently had the kidney transplant, died this morning."

He muttered an obscenity, steepled his fingers, and covered his mouth and nose with his hands. After a moment he said, "I'm sorry, Cat."

"Me, too."

"What happened?"

"It was mercifully quick. She rejected. Total shutdown of kidney function. Nothing went right. She died." She dusted the biscuit crumbs from her hands. "Her adoptive parents are devastated. So is Sherry. Jeff cried like a baby when we got the news. Everyone on the crew that produced the piece on her is grief-stricken. She'd become our . . . our poster child, a shining example of how an unfortunate child's future can be rerouted."

"She can still be your poster child."

"Alex, she's dead."

"I fail to see—"

"I meddled in these people's lives," she interrupted in a raised voice. "I made Chantal love them. I made them love her. They took her into their home, went through that ordeal, witnessed her pain, and suffered it with her. And what have they got to show for that emotional roller-coaster ride now?''

She made a sound of disgust. ''A televised funeral, that's what. Reporters swarming around Chantal's tiny casket and badgering them for a comment. Their grief is a media event. All thanks to me.''

She propped her elbows on the table and buried her face in her hands. ''I was feverishly working at my desk tonight, trying to get my mind off Chantal's death and onto something positive. But all I could think about was the trauma I'd put that couple through.''

''You really think you made them love her, and vice versa?'' He shook his head. ''You sure have an elevated opinion of your influence over people and their emotions.''

She raised her head and glared at him.

''You didn't force them to take her, Cat,'' he continued in a quieter, more sympathetic voice. ''They asked for the opportunity. They went through extensive training in order to meet the requirements. They wanted Chantal.''

''Alive. They wanted a living little girl, not a grave to visit on holidays. They wanted to share her childhood and watch her grow up.''

''Unfortunately, an adopted kid doesn't come with a lifetime warranty. No kid does. Sometimes they die, and that's just the way it is.''

''Please spare me the homespun logic. It's not making me feel better.''

''No, because you're enjoying your self-pity.''

Angrily she said, ''All I know is, if it hadn't been for me, those people wouldn't be grieving tonight.''

''Did they confront you about it?''

''Of course not.''

''Did they say, 'Ms. Delaney, why in hell did you put us through this? We were perfectly happy until you came along and foisted this sick kid on us.' ''

"Don't be ridiculous. They called me to say—" She broke off.

He leaned forward. "What, Cat? Go on. What did they call you to say?"

She cleared her throat and averted her eyes. "They called to thank me for helping place Chantal with them."

"Probably because the time they spent with her was the most rewarding time of their lives."

She sniffed and gave a brusque nod. "They said she'd been a blessing."

"So why are you second-guessing what you do? *Cat's Kids* is a worthy undertaking. What happened to Chantal is tragic, but she had love and caring when she needed it most, right?"

"Right."

"Given the chance, would you do it differently? Would you undo what was done? Take away the time they had together? Let Chantal die feeling lonely and unloved? Rob those people of what they called a blessing?"

She bowed her head, making her answer almost inaudible. "No."

"Well then?"

"You're right. Of course you're right." She offered him a sad smile. "This tragedy knocked me for a loop, that's all. I had some misgivings and needed someone with an objective point of view to allay my doubts. I also needed a good cry." She blotted her damp eyes with a napkin. "Thanks."

He waved off her gratitude.

The light coming from the kitchen fell on his dark hair and cast his features in sharp relief. Dean had said he looked like a thug. He did indeed have a rough-and-tumble demeanor. No doubt he was capable of inflicting pain.

But he had also experienced it. Otherwise, how could he understand it so well? His steely eyes and hard mouth were the result of it. With a single word or phrase, he could cut to the quick.

But with just as few words, he could extend sympathy and kindness. He wasn't soft, but he could be gentle. He could be a friend when one was needed.

"How's the book coming?" she asked, to fill the ponderous silence.

"At a snail's pace, although I've had a few productive days."

"That's good."

With that meager exchange, they'd exhausted the subject. He wouldn't expound beyond that, and she no longer expected him to. But just because there was a lapse in conversation didn't mean they stopped communicating. Their eyes met and locked, and the silence teemed with unspoken messages.

After a moment he eased the tray off his lap and set it on the table. Lowering himself to the floor beside her, he curved his hand around the back of her neck and drew her forward until her lips were scant inches from his.

"We've taken this as far as we can with our clothes on."

Chapter Twenty-six

*H*er troubling thoughts scattered like the feathery seeds of a dandelion, leaving her mind free to focus on his kiss. Nothing mattered except this moment. She needed his strength, his intensity, his unbridled hunger for her. She wanted him. Why be coy for coyness' sake?

Her arms encircled his neck. Their lips clung together as they knelt facing each other. He nudged her middle; she arched into him. He hissed a vulgarity. The desperation behind it was so wildly erotic that she rubbed against him for the sheer pleasure of hearing him repeat it.

They held a kiss while he removed her blouse. Cat tugged his shirttail from his waistband and ran her hands over his hard, fuzzy chest. He released her long enough to whip off his shirt and toss it aside, then he wrapped her in his arms and held her to him while his mouth again ravaged hers.

"You're kidding," he whispered when he slipped his

hands beneath her skirt. There was a smile behind his rough voice.

"Method acting," she replied on a soft breath. "Whenever Laura Madison's scenes called for sexiness, I substituted a garter belt and stockings for panty hose to help get me in the mood. Wearing them got to be a habit."

He caressed her bare thighs above the stockings. "It's a goddamn fantasy."

"Like something from one of your books?"

"Much better."

He removed her skirt, slip, and panties. Cat stretched out on her back on the carpet. With the cups of her bra barely covering her flushed breasts, her mons framed by a satin garter belt and lacy suspenders, her legs still encased in silk stockings, it was a wanton pose. She was shocked by her lack of modesty.

Alex's eyes never left her as he methodically unbuckled his belt and opened his fly. He stepped out of his trousers and underwear. His virile nakedness made her catch her breath. His belly was flat and hard, his limbs long and lean. He was muscular but not muscle-bound. Strong veins showed distinctly on his arms and hands.

Unabashedly, lustfully, she drank him in, from the arches of his feet, to his proud, heavy sex, to his unsmiling mouth and scar-slashed eyebrow.

He lay beside her, kissed her breasts through the cups of her bra, then lowered the lace and caressed her nipples with his tongue. Lifting his head, he gazed down at her. His thumb made several passes across her raised nipple.

"I could write this scene a thousand times and never get it this good." He watched her flesh respond to his touch. "The nuances of a woman's body simply can't be described."

He bent his head and took her nipple into his mouth, tugged on it with a strong flexing of his jaw. Responding to a current of sexual electricity, her back arched off the carpet. The demicups of her bra kept her breasts provocatively offered up to him. His tongue was nimble, his appetite carnal.

He ran his hands over her stomach and along the outsides of her thighs. She reached for him, stroked him, and he groaned elaborate curses. They kissed again, hungrily and greedily.

"Don't hold back, Alex," she whispered urgently. "Don't be soft with me."

"I have no intention of being soft."

"I want to know I'm a woman. I want to know I'm with a man. I want to be taken. I want—"

"You want to be fucked."

Placing a palm over each of her knees, he pushed them apart. But instead of slipping his hand between her thighs as she expected, he lowered his head. His open mouth found her center, his tongue moved inside her.

She was too stunned to cry out, even when, moments later, she climaxed. Her chest was heaving; her upper lip was beaded with perspiration; her hair clung damply to her neck and throat.

Alex's skin was also slippery with sweat when he levered himself above her and bridged her body with his arms. Eyes closed, face tense, he guided himself into her. Her body seemed to swallow him. It was a snug, glove fit, and his features formed a grimace of immense pleasure as his hips began a rolling motion, forward and back. Slowly, going deeper each time, he sank into her again and again.

Cat, who had thought it was over for her, was reawakened by his steady thrusts. She had never experienced lovemaking this intense, this soul- and mind-capturing. She surrendered herself to it totally.

He slipped his hands beneath her hips and tilted them up, holding her tightly. He seemed to concentrate on each delving motion, each slow withdrawal. But the tempo gradually increased. His breathing became rapid and ragged. Suddenly, his arms relaxed and he crushed her beneath him. But by then Cat was already spinning within her second orgasm.

When he came, it racked his whole body. Every muscle stretched taut, and the harsh, choppy sounds he made were like sobs.

It took a long while for them to recover, but Cat would have lain there forever, idly threading her fingers through his mussed hair, licking salty drops of sweat from his brow. He lay on her heavily, replete, but she didn't mind absorbing his weight. He had exerted himself, and that was thrilling to her.

He knew the mechanics of mutually satisfying lovemaking. He wrote about them. So it wasn't surprising that he was a skilled, passionate, and totally focused lover.

He was, however, as sensual as he was demanding. He'd drawn from her responses that were purely animalistic, without conscience. Her reactions had originated entirely and unapologetically in the senses. She'd had no control over them.

Yet, it had also been a cerebral coupling. Her mind had had intimate intercourse with his. They'd been perfectly in tune with each other's needs and desires, and had seen to their fulfillment. That's why she cherished this restful aftermath, this quiet moment when their breath and sweat mingled and seemed to emanate from one body instead of two.

He must have felt the closeness, too. Because perhaps the loveliest thing he did, just before his body withdrew from hers, was to place a soft kiss between her breasts where her scar had been.

She awoke first. Knowing he wasn't a morning person, she lay still and let him sleep. His hair was tousled and looked very dark against the pillowcase. Whiskers were beginning to sprout from his jaw and chin. There were a few gray ones in his sideburns, she noticed. His eyebrows were drawn into a slight frown, indicating that he was never entirely at peace. His private darkness shadowed him even in sleep.

The nightstand clock told her that she'd indulged herself long enough. She kissed his bare shoulder and slipped soundlessly from the bed. Downstairs, she dressed, gathering clothes that had been discarded with shameless abandon. Speaking softly into the telephone, she called a taxi.

While waiting for it to arrive, she cleaned up the remains of their dinner. On her way into the kitchen to dispose of the debris, she passed the door to the forbidden room but resolutely went by without pausing. She disposed of the trash, rinsed out their glasses, and poured herself a glass of orange juice, which she found in the refrigerator.

While leaning against the countertop sipping the juice, she toyed with the idea of opening that door again and taking a peek inside. His objection had worked in the reverse, whetting her curiosity instead of satisfying it.

Last night, his naked body had been hers to explore and exploit with unlimited access. They had engaged in the most intimate act between two people. Surely, now that their relationship had progressed to that plateau, he would no longer object to sharing that area of his life with her.

But what if he did object? Was it worth risking? No, she decided. She wouldn't trespass; she would wait for him to invite her.

The taxi arrived and she left his apartment without his waking up. She retrieved her car at the TV station and drove home, where she showered and dressed and tried to outline an agenda for the day. But her mind kept drifting back to the night before. Erotic recollections crowded her mind, leaving room for little else.

Her euphoria must have been apparent because Jeff remarked on it the moment she entered the office. "What happened? You win the lottery?"

She laughed and gratefully accepted the cup of coffee he extended to her. "Why do you say that?"

"Because your aura is visible to the naked eye this morning. You're positively glowing. I expected you to be upset over Chantal."

Her smiled faltered. "I'm still terribly sad, naturally, but not as negative about life in general as I was yesterday. A friend reminded me how marvelous it is to be alive."

"Would this 'friend' by any chance be the hunk novelist?" Jeff asked, winking.

"He is a hunk, isn't he?" she asked, giggling.

"He looked pretty good when he was here yesterday."

"You saw him?"

"Jeans and boots, et al."

She grinned. "That's my boy."

"He has that unmade-bed appearance, you know? The rumpled look women find irresistible."

Dean had criticized Alex's looks. Jeff obviously approved. "You didn't mention seeing him," she said.

"It was during that hullabaloo." He tugged his earlobe in embarrassment. "I admit I was star-struck and tongue-tied. I'd read his novels, and of course I knew you'd been seeing him. But I didn't think I'd ever have the pleasure of meeting him."

"I wish you'd paged me and told me he was here."

"You were surrounded by cops. Mr. Webster was on the warpath. Later, you seemed so upset that I hated to lay anything else on you. But I take it Mr. Pierce found you last night." He squinted as he appraised her. "Judging by your goofy grin, my guess is that it was a . . . uh, therapeutic evening."

"None of your business," she replied coyly, feeling herself blush.

Jeff was no fool. He smiled broadly. "Good. I hope you worked out all the kinks. You've been pushing yourself too

hard. In fact—'' His smile faltered and he cleared his throat.
"Can I speak candidly? Not as your assistant, but more like
a friend?"

Cat nodded him into a chair. He pinched up the creases of
his trousers and sat down facing her. "I hope I'm not . . .
That is . . ."

"Spit it out, Jeff."

"Well, in the last couple of weeks, you've seemed
distracted. Not that you aren't doing a terrific job," he added
hastily. "You are. You haven't let whatever is bothering you
interfere with work. You're as fabulous as ever. It's just . . .
I wondered if there's something on your mind. Something
besides Alex Pierce, that is."

Had her uneasiness been that transparent? Several close
acquaintances had commented on it—Dean, Alex, now Jeff.
She didn't want anything to cloud her sunny mood today, but
she welcomed an opportunity to talk about the two pieces of
mail she'd received. She wanted Jeff to second her opinion that
it was the handiwork of a kook, that it was nothing to worry about.

"You're very observant, Jeff. Actually I have been slightly
off balance lately."

She removed the two envelopes from her handbag and
handed them to him. Days ago she had begun carrying them
with her, perhaps with a subconscious hope that she'd have
just such an opening in which to show them to someone.

"Have a look," she said. "Tell me what you think. And
be honest."

After comparing the two identical envelopes, he read the
enclosed newspaper clippings. "Damn," he whispered after
he'd finished reading each of them twice. "Both died in
bizarre accidents and both were heart transplantees."

"An odd coincidence, isn't it?"

"I'll say. But what does it mean? Do you have any idea
who sent them?"

"No."

"I go through all the fan mail you receive. I don't remember seeing these, although you get so many letters they could have slipped past me. Or did they come through while Melia was still working with us?"

"They were sent to my home."

He looked at her with consternation. "How would a . . . a fan . . . get your home address?"

She shrugged. "That's just one of the things that disturbs me about them."

Jeff studied the envelopes and reread the articles. Cat watched his eyes moving across the lines of print. His initial reaction and comments hadn't been very encouraging. She had hoped he would tell her outright not to worry.

Instead, after he'd reread them, he asked, "Have you shown these to anybody else? Mr. Webster? The police?"

"No."

"Maybe you should."

"I don't want to be an alarmist."

"No one would accuse you of that."

"I don't know, Jeff." She sighed. "I don't want to send up flares and draw attention to something that's probably nothing."

He forced a reassuring grin as he returned the envelopes to her. "Well, you're probably right. I'm sure they're nothing to get upset about. Boy, some people don't have much to do, right?"

"Must not. They create dramas for themselves by meddling in the lives of celebrities. They live vicariously."

"Exactly. But . . ." He hesitated. "If you get another one, I think you should reconsider and take the matter to the police. Screw what they think. Let them think you're a hysterical female."

"Which I'm afraid is exactly what they'd think."

"At the very least you should consult the guards here at the station, alert them not to let any strange characters into the building."

"Which would exclude about three-quarters of the employees," she quipped.

"You've got a point." He flashed a smile but turned serious again. "Be careful, Cat. There're lots of nutcases out there."

"I know." She returned the envelopes to her purse and snapped it shut, effectively closing the discussion and resuming the role of boss. "I need to know the particulars on Chantal's funeral."

"Friday at two o'clock. And just so you'll know, Ron Truitt called from the *Light* earlier. He wanted a statement."

"I hope you told him to take a bullet train straight to hell."

"Not in those words, but that was the general message. I said you were, and would be, unavailable for comment."

"Thanks. If I'd spoken with him, I doubt I would have been that diplomatic. The man's a jackal, always on the scent of fresh blood."

Not wanting to dwell on the carnivorous reporter, she moved on. "Please have a flower arrangement from WWSA sent to the funeral home. I want to send something personally, but I'll make those arrangements myself."

By the time Jeff withdrew, he had instructions to consult Sherry and forge ahead with their shooting schedule. Last night's doubts about the viability of *Cat's Kids* seemed ludicrous now. They'd lost Chantal, but there were so many other special children who needed the program.

No matter what obstacles she encountered—bureaucracy, negative press, self-doubts—she must never call it quits. *Cat's Kids* was an entity larger and more important than she. Alex had helped her see it in a new perspective. In the overall picture, her personal setbacks were insignificant.

Just before noon, Jeff returned to her office with a message memo. "Your favorite novelist just phoned."

Her heart did a cartwheel as she reached for her telephone. "Which line?"

"Unfortunately, he's not holding. He said to tell you that he was in a hurry and only had time to leave a message."

Looking as nervous as the herald bringing bad news to the short-tempered queen, Jeff handed her the memo. "He was calling from the airport. Said they'd already announced his flight."

"Flight?" Her buoyant spirits sank like lead. "He's leaving town? Where's he going? For how long?" It was all written on the memo, but Jeff imparted the message verbally.

"All he said was that he'd be gone for several days and would call you when he got back."

"That's it?"

Jeff nodded.

She tried to keep her expression impassive, her voice stoic. It was an effort. "Thank you, Jeff."

Obsequiously, he backed out of the office and closed the door.

Cat neatly folded the memo, then stared at the square of lined paper as though it might offer an explanation that had thus far been withheld. It didn't.

She was crushed. She had hoped they'd have dinner together tonight. It had been only a few hours since she'd left him, but she yearned to see him.

That weakness made her angry with herself. He was certainly showing no signs of yearning. Here she sat, shackled by the blues, feeling like the only girl in the senior class who didn't have a date for the prom, while he was taking flight. Literally.

Her dejection quickly turned to pique. What had sent him out of town in such a hurry? Business or pleasure? What had been so damned important that he'd hotfooted it out of town without even taking the time to say goodbye?

Chapter Twenty-seven

$\mathcal{A}$lex wasn't particularly fond of New York City, but it fascinated him. It was a city of superlatives, epitomizing despair, dirt, and destitution, and glitz, glitter, and glamour. His reactions to it were always extreme, never lukewarm. He saw things within the same city block that could either exhilarate or disgust him.

He and his agent were having dinner in a small mom and pop restaurant on the West Side. Earlier in his relationship with Arnold Villella, on about his third trip to the Big Apple, Alex had eschewed the outrageously expensive meals at The Four Seasons and Le Cirque.

"If I can't pronounce it or don't know its origin, I won't eat it," he'd told his agent. Villella had called him a philistine but thereafter allowed Alex to choose where they dined.

Occasionally, if they had something special to celebrate, Alex permitted Villella to treat him to a late-night hamburger at 21. But Oswald's Cafe, overseen by the robust Hungarian immigrant himself, had become one of Alex's favorite places. The roast beef sandwiches were piled high with rare, tender shavings and served with a dark, grainy mustard so hot that it brought tears to the eyes.

Tonight, he wolfed down his sandwich while Villella tinkered with a bowl of goulash.

"You were hungry," the agent observed. "Didn't they feed you on the airplane?"

"I guess. I don't remember."

He remembered very little of the short flight from San Antonio to Dallas-Fort Worth, the brief layover, the nonstop to La Guardia, the cab ride into Manhattan, or anything else that had happened since last night.

Hot, juicy, noisy, tender, raunchy, gentle, frantic, slow, terrific, mind-blowing sex played hell on his memory.

He pushed aside his plate, and when the waiter came for it he ordered coffee. He was halfway through it when he realized that he and his agent hadn't exchanged a word in five minutes.

Villella had remained patiently silent. When dealing with penurious publishers, he had the instincts of a barracuda. But with the authors he represented, he was nurturer, disciplinarian, father confessor—adjusting his role to fit the needs of his clients.

Arnold Villella had agreed to represent Alex before he had published a single word. Most of the agents he had queried returned his first manuscript unread, their policy being that they didn't represent unpublished writers. Catch-22 of the publishing industry: You couldn't get published without an agent, and you couldn't get an agent without having been published.

But Villella had telephoned him in Houston on a Friday morning during a thunderstorm. Alex had a hangover, and Villella had to repeat himself several times before Alex could hear the message above the crashing thunder outside the window and inside his skull.

"I think your writing has promise. You have a raw but unique style. I'd like to represent you if you're interested."

Without delay, Alex flew to New York to meet the one person on the planet who believed his writing had promise. Villella was quick and inquisitive. He was opinionated and blunt. But not unkind.

When he discovered Alex's drinking problem, he had refrained from prying and said only that he had been associated with quite a few talented writers, many of whom were alcoholics. "While alcohol might have enhanced their imaginations, it was ruinous to their writing careers."

Upon returning to Houston, Alex checked himself into a rehab clinic, and, as he worked on revising his original manuscript, words seemed to eke from his pores along with the alcoholic poisons that had polluted his system.

Villella had earned his unqualified loyalty and trust. He was the only person in whom Alex confided, the only one who could criticize him without his taking umbrage. There was very little about him that Villella did not know, yet the agent had never passed judgment on him or his misdeeds.

"I'm sorry, Arnie," he said now. "I'm not very good company tonight."

"You'll get around to it," Arnie said.

"Around to what?"

"To telling me why you flew up here unexpectedly and asked me to avail myself for dinner."

"I hope you didn't have other plans."

"I did, but I can always juggle my schedule to accommodate my most important client."

"I'll bet you say that to all your clients."

"Of course I do," he replied candidly. "You're all like demanding children."

"I'll bet I'm the worst behaved, though."

Villella was too polite to agree but raised his hands, palms up, to indicate that Alex had spoken the truth. "How's the book coming?"

"Fine."

"That bad?"

Alex laughed with chagrin. "I'm trying to keep it in perspective. I continually remind myself that this is just the first draft."

"It won't read like a final one."

"I hope to God not." He hesitated, then said with uncharacteristic shyness, "In spite of the rough spots, I think it might be good, Arnie."

"I don't doubt that it's excellent. This is your most intricate and provocative plot so far. It's destined to be a bestseller."

"If I don't fuck it up."

"You won't. Relax. Have fun with it. It'll come."

"Are we talking about the book or sex?" Alex teased.

"I'm talking about the book. What are you talking about?"

Arnie's intuitive question swiped the grin from Alex's face. He signaled for a refill of coffee and, after it had been poured, closed his hands around the steaming mug.

"You're wound up tighter than an eight-day clock," Arnie observed. "What's wrong? You're not having relapses of depression, are you?"

"No."

"No more of those blackouts?"

"No. God no."

Villella referred to those hours—sometimes days—that Alex had lost to alcoholic blackouts. He would regain consciousness without being able to account for the period of time he'd been "gone." He would have no memory of what had taken place, where he'd been, what he'd done. It had been terrifying.

"This has nothing to do with drinking. I'm sober." He noticed a release of tension in his agent that Villella probably wasn't even aware of.

"Then if you're not anguishing over the book, not wrestling with the bottle, what is it?"

"I've been with a woman."

Villella blinked rapidly, and Alex could guess the reason for his agent's surprise. Villella knew about his sexual exploits. Most of them.

"This is different," he mumbled, glancing around self-consciously.

"Oh?" The agent's mood was suddenly upbeat. "This lady has tapped in to more than your keg of testosterone?"

"Yes. I mean no," he corrected himself querulously.

"Well, which is it?"

"She's not a bimbo. Not just a piece of ass. She's . . . Hell, I don't know what she is."

Villella folded one small hand over the other and settled them on the edge of the table, ready to listen. Alex continued to fidget. Finally Villella said, "This isn't like you."

"No shit."

"I can see you're deeply troubled. You hardly have what I would describe as a jovial, happy-go-lucky temperament, but I sense in you a desperation I haven't noticed since you first came to see me. Is this woman rejecting you?"

Images of Cat flashed through his mind: an inviting smile, an enticing glance, an encouraging response. Sweetness and sex. Wildness and whimsy. In turn, demure and demanding. His slightest touch had elicited sighs and murmurs of pleasure. Reprises of them echoed inside his head.

In a voice that grated like sandpaper, he answered, "No. She's not rejecting me."

"Then I fail to see how this budding relationship can be anything but enjoyable and healthy."

"It's her name."

"Her name? What do you mean?"

"It's Cat Delaney, Arnie. I've slept with Cat Delaney."

Villella gaped at him, wheyfaced with disbelief. "Good

God, Alex. What can you be thinking? I thought you'd had your fill of headlines. Yet you're seeing a woman who attracts media attention like a magnet. A woman who—"

"I know," Alex said impatiently, cutting him short. "I know it's crazy."

"Not only crazy, my dear boy. Extremely dangerous."

Chapter Twenty-eight

*I*t was difficult for Cat to keep her cool.

When she turned onto her street and saw Alex parked in front of her house, she practically floorboarded the accelerator. But by the time he met her halfway up the walk to the front door, she'd mustered some dignity and pride. She said an aloof hello.

"Have a nice trip?"

"So-so."

"Where'd you go?"

"New York."

"How was it?"

"Like New York."

"You left on the spur of the moment, didn't you?"

"Urgent business."

"Of course. The publishing industry is famous for its emergencies," she said sarcastically.

She unlocked her front door and stepped inside, then turned

to face him, blocking his entrance, just as she'd done the first time he'd appeared at her doorstep.

After their night together, she'd experienced the giddiness unique to newfound romance. In contrast, he'd skipped town. If an emergency had prevented him from speaking to her before he left, he could have called during the last several days. But he hadn't.

And now he was hardly displaying the lighthearted delirium of Gene Kelly in *Singin' in the Rain*. These were inauspicious signs that he hadn't felt the warm fuzzies after being with her that she had felt after being with him.

He looked tired and haggard. There were dark circles around his eyes, as though he hadn't slept since she'd left him in his bed three days ago. She struggled with the impulse to place her arms around him and keep them there until his hounded, haunted look disappeared.

"Did you go to that little girl's funeral?" he asked.

"How'd you know?"

"I called the TV station and was told you'd gone to a funeral and would be out for the remainder of the day. Bad scene?"

"Very. During the service, I kept thinking back on the day Chantal legally became their daughter. Everyone was so happy. They had a backyard barbecue to introduce her to their family and friends. The same family and friends were gathered at their house today." She sighed sadly.

"But there were no balloons or streamers. No gaiety. It wasn't quite the same." She stared into near space for a moment, then brought him back into focus. "What brings you by, Alex?"

"We need to talk."

His tone of voice and solemn expression were warnings that what he wanted to talk about was nothing she wanted to hear.

"Can I have a rain check? I'd be a lousy hostess right now. The funeral did me in. Another time would be better."

"There won't ever be a good time for this."

Cat could think of only one problem that would be this imperative and this grim. Her black mourning dress suddenly felt like chain mail. A crushing pressure seized her chest.

"Let me guess," she said. "You forgot to mention one tiny detail the other night before we slept together. You're married."

"No. I'm not married. And that's all I'm going to say while standing out on the front porch." He sidestepped her and went inside.

Once the door was closed, she confronted him. "You're not currently married, but an ex—"

"I've never been married."

"Hmm. This is worse than I thought. When was your last blood test?"

He placed his hands on his hips and glowered at her. "Give me a break."

If he didn't have a wife tucked away somewhere, and no ex was hounding him for usurious alimony, and he wasn't carrying a deadly virus, that left only one option. He was building up to a classic brush-off.

Damned if she'd give him the satisfaction. Squaring her shoulders, she tossed back her hair and went on the offensive. "Look, Alex, I think I know what you're going to say, so let me spare you the trouble, okay?

"I was emotionally fragile the other night and needed some TLC. You provided it. We're consenting adults. We practiced safe sex. We were sexually . . . compatible."

She paused to draw a deep breath, and hated that it sounded shaky. "But you don't want a lasting relationship. No commitment. No strings." Spreading her arms wide, she added, "Hey, that's cool. Neither do I."

She removed her earrings and stepped out of her pumps, thinking that those simple, ordinary actions would make her nonchalance more convincing.

"So you can stop looking like you're about to hurl chow on my Oriental rug. I'm not going to stamp my foot and make demands. I don't have a father who'll march you to the wedding altar with a shotgun in your back. I'm not going to slash my wrists, boil your bunny rabbit, or come after you with a butcher knife. This is not going to turn into a fatal attraction for you." She managed to form a cold, stiff, insincere smile. "So relax, okay?"

"Sit down, Cat."

"Why? Did I leave out a line of your carefully rehearsed monologue?"

"Please."

She dropped her earrings onto the hall table, led him into the living room, switched on a table lamp, and, folding her legs beneath her, curled up in the corner of the sofa. Picking up a throw pillow, she hugged it to her chest as a child would a teddy bear, for protection and comfort.

Alex sat down on the ottoman in front of the sofa, spread his knees, and stared at the floor between his feet. He looked like a prisoner watching the gallows being built outside his cell window.

Propping his elbows on his knees, he pressed his thumbs into his eyesockets and remained in that doomed-man posture for several moments before lowering his hands and looking at her.

"I wanted to sleep with you the minute I saw you," he said bluntly.

Mentally, she took a step backward and examined his statement from all angles. On the surface it sounded very romantic, but she didn't trust its simplicity. "I suppose I should be flattered. But I'm waiting for the ax to fall. What is it, Alex? Didn't I live up to your expectations?"

"Don't be ridiculous."

He shot to his feet and began to pace. Another bad sign. Men only paced when delivering bad news.

He stopped abruptly and turned toward her. "There's a lot of garbage in here." He tapped his finger against his temple. "A lot of shit went down before I left the Houston PD."

"I already know about your drinking problem."

"That was the effect, not the cause. I still haven't sorted it all out. I'm working on it, but it wouldn't be fair——"

"Don't fall back on that standard, trite b.s. about unfairness!" she cried. "Get to the point."

"Okay. Bottom line. I can't become involved in any sort of meaningful relationship right now. I thought you ought to know that before we get too deep."

For several moments she sat there huddled against the cushions, the pillow clutched to her chest. Then, tossing it aside, she vaulted off the sofa. Her heels made dull thuds on the floor as she marched to the front door and opened it wide.

He sighed and plowed his fingers through his hair. "You're pissed."

"Wrong. I'd have to give a damn in order to be pissed."

"Then why do you want me to leave?"

"Because there's not enough room in this house for me, you, and your gargantuan ego. The two of you must go. *Now.*"

"Shut the door."

She slammed it shut. "How dare you presume that I would be shattered by this. How dare you presume that our sleeping together meant more to me than it did to you. What gave you the idea that I wanted 'any sort of meaningful relationship' with you?"

"I never said——"

"Boy, you could teach the would-be studs in Hollywood something about ego. I've never met anyone as full of himself as you. Keeping your unfinished work under lock and key as though it were national treasure," she scoffed. "You might really be something if your cock could ever swell as big as your head."

"Very funny."

"Not at all. It's very sad."

Losing patience, he said, "I just didn't want you to expect something from me that I can't deliver."

"Then you've got what you wanted, because I expect less than zero from you. It was a one-night gig. Our glands had a terrific time together. It didn't mean anything beyond that."

"Bullshit," he said emphatically.

"You got off. I got off."

"Several times."

She saw red but kept going. "We each got what we wanted from the other. End of story."

"That's pure crap, and you know it, and I know it," he shouted. "If it hadn't meant anything, I wouldn't be here trying to explain myself, and you wouldn't be about to explode."

"Ordinarily you just love 'em and leave 'em without notice, is that it?"

"Yes."

She batted her eyelashes and splayed her hand over her chest. "Well, I'm honored by your consideration, Mr. Pierce. Truly I am," she drawled in a parody of a southern belle.

"Cut it out, Cat."

"Go to hell, Alex."

Glaring at her with frustration, he swore beneath his breath. After a moment he said, "We wouldn't be having this fight if . . . if . . ."

"Stop stuttering and give it to me straight. It's a little late for diplomacy. If what?"

He came closer, until he was looming over her. Lowering his voice to a sexy rasp, he said, "If it hadn't been so fanfuckingtastic."

Her heart was already racing with anger. His inflection made it flutter with awakening desire. She wanted to scratch out his eyes while also wanting to melt against him.

"You really have an inflated self-image, don't you?" she said, moving away. When she was at a safer distance, she turned to face him. "Do you expect me to swoon when you talk dirty? Who do you think you are, one of the heroes of those trashy books you hack out?"

He slammed his fist into his opposite palm. "Jesus, was Arnie ever wrong."

"Your agent? What's he got to do with this?"

"He advised me to level with you, to lay all the cards on the table. He said that would be the best way to handle the problem."

"You talked to your agent about how to 'handle' me?" Her voice rose to a shrill note of fury and disbelief. "Consider your 'problem' handled, Mr. Pierce. I'll even make your final farewell speech for you."

Aiming her index finger at his chest, she said, "Don't call me. Don't come to my house. Make no effort to see me or contact me. You're a prick. You're not a tenth as wonderful as you think you are. I don't ever want to lay eyes on you again."

She drew a deep breath before firing the last volley. "Did you get all that, you son of a bitch?"

Chapter Twenty-nine

*I*t was high tide, but Cat sat well away from the foaming surf. Her chin was propped on her raised knees, her arms linked around her legs. She stared at the horizon to which the sun had surrendered, but not without a spectacular fight. The sky was still alight with a vermilion glow that was gradually being relinquished to an encroaching indigo.

Sensing someone nearby, she turned and was astonished to see Dean making his way toward her. He dropped down beside her on the sand.

When she found her voice, she asked, "How'd you know I was here?"

"I called your office in San Antonio this afternoon. Your assistant informed me that you were taking a few days' vacation in Malibu. Were you going to come and go without even notifying me?"

"Yes," she replied candidly. "We didn't part on the best of terms."

He looked chagrined. "Actually I called today to apologize. I behaved like an idiot that night at your house."

"It's water over the dam. Don't worry about it."

She sensed him studying her profile. He hesitated, then said, "Forgive me for saying so, but you look a little worse for wear. In fact, you look like death warmed over."

"Gee, thanks."

"What'd he do?"

"Who?" When he said nothing, she turned her head. He was frowning at her for playing dumb. She returned her gaze to the waves. "I've slept with him."

"I guessed as much. So what's the problem? Is there another woman in the picture?"

"He claims there's not. I've seen no evidence of one."

"Dark dealings in his past?"

"Something he called 'garbage,' but he wasn't specific. I think it had to do with his resignation from police work. Plain and simple, he courted me, made me want to be with him, but he wants only recreational sex."

"And you're still attracted to him?"

Cat the Courageous always told the truth no matter how brutal it was, even to her own self-esteem. "I'd be lying if I said no."

"I see." He took it one step further. "Are you in love with him?"

As though her finger had been pricked, she gave a sharp cry and dropped her forehead onto her knees.

Dean said, "I take that as a yes. Does he know?"

"God, no. I played the scene well, I think. I gave him a tongue-lashing and ordered him out of my house. I even threatened him with my Lalique vase if he didn't leave. I doubt he took the threat of bodily harm seriously, but he left anyway."

Raising her head, she stared out across the waves, so steeped in misery that she wasn't aware of the tears on her cheeks. "I'm sorry, Dean. This must be awfully difficult for you. Thank you for listening."

He touched the corner of her lips where a tear had found a resting place. "The man's a fool to throw away the chance of having a relationship with you. What more could he want?"

"I doubt Alex knows what he wants. He's restless, searching for something."

"Or running away from it."

"Possibly. Or maybe he's just innately and unconscionably selfish."

Even as she spoke the words aloud, she didn't entirely agree with them. During their night together Alex had been tender and passionate, and as involved with her fulfillment as with his own.

Or was she deceiving herself in order to salvage a little pride? Probably. He was very good at charming and disarming. Surely he could take what he wanted from a woman and at the same time make her feel cherished.

She rolled back her heels and stared at the toes of her sneakers, thinking back to the instant when she'd first seen him. The chemistry had been instantaneous and explosive, something very powerful and like nothing she'd experienced before.

Just thinking about it now made her shiver. "Let's go inside," she said. "I'm getting cold."

Sitting at the kitchen bar sipping coffee, Dean said intuitively, "There's more on your mind than this crime novelist."

"I never could keep a secret from you."

"You can act convincingly for other people, but I can tell when you're troubled. Something was wrong the night I came to San Antonio. You denied it, but I knew you were lying. When are you going to confide in me, Cat?"

From the pocket of her sweater, she withdrew three

envelopes and slid them across the bar to him. "You might find these interesting reading."

He looked at her curiously, then opened the envelopes and shook out their contents. After reading each of the newspaper clippings several times, he looked up at her, mystified. "These were mailed to your home address?"

"The first and second ones came a couple of weeks apart. The third came the day I left."

Dean studied the envelopes. "These give nothing away."

"Except that they bear a San Antonio postmark."

"Three transplantees from different areas of the country. Three bizarre accidental deaths. A fall through a plate glass window, a drowning in an automobile, and a slip of a chainsaw. Jesus."

"It sounds like a Brian DePalma movie, doesn't it? Guaranteed to raise goosebumps."

Dean tossed the clippings onto the bar, his contempt obvious. "Some wacko with a macabre sense of humor sent them to you."

"Yes, that's probably all it is."

"You don't sound convinced."

"I'm not."

"Neither am I," he confessed. "Have you showed them to anyone else?"

"Jeff. The first two. He doesn't know about the third one."

"What was his opinion?"

"Basically the same as yours: a wacko playing a bad joke. He told me not to worry about them, then in the same breath said that if I received any more, I probably should show them to the police."

"Have you?"

"No. I've been stalling, hoping for an explanation."

"I'm sure they're no cause for alarm, Cat. But there's always the possibility that a kook who'd send anonymous messages through the mail is capable of doing something even kookier.''

"I realize that." Beyond frightening her, the clippings had resurrected doubts and ambiguities she'd laid to rest long ago.

"Dean," she began hesitantly, "you knew me before my transplant, perhaps better than anyone's known me. You went through the entire ordeal with me. You were around during my highs, and when I sank as low as I could sink.

"Likewise, you knew me equally as well following the transplant. You've literally been there through sickness and in health. If anyone could draw a personality chart on me, it would be you."

"I follow, but what's your point?"

"Am I different?" Her eyes met his directly. "What I'm really asking is, did the transplant change me?"

"Yes. Before it, you were dying. Now you're not."

"That's not what I mean."

"I know what you mean," he said, matching her impatient tone. "You want to know if you underwent a personality change following your transplant. Which will lead to the inevitable question: Is it possible for character traits of the donor to be transmitted to the recipient via the transplanted heart? Right?"

She nodded.

Dean sighed. "You're not seriously giving that bunk any consideration, are you?"

"Is it bunk?"

"Positively. Good God, Cat. Be reasonable."

"Bizarre things happen for which there are no scientific or logical explanations."

"Not in this instance," he said stubbornly. "You're an intelligent woman and probably know more about your anatomy than most students in premed. The heart is a pump, a mechanical part of the human body. When it's busted, it can often be repaired or replaced.

"I've seen countless hearts laid open during surgery. They're made up of tissue. None of them had little pigeonholes where fears and aspirations and likes and dislikes and love and hate were stored.

"The concept that the heart is a treasure trove of emotion and feeling has inspired some great poetry, but clinically it's total bullshit.

"However, if these clippings have disturbed you to the point of wanting to locate your donor's family, I'll do all I can to help you."

"I made it clear that I never wanted to know anything about my donor," she reminded him.

Dean was unaware of it, but on the night of her transplant, she had picked up a hint of her heart's origin. She wished she didn't know even that tiny clue. But, like a pebble in her shoe, she was constantly aware of it. Recently it had become even more worrisome.

"Maybe I should rethink my position," she said reluctantly.

He stood up and pulled her into a strong hug. "I'm sure these accidents are a wild coincidence. Someone has picked up on it and is playing a cruel prank on you."

"That's what I told myself after I received the first one. Even the second. Then I received the third. That's when I saw something that had previously escaped my notice. Apparently you didn't notice it either. Although I don't know how we could have overlooked something that significant."

He set her away from him. "What is it?"

"Look at the dates, Dean. Each of the fatal accidents occurred on the anniversary of the victim's transplant. And," she added slowly and quietly, "it's also the anniversary date of my transplant."

Chapter Thirty

❧

Alex stared into the black screen of his computer. The blinking green cursor wouldn't move. The damn thing hadn't moved for days—not since his fight with Cat.

She fought like her namesake, he thought, remembering how she arched her back and hissed at him, all but going for his face with her claws. A woman with her spirit hated like hell being manipulated, and he had blatantly manipulated her into bed with him. Her reaction had been about what he'd expected.

He rolled his head across his shoulders and rested his fingers on the keyboard as though getting down to business, for real this time.

The cursor continued its incessant, stationary blink. It seemed to be mocking him, winking puckishly, tickled to death that he'd come down with a bad case of writer's block.

For days he'd been trying to write a love—correction,

a *screw*—scene. Up to that point the book had been going fairly well. He'd even bragged about it to Arnie. The plot had been slowly but methodically unfolding. He had captured the setting so well that he could almost hear the dripping water in the sewer beneath the gritty city streets. His characters were innocently being led by him into perilous situations.

Suddenly and without warning, they'd balked. Every last one of them had dug in his heels and announced, "I'm not going to play anymore."

The hero was no longer capable of heroics and had turned into a sap. The villain had gone soft. The informers had turned mute. The cops had grown disinterested and inept. The central female character . . .

Alex propped his elbows on the edge of his typing table and plowed all ten fingers through his hair. The main female character had led the mutiny. Suddenly dissatisfied with the role he'd created for her, the bitch had cast it off and simply would not resume it.

This broad was no cream puff. She had a mouth as sassy as her ass, which he had described in lusty detail when he introduced her to his readers on page fifteen. But she was also extremely feminine and vulnerable, much more so than he had originally intended. He suspected that, while he wasn't looking, she'd taken liberties with that aspect of her personality. In a weak moment, he'd let her get away with it. Now it was too late to correct.

It was time for the hero's conquest of her, but the tenor of their bedroom scene wasn't developing as Alex had outlined it. Somewhere between his brain and his fingertips, the creative impulses had been redirected like the train tracks in a railyard. Some force other than himself was throwing the switches.

The hero was supposed to push up her skirt, tear off her panties, get in, come, get out, and leave her screaming invectives and threatening to sic her boyfriend, the villain, on him.

The scornful and sarcastic hero was to match her insult for insult and threat for threat, and leave her in the shabby motel room with her torn panties and orgasmic blush as mute testimonies to her gullibility and moral decay.

Instead, every time Alex tried to write the scene, his mind's eye saw it differently. The hero caressed his way beneath her skirt. Instead of roughly jerking down her panties, he slipped his fingers inside them. Touching her there nearly sent the poor bastard into orbit. He fondled her until she was ready and wet, and only then did he gradually work her panties down her legs.

Once inside her, he wasn't in any hurry to come and get out, either. She wasn't at all what he had expected; she was softer, sweeter, snugger. He completely ignored Alex's orders to nail her and get it over with.

Confused by the emotions that assailed him, and contrary to habit, the hero raised himself above her and looked into her face. A single tear was rolling down her cheek. He asked what was wrong. Was he hurting her?

Hurting her? Alex's mind screamed. *Where did that come from? He's not supposed to care if he hurts her.*

No, he wasn't hurting her, she told him. The only way he could do her harm was to tell her boyfriend the villain about this. *He* would hurt her. She was a victim of chronic abuse, she said. Did he believe she would stay with a slime bucket like the villain if she had a choice? No. Circumstance dictated that she stay with him.

That's crap! Alex mentally shouted. *She's a tramp. Can't you see that, you dope? You're being had. You're being screwed at both ends.*

The hero gazed into her limpid blue eyes, sank more deeply into her silky heat, breathed in the fragrance of her wavy red hair—

Wait a minute.

She was supposed to be a blonde. A bottle blonde. It said so on page 16. What had happened between page 16 and page 104 to change her hair color and her character? And when had he started using adjectives like *limpid* and *silky*? When he'd lost control of his own book, that's when.

The cursor continued to blink, unmoving.

Alex shoved back his chair and left the table. His fingers refused to strike the necessary keys and that's all there was to it. Hey, it happened. Even to the best of writers. Even Pulitzer prize winners got logjammed occasionally. No telling how good *The Grapes of Wrath* would have been if Steinbeck hadn't had creative lulls every now and then. Stephen King probably had off days when the words just wouldn't come.

On his way to the window, Alex noticed the near empty whiskey bottle on the bookcase. It seemed to be thumbing its nose at him.

When he'd left Cat's house, she was bristling with anger and brandishing a lead crystal vase. Acknowledging that her fury was more than a little justified, he'd driven straight to a liquor store.

The first swallow had tasted vile. The second went down more smoothly. Even smoother were the third and fourth. He didn't remember those that followed. He recalled retching violently, although he couldn't remember where.

He'd awakened at dawn, having to pee so badly that it hurt. His breath would have brought a bull elephant to its knees. He was befuddled, remembering nothing of how he'd gotten to the parking lot of a Kmart. He considered it a blessing that he hadn't killed himself or somebody else while driving.

Luckily, no one had called the police to report a drunk sleeping it off inside his car, parked next to the shopping cart return chute. He hadn't been mugged for his wallet or car.

He drove home, peed a liter or two, showered and shaved,

and ate aspirin until his head no longer felt like a two-ton ball bearing rolling around inside an oil drum.

He reread the material given to him when he'd left the rehab clinic and recited his AA prayer. Just as he was about to pour the whiskey into the toilet, he decided to keep it as a reminder that he was still a recovering alcoholic, that one drink was potentially lethal, and that answers couldn't be found at the bottom of a bottle. If they could, he'd have been able to slay his dragons long ago.

He'd drunk an ocean of booze searching for reasons for all the shit that had happened. His prayers to the Higher Power were usually in the form of questions. "Why did You suddenly decide to pick on Alex Pierce? Was it something I did? Something I didn't do?" He paid his taxes, contributed regularly to the Salvation Army, and was kind to old folks.

If it was that Fourth of July incident . . . He'd said he was sorry at least a thousand times. He couldn't possibly feel any worse about it than he did. He'd done what he'd had to do.

But apparently the Higher Power hadn't bought his rationalizations any more than his superiors in the department had. Feeling he'd been rejected by God himself, he began to crack under pressure. His moods had grown dark, his outlook on life even darker. Booze had become his one and only friend.

Now Arnie was his one and only friend.

Arnie. Right now, his hands would like two minutes with Arnie's throat. His well-meaning agent had advised him to come clean with Cat. But look where that had gotten him: she'd almost brained him with a vase. No matter what women claimed, he thought, they didn't really want honesty in a relationship.

Wouldn't it have been easier on both of them if he'd continued sleeping with her, taking the pleasure it rendered, and leaving the rest of it to Fate? But then, as Arnie had pointed out, he really would have been a shit.

Swearing, he ground his forehead against the window jamb. Cat was interfering with his appetite, his sleep, his rigid self-discipline, and his work. He was afraid to examine why she had so much control over his mind. He now mistrusted his instincts. The more he tried to sort things out, the more complicated they became.

There was only one certainty: Since his fight with Cat, he hadn't produced one readable page of manuscript.

If only sex with her hadn't been so damn good.

But it had been better than good. The best.

That's what he couldn't live with. That's what was tormenting him and turning his novel to crap.

Determined to regain control of this situation before he was forced to return the publisher's advance, he went back to his computer's blank screen and blinking cursor.

Since the scene wasn't unfolding as he'd originally outlined it, he'd go with it this way and see where it led. What could it hurt? He wasn't etching each word in stone. The pages could always be deep-sixed. Probably would be.

"What the hell," he muttered as he began pounding the keyboard with his rapid, two-finger system.

After a fleeting hour of relentless typing, he had five pages.

And they must be good, he thought dryly.

His cock could have driven nails through a brick wall.

Chapter Thirty-one

Y ou look rested." Sherry Parks took a seat opposite Cat's desk.

"Doesn't she?" Jeff sat down in the other chair. "The vacation was long overdue."

"I had a wonderful time," Cat told them. "Ate three squares every day. Slept so late it was indecent. Took long walks along the beach. In short, I was a sloth."

"Not entirely," Sherry said. "A walk along the beach can be a real workout."

"Actually I get a workout just dressing for it. Most people remove clothes before going to the beach. I have to cover every inch of skin." Because of the medication she took, she was particularly susceptible to sunburn.

Getting down to business, she flipped open the file folder Jeff had placed on her desk. The photo inside took her aback. "My! What a beautiful child," she exclaimed.

"Isn't he?" Sherry agreed. "That's Michael. Age three. This week Child Services placed him in a foster home."

"Under what circumstances?" Cat asked.

"His father is a real charmer," Sherry said sarcastically. "George Murphy. He's a so-called construction worker who can't keep a job because of his explosive temper and suspected drug use. He's constantly being fired. They live on his unemployment checks and what little Michael's mother can contribute."

"Is Murphy abusive?"

"According to their neighbors, he is. They've called the police numerous times to report domestic violence. He's been arrested, but she never presses charges. Apparently she's terrified of him," Sherry explained.

"Last month, the caseworker took Michael away for several days, but returned him to his mother when Mr. Murphy was arrested for possession of drugs. Unfortunately, he was released for lack of evidence."

"A lucky break for him," Cat remarked.

"You'd think so. But he didn't learn his lesson. His temper tantrums have gotten worse and more frequent. And, all of a sudden, they've been directed more toward the child than his mother.

"Michael suffered a 'fall' last week. He was X-rayed in the emergency room but released because no bones had been broken. The day before yesterday, his mother brought him to the hospital again. Mr. Murphy had pushed him into a wall. Michael was too addled even to cry. His mother was afraid he'd been permanently brain damaged."

"Was he?"

"No, it was just a slight concussion. Doctors kept him in the hospital overnight for observation. He was released to Child Protection Services yesterday and placed in a foster home."

"How is he now?"

"He cries for his mother but otherwise behaves well. In fact, almost too well. He has practically no communication skills. He indicated to his foster mother that he'd like a banana with his breakfast cereal, but he didn't know what it was called."

"Good God," Jeff whispered.

"This child has been so intimidated by his father that he's afraid even to speak," Sherry said sadly.

Cat continued to stare at the photograph. The boy had dark, curly hair, large, blue, expressive eyes, and long eyelashes. His lips were bowed, with little depressions in each corner. He was so pretty, he could have been mistaken for a girl if dressed differently.

She was indiscriminately drawn to all the children regardless of race, age, or sex. She empathized with all of them and tolerated even the most badly behaved. Behavior was usually an accurate barometer of the level of abuse they'd suffered. Their stories touched her, angered her, and sometimes made her ashamed to be a member of the human race, which could inflict such misery on its young.

But she was attracted to this child in a special, inexplicable way. She couldn't take her eyes off the photograph.

"I wanted you to see his case file," Sherry was saying, "because I think we'll eventually get him for *Cat's Kids*. His mother seems to love him, but she's terrified of Murphy. I'm afraid she won't cross him even to protect Michael. God only knows the abuse she suffers. I've seen this character, and, believe me, he looks capable of physical and emotional battering.

"Anyway, this time they're being jointly charged for abuse to a minor. Their overworked, underpaid, pro bono attorney is already talking plea bargain to keep from taking the case to trial."

"From what you've told us," Jeff said, "my guess is that they'll plead guilty to a lesser charge in exchange for losing custody of Michael."

This happened frequently. Some parents would actually give up their children in order to reduce their jail sentences. As shocking as the practice was, it was sometimes best for children to be permanently removed from parents who cared no more than that.

"You're probably right, Jeff," Sherry said. "Murphy will jump at the chance to get rid of the boy. Considering how overcrowded the jails are, he'll probably serve only a fraction of his sentence. He might even be sentenced only for time already served. It'd be a good deal for him."

"But tragic for Michael's mother," Cat said reflectively.

If this child were hers, she'd kill anyone who tried to take him away from her. But she didn't judge the other woman. Fear was a powerful motivator. So was love.

She said, "If she loves her child as much as you say, she might give him up to protect him from Murphy."

"In the long run, that would be the best thing for Michael," Sherry said. "*Cat's Kids* will find him a loving home. In the meantime, he needs to be integrated with other children. So I didn't think you'd mind if I brought him to the picnic."

Cat's head came up. "Picnic?"

Jeff cleared his throat and smiled sheepishly. "I was waiting until you got back to break the news."

Cat waited for an explanation.

"Nancy Webster got a bee in her bonnet," he said apologetically. "She called me at least a dozen times while you were away. Didn't Mr. Webster tell you that once she was placed in charge of something she became a steamroller?"

"Words to that effect."

"Well, he knows his wife well. She explained to me that organizing an elaborate fund-raiser takes months. So, in the interim, she's invited some potential contributors to a mini-fund-raiser. This weekend.''

"This weekend!"

"I asked why the rush," Jeff said. "Mrs. Webster said there's nothing on the social calendar this weekend. But for the next several months, just about every weekend is spoken for. So it's now or never.''

Cat took a deep breath. "Welcome back to the salt mine, Ms. Delaney.''

"Actually there's very little for you to do except show up on Saturday," Jeff told her. "I've already notified all the media. Sherry answered my S.O.S. She's done most of the legwork involved in rounding up the kids.''

"Including those who've already been adopted?" Cat asked. "I think we should have our success stories there. Especially in light of the negative publicity Truitt gave us following Chantal's death.''

"Jeff and I already thought of that," Sherry said. "We've included foster families, applicants to adopt, everyone we could think of who might be interested. Mrs. Webster said there was no limit to the number of people we could invite as long as we let her know an approximate head count by Thursday so she can inform the caterer.''

"A caterer for a picnic?''

"Barbecue with all the trimmings," Jeff told her. "But there'll be hotdogs for the younger kids because ribs might be too hard for them to handle.''

"Nancy's given this some thought," Cat said, tongue-in-cheek.

"Including the decorations and the band.''

"Band?"

"A country and western dance band from Austin," Jeff explained. Then breezily he added, "And Willie might drive down from Luckenbach, but he couldn't promise.''

"Willie Nelson? You're kidding."

"Nope."

"And she's pulling all this together by this weekend?"

"I'm telling you, if Norman Schwarzkopf had consulted her, he could have wound up Desert Storm in half the time."

Sherry stood to leave. "Personally, I can't wait. Everybody I've talked to is very excited. And I've always had a lech for Willie Nelson—braids, beads, and all."

After she left, Jeff gave Cat the rest of the details. "See, there really is nothing for you to do."

"What if I had extended my vacation for a few more days? I would have missed it."

"Nancy had a contingency. She planned to send a private jet for you, then return you to California to finish your vacation after the picnic."

"Money not only talks, it shouts."

"It certainly does." Jeff tucked his various files beneath his arm and stood. "You do look better, boss. I wasn't just flattering you."

"Thanks. I did a lot of thinking, but mostly I just vegged out." She hesitated to tell him about the third clipping she'd received, but decided that since she'd already confided in him, he should know about the latest development.

He expressed his outrage. "Who the hell is this creep?"

"I don't know. Dean didn't have any ideas either."

"Have you told Mr. Webster yet?"

"No, but I think I will. If some fruitcake barges in here and starts shooting up the place, Bill should be forewarned. This could involve the station's security."

"I doubt it'll come to that."

"So do I. I think this individual would be much more subtle." She then told him about the corresponding dates of the accidental deaths. "It was like a puzzle he wanted me to figure out."

"So when was your—"

"The fourth anniversary of my transplant is only a few weeks away."

"Jesus, Cat. This has ceased to be mystifying. These clippings could be outright threats. Don't you think it's time you went to the police?"

"Dean urged me to. But until an actual stalking crime is committed, what can they do? We don't know who my stalker is."

"But surely there's something to be done."

"I gave it a lot of thought on the flight home. Can I enlist your help?"

"You have to ask?"

"Thanks. Place calls to the morgues of these newspapers and ask for copies of any related articles. If follow-up stories were written about these accident victims, I want to see them."

"Are you looking for anything specific?"

"No. I'd like to know if there were criminal investigations or inquests as a result of the deaths. Or if there were any human-interest profiles written about the victims. That kind of thing."

He was more beautiful than she remembered. When she saw him, he took her breath. His curly hair was dark and endearingly unruly. He wore blue jeans and a western shirt. His cowboy boots looked new.

Cat knelt in front of him. His right index finger was hooked in the corner of his mouth. "Hello, Michael. My name's Cat. I'm so glad you could come today."

Sherry was holding the boy by the hand. "He's happy to be here. His foster mother told me so."

Above him, Sherry was sadly shaking her head, conveying to Cat that Michael wasn't mixing well with the other children. He seemed overwhelmed by the noisy crowd.

"This is the lady who sent you the new clothes, Michael," Sherry said to him. "Tell her thank you."

He stared at the ground.

"Never mind," Cat said. "You can thank me later. I haven't had a hotdog yet, have you?"

He raised his head and stared back at her through vacant blue eyes, giving no indication that he understood.

"Let's go get one together. Okay?" She extended her hand. Michael considered it for a long time before withdrawing his pruny index finger from his mouth and placing his hand in Cat's.

She smiled at Sherry and held up two crossed fingers. "We'll catch up with you later."

Cat matched her stride to Michael's slow shuffle. "I really like those boots," she remarked. "They're red like mine. See?"

She stopped and pointed down at her cowboy boots. She'd bought them at a boutique on Rodeo Drive in Beverly Hills, but Michael wouldn't know the difference.

He studied the likeness of their boots, then raised his head and squinted at her. It wasn't quite a smile, but it was a measurable response. Taking that as an encouraging sign, she squeezed his hand. "We're going to be good friends. I can tell."

The barbecue picnic was being held on the Webster estate. The band had set up in the Victorian gazebo on the banks of the pond where docile ducks gorged on bread crumbs thrown by the children. The air was filled with the mouth-watering aroma of mesquite-smoked meat. Picnic tables with red and white bandanna-print tablecloths had been set up beneath the trees.

Jugglers, mimes, and clowns strolled among the crowd, dispensing balloons and candy. Three of the Dallas Cowboys were autographing toy footballs. Two members of the San Antonio Spurs basketball team stood head and shoulders above everyone else.

After getting their plates of food, Cat and Michael selected one of the tables. While they ate their hotdogs, she jabbered, hunting for anything to which he would respond. But he didn't speak a word, not even when she introduced him to Jeff, who was a big hit with the children. Several clung to him as they made their way to the pond.

Michael was invited to come along and feed the ducks, but he shied away. Cat didn't press him. She did, however, notice that something else had attracted his attention.

She followed the direction of his absorbed stare. "Ah, you're a horse lover. Want to ride?"

He stared at her solemnly, but his eyes showed a spark of curiosity that hadn't been there before.

"Let's go take a closer look."

She wiped his face and hands with a napkin, then took his hand, which he was no longer reluctant to give her, and walked with him to the temporary paddock where four ponies were walking around an exercise wheel.

Once they reached the area, Cat sensed Michael's reserve, so she gave him time to mull it over. They stood and watched as the ponies went through their paces. After the third group of four children had been lifted off the ponies, Michael looked up at her inquisitively.

"Would you like to take a ride?" He nodded. "You got it, cowboy." She led him through the gate and into the ring. He selected the smallest of the ponies. "This one's my favorite, too," she whispered confidentially. "He's got the prettiest mane and the longest tail. And I think he likes you best, too. I saw him scoping you out."

Michael smiled shyly, and her heart nearly burst.

A man dressed like a cowboy was helping the other children mount, so Cat bent down to lift Michael into the saddle.

"Better let me. He's probably heavier than he looks."

She was brushed aside by a pair of hands she knew by sight and touch. Alex lifted Michael with ease and swung him into the saddle.

"There you go, Hopalong. Here're your reins. Hold them like this." He folded Michael's fingers around the strips of leather, then placed both hands on the pommel of the saddle. "Say, podnuh, I think you've done this before. You're a natural-born cowpoke." He gave Michael a companionable pat on the back.

"Everything okay here?" The man in charge checked to see that Michael was safely situated in the small saddle.

Cat placed her hand on the boy's thigh. "Michael? Are you ready?"

He had a white-knuckle grip on the saddle horn, but he bobbed his head up and down.

"I'll be right over there," she said, pointing to the spot. "I'll be watching you. I won't leave."

She took up her post at the railing in full view of Michael and waved at him. The "cowboy" made a kissing sound and the four ponies plodded forward in their controlled circle.

The boy's face registered an attack of abject terror, but it quickly passed. He glanced nervously at Cat out the corners of his eyes, afraid to move his head. She smiled encouragement and kept her eyes on him even when Alex moved into place beside her.

"Cute kid."

"What are you doing here, Alex?"

"I was invited."

"This is one social obligation you could have declined."

"I came because I wanted to make a contribution to *Cat's Kids*."

"Oh, please."

"It's true."

"So why didn't you mail a check?"

"Because I also wanted to see you."

She turned toward him and, for the first time, looked him straight in the eye. Which was a mistake. Because he looked good enough to eat. And the intensity with which he was looking at her brought back memories that were both wonderful and distressing.

She turned back to Michael and waved as he rode past. "Then you've wasted your time. Don't you remember the last thing I said to you?"

"You told me to fuck off."

She bowed her head and uttered a short laugh. "I don't think I phrased it quite that explicitly, but that was more or less what I meant."

"I've tried to contact you a hundred times. Where've you been?"

"I went to California."

"To cry on Dr. Feelgood's shoulder?"

"Dean's a trusted friend."

"How sweet."

"At least I know exactly where I stand with him."

"Damn right you do. And so do I. You're beholden to him. The pill-pusher takes full advantage of that."

"Dean is not a pill-pusher and my relationship with him—"

People were watching them, some with knowing smiles on their faces. Those who had attended Nancy's dinner party where Alex had been her date probably thought there was a hot romance between them.

Not wanting to create a spectacle, she pasted on a smile and returned her attention to Michael, who had become brave enough to bounce his heels against the pony's sides, imitating the older boy riding on the pony in front of his.

"Go away, Alex," she said under her breath. "You've made your position clear, and so have I. We've got nothing else to say to each other."

"I'm afraid it's not that easy, Cat. Charlie and Irene Walters are itching to meet you, and they'll be here soon.

They vowed they'd never speak to me again if I didn't personally introduce you to them." He took a step closer. "It was great of you to call and invite them."

"Since our scheduled first meeting went awry, I thought I should extend them a personal invitation."

"They also said that someone from the state agency called and set up another interview. Was that also your doing?"

"Sherry thought they sounded like perfect candidates to adopt and was disappointed when I told her about the mix-up. I'm sure she followed up."

"But you put in a good word for them."

She shrugged.

"Thanks."

She turned on him, barely containing her anger. "It's not up to you to thank me. I didn't do it for you. I did it for Mr. and Mrs. Walters. As you pointed out to me the morning we met, I shouldn't judge them by the company they keep. By all means, I'll be delighted to meet them when they arrive, but make yourself scarce. Now, if you'll excuse me, the ride is over and I've got to get Michael."

She pushed past Alex and went into the ring.

Chapter Thirty-two

Alex let her go. He was sensitive to Cat's position, especially at this function. She represented *Cat's Kids*, and vice versa. Everything she said and did reflected on the program. He didn't want to be responsible for any negative publicity, so he pretended that he was ready to end their conversation. He even managed a smile for anyone who might be watching.

As soon as Cat left the pony ride with Michael, Nancy Webster summoned her to the gazebo, where a crowd had gathered. Alex caught the word: Willie Nelson had arrived.

The singer sang a few songs. Cat, serving as honorary hostess of the event, remained on the platform with his band. She held Michael on her lap and even coaxed him to clap his hands in time to the music. He was still in her arms when she went to the microphone and made a few welcoming remarks, then urged those in attendance to contribute what they could for the children's special needs.

Following the short program, she stood and talked to the country/western star. Each time she laughed at something he said, Alex's gut tightened with uncharacteristic jealousy. Finally the performer departed with his ragtag entourage, which, in Alex's biased opinion, looked like an offshore drilling crew after a two-week shift.

Alex noticed, at about the same time as Cat, that Michael had cupped his crotch with one hand and was shifting restlessly from one foot to the other. Cat leaned down and whispered something in his ear. He nodded. Hand in hand, they made their way to the house and went in the front door.

Alex followed them inside. Away from spectators, he and she might be able to reach an understanding. Short of that, he would try and get her to agree to a meeting sometime later. She might think their short-lived relationship was over, but she was wrong.

He loitered in the Websters' living room, pretending to appreciate Nancy's collection of Hummel figurines and hoping to intercept Cat when she emerged with Michael from the powder room beneath the stairs.

He swore beneath his breath when Bill Webster beat him to it.

From the living room, he heard Webster greet her warmly. "Cat! Glad I ran into you. I've hardly seen you all evening."

"Hello, Bill. This is Michael. He needed a rest room, and the port-a-potties had long lines. I hope you don't mind that we made ourselves at home."

"Of course not. When a young man needs to go, he needs to go in a hurry." He chuckled. "What do you think of the festivities so far?"

"Everything's marvelous," she replied. "I'll never know how Nancy managed to pull it together in such a short time."

"This is nothing compared to the big fund-raiser we'll hold in the spring."

"I can't even imagine it."

Alex envisioned her making one of her funny faces. However, there was no humor in her voice when next she spoke.

"Bill, I need to talk to you about something important. Five minutes, first thing Monday morning?"

"Your tone makes me nervous, especially since you just returned from California. You're not thinking of quitting us and going back to *Passages*?"

"Absolutely not."

"Well then, what's on your mind?"

"It can wait until Monday."

"Sorry, Cat. I'll be attending a broadcasters' meeting in St. Louis. I leave tomorrow night and won't be back in the office until Thursday."

"Oh. Then I guess it'll have to wait till then."

"Don't be polite. If it's something that serious—"

"That's just it. I don't know. I wanted your opinion on whether or not it's serious."

"I've got five minutes now," he offered. "Let's go into my study where we can talk privately."

"I hate for Michael to miss the fun."

"He can play with my decoys."

"All right. I really don't think this should wait another week."

Alex heard the study door close. He stepped into the wide foyer and furtively glanced around. There was no one else in sight, so he crept down the hallway and stood outside the closed door. Listening carefully, he could just make out their words.

"The originals are at home locked in a drawer," he heard Cat say. "I carry these copies around with me. Read them, then tell me what you think."

Webster fell silent. Alex heard Cat talking softly to the boy, apparently trying to interest him in Webster's collection of decoys.

"Good Christ," Webster exclaimed. "How long have you had these?"

"Several weeks. What do you make of them?"

"My first impression is that whoever sent them is obviously mentally disturbed."

Outside the door, Alex frowned.

"Jeff's done some checking for me," Cat said. "There was one other short article written about the accident in Florida. None relating to the others. They were all ruled accidental deaths, which leads me to believe that I'm making a mountain out of a molehill. If the police don't suspect foul play, why should I?

"Still, I'm very disturbed over this. I thought you should be made aware because if something does happen, it could involve the television station and the safety of everyone there."

"Do you think that whoever sent these might actually come after you?"

Alex didn't hear her reply. Instead he heard his own name, spoken in question form. He spun around. Nancy Webster had just cleared the front door.

He grinned nonchalantly to cover his blatant eavesdropping. "Hi, Nancy."

"Have you seen Cat?"

"I saw her coming into the house and followed her this far. I think she brought the little boy in here to go to the bathroom. He apparently did the deed because I thought I heard her voice in here and was just about to knock."

Nancy moved past him and, without knocking, opened the door to her husband's study. "Bill? Cat? What's going on?"

The door swung open wide enough for Alex to see Bill seated in a maroon leather easy chair. Duck decoys were lined up on the ottoman in front of him. Michael was pushing them across the smooth leather. Cat was seated on the rug at Webster's feet.

Webster hastily shoved a handful of papers into his coat pocket. He looked startled and upset. "What is it, dear?"

Nancy looked like she'd been smacked in the face with a bag of wet cement. The tableau in the study was cozy and domestic. Alex knew that nothing untoward had happened, but he was constrained to silence.

"The fireworks are about to start," Nancy said with a stiff smile. "I didn't want you to miss them."

"Thank you for letting us know." Webster stood up and offered his hand to Cat. However, she came to her feet unassisted and lifted the boy into her arms.

"Come on, Michael. We can't miss the fireworks."

When she noticed Alex standing just beyond Nancy and realized that he'd overheard her conversation with Webster, her forced smile collapsed.

Cat carried Michael outside. She oohed and aahed over the pyrotechnics for the child's benefit, but her excitement was phony. Nancy possessively linked arms with her husband. Her enthusiastic comments on the fireworks also rang false. Webster was so withdrawn that he seemed not even to notice them.

Alex didn't see them at all. While the Roman candles exploded overhead, his hard gaze was fixed on Cat Delaney.

For the second time that evening, Nancy found Bill sequestered in his study. It was late. Everyone had left. The clean-up crew was due to arrive in the morning to haul off debris and set the grounds aright.

When she entered, he raised his highball glass to her. "You pulled it off with your usual style. Join me for a celebratory drink?"

"No thank you."

He'd had more than one and didn't need another. His face was flushed, and the whites of his eyes were turning pink. He rarely got tight, so when he did, the signs were noticeable.

"I'm exhausted," she said, extending her hand down to him. "Let's go to bed."

He ignored her hand. "You go on. I'll be up shortly. I'm going to have another short one." He poured more scotch into his glass. He grimaced when he took a sip. He wasn't drinking for enjoyment.

Nancy sat on the ottoman in front of his easy chair. "Bill, what's wrong?"

"I'm thirsty."

"Stop that!" she said sharply. "Don't insult me."

He seemed on the verge of arguing, then changed his mind. Closing his eyes, he raised the glass to his forehead and rolled it from side to side as though to iron out the frown lines.

"I saw your expression when you discovered Cat and me in here," he said. "I shouldn't have to explain myself, but I will. We were discussing a private matter."

"That's what I'm afraid of."

"It's not like that, Nancy. My God, give me some credit. She looks too much like Carla to ever become my lover."

"Then are you trying to replace Carla with her?"

He looked at her hard, his eyes no longer hazy from alcohol. "Is that what you think?"

She bowed her head and stared at her wedding ring as she turned it around her finger. "I don't know what to think anymore. Nothing's been the same between us since we lost Carla. Instead of climbing out of our grief, our lives have been on a gradual landslide. No matter what I do, I can't seem to stop it. I dread hitting bottom because I don't know what's waiting for us there."

She raised her head and looked at him with yearning. "Why don't you reach for me anymore, Bill?"

"I do."

"Not as frequently. And when you do, it's not the same as it used to be. I can feel the difference. I want to know what's interfering with our marriage. If you're not having an affair with Cat, what's going on?''

"How many times do I have to say it? *Nothing*. I have a lot of responsibilities. When I come home late, I'm tired. I can't get it up on command. Sorry.''

His sarcasm made her angry. She stood and headed for the door, then turned back before leaving. "Talking to you tonight would be a waste of time because you're drunk. Which is another indication that something is terribly wrong. I don't know what it is, but don't try and tell me that I'm imagining it.

"Carla was a delightful girl. We'll love her forever. You're close to all the children, but you and she had a special relationship. When she died, I know you felt that a part of yourself had died, too. If I could give her back to you, I would, Bill.''

She spread her arms helplessly. "I can't. But I refuse to lose more than what's already been taken from me. My whole life revolves around loving you. I plan to keep you and to restore our marriage to the way it once was. No matter what I have to do.''

Cat slept very little that night.

She couldn't get Michael off her mind. He was so emotionally and socially retarded that to draw him out would require an enormous amount of dedication. But the right parents could do it with love and patience, and the reward would be well worth the effort. Inside him was an animated little boy wanting desperately to be coaxed out.

Michael wasn't all that was on her mind, however. Seeing Alex had caused her to doubt all the positive resolves she'd made in California. It was galling how much she still wanted him.

His friends Irene´ and Charlie Walters had been as affable

as he'd described them. She was certain that once they completed the required parenting course, they would make excellent parents to one of Cat's Kids.

At any other time, she would have enjoyed meeting them and would have wished to spend more time with them. But the introduction had taken place shortly after the fireworks. Still fresh on her mind was the expression on Nancy Webster's face when she opened the study door and found her and Bill together. Clearly, Nancy had misinterpreted the nature of their private chat.

These worries, in addition to the stalker—as she referred to him for lack of a better term—continued to weigh heavily on her mind. Needing distraction, she spent Sunday afternoon shopping, then went to a movie that evening.

On Monday she and Jeff wrote thank-you letters to those who had made contributions to *Cat's Kids* at the picnic.

On Tuesday, they videotaped a segment with a five-year-old girl who was hearing impaired and had recently lost both parents in an accident.

That night when Cat returned home, she found among her mail a familiar envelope. It was identical to the three that had come before it. The content, however, was different.

Inside was a single sheet of white paper. Written to emulate newspaper copy was a story about the former soap opera star, heart transplantee Cat Delaney. It went on for several paragraphs, detailing her accomplishments, including *Cat's Kids*.

It was her obituary.

Chapter Thirty-three

It's weird all right, but it isn't criminal—know what I mean?"

Lieutenant Bud Hunsaker of the San Antonio Police Department wore checked polyester pants and black lizard cowboy boots with white stitching. His short-sleeved white shirt was stretched over a beer gut cinched by a tooled leather belt. His short, clip-on necktie lay diagonally across his chest. He had the bulk, the complexion, and the wheeze of an excellent candidate for a heart attack.

From the moment Cat had entered his office, he'd been gnawing on an unlit, soggy cigar and—if the direction of his stare was any indication—carrying on a dialogue with her kneecaps.

Now, he placed his meaty forearms on the desk and leaned forward. "Say, what's Doug Speer like? In person, I mean. He cracks me up, the way he's always getting the forecast wrong, then making a joke of it."

"Doug Speer works for another station," Cat replied with a brittle smile. "I don't know him."

"Oh, yeah, right. I'm always getting my weathermen mixed up."

"Can we please get back to these, Lieutenant?" Imperiously, she tapped the stack of paper she'd brought in with her and which now lay before him on his desk.

He rolled the cigar from one stained corner of his fleshy lips to the other. "Ms. Delaney, a lady like you, being famous and all, a public figure so to speak, you gotta expect a certain amount of harassment like this."

"I do, Lieutenant Hunsaker. When I appeared on *Passages*, I received lots of mail, including numerous marriage proposals. One man wrote a hundred times."

"There you go." Grinning with satisfaction, he leaned back in his creaky chair as though she'd made his point for him.

"But a marriage proposal per se isn't threatening. Neither are letters that gush praise or severely criticize my performance. By comparison, these are veiled threats. Especially the last one." She separated the fake obituary from the others. "What are you going to do about this?"

He shifted uncomfortably in his seat, and the chair groaned in protest. He picked up the single-spaced, typed sheet and reread the fabricated obit. Cat wasn't fooled by his feigned interest; she was being humored. He had already formed an opinion. Nothing short of an outright death threat was going to change his mind.

He snorted loudly and swallowed the gunk he'd sucked out of his sinuses. "The way I see it, Ms. Delaney, some weirdo is trying to bug you."

"Well, he's doing a damned good job of it, because I am bugged. I had deduced that much on my own. I came to you to find the weirdo and put a stop to the bugging."

"It ain't as easy as it sounds."

"It doesn't sound easy. If it were easy, I'd do it myself. The police are equipped to handle situations like this. Private citizens aren't."

"How d'ya figure we ought to handle it?"

"I don't know!" she cried in frustration. "Can't you trace the postmark? Or the typewriter? Or the brand of paper? Or the fingerprints on the paper?"

He guffawed and winked at her. "You've been watching too many cop shows on TV."

She wanted to rant and rave at him until she got him off his fat butt and out beating the bushes for her stalker. But sounding like a hysterical female would only confirm his opinion that she was making a brouhaha over nothing more than nuisance mail.

Rather than vent her temper, she said with chilly calmness, "Don't patronize me, Lieutenant Hunsaker."

His ingratiating smile slipped a notch. "Now hold on, I wasn't—"

"The only thing you haven't done is pat me on the head." She stood up and leaned across his desk.

"I am a rational, adult person, capable of deductive reasoning, because in addition to a uterus, I'm also equipped with a brain. I don't suffer from PMS, and I'm not given to vapors. The differences between you and me are so myriad we could fill an encyclopedia with a list of them, but the least of those differences is that I've got on a skirt and you're wearing trousers.

"Now, either you put down that disgusting cigar and start taking my problem seriously, or I'll jump rank and complain to your superior." She rapped her knuckles on his desk. "There must be some crime-solving method by which you could track down the person responsible for this."

His face had turned the color of raw liver; he knew she had him. He stretched his neck to relieve the tightness of his collar, straightened his tie, removed the cigar from his mouth, and dropped it into his lap drawer. Then, attempting to smile, he asked her politely to sit down.

"You know of anybody holding a grudge against you?"

"No. Unless . . ." She hesitated to voice her suspicions because she had nothing to substantiate them.

"Unless what?"

"There's another employee at WWSA—a young woman. She hasn't liked me since I began working there." She told him about her turbulent relationship with Melia King.

"She eventually confessed to throwing away my medication, but I don't believe she could have rigged a studio light to fall. She was rehired shortly after I fired her and seems to enjoy her new position. I see her every day. We have little to say to each other. There's no love lost, but I'm almost positive her resentment has nothing to do with my transplant."

"Ugly broad?"

"Excuse me?"

"What does she look like? Could be she's just pea green."

Cat gave a quick, negative shake of her head. "She's a stunner and could have her choice of men."

"Maybe she didn't welcome the competition."

His expression came close to a leer. Cat froze it into place with a frigid blast from her blue eyes. He harrumphed and again situated his wide rear end more comfortably in his chair. He picked up the obituary. "This language is sorta . . . unrefined."

"I noticed that, too. It doesn't read like authentic newspaper copy."

"And it doesn't give a cause of death."

"Because that would put me on the alert. I'd know what to expect."

"No one's actually approached you, issued threats, hung out around your place, anything like that?"

"Not yet."

Hunsaker grunted noncommittally, tugged on his lip, and

expelled a gust of breath. To buy more time, he read the newspaper clippings yet again. Before speaking, he cleared his throat importantly. "These're from all over the country. The sumbitch has been busy."

"Which I believe makes him all the more frightening," Cat said. "He's obviously obsessed with the fate of these transplantees. Whether or not he was responsible for their deaths, he has gone to great lengths to keep track of them."

"Do you believe he was behind these so-called accidents?" he asked, his tone suggesting that he didn't ascribe to that theory.

Cat wasn't sure whether she did, so she avoided a direct answer. "I feel it's significant that the dates of their deaths coincided with the anniversaries of their transplants, which also coincides with mine. That's too coincidental to be a coincidence."

Thoughtfully, he once again tugged on his lower lip. "You ever meet your donor family?"

"Do you think there's a connection?"

"It's as good a guess as any. What do you know about your donor?"

"Nothing. Until recently, I never wanted to know anything. But yesterday I contacted the organ bank that procured my heart and asked if my donor's family had queried them about me. They're checking the records of the agency that harvested the heart, so it might be several days before I get an answer. If no inquiry's been made into my identity, then we'll know that's a cold trail."

"How come?"

"Policy. The identities of donors and recipients are kept strictly confidential unless both parties inquire about the other. Only then do the agencies disclose information. It's up to the individuals whether or not to make contact."

"That's the only way somebody could find out who got a particular heart?"

"Unless they were able to tap into the central computer in Virginia and learn the UNOS number."

"Come again?"

She explained to him what Dean had recently explained to her. "UNOS, United Network of Organ Sharing. Each organ and tissue donor is assigned a number soon after retrieval. This number is coded to provide the year, day, month, and chronology of when the organs were retrieved and accepted by an organ bank. It's a tracking device to help prevent black marketing of organs."

He rubbed his hand over his face. "Jeez. This guy'd have to be smart."

"That's what I've been trying to tell you."

The more they hypothesized, the more frightened she became. "That brings us full circle, Lieutenant. What are you going to do to find him before he finds me?"

"Truth be told, Ms. Delaney, there ain't a lot we can do."

"Until I die in some freak accident, right?"

"Calm down, now."

"I'm calm." She rose to leave. "Unfortunately, so are you."

Moving faster than she had believed him capable of, he rounded his desk and blocked her exit at his office door. "It's puzzling, I'll admit. But at this point it's hardly life-threatening. No crime's been committed. And we don't even know if foul play was involved in these other deaths, do we?"

"No," she said tersely.

"Still and all, I don't want you to leave thinking I don't take you serious. How's this? How's about I have a patrol car cruise your street for the next few weeks, keep an eye on your place?"

Laughing softly, she lowered her head and squeezed her temples between her thumb and middle finger. He just didn't get it. Her stalker was too clever to be caught by a cruising squad car.

"Thank you very much, Lieutenant. I would appreciate any help you can provide."

"That's what I'm here for." His smile expanded, and so did his chest. "Prob'ly what this is, somebody's just trying to spook you. Get under your skin, you know?"

Eager to leave, she agreed.

Believing he'd solved her problem, he made a gallant gesture of opening the door for her. "You call if you need me, you hear?"

Sure, I'll call. And have you do what? Cat thought cynically. "Thank you for seeing me on such short notice, Lieutenant Hunsaker."

"You know, you're even prettier in person than you are on TV."

"Thank you."

"Uh, before you go, I's wondering . . . It's not every day I get a celebrity in my office. Could you sign your autograph for my wife? It'd really tickle her. Make it to Doris, okay? And you can put my name on it, too. If it's not too much to ask."

Chapter Thirty-four

What the hell are you doing?"

"Burning the bacon." Using a fork because she hadn't found a pair of tongs in any of the kitchen drawers, Cat lifted a slice from the sizzling skillet.

After her infuriating interview at the police station, she'd returned home and changed clothes. Too upset to work, she'd called Jeff and told him that she wouldn't be coming in. She needed a day off in which to think.

For almost an hour she'd deliberated over what her next move should be. Before she had fully formulated the plan, she was pushing a cart down the aisle of a supermarket, shopping for food to prepare for a man she claimed to despise.

"Hope you like it crisp." She laid the strip of bacon along with the others that were draining on a paper towel. "How do you like your eggs?"

"How'd you get in?"

"Through the front door. It was unlocked."

"Oh." He scratched his head. "Must've forgot to check it before going to bed."

"Must have. Over easy or scrambled?"

When he didn't answer, she cast a glance over her shoulder. He looked exactly as he had the morning she'd met him, except that this morning he had on boxer shorts rather than jeans. She tried to ignore how sexy he looked, his rangy body filling up the doorway with over six feet of rumpled, fresh-out-of-the-sack maleness.

"Over easy or scrambled?" she repeated. "I'm better at scrambled."

He placed his hands on his hips where the shorts rode low. "Any particular reason why you showed up this morning to cook my breakfast?"

"Yes. As soon as you put on your pants and sit down to eat, I'll tell you."

Shaking his head in bafflement, he turned and ambled out. By the time he returned to the kitchen dressed in a pair of threadbare Levi's and a plain white T-shirt, the food was ready. She poured them each a cup of coffee, set the filled plates on the table, and slid into a chair, indicating that he was to sit in the one across from her.

He threw his leg over the back of it and straddled the seat, his knees poking out on each side. Temporarily passing on the food, he sipped from his mug of coffee while studying her through the steam that rose from it—another reminder of the morning they'd met.

He said, "Does this have anything to do with the shortest route to a man's heart being through his stomach?"

"That theory bit the dust when blow-jobs were invented."

He chuckled, then laughed out loud, then picked up his fork and began scooping scrambled eggs into his mouth. He polished off a strip of bacon in two bites and drained his orange juice in one gulp.

"When did you last eat?" she asked.

"I think I ordered a pizza yesterday," he replied after a moment's thought. "Or maybe it was the day before."

"You've been engrossed in work?"

"Hmm. Is there any more toast?"

She put two more slices into the toaster. While waiting for it to pop up, she poured him a refill of coffee. His fingers closed around her wrist as he tilted his head back to look up at her. "Just feeling a domestic urge this morning, Cat?"

"Not really."

"Then is this an act of charity?"

"I hardly think you qualify."

"Peace offering?"

"Don't hold your breath."

"This is going to cost me, right?"

"Right."

"Can I afford it?"

"Unless you want the family jewels baptized with scalding coffee, you'd better let go of my wrist."

His fingers sprang wide, instantly releasing her. She returned the carafe of coffee to the hot plate and retrieved his two slices of toast, unceremoniously tossing them onto his plate.

"So we're still not friends," he commented as he slathered butter on his toast.

"No."

"Then I guess being lovers is out of the question."

Watching his strong white teeth sink into the slice of buttery toast made her tummy flutter. She carried her plate to the sink, rinsed it, and placed it in the dishwasher. She tidied up the kitchen while he was finishing his meal. He took his plate to the sink, then poured himself a third cup of coffee and took it back to the table.

Cat was cleaning crumbs off the table with a damp sponge when he hooked his arm around her waist and pulled her to him. He pressed his face into the giving softness of her middle, kissing her through her blouse, taking love bites, gnawing and growling affectionately.

She refused to respond. She kept her hands raised to shoulder level, well away from touching him. Finally he raised his head. "You don't like?"

"I like it a lot. You're very adept. But that's not what I'm here for."

He dropped his arms, and his face turned hard and angry. "If you didn't come here to make peace—"

"I didn't."

"Then why are you here?"

"I'm getting to that."

"Well do. If you didn't come over to play, I've got work to do."

She didn't respond to his anger. After washing her hands and pouring herself another cup of coffee, she rejoined him at the table, bringing her handbag with her. From it she withdrew the copies of the clippings and the obituary and pushed them across the table to him.

"Is this the top-secret stuff you showed to Webster the other night?" he asked.

"So you had eavesdropped. I thought so."

"A holdover habit from my days as a cop."

"Or just plain rudeness."

"Could be," he admitted with a shrug. "Nancy Webster thought you and her husband were having a tête-à-tête."

"As you know, we weren't."

"So why let her think the worst? Why not just tell her the truth?"

"Because the fewer who know about this, the better."

He picked up the papers and began to read. By the time he got to the second one, he was thoughtfully rubbing the scar that slashed through his eyebrow. Between the second and third one, he gave her a hard, inquisitive glance.

After reading the obit, he cursed softly and scraped back

his chair. Legs stretched out at an angle, spine concave, he rested the sheets of paper on his midriff and read each of them again.

When he was done, he sat up straighter, tossed the sheets onto the table, and looked at Cat. "You've got the originals?"

"Plus the envelopes."

"I heard you tell Webster that you'd been receiving these over the last several weeks."

"That's right."

"And you didn't see fit to mention them to me?"

"They weren't any of your business."

He swore.

"Okay, that was a cheap shot," she admitted. "I didn't mention them to anyone until I received the third one."

"Then who'd you tell? Besides Spicer. I know you must've showed them to Sweet Dean."

"I showed them to Jeff," she said, ignoring his sarcastic remark. "Then to Bill."

"Because the TV station's security might be compromised," he said. "I heard you tell him that. Who else knows?"

"No one. The fake obituary arrived in yesterday's mail. That was the last straw. This morning I had an eight o'clock appointment with a police detective." She frowned. "For all the good it did me," she said bitterly, "I could have better used the time to take a bubble bath."

"What'd he say?"

Almost verbatim, she recounted her conversation with Lieutenant Hunsaker. "My life could be in danger, but he was more interested in ogling my legs. Anyway, he tried placating me with a lot of nonsense about the occupational hazards of being a TV personality, as if I didn't already know. He reeked of cigar tobacco, cheap aftershave, and good ol' boy sexism.

"I cut him off at the knees, but the bottom line is that until something terrible happens to me, the police can't do much except cruise past my house a few nights a week. Can you believe that?''

"Unfortunately, yes." He regarded her for a moment. "This is what had you so jumpy that night we caught Spicer at your house, isn't it? And you're still jumpy."

Cat rolled her lips inward. She rubbed her damp palms up and down her thighs, drying them on her jeans. Now that she had cooked his breakfast and told him her predicament, she was suddenly nervous, partially because he could read her so well.

He sat motionless, scrutinizing her with eyes that seemed to miss nothing. "What do you want from me, Cat?"

"Help."

He made a scoffing sound. "From me?"

"You're the only person I know with a criminal mind." His eyes narrowed. "You've dealt with criminals. You've studied MOs. You know the psychological profile of a character who'd do something like this. I need your assessment. Is this the work of a prankster, or a psychopath? Should I dismiss this as garbage or take it as a warning?"

Dropping all vestiges of pride, she added, "I'm frightened, Alex."

"I can see that." He regarded her with his quiet intensity. "You're an easy target."

Nervously she ran her fingers through her hair. "I know, but I refuse to live in an ivory tower and become a prisoner of my success. There's always a chance that a fan is going to get crazy and become obsessive. Most just hound you for an autograph. But some will kill you. I attended the funeral of a young actress who was shot to death in her own home by a fan who professed to love her."

She shook her head sadly. "You'll learn, Alex, that the more famous you become, the less privacy and security you'll have."

"Authors have more anonymity than TV stars."

She conceded that, but remained reflective. "I enjoy being a celebrity. I'd be lying if I pretended otherwise. But I pay a price for it."

"Has anything like this happened to you before?"

She told him basically what she'd told Hunsaker about the mail generated by *Passages*. "I learned to differentiate between normal fan letters, even critical ones, and those that were written by someone obviously a little left of center. They raised goosebumps sometimes, but basically I ignored them. None ever disturbed me like this. Maybe I'm being silly and overreacting, but . . ."

"There's nothing here that's specifically threatening," he noted softly.

"If there were, I think they'd be easier to dismiss. As it is, they're just creepy. You can't fight something you can't see. But even though I can't see the danger, I sense it's there. It might just be my imagination working overtime, but lately, when I'm out, I find myself constantly looking over my shoulder. I feel . . ."

"Stalked."

"Yes."

He mulled over her subdued response. "What do you think it all means, Cat?"

"What do *you* think it means? I came for your opinion. In exchange for those damn eggs."

"I've had worse."

"Thanks."

He steepled his fingers and tapped them against his lips. Cat remained silent and gave him time to arrange his thoughts. He hadn't ridiculed her for being upset, although in a way she wished he had. She wanted him to tell her that she was needlessly worried about these cryptic messages.

"Here's what it looks like to me," he said. "But it's only a guess."

"I understand."

"Worst case scenario—"

She nodded.

"This much coincidence belongs in the Guinness book of records."

"I think so too."

"Taken independently, the causes of death were unusual but credible. Grouped together, they start to stink."

She drew in a shaky breath. "Go on."

"Considering the time and distance involved, the person who sent you the clippings probably didn't run across them by chance."

"He knew about the deaths."

"And might even be responsible for them. *If* it's established that they were homicides and not acts of God."

"So . . . so what are we dealing with here?"

"If he is responsible—and at this point that's still a big if—he's not your usual serial killer. He isn't picking his victims at random. Fate has chosen his victims for him. However, he's gone to a lot of trouble to seek them out and snuff them in very creative ways."

"What's his motive?"

"That's simple, Cat."

"The donor heart," she said huskily. Her chest felt very tight. Alex had said precisely what she feared he might. His hypothesis concurred with hers to the letter.

"These three transplantees received hearts on the same day you did," he said. "The psycho knew a heart donor, and, for some reason, he can't bear that his or her heart continues to beat. Obviously he isn't sure who the recipient is, so he's eliminating all the possibilities. One by one, he's icing the transplantees who got hearts on that particular day, knowing that sooner or later he'll strike the right one."

"But why?"

"To stop the heart."

"I know that, but why? If he were that close to the donor, he more than likely was the one to grant permission for transplantation. Why would he suddenly change his mind?"

"God knows. Maybe he just woke up one morning months after the fact and thought, 'Oh, my God. What have I done?' Donor families are called upon to make this decision hastily and under the worst of conditions. Maybe he felt pressured into donating. It began to haunt him, and he couldn't live with the guilt any longer. Ever read Poe's 'The Telltale Heart'?"

"This heart isn't buried. It's really beating."

"But, just like the character in the story, your stalker friend probably hears it constantly. It's haunting him, driving him nuts. He can't live with that and wants to silence the heart forever."

"Please . . ." She moaned.

He reached across the table and touched her hand. "Or we could be way off base, Cat. You asked me for an opinion. That's it. I hope it's wrong."

"But you don't think so."

He said nothing, but he didn't have to. She read the affirmation in his eyes. "For the sake of argument, let's say we're right so far. How did he track down these people, including you?"

She gave him the same explanation she'd given Hunsaker, telling him about the UNOS number.

Alex took time to reason it through. "Heart transplants still make news. He could have simply added up clues he had gleaned from here and there. Who knows? Until you know who the guy is, you won't know how he operates."

"He has to be affluent," she observed.

"Why?"

"Because in the past four years he's traveled all over the country."

"Ever hear of hitchhiking?" Alex asked. "Or hopping a freight? He had a year between each murder, so he could have worked odd jobs to support himself while making his way slowly toward his next victim.''

"I never thought of that," she said dismally. "It could be anyone."

"A businessman who travels strictly first class or a hobo. Whoever he is, the son of a bitch is smart and sly. He's adaptable, a chameleon. How else could he get close enough to these people to murder them without casting suspicion on himself?

"Like that woman in Florida. She fell through a plate glass window in her own home. Assuming she was pushed, he had to have been there in the house with her.''

"He could have passed himself off as a repairman," Cat ventured.

"Would she water her plants while a repairman was in the house?''

"Possibly."

"But unlikely. I picture her asking someone she knows and trusts to hold the stepladder while she reaches for the fern.''

Cat shivered. "He must be a monster."

"But he's not on a killing spree, not on a rampage. Instead he's controlled, totally focused on his mission, driven by revenge, or religion, or any one of a hundred other strong motivators.''

"It's interesting, isn't it? What motivates people to do the things they do." She looked at him askance. "Sometimes their motives make absolutely no sense. They care very little about how their actions affect other people, so long as their needs are served." Her words carried a double meaning, which he immediately caught.

"You still think I'm a shit."

"Oh, yes. Definitely," she said without mitigation, as though agreeing that world hunger should be stamped out.

"Don't I get credit for being honest with you?"

"I'm sure that even your honesty was self-serving."

"Cut me some slack, will you? Could you at least try to understand me?"

"I understand perfectly. You were horny, and I was compliant."

"I wasn't relying on you to get laid," he shouted.

"Then why didn't you get laid with somebody else! Why the big come-on, Alex? You made me fall hard, and you did it deliberately!"

He opened his mouth to speak, then decided against it. Shoving his fingers through his hair, he swore beneath his breath. Finally he said, "Guilty. I deliberately led you to believe that the impossible was possible."

"Why is it impossible?"

He remained silent, his lips set in a narrow, resolute line.

"What, Alex? What eats at you?"

"Nothing I can discuss."

"Try me."

"Believe me, Cat, you don't want to know."

"Well, whatever it is, sex isn't going to make you feel better about it."

He cocked his eyebrow meaningfully. "One of us is remembering wrong. I remember feeling not only better, but damn great."

"I don't mean physically," she said shortly. "Of course it felt good that way. It's that male thing that's incomprehensible to women. To this woman, anyway. Men can't distinguish the physical from the emotional. If it feels good down there, what else matters? Women—"

"He could be a she," he said suddenly, his body jerking as though he'd been shot.

"What?"

"A woman could be stalking you."

"Melia."

"Come again?"

Cat didn't even realize she'd spoken the name aloud. It was too late now. He'd want to know. "This woman at work. I've locked horns with her on several occasions." For the second time that morning, she related the difficulties she'd experienced with Melia King.

"I think I've seen her," Alex said. "A walking wet dream? Big tits, long black hair, full lips, legs that go on forever?"

"Little escaped your notice," Cat said dryly.

"She's hard to ignore."

"She's also spiteful and hateful, but I can't see her as a murderer."

"Everyone's a suspect, Cat. And everyone's capable of killing."

"I don't believe that."

"I once arrested a thirteen-year-old girl for whacking her mother while she was asleep. Motive? Mom had grounded her for wearing too much eye shadow. This was a sweet-looking kid with braces on her teeth and a Mickey Mouse poster on her bedroom wall. Murderers come in all shapes and sizes. This one is as slick as owl shit."

"If there *is* a murderer."

He glanced down at the three newspaper clippings. "The Justice Department should be notified."

That was a quelling thought. He must think this was even more serious than he was leading her to believe. "What would they do?"

"Assign an investigator to check out the deaths."

"That would involve a lot of time and red tape, wouldn't it?"

"I've never known any dealings with the federal government to move quickly."

"In the meantime, the anniversary of my transplant is barely a month away." She tried to smile. "I get the distinct impression that I'm next on his list. Or her list."

Alex picked up the obituary and read it again. "He wants

to get caught. If not, he wouldn't be sending you these. There's purpose behind the killings, but he doesn't do it instinctively or just for the thrill. He's committed to his warped ideal, and yet he knows it's wrong. He's begging to be stopped.''

''I just hope we can stop him in time.''

''Did you say *we*?''

''I can't do this alone, Alex. I don't have the connections or the experience. You do.''

''Breakfast is getting more expensive by the minute.'' He cocked his head to one side. ''What if I say no?''

''I don't think you'll refuse, because there's a lot of cop left in you. You took a vow to protect and serve. I don't think that commitment ended when you relinquished your badge. Even if I were a stranger you wouldn't turn me away. And if I died mysteriously, you'd never forgive yourself.''

He whistled. ''You play dirty.''

''I'm catching on.'' With characteristic candor, she laid it on the line. ''You're the last person I want to ask a favor of. It wasn't easy for me to come here this morning. If I had another option, I'd take it. Unfortunately, you're it.''

He mulled it over for less than ten seconds. ''Okay. I'll do what I can. But where do you suggest I start?''

''Here. In Texas.''

Obviously he hadn't expected such a definite answer to what had been a rhetorical question. ''Why?''

''I've never told anyone this before,'' she said hesitantly. ''I have one clue as to the origin of my heart. The night of my transplant, I overheard a nurse say that it was winging its way to me from the Lone Star state. I've always believed that my heart came from here.'' Trying to make it sound like a casual afterthought, she added, ''Maybe that's what drew me here.''

He leaned forward. ''You're dropping lots of juicy bait this morning, and I can't help but bite. What's that last statement supposed to mean? That you were drawn to Texas because your donor lived here?''

She shook her head, impatient with herself. "Dean says that kind of spiritual transference is impossible.''

"What do you say?''

"I agree.''

He arched an eyebrow, indicating that he'd noticed the lack of conviction in her voice. "But it's sure as hell a topic for stimulating debate, isn't it?''

"Maybe sometime we'll debate it. Right now, I need to find my stalker. The reference to Texas is the only clue I've got.''

"Fine. Standard operating procedure is that you go with what you've got.''

"One more thing, Alex. I tried to learn if my donor's family had ever made an attempt to contact me.''

"You did?'' he asked, surprised. "That goes against your resolve, doesn't it? You told me you never wanted to know anything about your donor.''

"I no longer have a choice. They're checking into the records. I'll let you know what, if anything, comes of that.''

"Good. Meanwhile, I'll start in Texas and work outward. I'll also see what I can turn up about these accidental deaths. There might be another common denominator beyond the victims being transplantees. But I don't promise anything.''

"I'll appreciate hearing whatever you learn.'' She got up and gestured toward the refrigerator. "There was food left. You're welcome to it.''

He followed her to his front door. "Don't leave yet.''

"We've concluded our business.''

"But not our argument.''

"There is no argument, Alex. We've agreed that you're a shit, and you now know how I feel about meaningless sex.''

"It wasn't meaning—''

"One thing strikes me as curious, though,'' she

interrupted. "Why'd you come clean so soon? You could have strung me along indefinitely. Why'd you ruin it for yourself? Did you suffer an attack of guilty conscience? Did Arnie threaten to withhold your royalty checks if you didn't behave like a good boy?"

Rather than respond to her caustic question, he bracketed her jaw with his hand. "You know the saying, 'Be careful what you wish for'? Well, I wished to sleep with you. I wished it to be mind-blowing. And it was. But I got more than I bargained for. It scared me. I didn't quite know how to deal with it." He touched the corner of her mouth with the tip of his thumb. "I still don't."

Chapter Thirty-five

$\mathcal{S}$o, that's where we are. I wanted you to know."

Cat had laid it all out for Jeff Doyle and Bill Webster and now sat back awaiting their reactions. Webster's office was quiet and serene, far removed from the chaotic activity in the newsroom.

She and Jeff sat side by side on a butter-colored leather sofa. The CEO sat in the matching easy chair. His relaxed posture was deceptive, however. He was obviously nettled by what Cat had told them.

"This detective . . . ."

"Hunsaker."

"Shrugged it off?"

"More or less," Cat replied. "Especially when the organ bank informed me that my donor family had never tried to trace me."

The result of that inquiry had left her both disappointed and glad—glad that she didn't have to deal with the personal aspects of her donor, but disappointed that she was no further along in identifying anyone who could possibly be her stalker.

"Lieutenant Hunsaker's indifference was exasperating," she continued. "But when I told Alex about it, he wasn't surprised. Unless a crime is committed, what can the police do? There's no probable cause on which to base an arrest, even if we knew whom to arrest, which we don't."

"There must be something that can be done," Jeff insisted.

"We're doing what we can," she told them. "Alex still has connections in the Houston Police Department, former associates who'll run computer checks for him, things like that. He has resources available to him that an ordinary citizen, like me, doesn't have." She gave a small smile. "Sometimes he fails to mention that he's no longer a cop. People still talk to him. He can be intimidating."

"Do you trust him?" Bill asked.

She looked sharply at him. "Why wouldn't I?"

He pointed to the manila folder in which she carried copies of the clippings, the obituary, and the envelopes in which they'd been mailed. "I think that's sufficient reason to be wary of any stranger who pops into your life."

"Alex Pierce is hardly a stranger to anyone," Jeff remarked.

"What do you know about him, Cat?" Bill persisted. "Except what's apparent, that he's physically attractive."

"I resent your implication, Bill. I haven't gone ga-ga over a handsome face. I haven't been blinded by desire."

"Don't get upset," he said placatingly. "I just meant—"

"You just meant that women think with their hearts rather than with their heads. We're the weaker sex, not savvy enough to recognize a wolf in sheep's clothing."

Vexed, she left the sofa and moved to the window. From this third-floor perspective, she watched the traffic on the expressway speed past. She gave her temper time to cool before turning back into the room.

"I'm sorry, Bill. You expressed a concern for my safety, and I nearly took your head off."

He waved off her apology. "You're under a lot of stress. Is it affecting you physically?"

"Beyond a few sleepless nights, no."

"We could suspend *Cat's Kids* for a few weeks, until this thing is sorted out."

"I'm sure Sherry would understand," Jeff said, seconding Bill's suggestion.

"No way. There'll be no changes in the way I live. My schedule remains as is. I'm not about to let this fruitcake direct my life."

"But if the stress becomes a health risk—"

"I feel great. My heart is fine. Promise." She touched the center of her chest. "But let's clear up that other matter before it festers. My personal life remains exactly that, so please keep your opinion of Alex to yourself. I need his help. That's the extent of it."

Self-consciously she went to the credenza where Bill's secretary had placed a coffee service. "Would anyone else care for coffee?" They declined.

Cat poured herself a cup, taking her time, involuntarily recalling those last few moments at Alex's front door when he'd bluntly told her that he still wanted her. He had tried to kiss her, but she'd left before giving her hormones a chance to kick in and cloud her judgment. Bill's implications weren't too far off the mark. Perhaps that's why she'd had such a knee-jerk reaction to them.

Now, as she turned to face her associates, she pushed thoughts of Alex aside and feigned amusement in her predicament. "It seems that someone is out to silence my tick-tock."

"I don't think it's anything to joke about." Jeff wore a stern frown that was incongruent with his boyish face.

"I agree, Jeff." Bill rubbed his palms together like a general about to impart his strategy to the troops.

"I'll send out a memo that no one is to be admitted into this building without prior clearance and only after showing accepted forms of identification. Cat, from now on you'll have an escort to and from your car to the employee entrance."

"Bill, that's—"

"No argument. Jeff, when she goes out on location shoots, see that one of the guards goes along. You can make room in the production van."

"We need someone riding shotgun?"

"Good idea, Mr. Webster," Jeff said, ignoring Cat's comment. She sighed and rolled her eyes, but Bill remained resolute.

She balked, however, when he suggested posting a twenty-four-hour guard at her house. "Absolutely not."

"It'll be at company expense," he told her. "You're a valuable commodity. We'll spare nothing to protect you."

"I'm not an objet d'art," she declared. "I'm a person. I refuse to have a muscle-bound gorilla in a cheap suit lurking around my house. I won't live like a prisoner in my own home. If you proceed, I'll take up residence in a hotel and no one will know where I am. I mean it, Bill. I won't give this wacko any more control over my life than he's already assumed."

After a few minutes of heated argument, he relented, but grudgingly. Soon after, she and Jeff left his office. "He's only trying to protect you, Cat," Jeff said as they rode the elevator down to the first floor.

"I appreciate his efforts, but we've got to keep this thing in perspective and not go to extremes. Lieutenant Hunsaker is probably right. I've built this up in my mind, and now my hysteria has become contagious."

"You've never been hysterical in your life," he said as he followed her out of the elevator. They turned right, toward the newsroom.

"Maybe hysteria was too strong a word. I am, however, letting a few pieces of mail spook me."

"Mr. Pierce didn't pooh-pooh them as crank mail."

"He's a novelist. I should have known better than to discuss this with him. He's got too active an imagination. He creates madness and mayhem on a daily basis. He took my vague ideas and embellished them into a suspenseful scenario that would make a great movie of the week."

"Good idea. I just might write it down and peddle it to Hollywood."

She and Jeff spun around at the sound of Alex's voice.

"But only if you promise to play the lead," he said to Cat amicably. "Hey, Jeff."

Both were surprised to see him. Cat recovered first. "I wasn't expecting you."

They'd had several telephone conversations since the morning she'd prepared breakfast for him, but they hadn't seen each other. For the past few days he'd been in Houston, and he hadn't notified her of his return.

"I ran across something that I think bears looking into. This afternoon I've got a meeting with a guy who's agreed to talk to me. It might be nothing, but I promised to let you know of any developments."

She turned to Jeff. "What's our schedule like this afternoon?"

"Fairly clear," he replied, his star-struck gaze remaining on Alex.

"Nothing that can't be rescheduled?" she asked.

Jeff shook his head.

"Hold it, Cat," Alex said. "Stick to your agenda. You're not going anywhere."

"Oh yes, I am. I'm going with you."

"Bad idea. I'll notify you if and when I learn something."

"That's not good enough. I'd go crazy waiting. I'm going."

"It won't be fun and it could be dangerous."

"So is sitting around waiting to be bumped off by a maniac. I'll be with you as soon as I take my medication." She started toward her office, then turned back. "If you leave without me, there'll be hell to pay."

She left him waiting in the newsroom reception area. Jeff retrieved her messages from the temporary secretary who'd taken Melia's place and brought them to her office.

"Sherry called."

"What about?" She replaced her prescriptions in her desk drawer and locked it.

"You aren't going to like it."

She straightened up and looked at Jeff. He frowned as he laid the memo on her desk. "Michael has been returned to his parents' custody."

"Oh, God."

"Their lawyer persuaded a lackluster prosecutor to drop the charges. Once again, George Murphy escaped jail by the skin of his teeth."

Cat envisioned the boy's sweet face and felt both anger and anxiety over the thought of him being emotionally and physically abused. "What's it going to take to get him out of there? Dismemberment? How could the caseworker allow this to happen?"

"Sherry promised that she would personally monitor the situation. Any further evidence of abuse and he's out of there."

"She can't be under their roof around the clock," Cat said dismally.

"For whatever it's worth, the caseworker said that Michael

ran into his mother's arms when he saw her. Said she embraced him and cried, covered his face with kisses. They were ecstatic over being back together.''

"I hope he survives without too many scars. All the children are special, but there's something about Michael . . .'' Her voice dwindled. When she realized that several moments had elapsed, she blinked Jeff back into focus.

"Anything else?''

"Dr. Spicer called from L.A. and wants you to call him back as soon as possible.''

"I'll call him tonight.''

"Better do it now. The secretary said he sounded harried.''

"All right. Ask her to place the call. In the meantime, keep an eye on Alex. Don't let him leave without me, even if you have to tie him to a chair.''

While she waited for the call to Dean to be put through, she separated Michael's file from the stack of folders on her desk. She was still staring at his photograph when the secretary beeped her to say that Dean was on the line.

"Hi!'' she said with forced cheerfulness. "It's good to hear from you.''

"How are you?''

"Fine.''

"You don't sound fine.''

"I've had a setback.'' She encapsulated Michael's history for him. "The lawyers probably struck a deal over a couple of beers, giving Michael's welfare very little, if any, consideration.'' She closed the file. "Enough of that. You're the voice of reason in an otherwise very weird world.''

"Don't jump to conclusions.''

"Uh-oh. More bad news? I don't think I can handle any more today. Will it keep?''

"It shouldn't.''

"Then give it to me straight. I don't have much time. In fact, I was on my way out.''

"It's about Alex Pierce."

Her heart bumped against her ribs. "Oh? What about him?"

"Thank God you're no longer seeing him. I just wanted to make certain that you never confided in him about those clippings."

She hesitated for a moment, then said quietly, "The truth is, I have. He's doing some detective work for me."

"You can't be serious!"

"I thought with his police experience—"

"He can't be trusted, Cat."

She didn't want to go around that block again. At least ninety percent of Dean's mistrust was founded on jealousy. "I needed his professional opinion, so I swallowed my pride and asked for it. He agreed to help me find my pen pal before I turn up dead from some dreadful accident."

"Listen to me, Cat." He lowered his voice to a confidential pitch. "I've done some checking into Mr. Pierce's background. They omitted quite a lot from the bio on his book covers."

"You did some checking? Why?"

"Don't get angry."

"Angry doesn't even come close. I'm incensed. I'm not a child, Dean, and you're sure as hell not my guardian."

"Well, somebody should be. You slept with the guy without knowing anything about him."

"I knew I wanted to sleep with him," she retorted.

Following a lengthy, hostile silence, he said, "There's something else you should know, something you might want to consider the next time he tries wooing you into his bed." He paused again, this time for effect. "Alex Pierce is a cold-blooded killer."

Chapter Thirty-six

$\mathcal{A}$lex drove well, plaiting his sports car through lanes of traffic with speed and skill. The console was narrow, the seats low and deep, enforcing intimacy. Her keen awareness of him was like a skin rash that continually itched. The more attention she gave it, the more irritating it became.

"You're uncharacteristically quiet," he said as he maneuvered around an eighteen-wheeler.

"Cat's got my tongue," she said.

"Cute."

"Hmm."

"Something wrong?"

"Other than having a maniac wanting to stop my heart? No, nothing beyond that." She exhaled and pushed back several stray curls. "I'm just not up to conducting clever conversation this afternoon, that's all."

"Fine with me."

He draped his right wrist over the steering wheel and

concentrated on his driving. Cat chastised herself for sulking. Following Dean's shocking news, she'd emerged from her office to find Alex flirting with Melia.

"That's the chick, right?" he'd asked as they made their way to the exit.

"That's the one."

"She seems harmless."

Cat shot him a dirty look. "Oh, she was oozing charm for you. Just don't forget that she tossed my life-perpetuating drugs into a Dumpster along with the remains of her Big Mac."

"I doubt she's an angel. She just didn't strike me as a killer. Do you know where she worked before?"

"No."

"Anything of her background?"

"No."

"I'll look into it."

I'll bet, Cat thought.

So, in addition to being subdued by fear, she was pouting jealously. In light of what Dean had told her about Alex, how could she be jealous of his flirtation with Melia? Her perspective was warped.

They drove in silence for a while, then she said, "You haven't told me where we're going."

"To a little town west of Austin. In the hill country. Been up around there?" She shook her head no. "Pretty country. You'll like it."

"This isn't a sightseeing excursion."

"It'd be better for both of us if it were."

They approached Austin from the south on Interstate 35, but Alex went west on a state highway that skirted the capital city. After another half-hour of driving, they passed through the small, scenic town of Wimberly. Over the last couple of decades, the community's slow pace and scenic surroundings had attracted artisans. On weekends, flea markets drew crowds that tripled the population. When the tourists went home, they rolled up the sidewalks again and life crawled by at a snail's pace for another week.

Beyond the city limits sign, Alex took a farm-to-market road that ran along a bluff overlooking the Blanco River.

"What kind of trees are those growing out of the water?" Cat asked.

"Cypress."

"You're right. It is very pretty."

"I've thought about buying some land around here. Building a house."

"What's stopping you?"

"Initiative, I guess."

The road narrowed and became bumpy. The sports car raised a cloud of gravel dust in its wake. Eventually they came to a building that sat a distance from the road in a grove of pecan trees. The edifice was perched on the bluff that descended twenty yards to the rocky riverbed where clear water gurgled over and between limestone boulders.

The building didn't live up to the natural beauty of its surroundings. Indeed, it was an eyesore. The corrugated tin walls were rusty. Painted on the north wall was a crude skull and crossbones. A dusty, tattered Confederate flag hung limply in the still air. There were no windows in the building, no name was posted, but a neon beer sign flickered above the recessed entrance. Two pickup trucks and a Harley-Davidson were parked outside.

Cat was about to make a joking remark about the disreputable-looking roadhouse when Alex turned into the parking lot. His car wheels crunched on the gravel as he pulled to a stop beside the motorcycle.

"You've got to be kidding."

"You've got to be quiet." Reaching across her, he unlatched the glove compartment. When it fell open, a snub-nose revolver nearly dropped into her lap. Alex picked it up, opened the cylinder to check that all the chambers were loaded, then clicked it back into place.

"I told you this wasn't going to be fun," he said. "Say the word and we'll leave."

She gave the entrance a doubtful glance, but cut her eyes quickly back to him. "No. If someone in there can clear up this matter, I want to hear what he has to say."

"Fine. But you're to keep quiet and play along no matter what happens. If you don't, if you start shooting off your mouth, you're not the only one who could get hurt. Got that?"

She hated being talked down to. Seething, she opened her door.

He grabbed her arm. "Got that?"

"Got it," she answered in the same grating tone.

Together they approached the foreboding entrance. Before going inside, she muttered, "If only I'd known, I could have worn something more appropriate. Like leather and chains."

"Some other time." He pulled open the door. "If you could act a little edgy it might help."

"Act?"

The atmosphere inside was so dank and dense it had texture. She couldn't see a thing for several moments, but Alex's eyes must have adjusted immediately because he pushed her into a booth along the wall, then left her to go to the bar.

It was being tended by a fat guy with mean eyes and a fuzzy black beard that hung to the middle of his chest. Arms that looked like hairy tree trunks were folded over his huge belly. He was gnawing on a matchstick and watching a bowling tournament on a black and white television mounted in the corner above the bar.

"Two beers," Alex said. "Whatever you have on draft."

The bartender stared at him, unmoving, for several beats. Then, as though for consultation, he cast his eyes down the length of the bar where two other customers sat hunched over their longnecks. Finally he spat the matchstick to the floor, grabbed the handles of two beer mugs in one hand, and filled them from the tap.

Alex thanked him, paid him, and returned to the booth. He slid in beside Cat. "Pretend to sip it."

"Won't they realize we're not drinking?"

"They know we didn't come to drink."

"Then they know more than I do. What *are* we doing here?"

"For now, we're waiting." He placed his arm around her and pulled her close. As though smooching, his lips settled against her ear beneath her hair. "I won't let anything happen to you. I swear it."

She nodded, but cast a worried glance at the two other customers. They had made quarter turns on their barstools and were staring at her and Alex, exchanging muttered comments.

A third customer, she now noticed, was at the video game machine at the other end of the bar. She could see only his back. He was skinny, his butt not even defined in the seat of his dirty jeans. He had stringy, unwashed hair that trailed over his neck to a point between his bony shoulder blades. He seemed to be playing more from boredom than any desire to win.

When his last rocket crashed with a high, shrill whistle, he turned away, tipped a longneck to his lips, and sauntered toward the bar. He eyed them curiously, then dropped onto a barstool and turned his attention to the bowling tournament.

Cat whispered, "How long do we have to—"

"Shh."

"I want to know."

"I said shut up and let me handle it!"

Alex's sudden shout astonished her into silence. She gaped at him while he swore beneath his breath and glanced nervously over his shoulder at the other patrons and the bartender. He gulped a swallow of beer and shot her a warning look as he slipped out of the booth.

Cat watched him sidle up to the skinny guy who'd been playing the video game. Alex ordered two more beers and sat down on the stool next to his. "Uh, excuse me. You Petey?" Cat heard him ask in an undertone.

The skinny guy's eyes never left the TV screen. "What's it to you, asshole?"

Alex leaned toward him and mumbled something that Cat couldn't hear. Petey guffawed. "Whadaya think, I'm fuckin' stupid? Jesus." He looked down the bar at the other drinkers and rolled his eyes. The bartender chuckled. "Fuck off," Petey said to Alex, hitching his head toward the door.

"Hey, look, I got—"

Petey came around, snarling like a wildcat who's tail had been stepped on. "Get the fuck outta my face, man. You got heat written all over you."

"You think I'm a cop!" Alex exclaimed.

"I don't care if you're the fuckin' Tooth Fairy. We got no business with each other." He turned back to the TV.

Alex, looking desperate, wiped his palms up and down his pants legs. "Dixie said—"

Petey whipped his head around, almost striking Alex's cheek with his stringy hair. "You know Dixie? Fuck, why didn't you say so? Are you the—"

"Nephew."

"Shit." Petey signaled the bartender. "Get me one of those."

He waited until he had a mug of draft, then motioned for Alex to pick up his two fresh beers. They made their way to the booth. Petey slid in across from Cat. "Hiya, Red." Eyeing her, he slurped the head off his beer. "This your old lady?" he asked Alex.

"Yeah."

Cat remained silent while Petey and Alex swapped stories

about Uncle Dixie. Their voices lowered to a covert tone so gradually that Cat hardly noticed until Alex said, "Thanks for agreeing to see me."

"My ass is fried if they figure out you ain't who you say you are."

"I know," Alex said grimly. "This is important or I wouldn't have asked Uncle Dixie to set it up."

"Will one of you please tell me what's going on?" Cat hissed.

"Stay cool, babe." Petey reached across the table and stroked her cheek. She slapped away his hand. He laughed and waved it in the air as though his nicotine-stained fingers had been scorched. "Hot tempered, hot in the sack, I always say."

"Chill out, will ya?" Alex said to her, loud enough for the others to hear. By now, two more customers had ambled in, a man who looked mean and tough enough to be a logger, and a woman who looked meaner and tougher than he. To the amusement of the other customers, she was exchanging amicable but lewd insults with the bartender.

"Dixie filled you in on what I want to talk about?" Alex asked in an undertone.

Petey nodded. "I remember it like yesterday. Better'n yesterday in fact. It ain't something you forget, ya know? Almost four years ago, a gang member slid under a trailer truck. Practically took his head off."

Cat sucked in a sharp breath. Petey looked at her, then back to Alex. "Are you sure she's cool?" he asked worriedly.

"She's cool. Go on."

"He went by the name of Sparky. Don't know what his real name was. Serious dude. Always reading books. Poetry, philosophy, shit like that. Had a lot of schooling. He was from back east somewhere, I think. Rich is my guess. Had those fancy mannerisms, ya know?"

"What was he doing with the gang?"

"Maybe Mom and Dad got pissed over something and kicked him out. Or he caught his old lady in the sack with her girl friend. Who knows?" Petey raised his bony shoulders in a shrug. "Anyway, he dropped his real name, came to Texas, and found us. He was cool. Everybody liked him okay. 'Xcept Cyc: Right off he and Cyc locked horns."

"Cyc?" Cat asked.

"The gang leader. Called hisself Cyclops 'cause he had a glass eye."

"What was his quarrel with Sparky?" Alex asked.

"What else? A squeeze. Hot piece of ass named Kismet. She'd been Cyc's old lady before Sparky came along. They hit it off real good. I think they really had a thing going. They liked to rack, sure, but I think it was more than that. You sense these things, ya know? Whatever, Cyc was pissed.

"Funny," he said, lowering his voice even more. "Cyc suspected Sparky of being a narc. He didn't do many drugs, see. A joint now and then. No heavy stuff."

"Was he a narc?"

"Not that I know of."

"What brought on the accident that killed him?"

"Cyc made a move on Kismet. Sparky charged him. They fought. Sparky won. He put Kismet on his bike and off they went. But Cyc chased them. Hell of a race. Sparky had to be going ninety or better when he hit that trailer truck 'cause it was like nothing I've seen before or since."

His oily hair barely rippled when he sadly shook his head. "Jesus. I'd followed 'em down out of the hills. Figured that Cyc would be the first to draw blood. That trailer truck beat him to it. Sparky was one big blood-slick on the highway."

Cat shuddered but remained silent.

"The paramedics scooped up the parts and piled them into the ambulance. We all followed it to the hospital. To save her life, Sparky had pushed Kismet off the bike right before they crashed. She was hurt, coupla broken bones, banged up beyond recognition. Cyc had managed to swerve and miss the truck, but his bike went out from under him. He was hurt too, but he was conscious.

"This emergency room dude approached us about Sparky being an organ donor and wanted to know how to contact his next of kin. We said as far as we knew Sparky didn't have no family. He mentioned something about presumed . . . uh . . . something where they can take the organs."

"Presumed consent," Cat said softly.

"Yeah. That's it. But he wanted one of us to give him the go-ahead. The rest of us agreed that since Cyc was the leader he'd have to make that decision. Cyc said, 'Sure. Cut the fucker's heart out and throw it to a dog for all I care.' So I guess they did."

Thirsty after the long monologue, Petey noisily gulped his beer before resuming the story.

"Kismet stayed unconscious for a coupla days. When she came to, she went apeshit. First because Sparky was history, then because Cyc let them mutilate him before he was buried. Cyc kept telling her the guy had no head left, so what difference did it make? But she went freaking nuts about it anyway."

"What happened to her?" Cat asked.

He shook his head. "The gang broke up after that. Our heart just wasn't in it no more." He laughed, showing yellowed, pointed teeth that made him look like a friendly rat. He looked at Alex meaningfully. "I moved on, ya know?" Alex nodded. "You gonna tell me why you're interested?"

"She's a heart transplantee."

Petey's eyes swung back to Cat with renewed interest. "No shit? Cool. You think you got Sparky's heart?"

Cat didn't even have to think twice about it. "No. I know I didn't."

Chapter Thirty-seven

I thought you'd turned up zilch about your donor," Alex said.

"That's true. But even without the agency's report, I'd have known Sparky wasn't my donor." Cat turned to Petey, who was hunched forward, listening. "I didn't get your friend's heart. You see, second to blood type, size is critical for a good match." She made a fist with her small hand. "I needed a heart this size. I'm too small to have received a grown man's heart."

Petey again revealed his jagged yellow teeth in a grin. "Sparky wasn't grown."

"I beg your pardon?"

"Don't you think I considered the size of the heart before following this through?" Alex grumbled. He looked at Petey. "Tell her what you told Uncle Dixie."

"Sparky was a runt," he said. "Pint size. Couldn't've been smaller if he'd been sawed off at the knees. He caught hell about his size from everybody, especially Cyclops. Behind his back, Cyc was always saying he didn't know how a pencil dick like Sparky could keep Kismet happy. Thing was, Sparky had a cock like a racehorse. What he lacked in stature, he made up for in that department.''

"How big was he?"

"At least nine inches," he answered, dead serious.

Cat shook her head. "How *tall* was he?"

"Oh. Five-two. Five-three at most."

"Stocky?"

"Shit, no. Don't you listen, lady?"

"Rarely," Alex put in dryly.

"I'm telling you, he was a pissant. Strong and quick, though," Petey added as he thoughtfully scratched his armpit. "He could hold his own in a fight. Landed Cyclops flat on his ass." He glanced nervously beyond Alex's shoulder. "Is that it? We gotta wrap this up, if you know what I mean.''

"Thanks, man."

"Anything for Uncle Dixie."

Cat watched in disbelief as Alex exchanged several folded bills for a plastic pillow filled with white powder. He slipped it into his jacket pocket, then stood and hauled Cat out of the booth.

By way of goodbye, Petey said, "Y'all mind if I finish your beers?"

The sun had slipped below the tree line on the distant hills. It was a beautiful twilight, especially in comparison to the gloomy interior of the bar. Cat breathed deeply to cleanse her nostrils of the stink of booze, smoke, and unwashed bodies.

She got into the car unassisted and rolled down the window, still greedy for fresh air. Alex slid behind the wheel and, saying nothing, drove for several miles before stopping at a crossroads.

Cat watched, aghast, while he removed the plastic pillow

from his pocket, pricked it open with his thumbnail and worked his finger inside, then rubbed the white powder into his gums above his front teeth.

He glanced at her. "Why're you looking at me like that? You can't be shocked. You're from Hollywood."

"I knew plenty of people who did recreational drugs, but I steered clear of them."

"You don't want to party with me?"

Her jaw was tense and set. "No, thanks."

"You sure? I thought later, when we got back to your place, you could brew us some tea."

"Tea?"

"Yeah. And we could sweeten it with this." He dumped some of the powder into her lap. She stared at it with apprehension, then looked at him. He winked at her. She dipped her finger into the white substance and tasted powdered sugar.

"Smart-ass," she muttered as she brushed the sugar off her skirt.

Chuckling, he pushed the car through the first four gears. "Petey's a narc. Works undercover. Deep cover. Has for years. Wouldn't surprise me if he's hooked on the stuff himself, but he wouldn't sell the real thing to a cop. Even a former cop."

"How'd you find him?"

"I started looking through death certificates and turned up several catastrophic deaths that occurred in Texas during the twelve hours before your transplant. This motorcycle accident was a good place to begin. Sure enough, after digging deeper, I discovered that the fatality had indeed been an organ donor.

"Then I asked a former associate at HPD if he knew of any agency—ATF, DEA, local police—that had penetrated a motorcycle gang in the last five years. He nosed around and turned up Uncle Dixie, who's supposed to be Petey's big distributor, but is actually the code word for a special narcotics unit out of Austin.

"I talked to the chief of the outfit. He was reluctant to set up a meeting with Petey; he only agreed to it because I was a former cop. I went out on a limb by taking you along. I hope you can keep your mouth shut and not blow his cover."

She shot him a retiring look. "Your meeting with Petey had nothing to do with drug trafficking. Why did you have to play out that scene? And why there?"

"If we'd met some other place and someone had seen him talking to a straight like me, it would have aroused suspicion. He can't afford that. He could lose his credibility, his contacts, and probably his life. Better that I looked like a duffus who dared to tread on Petey's turf looking to score."

"Well, you did look like a duffus."

"Thanks. Hungry?"

Five minutes later they were seated on opposite sides of a square table covered with blue and white checked oilcloth. In the center of it were grouped bottles of Tabasco and ketchup, a variety of steak sauces, salt and pepper shakers, and a sugar dispenser. Tanya Tucker was on the jukebox. Back in the kitchen, their flour-dredged, tenderized steaks were being fried in a vat of hot grease.

Cat resumed the conversation where they'd left it. "You're very adaptable, aren't you, Alex?" She squeezed a fresh lemon wedge into her glass of water, which was so large she couldn't get her hand around it.

"In my former line of work, being able to think on my feet was a requirement."

"Would you have used the gun today?"

"To save our lives? Damn right."

Trying to sound casual, she asked, "Did you ever have to shoot someone?"

He stared at her long and hard before saying, "When

you're a cop, you think you're trained to handle anything that might come down. But you're not. When you run into an unexpected situation, you do the best you can.''

That was the only answer she was going to get. She let the conversation lag while he stirred sugar into his iced tea. He was the next to speak. ''Where'd you get your training?''

''You mean my acting training?''

''I know you were an orphan who was reared in foster homes. Beyond that, I don't know anything about your life before you joined the cast of *Passages*. Where'd you grow up?''

She let herself be diverted, thinking that if she told him something of her background, he might be more open to discussing his. What Dean had told her today had disturbed her, but she didn't think it was as cut and dried as Dean had made it sound. She wanted to hear Alex's version of what had happened that fateful Fourth of July, but he wouldn't tell her if she asked. If he ever gave her an account, he would choose the time.

''I grew up in the South, actually. That's right,'' she said, noting his surprise. ''Alabama to be exact. After years of vocal coaching, I finally lost the accent.''

''What was little Cat Delaney like?''

''Skinny and redheaded.''

''Besides that.''

She picked up her knife and began tracing the checks in the tablecloth with its serrated blade. ''It's not a pleasant story.''

''I doubt it'll spoil my appetite.''

''Don't be too sure,'' she said around a shaky laugh. She began by telling him about her illness. ''I beat the cancer but was still puny for a year or so. One day, I felt so weak the school nurse volunteered to drive me home. My dad's car was in the driveway, which was unusual for that time of day. I went in—''

The waitress served their salads.

"I went inside through the back door, expecting to find Mom and Dad in the kitchen. But the house was very quiet. Later, I remembered that uncommon stillness, but at the time I didn't give it much thought and went looking for my parents."

Blood began pounding in her temples as, in her mind's eye, she followed that painfully thin child with unmanageable red hair, pale, skinny legs poking out of wide-legged shorts, new navy blue sneakers on her feet, moving soundlessly along the hallway where her baby pictures smiled down at her from dime-store frames.

"They were in their bedroom."

Alex stirred in his chair. She sensed him propping his elbows on the table and leaning forward, but she didn't take her eyes off the checked pattern of the tablecloth. She moved the knife blade along the straight edge of a blue square with the concentration of a child trying desperately not to color outside the lines.

"They were lying in bed. I thought they were taking a nap even though it wasn't Sunday. It took several seconds for me to figure out what all that red stuff was. When I did, I panicked and ran to the neighbor's house, screaming that something terrible had happened to my mommy and daddy."

"Jesus," Alex whispered. "What happened? Robbery?"

She dropped the knife onto the padded cloth. "No. Daddy took them both out with a pistol to the head."

She looked at him with the same defiance with which she had once faced the child welfare caseworkers, practically daring him to pity her.

"I spent the next eight years in the foster care system, being shunted from home to home until I could take responsibility for myself."

"What'd you do?"

"About what?"

"About school. Money."

"Your salad's wilting."

"Talk." He speared a leaf of lettuce that was dripping buttermilk dressing, but he didn't put it into his mouth until she resumed her story.

"After high school, I got a job as a typist for a large manufacturing firm. But I was going nowhere. Promotions were based on seniority, not merit. It was as unfair as the foster care system."

"What was wrong with it?"

"What wasn't?" She set down her fork and waved both hands in front of her face as though erasing what she'd just said. "Strike that. That was a gross generalization. Most foster parents are giving and self-sacrificing. It's the concept that needs reform."

"It beats putting kids in orphanages."

"I know." She decided she'd had enough of the salad and pushed aside her plate. "But a foster home is temporary, and the child—especially an older child—is fully aware of that. It's a home situation, and that's good. But it isn't *your* home. You're being allowed to live there, but only for a while. You're only visiting until you get too old, or do something wrong, or circumstances change, and then you'll be moved someplace else.

"You perceive the message as 'Nobody likes you enough to want you permanently.' And before long you begin to think you aren't worthy of love, and you start living up to everyone's low expectations—either real or imagined. 'You think I'm unlovable? Well, just get a load of this!' As a defense mechanism, you begin rejecting people and opportunities before they have a chance to reject you."

"That's an adult analysis."

"You're right. When I was in the system, I didn't realize I was self-fulfilling the prophesies. I was just a lonely little girl who felt unloved and unwanted, and who would do anything to get attention."

She laughed ruefully. "I pulled some real doozies. I hated feeling like a charity case." Her eyebrows pulled into a steep frown. "And then there are people—perhaps even good-intentioned folks—who don't have a clue how to rear a child.

"I hasten to add that this applies to natural parents as well as foster parents. They have no idea that they're inflicting emotional wreckage. A word, a look, even a pervasive attitude can destroy a child's self-esteem. People who would never dream of being physically abusive do irrevocable damage to a child's spirit."

"Such as?"

"I could bore you for hours."

"I'm not bored."

She eyed him suspiciously. "You're taking mental notes, aren't you? This will show up in a novel, right? The Perils of Cat Delaney. Believe me, Alex, the truth is worse than anything you could dream up."

"I know that from my days as a cop. Go on. This is off the record."

"I remember one Christmas," she said after a moment of reflection. "I was thirteen and by then had a grip on how the system worked. I knew never to expect too much. But there was another foster child living in the same house as I, a little girl about seven. The couple also had a daughter that age.

"Both the little girls wanted Barbie dolls for Christmas. That's all they talked about. To win Santa's favor, they did their chores, went to bed on time, ate their veggies. On Christmas morning, the couple's daughter unwrapped the Mattel megaseller in all her blond splendor. She got the real thing, dressed in a pink prom dress and matching high heels.

"The foster child got a brand X Barbie, a scaled-down, pale imitation. What that said to her was that she wasn't quite up to par, wasn't good enough to have the genuine article. Even Santa Claus didn't think so.

"And I thought *why*—why would someone hurt a child like

that? What could have been the difference in price between the two dolls? A few measly dollars? The cost of a rump roast? Wasn't a child's self-image worth more than that?

"I'm really in no position to judge because I've never been a parent. It's got to be the most challenging job imaginable. But it's not that hard to understand how hurtful an oversight from Santa Claus can be."

She drew a sigh. "I saw instances like that time after time. I would get so angry over the injustices that were heaped on kids. But, as I learned, the adult world is full of injustices too."

Their salad plates were removed and they were served their steaks. "Good Lord," Cat exclaimed. "This could qualify for a zip code."

The breading had been fried to a crunchy, golden brown. The meat inside was fork-tender. Alex cut into his. "What did you do after you left the typing job? That's a long way from a starring role in a soap opera."

"Obviously I needed more education. I'd saved every penny I could, but I still couldn't afford to attend college. So I entered a beauty pageant."

His fork halted midway between his plate and his mouth. "A beauty pageant?"

She took umbrage. "Is that so astonishing?"

"I figured you for someone who'd think beauty pageants are sexist and exploitive of women."

"At that point in my life, I was willing to be exploited for a chance at a twenty-thousand-dollar scholarship. So I invested in the best push-up bra ever engineered and added my name to the long list of hopefuls. Pass the rolls, please."

The bread was yeasty and soft and melted in her mouth. "Sinful." She moaned, closing her eyes and licking butter off her lips.

"If you think the roll is sinful, you ought to see the expression on your face."

Chapter Thirty-eight

❧

Alex's gaze was fixed on her mouth. "Do you realize that everything you do is sexual?"

"Do you realize that you have a dirty mind?"

"Indubitably." He lifted his eyes to meet hers. "You're a walking, talking turn-on. That's why every man you meet falls a little in love with you."

The statement was more disturbing than flattering. "That's not true."

"I can name three. No, four."

"Who?"

"Dean Spicer."

She raised one shoulder in a dismissive gesture. "Since I left California, we've been nothing more than good friends."

"Because that's the way you want it. He's still in love with you. Second is Bill Webster."

"You're way off base there. Bill adores his wife."

"She shares my theory."

Cat negated that with a firm shake of her head. "You're wrong. And if Nancy thinks there's anything besides friendship and mutual respect between Bill and me, she's wrong, too. Who else? Not that I'm buying any of this, you understand. I'm just curious."

"Jeff Doyle."

She laughed.

"If he weren't gay, he'd be in love with you," Alex insisted. "As it is, he merely worships the ground you walk on."

"You really are into fiction, aren't you? Who's number four?"

He let his piercing gaze answer for him.

"Do you expect me to believe that?" she asked.

"No."

"Good. Because it's a crock, and we both know it. You'd just like to sleep with me again."

"What are my chances?"

"Nil."

He grinned in a manner that said he didn't believe her. "Did you win?"

"What? Oh, the pageant? No."

"Too slender?"

"Too stupid."

"There's a story, right?"

She nodded. "During the preliminaries, we were required to mix and mingle with the judges. One of them was an oily character who was supposed to be a portrait photographer, but he looked like a crooked used car salesman to me. He was so earnest, so willing to put us contestants at ease, that his hands were constantly on us. Touchy-feely. The creepy kind of touching that makes you feel like you've stepped on a slug.

"Anyway, he would sidle up to us independently and

whisper things like, 'You've got what it takes, sweetheart.' Later we girls compared notes and came to the unanimous conclusion that he was a jerk and a joke. But as the week progressed toward the big competition on Saturday night, he became bolder, more familiar.

"His groping was no longer a joke, but none of the girls wanted to be the first to expose him for fear of jeopardizing her score. The old geezer knew this, of course. He was committing sexual blackmail and getting away with it. So I decided—"

"Let me guess," Alex interrupted. "You set out to right the wrong."

"Yes. I thought he should be revealed as the slime ball he was. During the dress rehearsal, he cornered me and began discussing my assets and enumerating ways in which he could help me make the most of them. I pretended to be breathless with excitement and gratitude, eager to hear more. So he suggested I join him in his room later, where he could go into more detail.

"We set a time. Before going to his room, I left a message for the committee chairwoman that he needed to see her as soon as possible."

"You set a trap."

"Hmm. Unfortunately, it backfired. Ms. Committee Chairwoman arrived at his door just in time to find him trying to wrangle me out of my blouse. He turned the tables, said I'd come to his room uninvited and offered him my lily white body in exchange for a high score on his tally sheet.

"I suggested that if she didn't believe me, she could consult the other girls whom he'd been groping all week. Which she did. But every last one of them chickened out.

"I guess that tacky tiara was more important to them than the truth. So, I was branded a slut who had compromised the integrity of the pageant and was promptly disqualified."

"I bet you had plenty to say then."

"Actually I was rather terse. As I recall, all I said was. 'Screw this. I'll become an actress instead.' "

Through the remainder of their meal and during the drive back to San Antonio, she told him the rest of her life story. After the fiasco of the beauty pageant, she'd sold everything she owned except for a few changes of clothes and bought a one-way Greyhound ticket to Los Angeles.

She worked at the fragrance counter of a department store. earning barely enough to pay for acting classes and a roach-infested apartment. When she was able to afford it, she put together a portfolio of photographs and began touting herself to talent agencies.

"Finally, out of the blue, an agent called and expressed an interest in representing me. At first I thought it was a prank call."

"I know the feeling." By now they'd reached the outskirts of the city. Alex took an exit off the freeway. "I felt exactly like that when I first heard from Arnie Villella. What was your first acting job?"

"A TV commercial. I spread a nonyellowing wax onto a vinyl floor. It aired nationally for over a year. The residuals were good. After that, I did more commercials, worked trade shows, pitching everything from household cleaners to Hondas, appeared in a few stage plays. Then my agent heard about the new character on *Passages*, and I auditioned for Laura Madison. You know the rest."

He stopped at an intersection and turned to her. "Say where."

"The TV station. My car's there."

He looked at her meaningfully. "Sure?"

She knew what he was asking, and had her libido been making decisions for her, the choice would have been much easier. "Yes, I'm sure."

As they headed to the TV station, Alex brought her up to date on the progress he'd made during his trip to Houston. "The Department of Justice was lukewarm on its promise to check into the accidental deaths of the three heart transplantees. The agent I spoke with sounded harried and indifferent."

"So we're on our own."

"More or less. At this point he wouldn't even consider asking the organ banks for confidential information, the UNOS numbers, etcetera. Not until it's determined that crimes have been committed, he said. So, with nothing more to go on, I began checking out death certificates."

"Thanks, Alex. You've done wonders with the little you had to go on. It would have been impossible for me to track down Petey."

"After what he said about Sparky's size—I think it's worth pursuing further, don't you?"

"Absolutely."

"I'll try and locate members of the disbanded gang. Although it'll probably be a wild goose chase. First I've got to find a former member. If and when I do, will he or she have had enough interest in Sparky to trace the destination of his donated heart? The odds aren't good."

"That woman—Kismet? If we could find her, she might know something."

"Yeah, but I'm sure Kismet was an assumed name."

"I doubt Cyclops was the name the leader was christened with, either."

"I doubt Cyclops was christened."

Forlornly, she stared through the windshield. As he'd said, the likelihood was extremely slim that they would identify her stalker in time to prevent a catastrophe. But she would continue exploring every open avenue. She wasn't going to simply wait for a fatal accident to befall her.

"Alex, you said earlier that you were checking into several

catastrophic deaths that would result in organ donations. What were the others?"

"One was a multicar accident on the Houston freeway. It happened during rush hour. There were a number of fatalities, but I haven't learned if any became organ donors. I've got a paid informer working that angle for me. He's an orderly in one of the major hospitals.

"The other was a case I was already familiar with. I didn't realize until I began looking into it again that it had happened around the time of your transplant."

Interested, she urged him to go on.

"For months it was a statewide news story. As a crime novelist, I was interested because it wasn't a run-of-the-mill murder. It happened in Fort Worth. Paul Reyes discovered his wife, Judy, and her lover in bed together. Reyes pulverized her skull with a baseball bat, but the paramedics managed to keep her heart beating until they got her to the hospital and declared her brain-dead. Meanwhile, Reyes had been taken into custody. From his jail cell, he gave permission for his wife's organs to be harvested."

"Did he go to prison?"

"No. That's the hell of it. His attorney argued for change of venue and got the trial moved to Houston, where he was acquitted."

"How could that have happened?"

"Technically, Mrs. Reyes's heart was retrieved before it stopped beating. He didn't actually kill her. It was a mistake for the state to go for premeditation instead of manslaughter. There was also some fancy legal maneuvering by his defense attorney. Combined, the trial resulted in an acquittal."

"Couldn't they get him for attempted murder? Or assault with a deadly weapon or something?"

"That would be double jeopardy. After the trial, Reyes disappeared. Hasn't been seen or heard of since."

Cat was excited. "This fits, doesn't it? Paul Reyes is still angry with his adulterous wife and obsessed with stopping her heart."

"That crossed my mind. I watched him when the verdict was read. His eyes had the fanatic gleam of a man possessed. I think he fully intended to kill Judy, and his only remorse was that he'd been denied the pleasure of doing it."

"People don't disappear without a trace. Someone knows where he is."

"I've already started trying to track down a family member who'll talk to me, but in the Mexican community, families tend to close ranks to protect each other from outsiders. Besides that, they become borderline hysterical whenever organ transplantation is mentioned."

Cat nodded in understanding. "The Spanish cultures traditionally reject the entire concept. They feel that a body should be buried intact, or the departed never finds peace and rest in the afterlife. We had several Hispanics among our transplant population in California. They're working to break through that cultural barrier, but with limited success. So Mr. Reyes's decision was probably unpopular with his and his wife's family."

"I'll keep probing."

"Does my blood type match hers?"

"Yes."

"So I could have received her heart."

"Conceivably. But there's the time factor to take into account."

Having arrived at the TV station parking lot, he pulled into the space beside Cat's car. After cutting the motor, he stretched his arm along the back of the seat and turned to face her. "Reyes attacked her in the middle of the afternoon. Your transplant took place early the next morning."

"But how long did Judy Reyes's heart continue beating

before they pronounced her brain-dead? It could have been hours, right? Which moves the harvesting closer to the time of my transplant.''

''That's speculation.''

Miffed over his lack of enthusiasm, she said, ''This has a lot of possibilities. Why are you throwing a wet blanket over it?''

''We're searching for facts, not possibilities. Don't jump to conclusions just because they're convenient. This must be methodically investigated.''

''Well, don't drag your feet.'' She tapped the crystal of her wristwatch. ''The clock is ticking toward the anniversary date.''

''I'm aware of that, Cat. Are you scared?''

She saw no virtue in equivocating. ''A lunatic has very subtly, but very definitely, threatened my life. Damn right I'm scared.''

''Then move in with me until we find him.''

''I can't believe you'd have the nerve even to suggest it.'' She clearly enunciated her words. ''It ain't gonna happen, Mr. Pierce.''

''Why not?''

''Because I don't want it to.''

''Liar.''

Cat saw red. She admitted to several character flaws, but lying wasn't among them. Furthermore, she despised lies and liars. He couldn't have insulted her more.

''You really value that appendage in your pants, don't you? We poor, frail females tremble at the thought of being deprived of it. Is that what you think?'' She laughed scoffingly. ''It was probably her husband's stupid male arrogance that drove Judy Reyes to take a lover.''

Moving like quicksilver, he whipped the revolver from beneath his jacket and aimed it at her head.

Chapter Thirty-nine

$\sim$

Cat thought she'd been shot, until she realized that the three sharp raps weren't emissions from the revolver but someone knocking on the car window.

She turned her head quickly. A rent-a-cop was peering into the car, his nose almost touching the foggy glass. Hastily she rolled down the window.

"Oh, Ms. Delaney, it's you," he said with surprise and relief. "This strange car parked next to yours? I came to check it out. Everything okay?"

"Everything's fine, thank you."

"Mr. Webster hisself sent down orders that we were to be on the lookout for anything peculiar goin' on."

He looked beyond her shoulder at Alex. Had he tucked the gun out of sight?

"You a friend of Ms. Delaney's?" the guard asked.

"Yes, he is," Cat replied before Alex had a chance to speak. "He gave me a lift back to my car."

Not one to be passed over, Alex said, "We're almost done here, buddy. Do you mind?"

"Everything's all right, really," Cat interjected, hoping that her smile looked genuine. "We were just chatting. I'll be leaving shortly."

"Well, okay, then." Self-importantly, the guard hiked up his belt and holster, as though to remind Alex—or himself— that he was armed and dangerous.

The standing joke around the TV station was that the guards had only one bullet among them, and that they took turns with it. Chances were his weapon wasn't even loaded.

Alex's was.

"I'll be right over yonder, Ms. Delaney, if you should need me for anything." He glared a warning at Alex, then ambled back to the building.

Cat rolled up the window. She'd managed to be civil with the guard, but when she confronted Alex, she gave vent to her temper.

"Are you *crazy*? How dare you point a loaded gun at me! You scared the hell out of me!"

"I wasn't aiming at you. I was trying to protect you."

"From *what*?"

"From a shadow I saw looming out of the darkness and approaching the window. I didn't know it was the guard."

"You could have waited to find out before pulling a gun."

"Which is a damn good way to get killed, wait and let the other guy get the jump on you."

"No, your way is much better. Shoot first and ask questions later. Isn't that what happened on the Fourth of July when you killed that man in Houston?"

Her angry words reverberated inside the car, then were followed by a startling silence that was broken only by her rapid, choppy breathing.

Alex's face turned to stone, and his eyes glittered like flint. "Who told you about that?"

Cat instantly regretted her outburst. "Alex, I—"

"*Who told you?*"

"Dean. Dean told me. This afternoon."

"I bet the son of a bitch got a charge out of that," he muttered. "Told you all the grisly details, did he?"

"Actually, the details were sketchy."

Alex snorted scornfully.

"I'd like to hear your side of it."

"Some other time." He reached across her and opened the passenger door, giving it so hard a shove that it almost sprang back on itself.

"Alex, I'm sorry. I shouldn't have brought it up. Not like that."

"Too late," he said curtly. "It's out. Now, you'd better go."

She hesitated, but it was apparent that he was furious and not in a mood to defend himself. She got out of the car and closed the door. He gunned the engine and sped from the parking lot, leaving her alone.

Cat was startled awake from a deep but troubled sleep. Before she could scream, he placed his hand over her mouth.

"It's me." He spoke in a low, husky whisper, but she instantly recognized his voice. "I need . . . this . . . I need you."

He lay down beside her, half covering her body with his. "Don't be afraid, Cat. Are you afraid?"

She shook her head.

Gingerly he removed his hand and replaced it with his lips. He kissed her lightly at first, then evocatively, exploring her mouth with his tongue.

When the kiss finally ended, he rested his lips against her throat. "Don't send me away."

He unbuckled his belt, unfastened his pants, and drew her hand inside. "It's been a bad night. I'm dying, baby." He used her hand to massage his solid erection. When her thumb rolled across the straining glans, he moaned.

Lowering his head, he nuzzled her breasts through her nightgown. "You want me. I know goddamn well you do. Don't you, Cat? Don't you?" He sighed her name beseechingly.

She murmured, mingling protest and consent, the former giving way to the latter. Cloth whispered against cloth as she bicycled her legs from beneath the covers. She parted his shirt. His skin was hot against her fingertips, her lips, and when he was at last naked and lying on top of her, she enveloped him in a welcoming embrace.

He gathered her nightgown in his hands, bunching it up inch by inch, until he slipped it over her head and tossed it aside. His hands moved down her torso from collarbone to hipbone, all ten fingers extended, touching as much of her as possible in one pass. He pressed his face into the giving softness of her belly; she clutched his head to her and locked her legs around his hips.

He kissed her navel, rubbed his cheek against the nest of tight, springy curls. His tongue traced the groove between her belly and thigh. Her heels dug into the mattress as she arched up, grinding her mons against his face.

He placed his hand between her thighs and slipped two fingers inside her. She gave a soft cry of surprise and pleasure.

"Don't come," he ground out. "Not yet. I want to be inside you when you come."

But she was very wet, and his fingers were nimble and deft. She fought the passion building inside her until she couldn't fight it any longer.

He seemed to know the exact moment of her surrender because he levered himself up and sank into her just as the first contractions seized her. The walls of her body closed around him like a tight fist.

"Ah, Christ, yes."

Moments later, replete, he lay heavily atop her, their skin so silky with sweat that their flesh seemed to meld.

After a while he raised himself to his knees. She wasn't ready for him to leave her. Doing a partial sit-up, she angled the upper half of her body up and placed her open mouth on a damp patch of hair-dusted skin low on his abdomen, just below his navel.

He tangled his hands in her hair and fell backward onto the mattress, bringing her with him. She bent over him and dabbed his stomach and chest with light kisses. She flicked his nipples with the tip of her tongue until they protruded stiffly.

When she took his sex in her hand, he was hard again. She straddled his middle and remained poised above him to heighten the anticipation, then gradually lowered herself onto his rigid length. He watched her through half-closed eyes as she rode him, her chest thrust out, her breasts high and proud. She was shocked by her own exhibitionism, her lack of modesty.

Holding her stare with his, he moistened his fingertips with his saliva and brushed them across her nipple. It shrank to a hard pebble that he gently pressed between his thumb and forefinger.

He slid his other hand into the mesh of their pubic hair and touched her center. The sensation was electrifying. Her head fell back on her shoulders; her hips pumped faster. He continued to stroke her there, barely glancing the slippery little nubbin with the pad of his finger.

Her release was shattering. Impaled on him, she bore down hard. He gripped her cheeks and held her anchored to him as, together, they experienced a drenching climax.

Then she collapsed on his chest, gasping, her heart drumming against his. He gathered her to him like a child and held her close, his lips moving in her hair, whispering. But because of the pounding of her own pulse, she couldn't distinguish the words.

Cat awoke with her head at the foot of the bed. She'd been covered with the corners of a sheet and a blanket, but the rest of the linens formed a tangled heap in the center of the bed.

She sat up, pushed her hair out of her eyes, and glanced around her bedroom. It was illuminated only by the gauzy grayness of predawn. The house was silent. She knew she was alone.

Sometime between ecstasy and sleep, Alex had left.

Or had she dreamed it?

No, their erotic interlude had been indisputably real. Her body bore the bittersweet imprints of it.

Chapter Forty

❧

It was three days before she saw him again. He didn't call or try to see her. Frequently during those three days, she thought that maybe the stress of the last few weeks had taken their toll on her sanity, and that she had imagined him sneaking into her house, into her bed, and taking her on the most thrilling sexual adventure she'd ever experienced.

But she had only to examine herself closely—her emotions as well as her body—to know that it hadn't been her imagination.

Any lingering doubts vanished when he popped his head inside the production van where she sat with Jeff, discussing the details of the *Cat's Kids* segment they were about to shoot.

He tapped on the side of the van. She raised her head from the file she'd been perusing. Jeff turned in his seat.

"Mr. Pierce," he said, showing his surprise. "Hi."

Alex acknowledged her assistant's greeting with a mumbled hello, but his eyes were fixed on her.

Her reaction to seeing him was a comical cliché. She went limp. Lifeless fingers dropped her fountain pen. It rolled off the edge of the folder on her lap and landed on the floor of the van.

"I'll just . . ." In tune with the awkwardness of the moment, Jeff stammered an excuse, then climbed out of the van and left them alone.

Alex continued to stare at her through the open side door. He was dressed in jeans and an unironed chambray shirt with the cuffs loosely rolled back to his elbows. It was a humid, airless day, but his hair looked wind-tossed.

"Hello, Alex. What brings you here?"

He glanced over his shoulder at the production crew setting up video equipment on the park playground. The video photographer was discussing camera angles with Jeff. The production assistant was checking microphones. The rent-a-cop, which Bill had insisted on, was leaning against a tree, smoking.

"I've never seen you work," Alex said, turning back to her. "Not on location."

"It's not as glamorous as it might seem when you're watching it at home."

"I'd like to stick around, if you don't mind."

So they weren't going to address it. Okay. If he wanted to pretend that the orgy hadn't taken place, fine. It was probably better this way. He'd come to her in the middle of the night, desperate and begging for physical and emotional release, an indication that he had weaknesses just like all other mortals. She'd responded to him without a whimper of resistance, an indication of her susceptibility.

They'd both exhibited a lack of self-control and common sense. She couldn't condemn him for using her without condemning herself for being so easily used. Why open it up for discussion? To spare themselves embarrassment, why not just pretend that it hadn't happened?

Besides, she wasn't sure she could speak freely in glaring daylight about what they'd done in the dark. Her cheeks were flushed just thinking about it.

"I don't mind if you watch," she told him. "But you'll probably get bored before we finish."

"I doubt that."

Jeff approached hesitantly. "Uh, Cat. Sherry just arrived with Joseph."

"Coming."

She tied on the sneakers she'd previously taken off. Alex gave her a hand down as she stepped from the van. "Thanks." For the benefit of Sherry, Jeff, and the production crew, she tried to appear casual, although her knees were still wobbly over his unexpected appearance.

Joseph soon took her mind off Alex. The boy's growth had been stunted by his crippling disease, so, although he was seven, he looked no older than four. His legs were in braces, but he was able to walk on his own. He had large ears and wore glasses with lenses so thick that they distorted the size of his eyes.

He was beaming at Cat as he hobbled forward. "I came to be on TV," he announced proudly.

Sherry Parks laughed. "Maybe I'd better warn you, Cat. He's a natural ham. Watch him, or he'll steal the show."

"It's good to see you again, Joseph." They'd been introduced at Nancy Webster's picnic. Looking down at him now, she narrowed her eyes and growled threateningly. "But if I catch you upstaging me, you're history. Remember, I'm the star!"

"Okay," Joseph said, laughing. "Does he run the camera?" He was pointing at Alex.

"No. He's only observing. This is Mr. Pierce, Joseph. He writes books."

"Books? No foolin'?"

"Pleased to meet you, Joseph." Alex shook hands with the boy as though he were an adult.

"You're tall."

"Naw, it's the boots." Alex raised his foot and showed the boy the riding heel of his boot. "Without these, I'm only five feet five."

Joseph's laugh erupted like bubbles from a bottle of champagne. Cat made a mental note to get that laugh on videotape. Who could resist it?

She made a round of introductions, then Jeff announced that they should get started. She took Joseph's hand and said, "Don't forget, I get all the best lines "

She and Joseph sat side by side on a merry-go-round. The production assistant put wireless mikes on them, and they recorded the interview segment first. She chatted with Joseph about inconsequential things until he was unmindful of the camera and completely relaxed.

"Would you like to be adopted, Joseph?"

"Sure. Could I have brothers and sisters?"

"Possibly."

"That'd be neat."

All his answers were disarming and endearing. They reshot the interview from a reverse angle so that, when edited, segments could be lifted from either camera angle, making it appear that the piece had been shot with at least two cameras.

Then she and Joseph walked among the Spanish moss-laden live oak trees while the photographer followed, carrying the camera on his shoulder.

When Jeff announced that they had all the raw footage they needed, Alex gave Joseph a high-five. "If you ever get a hankering to go into show business, I want to be your talent agent. Deal?"

Joseph's smile was radiant.

Cat knelt down and hugged him. "Let's hope for the best, okay?"

"Okay. But don't worry, Cat. If I'm not adopted, I won't be mad at you."

A hard lump formed in her throat. His father had split before he was born. His mother suffered from drug addiction and depression. When Joseph was three, the state had taken him from her. He'd been living in foster homes ever since. He deserved a family's love. And, with his charming personality and sense of humor, he'd be an asset to any family. She regretted having to return him to Sherry and continued to wave until they drove out of sight.

Alex dragged his sleeve across his sweating forehead. "You're right. It's not as glamorous or as easy as it looks. Two hours' work for a two-minute piece?"

"That's not counting all the postproduction time," Jeff. told him. "And the taping time would be doubled if Cat weren't such a pro. She rarely has to do more than one take."

She dropped a coquettish curtsy.

"Y'all coming?" the PA called from the van. The equipment had already been reloaded. The cameraman was in the driver's seat. He'd started the motor and had the van's air-conditioning going full blast. The rent-a-cop was grinding out his last cigarette, ready to climb into the van. He'd never challenged Alex or questioned his being there. Bill was wasting his money on that precaution, Cat thought.

Jeff headed for the van, but she held back and looked shrewdly at Alex. "You didn't come out here on an unseasonably hot day just to watch, did you?"

"It was interesting."

She placed her hands on her hips. "You're a little old for field trips. Come clean, Pierce. What's up?"

"I found Cyclops."

* * *

He was squatting beside his Harley, replacing a spark plug. It didn't really need the tune-up; he was tinkering just to keep his mind off his problems. If everything in his life ran as well as his bike, he'd be a happy man. His Harley was the only thing he could rely on to obey his commands without argument. Riding it never failed to give him a thrill.

Kismet was another matter.

He shot her a malevolent glance over his shoulder. She was seated on a yellow vinyl bean bag that she'd dragged into the shade of a scraggly cedar tree.

A few years back, she'd been the hottest piece of ass around. He'd been the envy of every man who knew him. Her temper had burned hot and fierce. She'd been afraid of nothing. Not even him.

Hell, back then, if he did something she didn't like, she'd light into him, sometimes drawing blood with her fingernails and teeth. They'd go at it until the fight turned into screwing, which it always did. Violence had been her biggest turn-on. The rougher the better. Bucking and heaving, she'd scream like a banshee when she came.

Now, the dark eyes that used to smolder hardly reflected light. They were dead eyes. She fucked like a corpse, too, tolerating him but never participating.

She even looked different. She kept her tattoo covered and tried to keep her hair tamed. He didn't remember the last time he'd seen her wearing something that showed off her figure. She didn't talk the same, either.

Trying to resurrect the old Kismet had become his life's occupation. She presented him with a constant challenge. The hellcat was in there, somewhere. Behind that vapid expression, the real Kismet was still sneering at the world. He knew it; all he had to do was come up with a way to draw her out.

Was she worth all the crap she put him through?

No way in hell. He'd have dumped her years ago, except for one major reason: That's what she wanted. She'd like it if he booted her out. For that reason alone, he planned to keep her till hell froze over. He had let her escape him once, and it had made him a laughingstock.

Although he'd gotten the last laugh, hadn't he?

Once Sparky was out of their lives, they'd picked up where they had left off. Well, not entirely. She'd never been the same. Most of the time, she looked through him as though he weren't there. The only thing that seemed to penetrate her indifference was fear. When she got good and scared of him, she turned to putty.

So scaring her had become his favorite pastime.

He stood now and wiped his hands on a faded red rag. "Get in the house."

His brusque order startled her. That was another thing that bugged him—her daydreaming. She had a private world that was closed to him.

"It's hot inside, Cyc," she said. "I'd rather stay out here where there's a breeze."

"I said, get in the house."

"What for?"

"What do you think?" he asked in a soft, taunting singsong. Reaching down, he grabbed her arm, nearly jerking it from its socket as he hauled her up. She cried out.

Just then a car pulled alongside the Harley and stopped. A man got out and looked at them over the roof of the car.

Cyc dropped her arm. "Who's that?"

"I don't know."

The tall, lean dude came toward them. He had calculating eyes and a mean slant to his mouth. *Cop.* Cyclops could sight heat a mile away. The guy probably had a piece in the small of his back beneath his windbreaker.

"Who are you and what do you want?" Cyc asked, facing his visitor aggressively.

"I'm looking for a guy who goes by Cyclops? Is that you?"

Cyc folded his tattooed arms across his chest. Smirking,

he tilted his head to one side, jiggling the silver cross that dangled from the hole in his earlobe. "What if I am?"

Ignoring the question, the man looked beyond him. "Are you Kismet?"

"Yes."

"Shut up," Cyc barked. "You don't have to talk to him." He glowered at the man, intuitively knowing that he meant trouble. "Who the fuck are you?"

"Alex Pierce."

"Doesn't ring any bells."

"No reason it should. But I've brought someone with me who wants to meet you."

He returned to the car and opened the passenger door, where he carried on a brief conversation with someone before stepping aside and helping her out. The late afternoon sun spotlighted her hair, identifying her instantly.

"Jesus, Mary, and Joseph!" Cyc exclaimed, his belligerent stance slipping.

The cop/dude never let more than an inch of space come between him and the redhead as they approached. She showed no such caution. Gutsy broad, Cyc thought. Tiny, but gutsy. You could tell right off.

"My name's Cat Delaney."

"I know who you are," he said. "Did you come for the kid?"

Kismet surged to her feet, dumping the tray of beads she'd held in her lap. They fell into the dirt, sparkling in the sunlight. "No! I won't let you take him again!" she cried.

"Mommy?"

Cyc jerked his head around. The kid was standing behind the screened front door, his finger hooked in his lower lip. He was staring at them with those wide, spooky eyes of his. When he stared like that, the little shit gave Cyc the creeps.

He was just about to order him back into the house when the redhead uttered a startled cry.

"Michael!"

Chapter Forty-one

$\mathcal{C}$at stared at the boy as if transfixed. He bolted through the screen door and ran to his mother, burying his face in her skirt. "You're Michael's mother?" Cat asked weakly. The woman nodded warily. Cat turned to the biker. "Then you must be George Murphy."

"Ain't that why you're here? To get our kid, so's you can put him on TV and get him adopted?"

Kismet began to whimper. Cat extended her hand to her. "No, I'm not here because of Michael."

Cyclops frowned. "If you didn't come after him, what are you doing here?"

Just as Sherry had said, Michael and his mother seemed to love each other. The boy was looking at Cat and smiling shyly in recognition, but his arms were still wrapped around his mother's legs.

Cat turned to the biker and gave him a contemptuous once-over. "Have you been sending me threatening mail? If you

329

have, I'm here to warn you that I've made it a police matter. If I receive any more—''

"Look, bitch—''

"Watch it, pal.'' Alex didn't raise his voice, but it was menacing enough to silence Cyclops. He had let the startling events unfold without making a single sound, but Cat knew that nothing had escaped his notice.

"This doesn't have to get ugly,'' he said. "Just answer the lady's question. Have you been sending her newspaper clippings through the mail?''

"I don't know what the fuck you're talking about,'' Cyc growled. "I don't know nothin' about no clippings. And if you don't get your ass off my—''

Cat broke in, "You were friends with a guy called Sparky.''

Kismet made an injured sound. "Sparky?'' she repeated breathlessly. "What about Sparky?''

"Shut the fuck up, will ya?'' Cyc shouted. He then turned his hostile, one-eyed glare onto Cat. "If you're looking for that little stump, you're shit out of luck, lady. He's been dead for years.''

"I'm well aware of that.''

"Then why come pestering me?''

"You gave permission for his heart to be harvested for transplantation. I had a transplant within a few hours of his death. It's possible that I received his heart.''

Kismet gasped before covering her mouth with her hand. Tears filled her eyes.

"I understand that you were very close to him,'' Cat said softly.

Kismet bobbed her head.

"That's ancient history,'' Cyc said. "What do you want from me?''

Alex answered. "Three people who received hearts on the same day as Ms. Delaney have died. We believe they were murdered by a donor family member who's having second thoughts.''

"Whoever is doing the killing has made it clear that I'm next on his list," Cat added.

"Gee, that's too bad," Cyc said sarcastically.

Alex took a threatening step forward, but Cat grabbed his sleeve and held him back. "I don't think they know anything about it, Alex.''

"He recognized you immediately. I saw it on his face.''

"She's on TV, for crissake!" Cyclops shouted. "What d'ya think, I'm blind and stupid?''

"I think you're an asshole.'' Alex fired back.

"Be quiet. Both of you. You're frightening Michael." Cat looked at Kismet. "Did you ever try to contact the recipient of Sparky's heart?''

"Yes, I did.''

Cyc turned around and glared at Kismet. "What the fuck are you talking about?''

As though she hadn't heard him, she spoke directly to Cat. "About a year after Sparky was killed, I went to the hospital where he'd died. They told me to call the organ, hmm . . .''

"The organ bank?''

"I guess so. They wrote down the phone number for me.''

Cyc took a hulking step toward her. "Will you shut your ugly face? You don't have to tell them nothin'. And where was I while you were sneaking off to the hospital?''

She continued to ignore him. "I called the number they gave me. The lady I talked to was nice, but because I wasn't related to Sparky, she wouldn't tell me anything. I pleaded with her. I wanted to know if—''

"I said shut up!" Cyc struck suddenly, cuffing her on the side of her head.

Cat couldn't have stopped Alex if she'd wanted to. He lunged for Cyc, put his hands around the man's throat, and slammed him into the exterior wall of the house.

"You touch her again, you go to jail, dickhead." His voice was quiet but steely. "But before that, I'd give you the fight you're looking for. I'd tear out your good eye and piss in the hole. By the time I got finished with you, you really would be blind and stupid. You'd be begging them to lock you up for a long, long time so I couldn't get to you again."

"Get outta my face, asshole." Cyc grunted. He was in obvious pain. Alex's knee was grinding his crotch. "I ain't gonna hurt her."

Cat noticed Michael. He was clutching handfuls of his mother's skirt in his tiny fists. He face was buried in the folds of fabric again. "Alex, the child."

The words worked like a magic wand. Alex relaxed his stance and released the biker. He backed away until he was standing beside Cat again, but he remained tense, poised for attack.

During their altercation, Kismet had remained docile, seeming impervious to it. Cat supposed that she was inured to violent outbursts, having been the victim of them so often. "Kismet," she said, "do you know anything about the recipient of Sparky's heart? Where it was sent? Anything?"

She shook her head, glanced at Cyc, then looked down at the ground.

Cat wanted to probe her for more information, but she didn't want to incur Cyc's wrath, which he would no doubt vent on Kismet and the child. Turning to the biker and making no attempt to conceal her scorn, she asked, "Will they be all right?"

"Why wouldn't they be?"

"Because several times you've put them in the hospital," she said contemptuously. "You're pathetic, you know that? You're nothing but a foul-smelling bully who beats up a woman and child in order to prove your manhood."

"Cat." This time Alex was warning her, speaking her name under his breath, out the side of his mouth.

Cyc flexed his fists at his sides. "We don't know nothing about your heart, or Sparky's heart, or any goddamn mail," he said with a snarl. "We particularly don't know nothin' about no murders. So get the fuck outta here before I get really pissed."

Alex grasped her arm. "Come on."

She let herself be led back to the car. Alex pulled out and drove away fast, putting distance between them and George Murphy.

"I can't believe it. All this time they've been in my files," she said in wonderment. "Cyclops and Kismet. How'd you find them?"

"Uncle Dixie keeps good records. Murphy has a score of misdemeanors to his credit. Several police departments in the state had kept track of him. SAPD had a dossier with his current address."

"When Michael appeared in that doorway . . ." She was still reeling from the shock. "He's so sweet and defenseless. I can't bear to think of him living with that brute."

"And the woman?"

"I think she loves her son very much. But she lives in fear of Cyclops."

"When he smacked her—"

"I wish you'd pulverized him."

He took his eyes off the road long enough to give her a surprised glance. "This coming from you, who accused me of shooting first and asking questions later. Which way do you prefer it? Make up your mind."

"Don't start, Alex. I've had my share of unpleasant encounters this afternoon. I need some time in my corner before going another round with you."

"You must be tired. I've never known you to give in so easily."

Kismet and Cyclops lived in a community southeast of San Antonio. It was a half-hour drive, most of which Cat spent staring sightlessly through the windshield. By the time they reached the city, dusk had fallen. Lights were coming on in homes and commercial buildings. Neon signs beckoned customers into restaurants and movie theaters.

"I wish I had no bigger problem than deciding which movie I wanted to see tonight," she said.

"You're in a funk."

"I have a right to be, don't I? We tracked down Cyclops but aren't any closer to finding my stalker."

"You don't think it's George Baby?"

"Do you?"

"I want it to be, but I don't think it is."

"Why do you want it to be, and why don't you think it is?"

"I want it to be because I'd love to nail that bastard's ass. He's a felony waiting to happen. Sooner or later he's going to wind up in Huntsville prison for a long stay. I'd rather it be before he hurts someone, particularly Michael.

"Second, I want this to be over for your sake. I want you to be able to sleep nights without worrying about whether you'll live to see tomorrow."

"Gee, thanks for cheering me up and boosting my morale." After a moment she asked again, "Why don't you think it's Cyclops?"

"He's too stupid, for one thing. This is a complex scheme, well plotted and well executed by someone with brains and patience. Cyclops has neither."

"You're probably right, but let's play devil's advocate and pretend that it's a distinct possibility. Cyclops lives hand-to-mouth, so taking to the road for unspecified periods of time wouldn't pose any problems for him."

"With Kismet and Michael in tow?" he asked.

"I suppose not. Besides, we've determined that my stalker gets close to his victims. No one in his right mind would let Cyclops get close."

"What about the woman? Maybe she acts as a lure to draw the victims in. Wins their confidence, perhaps their pity. Cyclops ices them."

Cat shot down that hypothesis with a firm shake of her head. "I don't think her self-effacement is a pose. She didn't strike me as conniving. Besides, Petey told us she was in love with Sparky. What reason would she have to want to stop his heart? I got the impression she's still in love with him, didn't you?"

"Yeah. And Cyc doesn't like it."

"So if he was jealous of Sparky when he was alive—"

"He could still be jealous. Kismet is carrying a torch even this long after Sparky's death," Alex said, completing her thought.

"He's not yet rid of his competitor."

"His old lady's still hung up on the short little guy who bested him not only in bed but in a knife fight. So he's out for revenge, bumping off anybody who might have gotten Sparky's heart."

She looked at him expectantly, as if they'd just discovered the cure for cancer. But her bubble of excitement burst quickly. "That brings us back to how he weaseled his way into the lives of those three victims. Cyclops isn't exactly the type to blend in. If someone close to him dies mysteriously, he's going to come under suspicion."

She gave a defeated sigh. "God, who could have dreamed that because I received a donor heart, I'd have a psychopath on my tail? And you want to know something really funny? Funny in the ironic sense, that is." She flattened her hand over her chest. "I never wanted to be treated in any special way because I was a heart transplantee."

"It does make you somewhat unique," he reminded her gently.

"But I don't ask for preferential treatment because of it. I want people to forget that I don't have the heart I was born with. Instead, that seems to be the only thing anyone thinks about when they're with me."

The guard at the WWSA employee parking lot recognized Alex's car this time and waved at them as they drove through the gate. He was smiling cagily, as if he were a key player in a romantic intrigue.

Alex cut the engine and turned to her. "That's not all I think about when I'm with you, Cat. Not by a long shot."

She resisted the allure of his closeness by cracking a joke. "You aren't going to rhapsodize on my hair and eyes and lips, are you?"

"If you like. Or I could get more carnal and wax poetic about the erogenous zones of your body, which on you include everything covered by skin. I know from experience."

It was an arrogant boast, yet it coaxed a purling response deep inside her. She strove to ignore it. "Save the lurid lingo for your novels. I'd hate you to waste all that soft-core dialogue on me."

He grinned. "I think you like it."

"What?"

"The soft-core dialogue."

She had vivid recollections of his whispers in her ear a few nights ago. Before she could be seduced by it again, she opened the car door. "Thank you for finding Cyclops."

"I plan to do some more investigating before we write him off."

"Let me know if anything turns up. Good night, Alex."

"Cat?"

She looked at him over her shoulder. He seemed to be at odds with himself over whether to voice his thoughts. Finally he said simply, "Good night."

They went their separate ways. She drove home, her emotions conflicted. He could have tried a little harder to wear down her defenses. She still would have said no, but he could have put forth more effort to persuade her to spend the night with him.

Her mind continued to grumble about it as she prepared for bed. She had just stepped out of the shower when her doorbell rang.

He had followed her home after all!

Belting her terrycloth robe, she quickly made her way through the house to the front door. Anticipation coursed through her like a fizzy wine. Her nerve ends were tingling.

But when she peered through the blinds, expecting to see Alex, she had a nasty shock.

Chapter Forty-two

❦

What do you want, Mr. Murphy?"

"I want to talk to you," Cyclops said. "Open the door."

She forced a laugh. "I'm not opening my door to you."

"If I want to come inside, there's not a fucking thing you can do to stop me. So why don't you save your door from getting trashed?"

"If you don't leave immediately, I'll call the police."

"You do, and the kid'll suffer for it."

She pressed her forehead against the door. It would be lunacy to open her door to him in the middle of the night, but as he'd pointed out, if he wanted to come in, a locked door wouldn't stop him.

Obviously he had followed her home from the TV station. How else would he know where she lived? Unless he'd been sending mail to her address for the past two months.

Either way, why was she debating with herself over whether to let him in? Why didn't she race for the phone and dial 911 in the hope that help would arrive before he could inflict much damage?

Michael, that's why. She didn't doubt for a second that Cyclops would make good his threat. Kismet might not be entirely innocent, but the child certainly was. It might be too late to save her, but Michael was worth putting up a fight for.

She unlocked the door and opened it.

He was physically imposing. Alex had been either awfully brave or awfully stupid to fight him. She tried not to quail from his size and his body odor as he pushed her aside and stamped into the entry. He turned his head this way and that, taking in his surroundings. There was a crystal bowl filled with potpourri on the hall table. He lifted it to his nose and sniffed.

"It's nothing you can smoke," Cat remarked.

He flashed a reptilian grin. "That's funny."

Still grinning, he returned the bowl to the table. "So this is how TV stars live. Classy. A lot better than the pigsty I share with my old lady and kid, huh?"

Cat declined to agree with the obvious. "What are you doing here at this time of night, Mr. Murphy? What's so urgent that you have to see me now?"

He strolled into the living room and threw himself onto her white sofa, planting his boots on the matching ottoman. "Hey, chill, okay? You came to see me first, remember? You started this, not me."

"Started what?"

"This shit about Sparky. I hadn't thought of that little runt in years, then you came along with your cop friend in his fancy car and stirred up a bunch of shit about him."

He snickered as his good eye traveled up and down her body. "Sparky's asshole was no higher off the ground than yours."

He made her skin crawl. She felt particularly vulnerable

standing before him wearing only her bathrobe. Which of the house phones would be easiest to reach from this room? How quickly could she dial 911? Was there a sturdy lock on her bedroom door? She didn't know. She'd never needed it before.

She called upon her acting skills to conceal her fear. "You're wrong about Mr. Pierce. He's not a cop."

He guffawed. "Who do you think you're bullshitting, lady?"

"I defer to your superior knowledge of policemen," she said beneath her breath, then left it alone. "Furthermore, why should it bother you that we asked a few questions about your friend Sparky?"

"Wasn't no friend of mine."

"So what do you care?"

"I don't. But it got me to thinking."

That must have been a stretch. "About what?" she asked.

He toyed with a silver button on his leather vest. "You think you got the little cocksucker's heart, right?"

"It's a possibility. But unless you came here tonight to confess to three murders, and to making threats to me through the mail, I don't see what concern it is of yours. So why don't you take your filthy feet off my furniture and get the hell out of my house?"

He winked at her with his good eye. "You're a regular chili pepper, aren't you, Red? You got a real smart mouth on you. Do you fuck as fiery as you talk?"

If she allowed him to provoke her, she would be playing right into his dirty hands. Instead, she folded her arms at her waist and tried to appear bored. "It's late, Mr. Murphy. Please state your business and leave."

He laid his head back on the pillows of the sofa, repositioned his feet on the ottoman, and nestled his butt deeper into the seat cushions.

She would have to burn that furniture.

"The little bastard's not mine."

"Pardon?"

Grinning in his mean, sinister way, he repeated, "Kismet's bastard's not my kid. Sparky knocked her up."

Concern for her furniture vanished along with her fear. Mindlessly, she sat down on the arm of an overstuffed chair. "You're not Michael's father?"

"Ain't that what I just said?"

"Sparky was his father."

"Yeah. It's a wonder Kismet didn't slip the kid after that accident, the way she was banged up and all. Been a hell of a lot better for me if she had, but the little sucker held on. Eight months after Sparky was wasted, his bastard was born."

Cat's mind was racing ahead of him now. She didn't need him to tell her the significance of this, but he did anyway.

"After you left, the kid jabbered 'bout seeing you at some picnic. He seemed real taken with you. Just like you are with him." His earring swung away from his cheek as he cocked his head and pretended to ponder life's mysteries. "Now I wonder why that is?"

Maybe he was more clever than she and Alex had given him credit for. It was frightening to think that his level of intelligence could equal that of his meanness.

"I don't know what you're getting at," she lied.

"The hell you don't," he said around a chuckle. "It ain't no accident that you and that spooky little dickweed hit it off. You got his daddy's heart. You . . . uh, what's a good word? You *connected* with the kid. Like kindred spirits. Karma and shit."

Michael's picture in Sherry's files had indeed had an inexplicable impact on her. Or was it inexplicable?

"I don't know for certain that I got Sparky's heart," she said huskily.

"I'm saying you did."

"Say whatever you like." She stood to signal that his visit

had come to an end. "But say it someplace else. Now that you've imparted your message, I don't think there's anything left for us to talk about."

"Well, that's where you're wrong, see? We got a lot to talk about."

"Such as?"

"Money."

That was the last thing she'd expected him to say. "What money?"

"The money you owe me."

She plopped back down onto the chair arm and regarded him with incredulity. "I'm not following you."

"Then let me spell it out for you. If Sparky had lived, he'd've had to put up with all the crap I've had to put up with. I took his kid and raised him—"

"Out of the goodness of your heart," she inserted sarcastically.

"Damn straight."

This time it was she who guffawed. "You took Michael because he came with Kismet, and you wanted her back after Sparky died. Not because you loved her, but because you couldn't tolerate being passed over for another man. You've been punishing her for it ever since."

He kicked aside the ottoman and surged to his feet. "The goddamn cunt begged me to take her back."

Cat forced herself not to recoil. He was a bully, and, like all bullies, he relished seeing fear in the eyes of his victims. He might slit her throat—or cut out her heart—with the knife sheathed in his belt, but she wouldn't give him the satisfaction of seeing her cowed.

"I've put up with her and her whelp for four stinking years," he said. "The way I see it, I got something coming to me for that."

"I don't think you really want what you've got coming to you."

"Listen, bitch." He poked her in the chest with his index finger. "You'd have died if it weren't for me. I told that doctor he could take Sparky's heart. You'd be history if I'd said no."

"That may or may not be true."

"I say it is. I want something in return for saving your skinny ass."

"Ah. Here's where the money part comes in."

"Now you're catching on."

"You want me to pay you for my heart?"

His narrow lips parted in a slow, sly grin. He reached out and yanked hard on a strand of her hair. "Knew the minute I clapped eyes on you, you were a smart chick."

Chapter Forty-three

❧

Alex was charged.

His creative juices weren't just flowing, they were spurting. His fingers couldn't move as rapidly as his brain fired signals, but he could live with that frustration as long as the words kept coming.

He'd finally shaken off the mind-numbing writer's block. He was back on track, better than before. As the clauses and phrases streaked through his mind, he transferred them to his computer screen.

The telephone rang.

"Son of a bitch."

He tried to ignore the intrusive ringing and continued to type. At this time of night it would probably be a wrong number anyway. Or Arnie. Arnie called every day or so to ask if he was still seeing Cat. When he said yes—he couldn't lie to his agent—he got a lecture on borrowing trouble.

The phone rang again.

Don't stop, he ordered himself. *Get this sentence down before it escapes you. If you stop now, it'll be gone forever. It'll disappear into that vast void that sucks in precise words and inspired phrases right after they peep at you from behind your subconscious and just before you can snatch them.*

The phone was on its fourth ring.

Ignore it. You've been waiting for a night like this for weeks, he reminded himself. *Everything's coming together. You've worked that knot out of your plot—granted, not quite in the way you expected, but maybe this way is stronger. The action is unfolding fast and furiously; the dialogue is good and crisp. It packs a punch.*

*Whatever you do, dumb ass, **don't** pick up the phone!*

He snatched up the receiver. "What?"

"Alex, can . . . can you . . . I wouldn't bother you, but . . ."

"Cat? Are you all right?"

"Actually no. I'm not."

"Fifteen minutes."

He dropped the receiver and turned off his computer, but not before saving the fine work he'd done. He crammed his feet into his running shoes, switched out the light, locked the door to his study, and raced from the condo.

Tom Clancy was probably interrupted all the time. He might have sold another million copies of *Patriot Games* if not for life's little interruptions. And Danielle Steele had nine kids. Think how many times a day she was interrupted.

Cat opened the door as he jogged up her front walk. "Thanks for coming."

"You're as white as a sheet. What happened? Why's your hair wet?"

"I washed it."

"You washed your hair? After calling me in what sounded like a life-or-death situation, you washed your hair!"

"Stop yelling at me!" She pointed imperiously toward the living room. "I had a visitor. Cyclops."

The biker had left a clear imprint of himself on her sofa and ottoman. Alex expelled his breath and raked back his hair. "Christ. How'd he get in?"

"I let him in."

"You *what*?"

"He threatened to hurt Michael if I didn't."

"He could have hurt you."

"But he didn't!"

"Now you're yelling. What'd he want?"

"Let's go into the kitchen," she said. "I've used a whole can of air freshener, but I can still smell him in here."

She led the way. Her cow-pattern kettle was simmering on the stove. She asked if he wanted a cup of tea. A belt of straight whiskey, maybe, he told her. But no tea, thanks.

She poured herself a cup, added a teaspoon of sugar, and sat across from him at her kitchen table. Her fingers looked translucent as she folded them around her cup.

"What'd he want, Cat?"

"Money."

"In exchange for Sparky's heart, right?"

Her eyes swung up to his. "How'd you know?"

"I've read about such. A person receives transplanted corneas, or a liver, or skin tissue. Once he's well, a member of the donor family shows up and demands payment."

"I've heard of it too," she said, nodding forlornly. "It was cited in our group sessions as one of the reasons for donors and recipients to remain anonymous." She crossed her arms over her chest and ran her hands up and down her arms. "But I didn't know anyone could actually be that mercenary."

"Cyclops could."

"He's so repulsive. Where he touched my chest and hair

with his dirty fingers, I felt like I'd been raped. I took a long, hot shower.''

She lifted the cup of tea to her lips but could barely hold it steady while she sipped from it. It clattered against the saucer when she replaced it. "I hated to bother you, Alex."

"No bother," he lied.

"I didn't know who else to call. I could have phoned that Lieutenant Hunsaker, but I have very little confidence in him.''

Alex supposed he should take that as a compliment. "You did the right thing. You shouldn't be alone tonight. Did you have any trouble getting Cyclops out of the house?''

"Not really. I called his bluff and told him that he'd get money from me over my dead body.'' With a weak smile, she added, "He said that could be arranged.''

"He could have killed you, you know.''

"I pointed out that killing me would be a dumb move if he wanted money from me.''

Alex considered it a miracle that Cyclops hadn't hurt her. At the same time, he was angry with Cat. "You played the smart-ass, didn't you? I can just hear you spouting off wisecracks. Why in hell did you wave those red flags in his face?''

"Well what would you suggest I do? Cringe and cry and show him how frightened I was? I also had Michael and Kismet to consider. He'll probably take out his frustration on them.''

"Was he frustrated when he left?''

"To say the least. I guess he thought he could intimidate me into writing out a check tonight. He was furious when I refused. I told him in no uncertain terms that I wouldn't give him a cent.''

"To which he said . . .''

"That I'd be sorry.''

Alex too was worried about Michael and his mother, but he wanted to allay Cat's concern. "He'll think long and hard before raising a hand to Michael again. Just a few weeks ago, he barely escaped a long jail sentence."

"I hope that's a deterrent, because blood ties won't stop him. Michael's not his child." She recounted what Cyclops had told her. "Maybe that explains why I became infatuated with Michael's picture before I even met him."

Alex leaned forward across the table. "What are you getting at?"

"Nothing."

"Come on, Cat. I raced to your rescue. Doesn't that entitle me to hear the nitty-gritty?"

"It's silly." She gave a small, mirthless laugh, a slight shrug, and tinkered with her spoon—all dead giveaways that she was stalling.

Finally she said, "From the time doctors began performing heart transplants, there has been discussion over whether characteristics of the donor could be passed to the recipient."

He took a moment to absorb that, then said, "Go on."

"Well, it's ridiculous, of course," she declared, a little too loudly. She took a moment to compose herself. "The heart is an organ. It's apparatus, physiological machinery. A person's *heart*, where his or her soul resides, is something entirely different."

"Then why did you automatically link your attraction to Michael to the possibility that his father was your donor?"

"I didn't."

"Yes, you did. And so did Cyclops."

"He doesn't care who donated what to whom," she said heatedly. "He just sees a way to make a buck. He hates Michael because he's Sparky's living legacy to Kismet. He's punishing her for choosing Sparky over him. He's made her life hell. No wonder she looks so haunted."

"They're not your responsibility, Cat."

She looked at him as though he'd just urinated on the American flag. "Of course they are! They're human beings, and they're in danger."

"I admire your altruism, but you can't save all the unfortunates of the world."

"If Cyclops hurts them, I couldn't live with myself. Could you? Doesn't a human life mean anything to you?"

He felt a wave of angry heat flood his face. "I'm going to ignore that because you're upset and, I hope, don't realize what you're saying. I'd like nothing better than to pound the shit out of George Murphy and see to it that he never touches Kismet and Michael again. But there are millions of victims just like them all over the country."

"I know I can't save millions, but I'd like to help them."

"You're not seriously thinking of giving him money?"

Their shouting match had depleted her energy. Her shoulders slumped forward, and she rested her head in her palm. "I would never surrender to blackmail, but he made it clear that if I don't, I'll regret it. One way or another."

Then she raised her head and looked at him. For the first time since he'd met her, she looked frightened. "Alex, I want to call it off."

"Call what off?"

"This insane search for my stalker. I haven't heard from him in almost two weeks. I'm convinced that someone with a perverted sense of humor was playing mind games with me, that's all.

"The phony obituary was his grand finale. He did what he'd set out to do—rattle my cage. But now he's finished playing his little game."

"You sure of that?"

"No, I'm not sure," she snapped. "But I don't want to overturn any more stones. Every time I do, there's an ugly worm underneath. I'm afraid to open my mail for what I might find. A one-eyed, tattooed biker with homicidal tendencies, whom I'd never even heard of until a few days ago, is now trying to extort money from me and threatening my life.

"I jump at my own shadow. I no longer feel safe in my home. I can't concentrate on my work. My appetite's shot to hell, and I don't even remember when I last slept through a whole night without waking up, listening for the bogeyman. I don't need any more of this crap."

"It's not that easy, Cat. You can't just call it off."

"I can. I am."

"Well I can't and I won't," he stated firmly as he came to his feet. "You don't close the files on an investigation just because you don't like the looks of the evidence you uncover."

"Oh, stop with the cop talk. You're no longer a policeman, and this isn't a bona fide investigation. Nor is it a plot for one of your novels. This is my *life*!"

"Right. And I'm trying to protect it. I'd like you to live past the fourth anniversary of your transplant."

"So would I." She paused and drew in a shuddering breath. His gut clenched. He wasn't going to like what was coming next. "That's why I'm going to California and stay with Dean till we're beyond the date. It's all arranged."

Alex placed his hands on his hips. "Oh really? When did you arrange it?"

"Before you arrived."

"I see. You called me to rush to your rescue, but I'm only a temporary wing for you to hover under until you can run back to Daddy Dean, is that it?" He snorted derisively. "And you accused *me* of using *you* just for sex."

He'd meant to offend her and he had. Tears sprang to her eyes, but, being Cat, she didn't crumble. "I'll see you to the door."

Dame Judith Anderson in her prime couldn't have looked or sounded more regally indignant as she rose from her chair and left the kitchen.

He followed, but only as far as the entryway, where he slammed shut the front door, which she was holding open for him.

"I'm not leaving you alone tonight, Cat." He held up his hands for silence before she could protest. "I'll sleep in the living room." He glanced at the dirty sofa and added, "I've slept on worse, believe me.

"Now, you can stamp your foot, rant and rave, whatever, but it'll be a waste of energy. Energy that I can tell you don't have. You can pout, pack for your trip, paint your toenails, anything you want, but until we have an indication of what Cyclops's next move is going to be, I'm not letting you out of my sight."

Chapter Forty-four

C yc could hardly believe his eyes when he
shuffled into the kitchen for his morning coffee. Kismet was
already sitting at the table. Her appearance nearly bowled
him over.

She was wearing makeup like she had when he'd first met
her. Applied with a heavy hand, it outlined and shadowed
her dark eyes. The nun's bun he despised was gone. Her hair
had been left free to fall around her shoulders in a wild tangle.

Missing too were the long skirts and shapeless blouses
she'd worn the past four years. She was back in the threadbare
jeans that fit her ass like a surgical glove. Her tattooed bosom
had been squeezed into a low-cut tight black tank top.

It was like she'd been sleepwalking since Sparky's death
but now had suddenly awakened. The startling transformation
had taken place overnight.

And it wasn't only skin deep. Her surly expression was
reminiscent of the old Kismet. The moment he entered the

room, she got up and poured him a cup of coffee, her movements quick and abrupt, the restlessness of years ago having returned. He would have suspected her of being wired if she hadn't sworn off drugs after the kid came along.

"Want some breakfast?" she asked.

Mistrustful of her sudden reversal, he said, "If I wanted breakfast I'd tell you, wouldn't I?"

"You don't have to be an asshole about it."

She refilled her coffee cup and returned to the table. Picking up her lit cigarette from the ashtray, she took a drag and aimed a plume of smoke toward the ceiling. She'd given up cigarettes while she was pregnant and hadn't smoked again.

Now, as he watched her full, red lips close around the filter of the cigarette, his loins filled with desire. He'd seen her like this a thousand times—angry and kinetic—but it had been a damned long time. Until this moment, he hadn't realized just how much he'd missed her sassiness.

But Cyc was suspicious by nature and rarely took things at face value. "What got into you?" he asked.

She ground out the cigarette by impatiently jabbing it against the amber glass. "Maybe you knocked some sense into me last night."

"You had it coming." He'd worked her over good for making him look like a goddamn fool in front of the Delaney bitch and her cop boyfriend. The bruises hardly showed beneath her heavy makeup.

"I can't believe she refused to give you any money."

Over a bottle of booze and a few lines of coke, he'd told her about his unproductive visit with Cat Delaney. "Don't worry. She'll come around."

"But when?"

"Soon as I think of something." He slurped his coffee.

"Who does she think she is? If not for Sparky, she'd be dead."

"She says she might have got somebody else's heart. It might not've been Sparky's."

"Even if it wasn't, she owes me," Kismet said, tossing her head defiantly. "We've had to struggle these last four years, while she's been living high on the hog. It's not fair."

"We'll get some money from her. I just gotta think up a plan."

"I've been doing some thinking of my own."

His good eye narrowed to a sinister slit. "Oh yeah? What about?"

"We've gotta make a move before that cop friend of hers starts filling her head with bullshit. He could ruin this for us."

She came out of her chair as though the seat of it had bitten her on the butt. Charged by caffeine and nicotine, she began to pace.

Cyc agreed with what she was saying, but it would look like weakness if he complied too soon. "You stay out of it," he said crossly. "I got the situation under control."

She whirled around and angrily confronted him. "The hell you do! You let her buffalo you with her pretty face and big blue eyes. For all your threats, you came up empty."

He came out of his chair like a shot and slapped her hard across the cheek. To his astonishment, she hit him back. Her palm landed against his ear with a loud smack that hurt his eardrum. Nevertheless, he heard every word of what she hissed at him.

"I'm not going to take that shit from you anymore, you son of a bitch. You've hit me for the last time."

Her turnabout was exciting, but there was a limit to what he'd allow. He wanted her somewhere between the spitfire she'd been and the calf-eyed dishrag she'd become.

"I've got something you'll take."

Grasping her by her plump upper arms, he shoved her against the countertop and pinned her there with his body.

She struggled to be released, which he had to do in order to unfasten her jeans. While his head was being pummeled by her flailing fists, he managed to work the tight jeans down her legs and off her bare feet.

She tried to run from the room, but he grabbed a handful of her hair and yanked her back. He lifted her onto the table and pushed apart her thighs. Flattening his hand on the center of her chest, he held her down while he undid the buttons of his jeans. His cock sprang free.

Cyc grunted with pleasure and surprise when her hand formed a tight fist around it. She pumped him greedily, eagerly, like she'd done years ago when she couldn't get enough, when she'd made sex a contest of wills and stamina that she won as often as not.

He pushed up her top and clutched her breasts, pinching her large nipples. Then, turning her head, she bit his arm. He slapped her again, leaned over her, and bit her nipple hard before sucking it like his life depended on it. She squirmed beneath him, she clawed his bare back, she cursed him viciously.

He drove himself into her with such force that the table legs scraped across the floor and he almost lost his balance. She clamped his hips with her strong thighs, crossed her ankles at the small of his back, and sank her fingernails into the cheeks of his ass.

He came almost instantly, but so did she. She flung her arms back over her head, knocking coffee cups and the ashtray to the floor. She thrashed her head from side to side, whipping her hair around. Her teeth clamped down so hard on her lower lip that they broke the skin. Even long after it was over, her breasts continued to rise and fall.

Cyc rubbed them roughly with his callused palms. "Great tits."

She purred deep in her throat and began moving restlessly, arching her back, shifting the position of her legs. Her face was flushed, her lips bruised and swollen. A bead of blood appeared on her lower lip. A damp strand of hair lay across her throat. She looked at him through drowsy, half-closed eyes, smiling the wicked smile he remembered well.

"Your pussy has pythons in it. I always said so."

She laughed lustily. "We're gonna be rich, Cyc. *Rich*."

"Damn right." He tried to withdraw, but she locked him within her thighs.

"Where do you think you're going?"

His heart rate accelerated. Once had never been enough for the old Kismet. She *was* back.

"You made quite a mess down there," she whispered, her smile lewd. "Clean it up."

She clasped his head between her hands and pushed it down between her thighs.

Chapter Forty-five

*H*e tapped on her bedroom door. "Cat?"

"I'm almost ready. Has the taxi arrived?"

"No, but Cyclops has."

She opened the door with a swift yank. Alex was checking the cylinder of his revolver. Seeing the loaded weapon made her shiver.

"They drove past once and must have circled the block," he told her. "I just saw them turn the corner at the end of the street. They're headed this way."

" 'They'?"

"He's got Kismet and Michael on the bike with him."

"Good Lord."

"Right," Alex said grimly. "My guess is he'll use them like hostages to soften you up."

Following their quarrel the night before, Cat had retired to her bedroom and packed for her trip to California. Once that was done, she'd turned out the lights and gone to bed. but not to sleep.

She could hear him moving about the other rooms of the house, probably checking windows and doors to make certain they were locked. In spite of her anger at him, she was glad he'd stayed. She felt much safer having him there, keeping vigil.

When they'd met in the kitchen this morning, they'd behaved like polite strangers. He'd offered to pour her a cup of coffee from the pot he'd brewed, and she'd thanked him for it. He'd asked the time of her flight and offered to drive her to the airport.

"Thank you, but I've called for a taxi to pick me up here."

"Fine," he'd replied.

She had then returned to her bedroom to shower and dress. They hadn't spoken again. Now she followed him down the short hallway into the living room. "Maybe they won't stop when they see your car out front," Cat said hopefully.

"I parked it in the garage after you went to bed."

"Oh."

"It'll work to our benefit if they think you're alone. We've got the element of surprise on our side."

She parted the slats of the blinds in one of the front windows and watched as the motorcycle moved slowly down the street toward her house.

From his position at the adjacent window, Alex said, "Go back to your room, Cat. Wait there until I've had a chance to feel out this situation."

"No way."

"This isn't the time to— Whoa!" he exclaimed suddenly. "That *is* Kismet, isn't it?"

Cat had to look beyond the clothes and makeup to be certain. If Kismet hadn't been carrying Michael in her arms, she wouldn't have recognized her.

As she brazenly sauntered up the walk, her hips swung provocatively from side to side. Yesterday, she could be cowed with a look. Today, she seemed ready, even eager, to take on any opponent brave enough to cross her.

She gave the doorbell three strident jabs. Cat glanced at Alex. He motioned for her to open the door, then stepped to the other side of it so that when it was opened, he would be concealed.

Cautiously, Cat unlocked the door and pulled it halfway open.

Instantly noticeable were the unshed tears welling in Kismet's eyes. They were incongruent with the whorish makeup and the swaggering self-confidence with which she'd approached the house. Then Cat noticed that her lips were trembling.

"Please," she whispered. "Please help me."

Despite the unflattering description Cat had given Alex of Lieutenant Hunsaker, he was willing to extend his fellow cop the benefit of the doubt. Unfortunately, Hunsaker lived up to expectations. The moment he strutted into Cat's living room, Alex pegged him as a buffoon. His ego was as inflated as his beer gut.

"Looks like destiny brought us together after all," he said to Cat, smiling broadly. Specks of tobacco resided in the corners of his lips.

"Looks like."

"The wife sure did appreciate the autograph."

"Thank you. Lieutenant Hunsaker, this is Patricia Holmes and her son, Michael." He acknowledged the introduction to Kismet with a curt nod.

While waiting for the police to arrive, Cat had remained in the bedroom with Michael and Kismet. When they emerged, there wasn't a trace of the harsh makeup on

Kismet's face. Her hair had been neatly secured with a clip. She was wearing a pair of coveralls, probably the only item in Cat's closet large enough for her.

Cat turned Hunsaker toward him. "And this is Alex Pierce."

"Pierce." The detective shook his hand.

"Alex is a former policeman," Cat informed him.

" 'S that right? Where 'bouts?"

"Houston."

"Houston, huh?" He looked Alex up and down. "How come you left the force?"

"None of your business."

Taken aback, Hunsaker said, "No need to get defensive."

"I'm not. Just stating a fact."

He noisily cleared his throat and gave his slipping belt a tug. "Okay, who's gonna fill me in on what happened?"

"Alex?" Cat prompted. "You saw more than we did."

He outlined what had happened the preceding day and earlier that morning, ending with Kismet's tearful plea at Cat's threshold.

"Cat didn't ask any questions. She pulled her and the boy inside and bolted the front door. Ms. Holmes was terrified. She said that if Cyclops got his hands on her, he'd kill her for betraying him. Michael was scared too. He didn't understand what was going on, but he sensed his mother's panic. I told Cat to take them into her bedroom."

"That's when I called you, Lieutenant," Cat chimed in. "But I was afraid of what Cyclops might do."

"I told her not to worry, that I'd stop the bastard cold before he made it into the house." Hunsaker cut his eyes toward the revolver lying on the table. "It's no longer loaded," Alex said.

"What about the biker?" Hunsaker asked. "This Cyclops character. What'd he do then?"

"He hadn't expected Cat to pull Kismet into her house

and slam the door. Consequently, he sensed right away that something had gone awry. He shouted from the curb, asking what the hell was going on. When I didn't answer, he started looking agitated.

"I don't know what the hell took you so long to get here, Hunsaker," Alex continued. "If you hadn't dragged your feet, Cyclops could be behind bars by now awaiting indictment for assault and extortion."

The detective ignored the criticism and turned to Cat. "He tried to get money from you last night?"

"That's right." She recounted Cyclops's visit.

"He doesn't sound like somebody you'd want to mess with," he remarked when she was finished. "Why didn't you call me?"

"Because she called me," Alex said. "I stayed here the rest of the night."

Hunsaker must have taken the implication for what it was. He harrumphed and said, "What about this morning? Why'd he come back?"

"Ms. Holmes tricked Cyclops into bringing her and Michael along to strengthen his argument," Alex said. "Once she disappeared into the house, his animal instincts must have warned him that he'd been double-crossed, and that he'd be screwed for sure if he didn't get out of here."

"So he took off?"

"Yeah. But not before yelling, 'I'll kill you, Kismet. You and your brat.' I can't quote him accurately within Michael's hearing, but all I omitted were a few adjectives. Then he roared away. There's a dangerous criminal now at large," Alex added as a mild rebuke for the detective's delay.

Hunsaker turned to Cat. "Do you have anything to add?"

"Only that Alex and I witnessed Mr. Murphy striking Ms. Holmes yesterday afternoon at their house."

This was getting too complicated for him. He scratched his head. "I'm unclear on why you went out there."

"We were following up a clue into that other matter I discussed with you in your office," Cat said.

"Those clippings, you mean?"

"Yes. I thought Cyclops might be the one sending them."

"Was he?"

She looked at Kismet, who vigorously shook her head. "I don't believe so," Cat said. "But he still belongs behind bars. You can check with Child Protection Services. There've already been several complaints against him for abusive treatment of a child. He was released due to a lack of initiative by the prosecutor."

"What about her?" He hitched his thumb toward Kismet.

"She was also implicated, but only because she couldn't stand up to Cyclops for fear of reprisal."

Hunsaker indicated the soiled sofa. "Mind if I sit?"

"Not at all," Cat said.

He lowered himself to the edge of the cushion and addressed Kismet, who was seated in a chair, holding Michael on her lap. Acting as a buffer, Cat sat on the arm of the chair.

"What've you got to say for yourself?" Hunsaker asked.

Kismet glanced apprehensively at Cat, who took her hand and squeezed it encouragingly. "Tell him what you told me."

She blotted her tears and nervously wet her bruised, swollen lips. "Yesterday, after they left," she nodded toward Cat and Alex, "he came up with this plan on how to get money from her for Sparky's heart."

"Who's Sparky?"

Alex filled in the gaps. Hunsaker hung on every word. "Jesus, this is complicated," he grumbled, turning back to Kismet. "Cyclops wanted money in exchange for this Sparky's heart. And Sparky was your boy's natural daddy, right?"

Kismet nodded and ran her hand over Michael's head. The

boy hadn't been out of her reach since Cat had pulled them inside. No one could doubt her devotion to him.

"Cyc came home real late last night. He was angry because Ms. Delaney had refused to give him any money," Kismet told the detective. "He said she laughed at him."

Alex was aghast. "You laughed at him? You didn't tell me that. Are you crazy?"

"No, I'm not crazy."

"Quiet!" Hunsaker ordered. He looked balefully at Alex. "Pardon the interruption, Ms. uh, Holmes, is it? Go on."

"Cyc did some lines and got real mean. I tried to stay out of his way, but he still worked me over pretty good. After he passed out, I laid awake trying to figure out what to do."

Her dark eyes began to shimmer with fresh tears. "Ms. Delaney seemed like such a nice lady. I'd seen her on TV, helping those kids. She was good to Michael at that picnic."

"What picnic?"

"Irrelevant," Alex snapped. "Let her tell her story, why don't you?"

"I'm not the one who keeps interrupting. You are." Hunsaker signaled for Kismet to continue.

"I didn't want Cyc to bother Ms. Delaney. But I was so happy to know that maybe Sparky's heart had saved the life of someone like her. And the way she stood up to Cyc gave me courage. So I decided to stand up to him too."

"Except that she had no money, no transportation, and no one to call for help," Cat interjected. "If she had tried to run away, she wouldn't have gotten very far before he found her."

"And he'd have hurt me and probably Michael," Kismet said. "I knew my only chance was to outsmart him. So this morning, I . . ." She swallowed convulsively.

Cat placed her arm around her. "Go on, Patricia," she urged gently. "You're almost finished."

Kismet nodded. "I gave Michael a downer last night so he'd sleep late this morning. That was wrong, I know, but I couldn't . . . I didn't want to risk him seeing . . . I got Cyc all turned on, you know? I had to pretend that I liked it. I had to convince him that I'd gone back to being the way I was before I fell in love with Sparky." She began to cry in earnest.

"You did what you had to do, Patricia. No one in this room is in a position to judge you."

Cat's soft, understanding, woman-to-woman tone shut out Alex and Hunsaker as effectively as the closing of a steel vault door. Kismet had used sex to barter for her life. A few men might be able to empathize. But it really took another woman to comprehend the utter debasement of that.

At that moment, just being a man made Alex feel guilty by association. He wondered if Hunsaker felt as he did. Probably not. Hunsaker was too thick-headed to grasp anything that abstract. But at least he had the sensitivity to look away and remain quiet until Kismet had composed herself enough to continue.

"Afterward, I convinced Cyc to drive me here and let me have a go at Ms. Delaney. I said I'd use Michael, since she really cared for him. Cyc didn't like the idea, but I argued that since he hadn't gotten money from her with threats, he ought to let me try and play on her sympathy. He finally gave in."

She pulled Michael closer to her. "That walk from the curb to the front door seemed to take forever. I was scared stiff Cyc would catch on to my plan before I reached the door."

When she turned to Cat, her expression bordered on worshipful. "I don't know what I'd've done if you'd slammed the door in my face. I can never repay you."

"I only want to see you and Michael safely away from that brute."

"Do you wanna press charges?" Hunsaker asked Kismet.
"Yes."

"You sure? Sometimes you gals chicken out when it comes right down to it."

"She's not going to chicken out," Alex said testily.

"And I certainly won't," Cat said. "He threatened my life and theirs if I didn't give him money. That's extortion. I'll testify against him. You can depend on it."

"But you've got to find him first," Alex said to Hunsaker. "In the meantime, we've guaranteed Ms. Holmes and Michael a safe place to live."

The detective came to his feet. "There's a lot of paperwork involved. Will y'all be able to come to my office this afternoon and give your statements?" They agreed on a time. "I'll put out an APB for George Murphy. I've got a description of him and his Harley. We'll have him in custody in no time."

"You won't find him," Kismet said with quiet certainty. "He's got dozens of places to hide. There're people who'll hide him. You won't find him."

Alex was afraid she might be right, but he kept this grim opinion to himself. If and when Cyclops was captured, it would likely be attributed to the biker's carelessness rather than to the efficiency of the police.

Hunsaker, on the other hand, made boisterous promises that Cyclops would soon be in police custody. "You relax and let us handle everything from here on, little lady." He ruffled Michael's hair. "Cute kid."

"Thank you for coming," Cat said as he lumbered to the door.

"You never figured out who was sending you those mysterious clippings?"

"I'm afraid not. That's what I was after when I stirred up this hornets' nest. Of course, I'm glad I did. Patricia and Michael have been liberated." Alex realized that as a sign of respect, Cat now referred to Patricia only by her real name. Kismet was a thing of the past.

"Have you received any more crank mail since you came to see me?" Hunsaker asked.

"No."

"There you go," he said, pleased with himself. "You'll probably never know who sent it. I figured all along that it didn't amount to anything."

Cat had better manners than Alex could fathom. In spite of Hunsaker's gross condescension, she graciously thanked him for his time and assistance.

"I forgot to tell you," he said to Cat after closing the door on the detective. "While we were waiting for Hunsaker to get here, your taxi came. I tipped the driver ten bucks and sent him away."

"Thank you. I'd forgotten all about it."

"Will you still be going to California?"

"Not until I'm certain that Patricia and Michael are in a safe place. I called Sherry—she's working on it."

She arrived half an hour later. "I've found a house I think you'll both like," she told Patricia and Michael. "There are three other women and their children living there, along with a full-time counselor. Two of the children are near Michael's age, so he'll have playmates. You'll have your own bedroom and bath and all the privacy you want. But you'll eat with the other families and be expected to do chores."

Patricia couldn't believe her good fortune. She was overwhelmingly grateful and cried unabashedly. "I'll be glad to do anything. I'll do my chores and everybody else's, so long as Cyc can't find us."

Shortly, they gathered at the front door to say their goodbyes. "You'll be safe," Cat stressed to Patricia. "If you need anything, or just want to talk, call me. You've got the number I gave you?"

"In my pocket."

Cat, who'd been holding Michael during the exchange, hugged him tightly, then passed him to his mother. "I'll want to visit you soon, if it's all right."

"Yes," Patricia said eagerly. "We'd like that, wouldn't we, Michael?" He nodded shyly.

Cat was getting choked up. "Goodbye for now. Sherry will take good care of you."

"I'll walk you to the car," Alex offered when he noticed that Patricia look fearful of going outside. "Might not be a bad idea to double back and take a circuitous route to make certain you aren't being followed," he suggested to Sherry.

"In situations like this, that's standard operating procedure," she said with a smile.

He stepped onto the porch and, after scoping out the immediate area, gave them the all clear. Patricia held back and clasped Cat's hand. She spoke earnestly and swiftly, as though if she didn't rush the words, she might never have the nerve to speak them.

"You're such a good person. So kind to people. Sparky was the only other person I've known who was like you. I think you *must* have his heart."

Chapter Forty-six

Work was Cat's panacea. Even while suffering a serious heart condition, she'd worked grueling hours on *Passages*. When depressed, she worked. When happy, she worked. In her present predicament, she sought respite in work.

She had called Jeff Doyle earlier, explaining why she wouldn't be in until after lunch. "I'll fill you in on the details when I get there."

He held her to that promise. In the privacy of her office, he listened to her story with mounting disbelief. "My God, Cat. This George Murphy sounds like a barbarian. He could have killed you."

"Well, he didn't."

"Why don't you stick to your plan to go to Los Angeles? Maybe you should leave town for a few days."

"I've already called Dean and canceled the trip."

To go to California now would be the coward's way. It

wouldn't be very confidence-inspiring to Michael and Patricia if she assured them of their safety from Cyclops, then hightailed it to the West Coast. She'd decided that instead of running away to escape, she would bury herself in work.

"At least take the rest of the afternoon off," Jeff urged. "We'll catch up."

"No. This is where I need to be. Did I miss anything important this morning? Bring me up to date, and let's get busy."

She returned calls, dictated a score of letters, and scheduled two location shoots with the production crew for the upcoming week.

"For the Wednesday shoot, I've made arrangements with the same old cowboy who brought the pony ride to Nancy Webster's picnic," Jeff told her. "He loved the kids and said he'd be glad to help us anytime, free of charge."

"That's great. The kids'll love it. Michael certainly did."

"Cat, what you did for him and his mother . . ." Jeff let it hang until she looked up at him inquisitively. "It really was terrific of you to take such a personal interest." He hesitated. "Do you think you got Michael's father's heart?"

"I don't know, and I don't want to. I would have helped any woman and child trapped in similar circumstances. It's enough for me to know that they're safe and have been given a fresh start."

After delivering them to the shelter, Sherry had called to report that Patricia and Michael had been cordially welcomed by the other battered families living there.

"Patricia's already volunteered to earn extra money for the shelter by stringing beads," Cat told Jeff. "She sells them to a vendor in the Marketplace. Over time and with some training, I think she could become quite an artist."

"Without you, she'd never have had the chance."

Cat gnawed her lower lip thoughtfully. "If Sparky had survived the accident, their lives might have taken a different turn. They might have separated from the bikers' gang when they learned she was pregnant with Michael.

"They'd have reared him together, with love and caring. She might have developed her artistic skills. I've been told that Sparky was extremely intelligent, interested in literature and philosophy. He might have become a teacher or a writer."

"That's a rosy fantasy, Cat. It probably wouldn't have happened that way at all."

"But we'll never know, will we? Because Sparky died."

"And someone else lived," Jeff said softly.

She glanced up quickly, yanking herself away from her disturbing thoughts and clearing the emotional knot from her throat. "Yes, someone else lived."

Later that afternoon, Jeff poked his head into her office. "Mr. Webster just called from upstairs. He wants to see us."

"Right now? I'm up to my armpits in paper."

"He said it can't wait. Any reason why he should be upset?"

"Did he sound upset?"

"Very."

She hadn't seen Bill for several days. When his unsmiling secretary escorted her and Jeff into his office, he showed a marked lack of cordiality. "Sit down, please."

Once they were seated on the leather sofa, he gestured toward his other guest. "This is Ronald Truitt. As you know, he's the entertainment columnist for the *Light*."

So, this plump, fortyish nerd with the receding hairline was Ron Truitt, her journalistic nemesis, the critic from hell.

He was having a nicotine fit. A pack of Camels was in his shirt pocket. He patted it periodically, as though to reassure himself that the cigarettes were still there, even though he couldn't smoke them.

He was trying to appear at ease and nonchalant, but he

wasn't doing a very good job of it. His legs were bouncy, he fidgeted nervously, and he blinked too frequently.

Cat didn't acknowledge Truitt but turned to Bill. "What's going on?"

"As a professional courtesy, Mr. Truitt came to warn me about the contents of his column appearing in tomorrow's newspaper. I thought you deserved to be warned of it, too."

"Warned? That has an ominous ring to it."

"Unfortunately, the column has ominous overtones."

"Regarding *Cat's Kids*?" Jeff asked.

"That's right." Bill turned to the journalist and signaled that he had the floor. "I'll let you speak for yourself, Mr. Truitt. But it should be stated beforehand that everything said in this room is off the record."

"Sure." Truitt sat up straighter and, unnecessarily, flipped open a spiral pad to consult his notes. Cat recognized playacting when she saw it.

"I got a call late this morning," he said, "from a man who called himself Cyclops."

"Cyclops called you?" Cat exclaimed.

"Then you know him?" Bill asked.

"Yes. His real name is George Murphy, and he's wanted by the police. Did he tell you where he was calling from?"

"No." Truitt's grin was brittle. "And he said you'd probably turn the tables and try to make him out the bad guy."

"He *is* the bad guy. He's guilty of a list of crimes as long as my arm, starting with child abuse and ending with extortion."

"Maybe," Truitt said. "But he's alleged that you're no saint."

"I never claimed to be," Cat snapped. "But that's beside the point. Don't you have anything better to write about than a name-calling contest between me and a coke-snorting biker who's being sought by the police?"

"This is somewhat more serious than a name-calling contest," Bill said. "You see, Cat." He paused, then dropped the bomb. "Mr. Murphy has accused you of child molestation."

She was too astonished to speak. She gaped at Bill, then looked at Truitt.

"That's right," he said. "Cyclops told me that you had sexually molested his stepson during a picnic at Mr. Webster's house."

"He doesn't have a stepson," she rasped.

"A kid named Michael?"

"Michael's mother is not married to Mr. Murphy. Legally, he's not the boy's stepfather."

"Well, anyway, he raised the question of whether his kid was the only one you've molested. You certainly have an opportunity to take advantage of many."

"I can't believe this." She gave an incredulous laugh. But no one else was smiling, especially not Webster. "Bill, say something. Surely you don't think—"

"What I think is irrelevant."

She turned to the journalist. "Surely you're not going to print this. First of all, it's ludicrous. Second, without corroboration you'd be leaving yourself open to a libel suit of astronomical proportions."

"I've got corroboration," he said confidently.

Again she was flabbergasted. "From whom?"

"I'm not at liberty to say. My second source chooses to remain anonymous, but I assure you that he or she is in a position to know what they're talking about."

"He or she doesn't know anything!" she cried. "How'd you come across this second source?"

"I started nosing around, talking to people."

"You're making a serious mistake, Mr. Truitt," Cat said evenly. "If you print that column, it could cost you and your newspaper dearly. Anyone who knows me, knows that I do everything within my limited power to rescue children from all forms of abuse—physical and sexual as well as psychological and emotional. If George Murphy wants to accuse me of something, he should make it something more credible.''

''But you're in an excellent position to win the trust of many children, aren't you, Ms. Delaney?'' Truitt asked.

''That's a despicable implication and I refuse to honor it with a response.''

He scooted to the edge of his seat, a shark who smelled blood and was moving in for the kill. ''Why'd you give up a successful career as a soap opera star to do a local program like *Cat's Kids*?''

''Because I wanted to.''

''Why?'' the reporter persisted.

''Well, not so I'd have a source of children to molest!'' she shouted.

''Cat.''

''Well, that's what he's getting at, isn't he?'' She shouldn't be yelling at Jeff. He was only trying to calm her down. After taking a moment to compose herself, she spoke to Truitt in a softer, more reasonable voice. ''I gave up my former career because I wanted to do something meaningful with the rest of my life.''

He made a comical grimace of skepticism. ''Let me get this straight. You gave up an enormous income, stardom, and fame for far less money and four measly minutes of airtime each week?'' He shook his head. ''It just doesn't wash. Nobody's that noble.''

Cat wasn't about to discuss her motives. They were intensely personal. Furthermore, she didn't owe this mean-spirited, chain-smoking hack any explanations. She wanted to throw that into his smug face, but for WWSA's sake, she responded more diplomatically.

''You have nothing whatsoever to substantiate this

ridiculous accusation. Cyclops is hardly a credible source. He's not even articulate."

"I have two sources, remember? The other one is quite credible and articulate."

"Your sources are a reputed criminal and someone who doesn't even have the guts to come forward and accuse me to my face."

"Woodward and Bernstein started with less and ended up frying an administration and making history."

"Charity prohibits me from pointing out how far you are from a Woodward or a Bernstein, Mr. Truitt."

He merely grinned, flipped down the cover of his spiral pad, and stood. "If I turned my back on a story this hot, I'd be drummed out of the press corp."

"It's a lie," Cat said. "A bizarre, unfounded lie."

"Can I quote that?"

"No," Webster said, rising from his chair. "We're still off the record. Ms. Delaney isn't making an official statement at this time."

"Bill, I'm not afraid to—"

"Please, Cat," he said, cutting her off. "You'll be hearing from our public relations department later this afternoon," he told Truitt as he escorted him to the door.

After he left, the silence in the room was funereal. Cat was seething. She glared at Bill, following him with her eyes as he returned to his desk and sat down heavily.

"I'm waiting for an explanation, Bill," she said, rising to her feet. "Why did you sit there mutely and let me be slandered? Why'd you even give him an audience?"

He held up both palms. "Sit down, Cat. Get a grip on yourself and listen to reason."

She sat down, but angrily lashed out, "Do you think I'm a child molester?"

"For God's sake, of course not! But I have to consider what's best for the station."

"Ah, the station. As long as it remains inviolate, my reputation can be thrown to a pack of wild dogs and ripped to shreds."

He looked momentarily chagrined. "We can't stop him from writing and printing the column. All we can do at this juncture is batten down the hatches for the storm it will surely generate. I'll have the public relations department begin gathering character references. You can work with them on an official statement."

"To hell with that," she said. "I won't honor such a heinous lie with a denial." Her eyes smarted with sudden tears. "How could anyone believe that I would harm a child?"

"Your viewing public won't believe it, Cat," Jeff said with conviction. "Not for a second."

"I don't believe they will either," Bill said. "Once the story's printed, there'll be nothing more to say on the matter because there's nothing more to it. Your fans will regard it for what it is, a malicious attack on you by someone who obviously holds a grudge."

"It'll blow over. In a few weeks it'll be forgotten." He paused before adding, "During that time, I'm suspending the production and airing of *Cat's Kids.*"

She didn't trust her hearing. For several moments all she heard was a terrific roaring in her ears. "You . . . you can't possibly mean that."

"I'm sorry. That's my decision."

"But that's tantamount to admitting guilt," she cried. "Bill, I implore you not to take that action."

"You know that I wholeheartedly approve and support the work you've done. It's important to the station. It's made a significant contribution to the community. I want it to resume in due time.

"It also goes without saying that I have a tremendous amount of respect and regard for you, Cat. I hate to disappoint you like this. I'm sure you view my decision as a betrayal, but it's my unpleasant responsibility as CEO to consider what's best for everyone, including you.

"Until this episode is over, I don't think your face should appear on television screens, serving as a reminder of the damaging story." His somber expression and tone underscored that his decision was final.

Cat stared at the floor for several moments, then finally raised her head and stood up. "Very well, Bill. I understand your position. You'll have my resignation by the end of the day."

"What!" Jeff exclaimed.

"Cat—"

"Listen to me, both of you. If that story gets printed, *Cat's Kids* is tainted forever. I could deny the ugly allegations until I'm blue in the face, but it wouldn't do any good. People are prone to believe the worst, especially if they read it. If it's in print, it must be true, right?

"Bill, you said you must consider what's best for the TV station. Well, *I* must consider what's best for the children. Whether Mr. Truitt or anyone else believes it, their welfare was my sole reason for starting *Cat's Kids*. They're still my primary concern.

"They're already innocent victims. I don't want them to be victimized again by eliminating what might be their last hope. If I'm out of the picture, you can change the name of *Cat's Kids* and continue the program. I urge you to start shopping for my replacement immediately."

Chapter Forty-seven

$\sim$

What do you want?"

"I thought you might need some tender loving care. I brought cheeseburgers." Jeff held up a white paper sack so she could see it through the peephole.

"Are they chock-full of fat calories?"

"The sack is almost too heavy to lift."

"In that case . . ." Cat unlatched her front door. Stepping out onto the porch, she gave a wave, then went back inside with Jeff and locked the door.

"What was that all about?"

"Did you notice the car parked down the street? It's a surveillance cop. Until they locate Cyclops, Lieutenant Hunsaker is keeping a twenty-four-hour watch on the house."

"Good idea."

"Alex's idea. I feel like a fool with all this cloak-and-dagger stuff."

They went into the kitchen and began unloading the fast food.

"Early this afternoon, when we went to the police station to give our statements, Alex convinced Hunsaker that my house should be watched in case Cyclops returns. Mmm. These are delicious," she said, devouring another french fry. "Thanks."

"I figured you hadn't eaten."

"I hadn't. I didn't even realize I was hungry."

"Where's Mr. Pierce now?"

"How should I know? I don't keep track of him and vice versa."

She sounded defensive because that's how she felt. Alex hadn't called. Although he knew she wasn't going to California, Cat suspected that he was still angry with her for calling him to her rescue, then spurning him in favor of Dean. That hadn't been her intention, but that's how he'd perceived it.

He'd turned her over to Hunsaker, then washed his hands of her. She wanted to hear his opinion on this latest chain of events but decided against contacting him. He would have to make the next move . . . if there was one.

"I thought he might be staying here with you," Jeff said.

"He did last night." She rubbed her forehead, trying to stave off the headache that always seemed to seize her whenever she tried to make sense of her undefined relationship with Alex. "Mind if we don't talk about him?"

"Not at all. You got ketchup?"

"In the door of the fridge. But use it sparingly. As of this afternoon, I'm unemployed."

"You don't mean to make that resignation stick, do you?"

At first the cheeseburger and fries had smelled delicious. Now, with the reminders of Alex's desertion and Truitt's column, the food was making her queasy.

"I'm in a quandary over what to do, Jeff. Everything's in

such a muddle." She laughed without humor. "You know, I really had it good when my only problem was a terminal heart condition.

"Now, my love life is in shambles. I've got a biker fiend out to skin me. My reputation is about to be trashed by a jugular-seeking journalist, and there's nothing I can do to prevent it." She flashed him a dazzling smile. "Of course, looking on the bright side, in two days a homicidal maniac is likely to spring from nowhere and do me in, saving me from all my other trials and tribulations."

"Two days? Jeez. I hadn't realized."

"Time has flown since I met Cyclops and got involved with Patricia and Michael. The anniversary date sort of crept up on me, too."

"Mr. Pierce isn't any closer to learning who sent those clippings?"

"We knocked around the idea that it might be Cyclops. But after thinking about it, we crossed him off as a possibility. He's not clever enough."

"What about Paul Reyes? Any word on him?"

She had shared with Jeff what Alex had told her about the three incidents that had occurred shortly before her transplant. Per her request, he'd checked the library for newspaper stories relating to them. As a result of his research, they'd read every available account of the Reyes murder trial.

"Alex is still trying to locate a relative who'll talk to him."

"What about the lover?"

"The lover?" she repeated, perplexed. "I don't know."

"Or did any information come out of the multicar accident on the Houston freeway?"

"Not that I know of. I'd almost forgotten about that."

Her telephone rang and she excused herself to answer it. "Hello?"

"Where are they?"

Her heart gave a lurch. "Cyclops?"

Jeff's eyes popped wide. He dropped his hamburger and came out of his chair so fast it fell over backward. "Should I get the cop?" he asked in a stage whisper.

She shook her head and waved him to be silent. As it was, she could barely hear Cyclops over the racket in the background on his end.

"I'm warning you, bitch. You'd better tell me where they are."

"They're someplace where you'll never find them." She spoke calmly and without fear, although her heart was pounding. "They're safe from you. You can never hurt them again."

"Maybe. Maybe not. But I can sure as hell find you, can't I? I know where you work and where you live. None of this would've happened if you hadn't started meddling."

"You won't find me at work. I don't work for WWSA anymore, thanks to you."

"Huh?"

"Don't play dumb, although I realize that's asking a lot. On the other hand, maybe you're smarter than you pretend to be. Only a cunning but twisted mind could devise a lie like that one you told Mr. Truitt."

"Who?"

"The columnist for the *Light*."

"The what? What the fuck are you talking about? Hey, is this call being traced? Are you talking bullshit just to keep me on the phone? *Shit!*"

The line instantly went dead.

Cat continued to hold the receiver to her ear long after she'd gotten a dial tone. Finally she hung it up, but continued staring at it thoughtfully.

"What'd he say?" Jeff asked.

"He, uh . . ."

"Did he tell you where he was? Cat? What's wrong? Cat?"

It took her a moment to shake off her puzzled daze and bring Jeff back into focus. "He's still issuing threats."

"You mean accusing you of child molestation wasn't enough?"

"Cyclops claims not to know anything about that. As strange as it may sound, I think he's telling the truth."

Jeff shook his head in bewilderment. "I don't get it."

"Neither do I."

"Truitt said Cyclops called him. He couldn't have made up that name."

"I don't believe he made it up," Cat said.

"Then he's lying?"

"No, someone called Truitt, all right. And identified himself as Cyclops."

Understanding dawned on Jeff's face. "But it could have been anyone. Probably the same guy who sent you those articles."

"Exactly. This person's omniscient. He seems to be living inside my skin with me. He knows everything that happens almost as soon as I do, including my dealings with Cyclops. Or maybe I'm jumping to conclusions."

With a groan of frustration, she pressed the heels of her hands against her temples. "I don't know what to think anymore, or what to do."

"Hang in there, Cat," Jeff said sympathetically. "Let's approach this pragmatically. Assuming your stalker concocted the child molestation story and called Truitt, who corroborated it? Truitt's ambitious and nasty, but he doesn't strike me as a fool."

"Me either."

"So I don't think he'd stick his neck out unless he really had a second source backing up the allegations."

They bandied it back and forth until Cat's headache grew unbearable. She hadn't slept but a few hours the night before.

Since awakening this morning, she'd dealt with Patricia's unexpected arrival, Truitt and his bad tidings, then Bill's betrayal, and now this.

Her brain was filled to capacity with disturbing data; she couldn't force any more into it. "We're going in circles, Jeff," she said at last. "If you'll forgive me, let's call it a night. I'm going to take a long, hot bubble bath and try to get some sleep."

"I'll be glad to stay with you tonight if you want company."

"Thanks. But I've already got a watchdog—he's parked down the street."

At her front door, Jeff hugged her awkwardly. "Please reconsider your resignation, Cat."

"It's already been submitted."

"But Mr. Webster had already left for the day when you took it upstairs. It's not official until he opens it. Wait and gauge the effect of Truitt's article. It might not turn out the way we expect." He earnestly pressed his point. "You can't walk away from *Cat's Kids*. You and it are one and the same."

"That's what everybody said about me and Laura Madison. The character no longer exists, but the show goes on every day at noon."

"This is different. *Cat's Kids* is your life's mission. It's too important to you. To all of us."

She tried to alleviate his concern with a joke: "You don't fool me, Doyle. You're just trying to protect your job!"

Cat watched him move down the walk and get into his car, then she checked to see that the unmarked police car was still there. At first she'd been opposed to having someone on watch outside her house. Now she drew comfort from knowing that help was nearby.

Cyclops might come back. He was still bloodthirsty. But she truly believed that he knew nothing of the story given to

Truitt. A sneak attack wasn't Cyclops's style. A knife, yes. But not subterfuge.

If he hadn't called Truitt, who had? And how had the caller known to identify himself as her enemy, Cyclops? Who was privy to that much information about the events in her life? Who was Truitt's secret second source?

Still searching for answers, Cat immersed herself in the bubble bath.

Chapter Forty-eight

❧

*H*e grimaced with the force of his thrusts. Blood coursed hotly through his veins. His forehead was beaded with sweat. It rolled into his eyes and made them sting.

He was breathing as though running an uphill marathon, pushing himself to his physical limit, seeking escape from his guilty misgivings, absolution for his transgressions. He didn't delude himself that this was making love. It was self-flagellation.

He took shameless advantage of her sensuality. She never said no. He could take her without a word of affection or a tender caress, and she never complained. She performed on command. The more he demanded, the more she gave.

Her compliance wasn't founded on love, either. And it wasn't charity. She had selfish reasons for wanting to keep him happy and remain his lover. They each took from the affair exactly what they wanted.

The sex was always lusty. Dirty. The raunchier it was, the

more appropriate it seemed. The relationship was illicit. They were already sinners. So they lost nothing by satisfying their basest appetites and acting out their most lascivious fantasies.

Reaching beneath her, he fondled her breasts. His belly made wet, smacking sounds against her buttocks. She didn't like it this way, but her own eroticism governed her. She bowed her back like a cat. Her sharp fingernails clawed at the sheet. She cursed him even as she began to shudder in climax. Sweating profusely, heart pounding, he came at the same time. She fell face first into the bedding; he collapsed on top of her.

After a while she mumbled, "Get off. You're crushing me."

He flopped onto his back, flinging his arms wide, still trying to regain his breath. She crawled on all fours to the edge of the bed, then got up and put on a robe.

"Did I hurt you?" he asked.

"That's part of it, isn't it?"

"I know you'd rather not do it like that."

"I'm sure cavewomen found it very romantic."

He searched her expression for sarcasm and found none. She was rarely critical.

The doorbell rang, surprising them both. He propped himself on his elbows. "Who could that be?"

"I'll have to go see."

"Ignore it."

"I can't. It might be my kid brother looking for a place to crash."

"While I'm here?" he asked in alarm. The idea of someone seeing him at her apartment made him uneasy.

"Relax. He doesn't ask questions. What I do is my business."

She made certain her robe was securely belted, then jogged downstairs and answered the door. "What in the world are you doing here?" he heard her exclaim.

"Hello, Melia. May I come in?"

It wasn't her brother. It wasn't anybody's brother. It was Cat.

"Jesus," he groaned, dragging his hand down his flushed face. The sweat cooling on his body gave him a chill, and he shivered.

"What do you want?" Melia asked ungraciously.

"We need to clear the air. May I come in?"

He heard the door close and pictured the two women squaring off.

"Okay, you're in," Melia said. "Now what?"

"It's been you all along, hasn't it? You're the one playing dirty tricks."

"I don't know what the hell you're talking about," Melia said heatedly. "Where do you get off, coming over here in the middle of the night without an invitation and start talking nonsense? Jesus! You've gotta be the most paranoid person in the world. I think you need a psychiatrist."

Cat didn't back down. "The clue was there all the time, only I didn't see it until tonight while I was soaking in my bubble bath. Then, *voilà!* Your name just popped into my head. King."

"I know my name," Melia said drolly.

"But that's not your legal name, is it? That's not the one you were born with. Your birth name was Reyes. You've Anglicized it to King."

"Is that right?"

"I'd bet on it. And you were related to Paul Reyes."

"Who?"

"Paul Reyes."

"Maybe. I don't know all the twigs on my family tree."

"You'd remember this twig," Cat said. "He made headlines after killing his wife with a baseball bat. He stood trial for murder, but was acquitted."

"Look, I don't have a clue what you're talking about. I

don't know anybody named Reyes. So why don't you get the hell out of my house?''

Cat plowed on relentlessly. ''Paul Reyes donated his wife's heart for transplantation.''

''As if I care.''

''I think you care very much. I think he cares very much, too. He cares so much, he wants to stop his unfaithful wife's heart. How does it work? Let's see. You find the transplantees and set them up, then he comes in to make the kill, right?''

''I don't—''

''Of course it's you!'' Cat said. ''You had access to everything that crossed my desk. You were privy to incoming and outgoing calls. You knew everything that went on in my life.''

''All I know is that you're a freaking nutcase,'' Melia shouted.

''All station personnel were invited to the barbecue, so you saw me there with Michael. Today, you heard about my encounter with Cyclops. You knew Truitt was no fan of mine or *Cat's Kids*. He'd be eager to hear even a breath of scandal about me.

''So you had someone call him, probably Reyes himself. He identified himself as Cyclops and told that outlandish story. Then, when Truitt began investigating the allegations, you were all too willing to corroborate them. What could be worse—a program designed to help children is actually a hotbed of molestation and abuse.''

''You've got one active imagination, lady.''

''I didn't imagine that studio light falling on me.''

''I had nothing to do with that!''

''I didn't imagine my medication being thrown into a Dumpster.''

''I was pissed at you.''

''Why?''

''For being such a bitch!''

"Or for having a heart that you and your family want stopped."

"I already told you, I don't even know anybody named Reyes."

"Judy Reyes was screwing around. The whole family was offended, right? You appointed yourself the avenger."

"I can't believe this!"

"Oh, I can," Cat said. "Once I got the clue about your name, everything else fell into place. You've been harassing me. The light, the clippings sent anonymously, the story told to Truitt. Those were planned to weaken me. Break me down. Make me vulnerable.

"Then, when I showed up dead—maybe by suicide?— everyone would say, 'You know, she's been acting awfully weird. For months she's been on the verge of flipping out.'

"Tell me, Melia, how did you and Paul Reyes plan to kill me? Run me off the road and make it look like an accident? Poke pills down my throat to seem like an overdose? Another accident in the studio? What?"

"Stop yelling at me," Melia threatened. "I don't know anything about this."

"The hell you don't."

"Okay! Sure I know you've been getting some anonymous mail, but it didn't come from me. I didn't rig that studio light to fall, either. Do you think I shimmied up a pole and unbolted it? Get real."

"This is real," Cat said emphatically. "You came to work at WWSA shortly after it was announced that I would be moving here. You made that happen. And you've hated me from the minute you laid eyes on me," Cat accused.

"I don't deny that. But it has nothing to do with your stupid heart!"

"Then what?"

"She thought I had a romantic interest in you."

Bill Webster watched from the second-floor gallery as Cat

looked up. When she spotted him, her features went slack with disbelief. Her wide blue eyes followed him as he descended the stairs. He'd pulled on his pants and shirt, but his feet were bare.

He knew it was apparent that he'd just come from Melia's bed and that he didn't have a prayer at self-defense. Babbling excuses or denials would cost him what shreds of dignity he had remaining.

"There's only one logical conclusion you can draw from this awkward situation, Cat." He glanced at Melia, who looked as disheveled as he, if not more so. "In this instance, appearances aren't deceiving. It's exactly what it seems."

He moved to the small cabinet that Melia kept stocked with liquor for him. "I need a drink. Ladies?"

He poured himself a stiff scotch and drank it in one swallow. Melia settled into a corner of the sofa. She was studying her fingernails and looking somewhat bored. Cat appeared to have taken root in the center of the floor.

"I upbraided Melia severely for what she did with your medication," he began. "It was a childishly stupid stunt, and I warned her that nothing like that was ever to happen again."

"He chewed my ass," Melia said with a pout.

The fiery accusation in Cat's eyes was quelling, but he forced himself not to flinch.

"I regret that you learned about . . . this," he said. "But since you were falsely accusing Melia, I felt compelled to step in and set the record straight."

At last Cat spoke. "This is unbelievable. And yet it explains so much, like why you rehired her after I'd fired her." She expelled her breath in disgust, a reaction that didn't surprise him. "You know that Nancy suspects you're having an affair with me?"

"We haven't discussed it," he lied.

"Why would you sleep with *her*," she nodded contemptuously toward Melia, "when you're married to a wonderful woman like Nancy?"

"If she's so bloody wonderful, what's he doing in my bed?" Melia asked. "Screwing his brains out, that's what," she added smugly.

"Please, Melia, let me handle this." To Cat he said, "This is my business, Cat. You've made it clear on several occasions that you don't welcome my interference in your private life. I deserve the same courtesy."

"Okay. Fine," she said shortly. "But I think your mistress is the one who's been harassing me."

"You're wrong," he said simply.

"I haven't had time to check her credentials and find out where she's been and what she's been doing the last few years, but I intend to. And if I discover that she's been anywhere near those three transplantees who died, I'll notify the Department of Justice."

"I've lived in Texas all my life," Melia said. "And for your information, my father's name *is* King. I'm only one-quarter Hispanic, so that shoots this Reyes theory of yours all to hell. And anyway, I don't give a damn where your heart came from. I just didn't want you to think you could waltz in here and take Bill away from me."

"He doesn't belong to you."

Melia snorted. "Oh, yeah? If you'd gotten here about five minutes earlier, you'd know otherwise. I had him on his knees."

Bill felt his face turning red. "Melia was jealous of you when you first arrived," he told Cat. "She thought I might replace her with you. I've assured her that's not the nature of our friendship."

Cat turned back to Melia, who was idly combing her fingers through her long hair. "I don't believe your innocent act. At the very least you corroborated that ridiculous story about child molestation, didn't you?"

Melia's hand fell to her side. Her dark eyes flickered

guiltily. Bill stepped closer to her. "Melia? Did you?" She looked up at him, her expression sullen. And guilty. He had an intense desire to slap her hard across the face. *"Answer me."*

She bounded off the couch. "This guy calls me today, okay? He repeats what some biker named Cyclops had told him over the telephone and asked if I knew anything about it. I told him, sure. I saw Cat Delaney with that kid at the barbecue. She carted him around all night, acted real taken with him. Truitt asked if she'd had any opportunities to be alone with the boy. Again I said, sure. With my own eyes I saw her take him into the house when no one else was around.

"Then he asked if this could be tied to that other incident, when the couple backed out of that adoption. Could that little girl have possibly been one of Cat's victims, too? I told him I'd better not address that because I'd been on the staff of *Cat's Kids* when it happened and didn't want to incriminate myself along with her."

"My God," Cat whispered with a mix of repugnance and awe. Then she turned to him. "You'd better keep her happy, Bill. If you ever end this shabby little affair, God only knows the havoc she'll wreak on your life. Not that you don't deserve it."

Her anger continued to build. "Her unfounded jealousy of me almost destroyed *Cat's Kids*. She could have undone everything we've accomplished. Her lie could have affected dozens of children's lives. They would have been deprived of a future, and all because of that . . ." She flung her hand toward Melia. "Is she worth it?"

"I won't allow you to pass judgment on Melia and me, Cat," he said in a feeble attempt to defend himself. "However, I am sorry that you were hassled today."

"Hassled?" she repeated, implying what a ludicrous understatement that was. "Being sorry isn't enough. You can't fix this with an apology."

She lifted the cordless phone off the end table and pitched it to him. "I'm sure you know the managing editor of the *Light*. Call him. Stop them from printing that story."

"That's impossible, Cat. It's too late. I'm sure it's already being printed."

"Then you'd better trot down there and pull the plug on the presses yourself. If you don't stop that story, I swear they'll have another one tomorrow that will totally obscure the one about me! I'd hate to do that to Nancy, but I would in order to safeguard *Cat's Kids*. And you know me well enough to know that I'm not bluffing."

She glared at Melia. "As for you, you're a slut. A silly, malicious, spoiled slut."

Then she turned her contempt onto Bill again. "And you're a joke. A pathetic, middle-age-crazy cliché, trying to recapture your youth with your pecker. And to think I once admired you."

She sneered scornfully, then moved to the door. "I suggest you make that call before it gets any later."

Chapter Forty-nine

With barely an hour to go before dawn, Cat returned home. When she'd left Melia's apartment, she'd been too upset to sleep. But that had been hours ago. Now she felt she could sleep for a month. She stepped out of her shoes and pulled her shirttail from the waistband of her jeans as she headed for her bedroom.

"Where the hell have you been?"

The voice boomed out at her from the darkness of her living room. "Damn you, Alex!"

"I've been waiting on you half the night."

He switched on the table lamp and blinked against the sudden brightness. Then he rose from the easy chair in which he'd been lounging. "Where the hell have you been all this time?"

"Driving."

"Driving?"

"San Antonio doesn't have a beach, so I made do."

"Is that supposed to make sense?"

"Not to you. It does to me. What are you doing in my house? I didn't see your car outside. How'd you get in?"

"My car's parked on the next block. I walked through the backyards and broke in through the kitchen window, same as I did before. It's a flimsy lock. You should have it replaced. Why wasn't your alarm set?"

"I figured it wasn't necessary since there's a cop parked down the street watching the house."

"Getting past him was a snap. If I can do it, someone else can."

"So much for Hunsaker's surveillance," she muttered.

"Why wasn't he tailing you?"

"He tried to follow me when I left. I told him I was only going out for milk and bread and would be right back. Just now, when I drove past, I caught him yawning. I think he was waking up from a long nap."

"Figures. You okay?" She nodded. "You don't look okay. You look like shit," he said candidly. "Where'd you go on this drive that lasted for hours?"

"Nowhere. Everywhere. And stop grilling me. You're the intruder here, not me. I'm hungry."

Her hopes for getting to sleep anytime soon had been dashed, so she decided she might just as well appease her hunger. She hadn't eaten since the few bites of the cheeseburger that Jeff had brought her earlier.

Alex followed her into the kitchen. She took a box of cereal from the pantry and shook some into a bowl. "Want some?"

"No thanks."

"Why were you waiting for me?"

"Later. Let's hear from you first. Where'd you go and why? What's been going on since you left Hunsaker's office yesterday afternoon?"

Around a mouthful of granola, raisins, and slivered almonds, she said, "You wouldn't believe it."

"Give it a shot."

She motioned for him to sit down. He straddled one of her kitchen chairs. Between bites she told him about Ron Truitt and all that had ensued after he'd dropped his bombshell. "As it turns out, it wasn't Cyclops who called him."

"How do you know?"

"Last night, while Jeff and I were sitting here and I was crying in my beer over the pending demise of *Cat's Kids*, the biker from hell called. He's not too happy with me, but he pled ignorance to the scoop given to Truitt."

"He could have been lying."

"Possibly, but that's not the impression I got."

"If not him, who?"

"That remains a mystery. But I know who corroborated the story. Melia King. You remember her," she added sweetly. "The walking wet dream?"

Alex wasn't amused. "That makes sense," he said grimly. "There's been bad blood between you two from the get-go."

"And now I know why. She's been sleeping with— euphemistically—the man who's suspected of having the hots for me."

"Webster!"

"I can't tell you what a blow it was to my ego to discover that he prefers her to me," she said caustically. Then she recounted for him the scene at Melia's apartment.

"That son of a bitch," Alex said, hitting the table with his fist. "I knew he was a slippery bastard. Didn't I tell you?"

"I've always thought of Bill as being extremely astute. Even shrewd, but in a constructive way. As it turns out, he's a lying, cheating adulterer. And in my opinion that's the lowest life form on the planet. I don't understand why that's such a hard commandment to keep. If you want to screw around, you don't get married.'' She noticed Alex's wince. ''You don't agree?''

''I agree that it looks good on paper. It's rarely that simple. Sometimes there are extenuating circumstances.''

''Rationalizations, you mean. But I don't see how Bill could even rationalize this affair.''

She was furious with him, but she also felt a keen sense of loss. Bill Webster certainly wasn't accountable to her for what he did in his private life. All the same, she felt betrayed by a man she had admired and respected. The betrayal hurt.

''Why would he jeopardize his marriage to a classy lady like Nancy for that sulky little tramp?''

''Maybe Melia delivers the goods.''

''I'm sure she does. What really upsets me is that Nancy thinks I'm the delivery girl.''

Finished with her cereal, she left the table and began making coffee. ''I could throttle him. *Cat's Kids* was almost destroyed because he can't keep his pants zipped. All during this showdown, he tried to maintain his dignity, but I could tell he was embarrassed. I hope he was mortified. I hope he gets a bad case of the palm-sweats the next time he, Nancy, and I are in the same room. Coffee?''

''Please.''

She returned to the table with two cups of the fresh brew. ''After leaving Melia's, I was too upset to come home, so I drove around for hours, trying to make sense of everything.''

''Do you think Webster can halt the story?''

''I think he'll go to any lengths to try. Short of that, he'll demand a retraction of equal length and prominence, and insist that the newspaper accept full responsibility for the error.''

She smiled wanly. ''Having avoided that disaster, I've only got to worry about living through the day after tomorrow.''

"It's nothing to joke about."

"You're telling me."

"There is some good news."

"I could use some."

"Irene Walters called this afternoon. Guess who's spending the weekend with them? Joseph."

Gladness spread through her chest. "That's . . . that's wonderful. Oh, I hope it works out. He's so clever. So sweet. And I'll never forget him telling me that he wouldn't be mad at me if he wasn't adopted."

"My guess is he's a shoo-in," Alex said, chuckling. "She said they saw the segment on him and fell instantly in love. They have to complete the parenting course, but in the meantime, he's going for a visit. Charlie wants to start teaching him how to play chess. Irene's got a list of his favorite foods. They're even sprucing up Bandit so he'll make a good first impression."

Not until he reached out and stroked her cheek did she realize they were wet with tears. "That is good news. Thanks for telling me."

He wiped her cheeks dry with a napkin, then stared deeply into her eyes. "Who called the newspaper, Cat?"

"I don't know."

"I'm guessing it's your original stalker."

"Me too. He's still out there, playing with me. But how'd he know about Cyclops?"

"Your phone could be tapped. Your house could be bugged." He paused. "Or . . . it could be someone close to you, someone you trust and would never suspect."

The coffee she'd drunk turned rancid in her stomach, because Alex's conclusion matched the one she'd reached on her long drive through the sleeping city.

She stood up quickly. "I need a shower."

"Better hurry." He checked his wristwatch. "Our flight's in two hours."

"Flight?"

"That's what I came to tell you. I've tracked down Paul Reyes's sister. She lives in Fort Worth and has agreed to talk to us."

Chapter Fifty

❧

They got caught in morning rush hour traffic and barely made it to the airport in time to catch their flight. Less than an hour later, they disembarked at Love Field in Dallas, where Alex had reserved a rental car.

"This thirty-mile drive to Fort Worth will take longer than the flight," he remarked as they left the airport.

"Do you know where you're going?" Cat was looking at the city's glittering skyline. She'd never been to Dallas and wished this trip were merely for sightseeing.

"Mrs. Reyes-Dunne gave me directions. Anyway, I know the general vicinity."

"How'd you locate her?"

"I once worked a case with FWPD and became good buddies with one of their detectives. Several days ago I called him and asked if he remembered the Reyes case. Hard to forget it, he said, although he hadn't followed it much after the trial was moved to Houston.

"As a favor, I asked him to track down some of Paul Reyes's family and explained why. I stressed it wasn't a police-related matter.

"A few days later, he called and told me he'd located Reyes's sister. He said she was wary, so he left the choice up to her. He gave her my number in case she decided to talk. Lo and behold, when I got back from Hunsaker's office yesterday, she'd left a message on my machine. I called her back and she agreed to this appointment."

"Did she give you any information over the phone?"

"No. She only confirmed that she was the sister of the Paul Reyes I was looking for. All her answers to my questions were guarded, but she was interested in the prospect that you might have received Judy Reyes's heart."

Following both the road map and his instinct, he navigated the labyrinth of expressways connecting the two cities. One community seamlessly merged with another to form a large suburban sprawl.

Alex found the street they were looking for in an older neighborhood west of downtown Fort Worth, off Camp Bowie Boulevard. He parked at the curb in front of the neat brick home. The front yard was shaded by a large sycamore tree. Fallen leaves crunched beneath their feet as he and Cat made their way up the walk.

A pretty Hispanic woman stepped onto the porch to greet them. She was dressed in a white nurse's uniform. "Are you Mr. Pierce?"

"Yes, I am. Mrs. Dunne, this is Cat Delaney."

"How do you do?" The woman shook hands with both of them. She held on to Cat's hand for a long time while visually exploring her face. "You think you got Judy's heart?"

"It's possible."

The woman continued to stare at her, then, remembering her manners, gestured them into the wicker chairs on the porch. "We could go inside if you'd rather."

"This is fine," Cat said, taking a seat.

"I like to soak up all the fresh air I can before reporting to work."

"You're a nurse?"

"Yes, at John Peter Smith, the county hospital. My husband is a radiologist there. I'm currently working the late shift." She glanced up at the sky. "I miss daylight."

Then she turned to Alex and said, "I'm not sure why you wanted to see me. You were rather vague over the telephone."

"We're interested in locating your brother."

"That's what I was afraid of. Has he done something wrong?"

Cat glanced at Alex to see if he found any significance to those two innocent statements. Obviously he did. He was sitting on the edge of his seat—literally.

"Has your brother been in trouble since he was acquitted of his wife's murder?"

Mrs. Dunne answered Cat's question with one of her own. "What do you want with him? I won't tell you anything until I know what brought you here."

From a manila envelope Alex withdrew the newspaper clippings that had been sent to Cat. He passed them to Reyes's sister. "Have you ever seen these before?"

As she read the newspaper accounts, it became increasingly clear that they disturbed her. Behind her glasses, her eyes filled with apprehension. "What do these have to do with Paul?"

"Possibly nothing," Cat said gently. "But I'd like to call your attention to the dates on them. It's tomorrow's date. It's the date on which these three, supposedly unrelated deaths occurred. It's also the anniversary of your sister-in-law's murder and my transplant.

"We—Mr. Pierce and I—don't believe those three transplantees died accidentally. We think they might have

been killed by a donor's family member who wants to stop
the donated heart on the date it was harvested.''

Mrs. Dunne took a tissue from her pocket and blotted her
tears. "My brother loved Judy to distraction. What he did to
her was horrible. I'm not condoning it. He acted out a fit of
jealous rage, but not because he hated her. He loved her so
much that when he saw her with another man . . .''

She paused to dab at her nose. "Judy was very pretty, you
see. She'd been the love of his life since they were children.
She was intelligent, much smarter than Paul. Because of that,
he'd placed her on a pedestal.''

"The top of a pedestal can be a lonely place," Cat
remarked.

"Yes. I think that's true," the nurse agreed. "I don't
excuse Judy's adultery, but I can understand it. She wasn't
an immoral woman. In fact, she was devoutly religious.
Falling in love with another man must have been a tremendous
personal conflict for her.

"I'm sure if you could ask her now, she would say that
Paul was justified in what he did, and that she forgave him.
I doubt she would ever forgive herself for the destruction she
caused in his life and that of their children.''

She cleared her throat. "I also believe Judy would still be
in love with this man. It wasn't a casual affair. She loved
him enough to die for him.''

Cat remembered Jeff asking her about the lover; her own
interest had been piqued. "What happened to him?''

"I wish I knew." Mrs. Dunne's voice conveyed her bitter
antipathy. "The coward ran. He never came forward. Paul—
none of us—ever even knew his name.''

Cat touched her hand. "Mrs. Dunne, do you know where
your brother is?''

She divided a cautious glance between them. "Yes.''

"Could you arrange for us to talk to him?''

No answer.

Alex leaned toward her. "Is there a remote possibility that he sent Ms. Delaney these clippings and the phony obituary as some sort of warning? I know you don't want to incriminate your brother, but is there even a slim chance he committed three murders in order to stop Judy's heart?"

"No! Paul's not a violent man." Realizing the absurdity of that statement in light of the crime he'd committed, she amended it. "Only that once. Judy's betrayal drove him crazy. Otherwise, he could never have raised a hand to her."

Cat said, "What prompted him to donate her heart for transplantation?"

"I . . . I asked him about that later. Some members of the family were very upset over that. Paul . . ." Her eyes fluttered behind her glasses.

"What? What'd he say?"

Softly she replied, "He said, for what she'd done, she deserved to have her heart cut out."

Alex turned to Cat and looked at her meaningfully. "And now he can't live with knowing that her unfaithful heart still beats."

"My brother isn't harassing Ms. Delaney," Mrs. Dunne said sharply. "I'm sure of it. He wouldn't punish anyone else for the sins of Judy and her lover." She stood. "I'm sorry, but I must leave for work soon."

"Please," Cat said, standing and grasping her hand. "If you know where your brother is, please tell us."

"He dropped out of sight after the trial in Houston," Alex said, prompting her. "Why, since he'd been acquitted?"

"For the girls' sake. His daughters. He didn't want to be an embarrassment to them." She glanced over her shoulder into an open window on the porch. "They live with my husband and me. We have legal custody."

"Does Paul come to see them?"

She hesitated. "Sometimes."

"How does he support himself?" Her failure to respond

didn't deter Alex. "Could he have traveled to these other states? Have there been extended periods of time when you didn't know where he was?"

"If you know anything, please tell us," Cat urged. "It could save lives. Mine and his. Please."

Mrs. Dunne sat back down, bowed her head, and began to cry. "My brother has suffered such heartache. When he killed Judy—and he killed her despite the jury's ruling—he died himself. He's still deeply disturbed. But what you're suggesting he's capable of is so terrible, I—"

"Has he recently been in San Antonio?"

Mournfully, she shrugged. "I don't know. I suppose it's possible."

Cat and Alex glanced at each other, excited now.

"But he recently showed up here," she added.

"He's here? In the house?"

"No. He's here in Fort Worth."

"Can we see him?"

"Please don't ask that. Can't you leave him alone?" She sobbed. "Every day, for the rest of his life, he has to live with what he did."

"What if he harms Ms. Delaney? Will you be able to live with that?" Alex asked her.

"He won't harm her."

"How do you know?"

"I know." She removed her glasses and dried her eyes. Then, in a very dignified manner, she replaced her glasses and stood up. "If you insist on seeing him, come with me."

Even from the outside the facility looked foreboding. Most of the windows had bars. They were required to pass through a series of security checks before being admitted into the ward.

"I'm not sure this is a good idea." The staff psychiatrist shook his head doubtfully. They had already explained the situation to him and asked his permission to talk to Paul Reyes. "I haven't had time to complete my analysis. My patient's well-being is my first priority."

"Your patient might be implicated in three murders," Alex said.

"But if he's locked up here, he can't harm Ms. Delaney. Certainly not tomorrow."

"We need to know if Reyes is the one who's been stalking her."

"Or rule him out as a suspect."

"Exactly."

"You're no longer a police officer, are you, Mr. Pierce? What jurisdiction do you have here?"

"Absolutely none."

"We just want to see him and ask him a few questions," Cat said to the doctor. "And gauge his reaction to seeing me. We wouldn't do anything to jeopardize his mental health."

The psychiatrist turned to Reyes's sister. "You know him best, Mrs. Dunne. What's your evaluation?"

He trusted her opinion because she was a psychiatric nurse on staff in the women's wing of the hospital. She'd explained that to Alex and Cat on the way over.

"If I thought it might be harmful," she said, "I wouldn't have brought them. I think seeing him will cancel their suspicions."

The doctor weighed his decision thoughtfully. Finally, he agreed. "Two or three minutes, max. No tough stuff." He addressed the last remark to Alex. "Burt will go with you."

Burt, a black man in white pants and T-shirt, was as physically imposing as an NFL linebacker.

"How is my brother today?" Mrs. Dunne asked him.

"He did some reading this morning," he replied over his wide shoulders as they followed him down the corridor. "I think he's playing cards in the rec room now."

They entered a large, bright room where ̣atients were

watching television, playing board games, reading, and milling about.

"That's him." Alex pointed out Paul Reyes to Cat. "I recognize him from his trial in Houston."

Reyes was slightly built and partially bald. He was sitting apart from the others, staring into space, seemingly in a world of his own. His hands were loosely clasped between his knees.

"He's been medicated," Burt told them. "So y'all should be able to have a quiet visit. But as the doc said, if the patient gets upset, you'll have to leave right away."

"We understand," Mrs. Dunne said.

Burt withdrew, but only as far as the door. Cat noticed several other uniformed personnel mingling with the patients. Looking around, she felt compassion for each of them. They were grown men, but as dependent as children, living in confinement, locked inside walls and their own emotional misery.

Mrs. Dunne seemed to read Cat's depressing thoughts. She said, "For what it is, this is an excellent facility. We have wonderful, caring doctors on staff."

Her brother hadn't noticed her yet. She regarded him with pity. "Paul arrived at the house unexpectedly three days ago. We never know when he's going to pop in or what condition he'll be in when he does. Sometimes he'll stay for a few days and everything will be fine."

Her eyes clouded. "Other times, we're forced to commit him to the hospital until he gets better. Like this time. He was extremely depressed when he arrived. I attributed it to the date. Tomorrow, it will be four years since . . . But you know that."

Cat nodded.

"He began behaving irrationally. The girls love him, but they were frightened. My husband and I brought him here for analysis. We were strongly urged to commit him so he could undergo complete psychiatric testing.'' Tears filled her eyes as she gazed at her brother. "Is it absolutely necessary for you to disturb him?"

"I'm afraid so," Alex replied, giving Cat no opportunity to speak. "If only for a minute. We'll make it as easy and brief as possible."

Mrs. Dunne placed her fingertips against her lips to keep them from trembling. "When we were children, he was so sweet. Never in trouble. Kind and gentle. If he killed those people, I know he didn't mean to. It was another personality living inside him, not my sweet Paul."

Alex laid a consoling hand on her arm. "We don't know anything for certain yet."

Mrs. Dunne led them to her brother. She placed her hand on his shoulder and softly spoke his name. He raised his head and looked up at her, but his eyes were vacant.

"Hello, Paul. Are you having a good day?" She sat in the chair beside his and covered his listless hands with hers.

"Tomorrow's the day." His voice was hoarse, as though his throat was very dry from disuse. "That's the day I found her with him."

"Try not to think about it."

"I always think about it."

Mrs. Dunne nervously moistened her lips. "Someone wants to see you, Paul. This is Mr. Pierce. And this is Ms. Delaney."

While she was speaking, he gave Alex an indifferent glance, but when his eyes moved to Cat, he suddenly sprang out of his chair. "Did you get the things I sent you? Did you? Did you?"

Instinctively, Cat recoiled. Alex stepped between her and Reyes. Mrs. Dunne grabbed her brother's arm. Burt came running and would have subdued the patient if Cat hadn't intervened.

"Please," she said, stepping out from behind Alex. "Let

him talk." Speaking directly to Reyes, she asked, "Did you send me those clippings?"

"Yes."

"Why?"

Despite her fearlessness, Burt had a firm grip on Reyes's upper arm. Mrs. Dunne still had hold of the other. "You're going to die. Like the others. Like that old lady. And the boy. He drowned, you know. Hours in the water before they found him. The other one . . ."

"Severed his femoral artery with a chain saw," Alex said.

"Yes, yes." He sprayed them with spittle. His eyes glowed feverishly. "Now you. You're going to die because you got her heart!"

"Oh, my God," his sister moaned. "Paul, what have you done?"

"Did you kill those three people, Reyes?" Alex asked.

His head made a quick swiveling movement, very much like an owl. He fixed his wide, wild eyes on Alex. "Who are you? Do I know you? I know you!"

"Answer the question. Did you kill those transplantees?"

"I killed my whore of a wife," he shouted. "She was lying with him. I saw them. So I killed her. I'm glad. She deserved to die. I wish I could kill her over and over again. I wish I could have killed him, too, and licked his blood off my hands."

He was growing more agitated by the second and began struggling against Burt's restraint. Burt called for assistance. Because of the commotion Reyes was creating, other patients were becoming restless and anxious.

The doctor rushed in. "I was afraid of this. Out of here, now!" he shouted.

"Wait! Just a second more, please." Cat stepped closer to Reyes. "Why did you bother to warn me?"

"You got a heart. I read about you. Do you have Judy's heart?"

Somehow managing to wrestle free of Burt, Reyes lurched forward and splayed his hand over Cat's chest. "Oh, Jesus. Oh, God," he groaned when he felt her heartbeat. "My Judy. My beautiful Judy. Why? Why? I loved you. But you had to die."

"Paul," his sister cried in a ragged voice. "God forgive you."

Burt's massive arms encircled the patient and pulled him away. Alex shoved Cat aside. She'd been stunned by Reyes's action and yet strangely moved. The man's agony was intense. He'd been driven mad by love and guilt and rage. She felt more sympathy than fear.

Alex placed his arm around her. "You okay?"

She nodded, watching with pity and horror as Reyes struggled with Burt, who was having difficulty holding him back as he strained forward, yelling, "You'll die!"

The cords in his neck bulged against his skin. His face was mottled and distorted. "Tomorrow. That's the day. Like the others, you'll die."

The doctor plunged a syringe into Paul Reyes's biceps. He seemed impervious to the jab of the needle, but almost instantly he slumped against the burly attendant.

He struggled to focus on Cat one final time. "You'll die, too," he rasped.

Then he succumbed to the powerful drug.

Chapter Fifty-one

"What're you thinking?" Alex handed her a glass of soda, then stretched out on the chaise lounge next to hers.

They were relaxing on his deck. The sun had set, but it was still light. Steaks were grilling on the hibachi. Periodically, fatty juice dripped onto the smoldering coals and, with a sizzling hiss, sent up a cloud of aromatic smoke. Cat hadn't talked much during the return flight to San Antonio. When he suggested picking up something to cook at his place, she'd agreed out of indifference. Sensing her need for introspection, he hadn't pressed her for conversation until now.

She took a sip of soda, then, with a sigh, laid her head back and gazed up at the deep lavender sky. "I can't really believe it's over. I thought I'd feel more . . . relieved. And I am," she hastened to say. "But I keep seeing him screaming at me."

"He can't make good his threats, Cat. There's no reason for you to be afraid anymore. After what we heard today, which was practically a confession, Paul Reyes will never leave that institution.

"The Justice Department will check into his activities for the past several years. My guess is they'll find that his path crossed those of the transplantees who died.

"If he's indicted, he'll probably be declared incompetent to stand trial. But if his mental condition ever improves and there is a trial, he'll no doubt be convicted and sentenced to life in prison. Either way, you're safe from him."

"I don't actually fear him, Alex. I pity him. He must have loved her terribly much."

"Enough to bash in her skull?"

"Exactly." She gave a serious answer to his caustic question. "When he pressed his hand over my heart, I saw more pain than hatred in his eyes. His wife's unfaithfulness destroyed him. He was outside himself when he picked up that baseball bat. He killed her, but he still loves her and grieves for her. Maybe that's why—"

"What?"

"Never mind. It's crazy."

"Tell me anyway."

"Maybe that's why he gave his consent for her heart to be harvested. He wanted to kill her, but he didn't really want her dead."

"Then why'd he bump off three people to stop her heart?"

She gave him a weak smile and shrugged. "That's a definite hole in my theory. I told you it was crazy."

He swung his feet off the chaise and sat up to face her. "You know, in another life, you might have done police work yourself, Cat Delaney. You have a knack for deductive reasoning." He looked deeply into her eyes. His voice lowered to an intimate pitch. "I'm glad it's over for you."

She took a deep breath and let it go slowly. "So am I."

"Ready for supper?"

"I'm starving."

Food would slake her hunger. She wished there were an instant erasure for memory. The scene at the mental hospital would stay with her for a long time.

Mrs. Reyes-Dunne had been distraught. Weeping, she had confessed to them that she had lied about the clippings; she had seen them before.

"I was doing Paul's laundry and came across them in his suitcase," she had said. "At the time, I wondered where he'd gotten them since they were from out of state. But I never brought it up. The less said about heart transplantation, the better.

"You see, some members of our family were as upset with him for donating Judy's heart as they were that he'd killed her. Some thought she had it coming. Machismo, you know?"

Cat and Alex had nodded their understanding.

"His wife was found cheating, so killing her was justifiable. But taking her organs, and not burying them intact, violated religious and cultural traditions."

As she talked, her distress increased. "Maybe if I'd said something to Paul when I found the clippings, you would have been spared this terrible ordeal," she had said to Cat.

"If I'd realized the extent of Paul's insanity sooner, those other people wouldn't have died. I know what drove him to kill Judy, but I can't believe that my brother would cold-bloodedly murder a stranger."

"He was rekilling Judy, not the other individuals," Alex had reminded her.

"I realize that. All the same, I can't believe Paul is capable of doing such a thing."

Both Cat and Alex had tried to console her, but to little avail. She knew, as they did, that her brother would be institutionalized for the remainder of his life. He would never recover from his beloved Judy's infidelity. His daughters would grow up without either parent and would always bear the stigma of their father's crime.

Cat knew what that was like. Her heart went out to the girls, whom she'd never met.

She and Alex sat down to dinner and feasted on the steaks, baked potatoes, salad, and a pecan pie that Cat had selected from the supermarket bakery.

Alex pushed aside his empty plate and leaned back in his chair, stretching out his long legs. "You know what impresses me most about you?"

"The amount of food I can consume at one sitting?" she joked, patting her full stomach.

"That, too," he said, grinning. "For a skinny gal you can sure pack it away."

"Thank you, sir," she drawled. "I don't recall ever receivin' such a flatterin' compliment."

When his laughter subsided, he turned serious. "Actually, I was going to say that I'm impressed by your courage. Today you held your ground even when Reyes touched you. Something as traumatic as that . . ." He shook his head. "Anybody else would have freaked. I've never known a woman—and damned few men—as brave as you. I mean that, Cat."

She absently stabbed her fork into the remains of her pie. "I'm not brave, Alex."

"I disagree."

She dropped her fork and looked at him. "I'm not courageous. In fact, I'm a coward. If I were brave, my parents wouldn't have died."

He cocked his head. "How do you figure that?"

She'd never told anyone what really happened that afternoon the school nurse brought her home early—not the child welfare personnel, not the counselors who tried to determine how badly the experience had affected little Catherine Delaney, not any of her foster parents, not Dean. No one.

But now she felt an overwhelming need to unburden herself to Alex.

"It didn't happen exactly the way I told you before," she said quietly. "The nurse brought me home from school early. It was odd to see my father's car in the driveway. Ordinarily he would have been at work at that time of day. He rarely took off, even on the weekends. You see, he had to work extra long hours to pay my medical bills. Even at that, he'd gone into debt, and the creditors were howling.

"I didn't understand all the terminology. Words like *second mortgage, lien, collateral,* weren't in my vocabulary yet. But those words frequently entered into my parents' subdued conversations."

Stalling, she folded her napkin very neatly and laid it beside her plate. "That day, the moment I stepped through the kitchen door, I sensed that something was wrong. The house had a . . . *feel* to it that I've never felt before or since. A chill went through me that had nothing to do with the temperature. Premonition, I guess. Whatever it was, I dreaded walking down the hallway to my parents' bedroom.

"But I forced myself. Their bedroom door was open a crack. I peeped in. They weren't dead like I told you, like I've told everyone. My mother was on the bed, propped against the pillows. She was crying.

"Daddy was standing beside the bed. He was holding the pistol at his side and talking to her quietly. I didn't realize until later that he was explaining to her why taking their lives was the only way out of their financial crunch.

"I mistakenly thought he was talking about killing *me*. He was saying things like, 'It's the only way. It'll actually be better for Cathy this way.' He was the only one ever to call me Cathy," she added with a rueful smile.

"I knew I'd cost them a lot of money. But beyond the financial considerations, they'd been put through hell. Instead of fussing over ballet costumes, my mother had to figure out creative ways to cover my hairless head after chemotherapy. My illness had actually changed her more than it changed me. I also recovered faster. Mother didn't bounce back as quickly.

"So when I heard Daddy talking about a speedy solution to all their problems, I figured they were going to snuff me in order to save themselves a lot more grief and expense. This was an eight-year-old's rationale, remember. I understood just enough of what was being said to panic. I crept to my room and hid in the closet."

She paused and pulled her lower lip through her teeth a few times. "While I was crouched there in the dark, I heard the gun blasts. I realized that I'd been wrong. Terribly wrong. That's when I decided to remain hidden forever. I figured that I'd eventually starve to death or die of thirst. Even at that tender age, I had a dramatic flair," she added with another sad smile.

"Finally, one of our neighbors came over to borrow something. When no one answered the door, she came inside and sensed, as I had, that something wasn't right. She discovered Mother and Daddy. I still didn't reveal myself. Not even when the police and ambulance arrived. Someone called the school office and learned that I'd been taken home. Only then did they search the house and find me. I was afraid I'd get into trouble, so I pretended that I'd come home and found my parents already dead. I didn't tell them the truth— that I could have prevented it."

"That's not the truth, Cat."

She vetoed his soft argument with a brusque shake of her head. "If I'd gone into the bedroom—"

"He would probably have killed you too."

"But I'll never know, will I? I should have stopped him.

I should have run outside and screamed for help. I should have done anything but hide. I should have realized what he was about to do—maybe I did, subconsciously."

Alex came around the table and pulled her to her feet. "You were eight years old."

"But I should have understood what was happening. If I hadn't been so cowardly, I could have saved them."

"Is that why you've taken it upon yourself to save everyone else?" He caught her by the shoulders. "Cat, Cat," he whispered, wiping the tears from her cheeks with the pads of his thumbs.

"You're remembering what happened through the mind of an adult. You were a child. Practically a baby. Your parents were weak, not you. They copped out, you didn't." He pulled her close and pressed her head against his chest.

"When I was a cop I saw it happen dozens of times. Someone who'd reached the end of his rope took himself out, and anybody else who happened to be around. If your father had known you were in the house, chances are very good you'd have been blown away too. Believe me."

He held her tighter, lowered his head, kissed her temple. "Hiding in the closet saved your life."

She wasn't entirely convinced, but she grasped every persuasive word. For years she'd needed someone to tell her that she'd done the right thing.

She clung to Alex as tenaciously as she clung to his reassurances. Eventually his lips sought hers, which hungrily reacted to his touch.

Chapter Fifty-two

Desire overtook them. They kissed madly. She loved the scratchy feel of his beard against her face, loved the way his hair curled around her fingers, loved the sight, smell, and taste of him. Loved Alex.

There were still things that needed to be worked out, but now she knew she loved him. When he said, "Let's go upstairs," she placed her hand trustingly in his and followed him.

When they reached the second floor landing, they paused to kiss. It got out of hand. Within seconds they were against the wall, frantically wrestling with clothing until he was planted solidly inside her. It was hard and fast and soon over.

Supporting her on his thighs, he stumbled into the bedroom. Together they fell across the bed. His hands were everywhere at once, moving over her possessively, impatiently stripping off clothing until they were naked.

He nipped her tummy with his teeth and slipped his hands

417

beneath her cheeks. He massaged the backs of her thighs, his fingers making flirting passes between them until she thought she'd die of anticipation.

"God, Alex, touch me."

He separated the lips of her sex, exposing it to the silky strokes of his tongue and the gentle suction of his mouth, which resulted in another orgasm.

Then she reversed position and took his erection into her mouth. She loved the musky taste, the velvety texture of it against her gliding tongue, the firm, smooth feel of it inside her mouth.

She gave herself over entirely to loving him, but he pulled away, rose above her, and entered her swiftly.

Suddenly he became very still and gazed down into her face. She opened her eyes and looked at him, puzzled by this unexpected respite from their frenzied lovemaking.

"This is too important to rush." Holding her stare, he pressed deeper.

She gasped softly. "I love you, Alex. No, don't say something you don't mean. Just kiss me."

His mouth made slow love to hers; their bodies followed suit. Even when it was over, he remained nestled inside her.

"It's never felt like this," she said with a sigh. "Only with you. For the first time, I feel really one with another person. This depth of feeling, this merging of body, mind, and soul is incredible."

He squeezed his eyes shut. In a rough voice, he said, "Yes, it is."

"You know," she said, her words muffled by her pillow, "if we keep this up, I'll have to add another pill to all those I already take."

They lay like spoons beneath the sheet, her bottom fitted snugly against his lap. His arm was curved around her waist, holding her close.

"Birth control, you mean?"

"Hmm."

"Don't bother," he said. "I'll see to it that you don't get pregnant."

"Or we could skip the precautions altogether." Mischievously, she turned her head and grinned at him over her shoulder. "Don't blanch, Pierce. If I got pregnant, the baby would be my responsibility alone."

"The hell it would. But that's not the reason I blanched. You're not supposed to have children, are you?"

"It's not recommended. But several heart transplantees have. So far, mothers and babies are doing great."

"Don't risk it. Too many things can go wrong."

"You're such a pessimist."

"I'm a realist."

"You sound angry. Why? I was only teasing."

He hugged her tighter. "I'm not angry. I just don't want you taking unnecessary chances with your life. It's nothing to tease about."

"I've always wanted a baby," she said wistfully. One couldn't have everything, she reminded herself. And look at how many blessings she'd received, the greatest of which was now holding her protectively. She could feel his breath in her hair. Even that was comforting.

He was so handsome, so virile, so . . . everything. Images flashed through her mind, chronicling every moment they'd spent together.

He must have sensed her silent laughter because he nudged her butt with his knee. "What's so funny?"

"I was just thinking about the threat you issued Cyclops. It was the grossest thing I'd ever heard."

"About tearing out his good eye and—"

"Don't repeat it, for heaven's sake! Where'd you come up with such an expression?"

"Where else? On the streets. Or in the locker room. You

hang out with cops long enough, your mouth starts spewing garbage.''

He'd opened a window of opportunity.

After a moment of silence, she asked quietly, "What happened, Alex? Why did you leave the Houston Police Department?"

"Spicer already told you. I killed somebody.''

"I assume you shot someone in the line of duty.''

He waited a long time before saying anything. No longer relaxed, every muscle in his body had tensed up. "Not just someone. Another cop.''

No wonder it was a blot on his memory. Policemen were like a fraternity. Universally, they regarded one another as brothers. "Do you feel like talking about it?''

"No. But I will.''

"Hunsaker here.''

"Lieutenant, this is Baker.''

"What time is it?''

He switched on the nightstand lamp. Mrs. Hunsaker grumbled and burrowed deeper into her pillow. He hadn't been asleep. The chili he'd eaten for supper was burning a hole in his gut. He kept belching the six-pack he'd drunk with it. He'd been on the verge of getting up to take an antacid when the telephone rang.

"Sorry to call so late,'' his subordinate apologized. "But you told me to let you know soon's I finished that report.''

Baker was a young rookie, still wet behind the ears and eager to please. He treated every pissant assignment as if it were an investigation into the assassination of JFK.

"What report?'' Hunsaker asked around a sour belch.

"On those friends of Cat Delaney's? You gave me a list of names and told me to check 'em out? Well, I just got finished, and wondered should I leave the file on your desk or not?''

"Hell, I'm sorry, Baker. I forgot to tell you. I closed the file on that."

"Oh. Really?" He was clearly disappointed.

"Yeah, Ms. Delaney called late this evening. She located the guy who'd been hassling her in a loony bin in Fort Worth. He confessed to the whole thing. I pulled off the surveillance, but forgot about that report I'd asked you to do. Sorry. At least you'll get overtime, right?"

"Right."

Hunsaker belched again. He needed to pee. "Was there something else, Baker?"

"No . . . well . . . sorta."

"Spit it out, Baker."

"It's just sorta . . . ironic, I guess is the right word. 'Bout that writer. Pierce."

And when Baker told him what he'd uncovered, Hunsaker too thought it was ironic. In fact, it was earthshaking.

"Jesus," he said, dragging his hand down his face. "Stay put, Baker. I'll be there in twenty minutes."

"If it's too painful for you to talk about, Alex, you don't have to."

"I don't want you thinking it's worse than it is. It's already pretty bad."

He took a moment to collect his thoughts. "We'd been trying to shut down this drug ring for years, but they always seemed to be one step ahead of us. Several times they'd squeezed through our net. We'd show up at the distribution center, and they'd have just pulled out.

"We finally got a reliable tip, but it had to be acted on quickly. We scheduled a raid for the Fourth of July. They wouldn't expect it on a holiday.

"The operation was so secret that only the officers directly involved were aware it was coming down. We were all nervous, but eager to nail these bastards.

"We arrived at the house. They hadn't been forewarned this time. The point guys busted in and took them completely by surprise.

"I raced down the hallway toward the bedrooms, kicked in one of the doors, and came face to face with one of our guys. He'd been my partner when we were rookies. It'd be hard to say who was the most surprised.

"I said, 'What the fuck are you doing here? You weren't scheduled on this bust.' And he said, 'That's right, I wasn't.'

"Suddenly it occurred to me what he was doing there. And at the same instant, he went for his gun. I dropped and rolled and aimed. Not at my old partner, not at a man I thought was my friend. But at a dirty cop, a goddamn crack dealer. I shot him in the head."

Against her back, Cat could feel the rise and fall of his chest, the thudding of his heart, and knew how difficult it was for him to talk about it.

"You did what you had to do, Alex."

"I could have wounded him. Instead, I shot to kill."

"He would have killed you."

"Maybe. Probably."

"Surely you were cleared of any wrongdoing."

"Officially. Raids like that have a way of getting fucked up. Something unexpected always happens. When the smoke cleared, a cop was dead, and I had killed him. If an operation goes sour, someone has to take the fall.

"So the word coming out of the department was that this cop was working undercover, and that I mistook him for one of the bad guys and fired my weapon before making positive identification."

"That was grossly unfair!"

"They covered their asses. They didn't want it known that one of Houston's finest was a drug dealer. Instead, he received a hero's funeral, twenty-one-gun salute, the whole shebang."

"Why didn't you speak out?"

"Come forward with the truth?" he said scoffingly. "It would have looked like I invented a lie to cover my mistake. It would've been my word against the department's. Besides, the guy had a wife. She was pregnant with their first kid. I couldn't sling shit on him without it landing on them, too. She didn't know anything about his moonlighting."

"How do you know?"

"I just know. Besides, she never tried to retrieve the money he had stashed away. It stayed in a safe deposit box while she and the baby went to live in Tennessee with her folks."

Cat turned to face him. Lovingly, she touched the scar in his eyebrow. "I'm sorry, Alex. I wish I could undo it for you."

"So do I," he said with a grim smile. "After that, I was like a big boil on the department's butt that just kept festering. I dreaded work every day. The cops who didn't know any better despised me for the alleged screwup. The cops who did know were wary of me, wondering if I'd spill the beans after all. I was a pariah. For all practical purposes my career was over. Eventually I gave them what they wanted—my badge."

"Your first career was over," she amended. "Because that's when you started writing brilliant fiction."

Now she understood why his novels painted unflattering pictures of the inner workings of police departments. His heroes were the mavericks who exposed dirty politicians and cops on the take, usually at tremendous personal sacrifice.

She nuzzled his chest. He sank his fingers into her tangled hair and pulled her head up. "Life's a bitch, all right, but it does have its compensations."

"Such as?" she asked seductively.

"Such as you." Drawing her mouth up to his, he kissed her.

* * *

Cat awoke suddenly, as though someone had called her name.

For several moments she lay tense and motionless, listening. But all she heard was Alex's rhythmic breathing. Gradually her body relaxed. She basked in his warm, protective nearness.

Recalling their recent lovemaking, she blushed at her immodesty. With him, she'd become utterly shameless. She felt free to express her sexuality . . . and, God, it was glorious.

She gazed at his sleeping face. The frown between his eyebrows was now relaxed. The stern line of his mouth had softened. In sleep, he was released from the memory that haunted him.

If she could forgive the frightened young girl who'd hid in the closet, Alex could forgive himself for shooting his former partner. With each other's help, they'd work through their personal nightmares.

Needing to use the bathroom, she eased off the bed, pulled on his shirt, and went downstairs. She didn't want to disturb his sleep by flushing the toilet.

With the help of the streetlight filtering through the blinds, she found her way to the powder room beneath the stairs. When she came out, she realized how wide awake she was.

She'd been up all night the night before. Yesterday had been a long, taxing day. They'd made love until exhaustion overcame them. Yet now, after only a few hours' sleep, she felt refreshed. It was still hours before dawn, but she was too keyed up to go back to bed.

Was she hungry? No.

Thirsty? Not really.

Suddenly, the door to the closed room seemed to shout at her. She stared at it for several moments, knowing she should resist its magnetic pull. But her innate curiosity wouldn't let her.

If she went in now, what would it matter?

Alex hadn't welcomed her intrusion before, but that had been in the early stages of their relationship. They'd barely known each other then. The situation was different now. They'd been intimate, physically and emotionally. They'd shared their secrets. Surely his silly no-trespassing rule no longer applied.

She tried the door and discovered it was locked.

It was just as well. She knew she shouldn't go in before okaying it with him.

Nevertheless, she stood on tiptoes and ran her hand along the top of the jamb, where she found a thin brass key. She took that as a good omen. If he really didn't want her in there, why would he leave the key so accessible?

She inserted the key into the lock. It opened with a soft metallic click. She paused to listen, but there were no sounds coming from upstairs. She went in and closed the door behind her before turning on the light.

The room was a crushing disappointment. If she were designing a writer's retreat, she would make it cozy and interesting. It would have paneled walls, ancient Turkish rugs, and massive leather furniture. Perhaps with a globe standing in one corner. Shelves would be filled with limited first editions and collectibles that reflected light from quaint Tiffany lamps.

Alex's workshop was just that—a workshop. It was utilitarian, disappointingly unattractive, lacking in character, aesthetically void. His computer terminal and printer sat on a folding table with metal legs and a Formica top. Beside it was a fax machine.

He had a quantity of books that ranged from encyclopedias to fiction bestsellers, but they weren't leather-bound and arranged in antique oak bookcases. They were stacked haphazardly on gray metal shelves. The telephone sat on a stack of phone directories.

In the corner of the room was the desk where he obviously did his paperwork. It was cluttered with correspondence, faxes, a bank statement, a coffee-stained legal pad with illegible scribbles connected by arrows and asterisks, and a stack of file folders. The folders had been hand-labeled and had seen a lot of use; their edges were frayed and curled.

Cat's attention moved past the messy paperwork to a framed photograph. She picked it up to take a closer look at the smiling couple. It pictured Alex with a wide, curving mustache. She must remember to tease him about that.

With him in the snapshot was a very pretty young woman. Like him, she was dressed in cut-off jeans and hiking boots. She was perched on a boulder; he was crouched behind her. In the background was a mountain range that looked like the Rockies.

Vacation pictures. He'd shared vacations with this woman.

Cat berated herself for feeling jealous. Naturally Alex had had other romantic involvements. Probably some of them had been serious. She couldn't let one photograph cause her to react like a jealous adolescent.

Forget it, she told herself, returning the frame to its former place.

The wall behind the desk was covered with cork board. Very little of the cork showed because almost every square inch of it was covered. There were typed notes, tear-sheets from newspapers and magazines, and handwritten memos on scraps of paper. Thinking that all the materials posted there must pertain to his work in progress, Cat leaned forward and began scanning them at random.

It took her only moments to realize that they all related to one subject. And it wasn't crime or police corruption. It was organ transplantation, specifically heart transplantation.

One item in particular caught her eye. It was a duplicate of one of the clippings that Paul Reyes had sent her. Except that the one speared by the bright yellow thumbtack on Alex's bulletin board wasn't the photocopy she'd given him weeks ago. This was an original. It was turning yellow at the edges. It was two years old.

Her knees gave way and her bottom landed hard on the desk chair. "Get a grip, Cat," she muttered. It was too early to jump to conclusions. There must be a logical explanation for this. It just hadn't revealed itself yet.

Alex was researching heart transplantation for one of his books. Yes, that was probably it. He hadn't wanted to tell her because . . . Why?

Why hadn't he told her? Why all the secrecy?

The answer might be in the files. The one on top of the stack was labeled AMANDA. Cat flipped back the cover. Her heart jumped. Smiling out at her from a close-up portrait was the same woman as in the vacation snapshot.

She had arresting, laughing eyes, an intelligent face. What exactly had been the nature of her relationship with Alex? Cat wondered. She craved to know, but dreaded finding out.

She moved the photograph aside in order to read the next document in the file. "Oh, God." It was Amanda's death certificate.

Whatever their relationship had been, it had ended with her death. Poor Alex. If he'd been seriously involved with Amanda, losing her must have been tragic for him. That accounted for some of his cynicism. Her untimely death, coupled with the shooting of his former partner, explained why he'd turned to alcohol for comfort. Had he lost Amanda before or after the shooting?

Cat checked the date on the death certificate, and clapped her hand over her mouth to stifle her gasp.

When she started breathing again, it sounded loud and harsh in the silent room. Her heart was racing. Frantically, she pushed aside Amanda's file and read the label on the one beneath it, although she was almost certain what she would read.

DANIEL L. LUCAS, a.k.a. SPARKY.

She knew before looking what name she would read on the next file. She was right. JUDITH REYES.

Hands shaking, she rapidly opened the other folders in the pile. They were labeled with the names of the transplantees who had died under mysterious circumstances. Each file contained extensive notes, detailed descriptions of the fatal accidents, copies of autopsy reports and police reports, files that only a cop—or an extremely clever ex-cop—could obtain.

The last file in the stack was labeled with her name. Shakily she thumbed through it. Her life was well documented, especially the years since her transplant. There were dozens of photographs of her, some years old, some as recent as last week, some posed, others candid, obviously taken with a telephoto lens.

She hastily scanned the other files. They were equally as extensive. It would have taken years to compile this much information. He couldn't have started weeks ago when she asked his help in tracking down her stalker. Hours, days, years of dogged investigation were represented here. Each death had been thoroughly researched—or recounted.

Her mind refused to accept what that implied.

Suddenly the door behind her burst open. Cat sprang from the chair and spun around.

Alex, his eyes glinting murderously, bore down on her.

Chapter Fifty-three

I told you never to come in here.''

Cat's mouth was dry. But rather than show her apprehension, she went on the offensive. ''What are you doing with all this stuff? How'd you collect it? What does it mean? You were interested in heart transplantation long before we met. Why? Who was Amanda?''

''You shouldn't have snooped into my personal files.''

''I want to know why you've got these files, Alex. *Who was Amanda?*'' she repeated loudly.

''A woman I knew.''

''A woman very close to you.''

''Yes.''

''And she died.''

''Yes.''

Behind her back, her hands gripped the edge of the desk. ''According to her death certificate, she died hours before my transplant. Was she by any chance a heart donor?''

After a brief hesitation, he curtly bobbed his head.

"So why didn't you ever mention her to me? Wait!"

Her thoughts were racing past with such confusing speed that she couldn't organize them. Something had triggered her memory of what had been said in conversation the night before last, although now it seemed years ago.

"The wreck on the Houston freeway," she exclaimed. "Jeff mentioned it to me the other night. I'd almost forgotten it. Was Amanda a casualty of that?"

"No."

Air rushed out of her lungs. "Who was she, Alex? Damn you, tell me! You went on vacations together. It was obviously a meaningful relationship."

"Very."

Tears stung her eyes. "You had a very meaningful relationship with a heart donor, but you never mentioned that to me? Why?"

"It doesn't matter. Not any longer."

He moved forward; she took a hasty step backward. "I believe it matters a lot," she said breathlessly. "Otherwise we would have speculated openly about her the way we did Sparky and Judy Reyes. What aren't you telling me about Amanda?"

Feeling as though she was about to suffocate, she clutched her throat and swallowed convulsively. "How did she die?"

"Cat—"

"Answer me! *How did she die?*"

"Of an embolism in her brain. During childbirth."

"Childbirth?" she croaked, barely loud enough to hear. "And the baby? What about the baby?"

"Stillborn. My son strangled on the umbilical cord."

A small cry of anguish escaped her. "*Your* son. Amanda was your wife?"

"We never were married."

"A technicality, right? You were committed to her, and she to you."

"Totally."

"You loved her."

"More than my own life."

Reflexively, Cat swiped at the tears streaming from her eyes. "And you believe I got her heart."

He came toward her with his arms outstretched, but again she recoiled, which made him angry. "Dammit, stop backing away from me. You've got to calm down and listen to me."

"Oh, I'm a good listener," she said with a self-directed scornful laugh. "I take everything at face value. I believe whatever I'm told without question. I never look for double meanings or hidden agendas. I trust blindly."

A sob rose out of her chest with such force that it was painful. "You bastard! You haven't been making love to me! You've been making love to Amanda!"

"Listen—"

"No! I'm through listening." Tormented by the implications of what was happening, she ground the heels of her hands against her temples. "When I think of how elaborately you planned all this . . . And you did plan it, didn't you? It's been one grand charade. The whole thing. Our meeting, everything?"

"Yes," he admitted tersely.

Her chest caved in, forcing another harsh sound from her throat.

"Irene and Charlie Walters had applied for one of your kids," he said rapidly. "I hoped to meet you through them. Eventually. I certainly didn't plan on Irene's brother in Atlanta getting sick, or on you showing up that morning."

"I can't believe this."

"But there you were and I felt an instant . . . something. You felt it, too."

"Love at first sight," she said, sneering. "You think Amanda's heart gave a little leap of recognition when I saw you?"

"Jesus," he muttered, plowing his fingers through his hair. "I don't know what to think anymore. All I know is that I'm in love with you."

"No. You're in love with Amanda."

"What I did was—"

"Despicable. Underhanded. Contemptible. Shitty!"

"All right! You're right. I'm a shit. I admitted that a long time ago." He bit back whatever angry words were to follow. His head dropped forward. For several moments he stared at the floor. Finally he raised his head and said softly, "Before you can forgive me, you'll have to understand how much I loved her."

Cat was too upset to speak. He used her silence as an opportunity to defend himself.

"Amanda pressured me to get married, but I refused because of my job. Sometimes I was gone for days at a time. When I walked out the door, she never knew if she'd see me again, or if some punk would pass his gang's initiation by doing a cop. That kind of life is hell on relationships. I wanted her to feel free to walk out anytime. No strings.

"Shortly after the shit came down in the department, she let herself get pregnant. At first I was angry, then scared. But she was so goddamn positive about the baby that gradually I came to love the idea. The new life growing inside her was like a spark of hope, you know?

"When word got to me that she was in labor, I sped toward the hospital, but I was detained by that pileup on the freeway. When I finally made it there . . ." He rubbed his eyes. "I went a little crazy when the doctor said they'd already declared her brain-dead."

Cat's eyes were still streaming tears, but she was no longer angry. She was captivated by the tragic story. Intermittently she hiccupped small sobs. Otherwise she didn't interrupt.

"The agent from the organ bank introduced herself to me. She didn't pressure me. I'll give her that. She was apologetic for the intrusion at that most difficult time, but reminded me that Amanda had designated on her driver's license that she wished to be an organ donor if anything ever happened to her.

"That's considered a legal document. Even so, she said they wouldn't proceed with retrieval without my permission. Amanda had no living relatives. The decision was entirely up to me.

"Someone desperately needed Amanda's heart, she said. Without it, the other person would die. The organ had to be harvested quickly. Haste was imperative. So if I could please grant permission . . ."

His voice trailed off, and Cat knew he was no longer with her. He was back in that hospital corridor, numbed by grief, being asked for permission to cut out his lover's heart.

"We were together for five years, but I never gave her what she wanted most, and that was my name. It wasn't a popular name around Houston at that time. I thought she'd be better off without it. Or maybe I was just too goddamn selfish.

"I knew I loved her," he continued. "I knew I wanted to live with her and our baby for the rest of my life. But I didn't realize how much I depended on her emotionally until she wasn't there anymore.

"Ironically, I'd resigned from HPD that day, something she'd been urging me to do since the shooting incident. She wanted me to devote all my time to writing. She believed in my talent. At least that's what she told me," he said with a poignant smile.

"After burying her, I emptied our apartment, threw away

all the baby stuff, and stayed drunk for several months. It wasn't until after I got sober and linked up with Arnie that I thought to inquire about her heart recipient.

"Since the procurement agency wouldn't tell me anything, I became obsessed with finding the recipient myself. It haunted me to know that her heart was living inside someone else.

"I began reading newspapers from every major city published on the date of her death and for several weeks afterward. I searched for stories about heart transplants. If recipients are media savvy, they can sometimes discover who their donors are just by reading the headlines. I thought it might work in the reverse.

"I read everything available on the topic. I learned the criteria necessary to make a good organ match. I wrote down those criteria and sketched a profile of the recipient, much as I would for a character in one of my books.

"Your transplant had been a media event. Using former police contacts, bribes, any method I could devise, I learned from hospital personnel in California the time your transplant had taken place. It was cutting it close, but still possible. Your blood types matched. You were comparable in size. The more I researched it, the more convinced I became that you got her heart.

"I was actually planning a move to Los Angeles to try and meet you when it was announced that you were coming to San Antonio. I moved up here from Houston immediately." He paused. "You know the rest."

"I know you're a sneaky, lying son of a bitch."

"At first, yes. Seeing you through that screen door hit me like a blow to the gut. I *knew*," he said, making a fist for emphasis. "I knew I was right. The more I was around you, the more convinced I became. You have traits that are so similar to hers."

"I don't want to hear this."

"Your expressions remind me of her. Your likes and dislikes are the same. You even have the same sense of humor, the same optimistic attitude."

"Stop it!" She covered her ears.

"I had to make love to you, Cat. I had to."

"You used me like a medium."

"Yes," he said, his voice becoming a hiss. "I had to see if I could reach her. Feel her. Touch her just once more."

"Ah, God!" Cat cried, shattered by hearing him admit it.

"And I did feel a cosmic connection. But was it Amanda? Or was it you? What happened between us had been so good that I started feeling guilty for betraying her."

"Surely I wasn't the first woman you'd been with in four years?"

"No. But you're the first one I'd been with where it meant something, where I woke up knowing your last name. That's why I broke it off with you. I no longer trusted my motives. I was falling in love with you, and it had nothing to do with Amanda.

"I no longer wanted to know if you had her heart. I nearly swallowed my tongue that morning you told me you'd asked the organ bank about your donor. Immediately after you left, I called the agency that had retrieved Amanda's heart and canceled my long-standing request for information. If you'd gotten her heart, I didn't want to know. At that point, all I knew or needed to know was that I loved you."

"Do you expect me to believe this drivel? As for this . . ." She swept the files to the floor, scattering their contents. "You've gone to a hell of a lot of trouble for nothing. For all either of us knows, I don't even have her heart!"

"I'm ninety-nine percent sure. I didn't experience that tug of recognition with any of the others."

"It's still only a—" She broke off abruptly when the realization of what he'd just said hit her full force. "The others? The other transplantees? You met them, too?"

Her tears dried instantly and she saw the truth with crystal clarity. "Oh my God. It's *you!*"

"Cat—"

She charged him, ramming both fists into his chest and taking him off guard. He lost his balance and careened into the shelves, knocking books to the floor. Cat ran out the door and slammed it behind her.

She raced down the hall, through the living room, snatching his car keys from the end table. The front door was locked. Her nerveless fingers grappled with the bolt. She heard his bare feet running on the carpet behind her. Without an instant to spare, she shot through the front door and dashed to his car.

He came sprinting after her. "Cat, wait a minute," he shouted.

"So you can kill me like you did them?"

She pushed the gear shift into reverse and tromped on the accelerator. The tires squealed on the pavement and spun out of control. He was almost within grasp of the door handle before she was able to get traction and speed off into the night.

Chapter Fifty-four

‿ঐৎ

Where was that stupid bitch?

Only Kismet wasn't so stupid, Cyclops bitterly reminded himself. Like an asshole, he'd fallen for her act.

For days he'd been mulling over how he could find her. So far, he'd had no brilliant ideas. It would have been a miracle if he had. His brain was pickled. He'd been subsisting on a continuous cycle of booze and drugs.

He'd asked around, but none of his acquaintances knew where any women's shelters were. His inquiries had resulted only in smart-ass remarks about how he couldn't keep his old lady under wraps. They'd laughed at him.

Damn! He had to find her and drag her back, if for no other reason than to save face with his friends. He was even losing the respect of his enemies, which was worse.

When he did get his hands on her—and he was certain it was only a matter of time before she came crawling back to him—he'd make her sorry she'd ever double-crossed him.

She wouldn't have gotten so brave if not for that Delaney broad. The blame for all this really belonged to her. She'd shown up out of nowhere and gotten Kismet worked up about Sparky again.

Keeping Kismet in line was a cinch. All he had to do was threaten the kid and she became as meek as a lamb. There was no limit to what she'd do to protect Sparky's spooky little bastard. But he could hardly control her, much less punish her the way she deserved to be punished, if he couldn't even find her.

Only one person could tell him where Kismet and her whelp were hiding. Well, actually two people, but he'd just as soon not tangle with that Pierce character unless it was absolutely necessary.

In any event, sitting on his butt and brooding wasn't accomplishing anything. He'd thought the situation through till he was sick of thinking. It was time to take action. The heat would have cooled by now. The cops would have other things on their minds; they wouldn't be looking for him.

He came to his feet, reeling drunkenly before gaining enough equilibrium to make his way to the exit of the bar. The night air was chilly and bracing. It sobered him somewhat.

As he mounted his Harley, he patted it as though it were a living thing. When he gunned the powerful engine, he welcomed the familiar thrumming that vibrated up through his thighs and sex and belly. It imbued him with a sense of manliness and confidence, which the fiasco with Cat Delaney had squashed.

If he let that redheaded bitch get away with screwing up his life, he'd just as well hand her a butcher knife and let her castrate him.

"No way in hell," he snarled as he roared off into the night.

* * *

Bill Webster had spent a sleepless night.

For the umpteenth time he checked the clock on Melia's nightstand. It was now past midnight. He threw off the covers and climbed out of bed. His pants were neatly folded over the chair. He was stepping into them when Melia sat up and groggily spoke his name.

"Sorry I woke you," he said. "Go back to sleep."

"Where are you going?"

"It's time I left."

"Now? I thought you told Nancy you'd be away all night."

"I did."

"Then why don't you wait until morning?"

"It is morning."

She frowned, disinclined to split hairs at that ungodly hour. "I hate waking up alone," she said crossly.

"It can't be helped this morning."

"What's your rush?"

"There's something I've got to do."

"At this time of night?"

"The sooner the better," he said cryptically.

She tried her sexy best to lure him back into bed, but couldn't persuade him. He left in a hurry, without even kissing her goodbye.

Alex cursed viciously as he watched the taillights of his car disappear around the corner, but he didn't waste time on regret.

He hurried back inside, ran up the stairs to his bedroom, and pulled on some clothes. He retrieved his revolver from the top bureau drawer, grabbed a handful of bullets, and dropped them into the breast pocket of his shirt as he raced back downstairs.

On his way out the door he glanced at his wristwatch and cursed again.

His motorcycle was still in the shop. So, with the grip of the pistol, he broke out the driver's window of his neighbor's BMW. Within seconds he'd hot-wired the ignition.

As he sped away, he looked at his watch again. He was no more than five minutes behind Cat.

She was too frightened to cry. She would cry later. After he was behind bars and she was safe, she'd give vent to her heartbreak. Right now, she had to concentrate on surviving.

It had been Alex all along. There was a possibility that she had his dear Amanda's heart, so he planned to kill her as he had the others. Today was the day—the anniversary of a day that had meant new life for her, but unbearable grief for him.

He'd said he was haunted by the thought of Amanda's heart beating inside another body. So he had tracked possible recipients and, using his bluffing skills, gotten close enough to kill them without arousing suspicion. Then he conveniently moved on to his next victim and laid the next trap.

Who better to commit such perfect crimes—which the authorities hadn't even deemed crimes—than a former policeman who wrote ingenious novels? He knew how to cover evidence and plug up holes in a plot.

Cat shivered, and only partially because all she had on was his shirt. The leather upholstery was cold against her bare bottom, and her arms and legs were pimpled with goosebumps.

As soon as she reached her house, she would call Lieutenant Hunsaker. But first she had to get there. She kept one eye on the rearview mirror. Although she'd left him afoot, he was resourceful. She half-expected another car to overtake her.

That would be perfect, wouldn't it? He could force her off

an overpass, then speed away. Her death would be ruled an accident, and no one would suspect him because she'd been killed while driving his car. Yes. That would make a believable story. She'd spent the night with him, but had left early in the morning to return home. He'd loaned her his car.

"I can't believe it," he'd say when notified of her death. He would mourn and look bereaved. And they'd believe his innocence.

Just as she had.

Why hadn't she listened to Dean? To Bill? They'd warned her about him. They'd sensed his duplicity. Why hadn't she? His "dark side," as she'd preferred to call it, was so dark it was murderous.

He'd played his role so well, with the finesse and skill of a master. First he'd pursued her, disarming her and charming her. Then he'd spurned her, making her want him even more. Then he'd become her friend and confidant just when she most needed one. And finally he'd become her lover in the strictest sense of the word. She'd professed her love out loud. And all the while—

She was sobbing dryly as she took the exit ramp at triple the recommended speed. She tightly gripped the steering wheel and navigated the few remaining blocks to her house, reminding herself that she couldn't dwell on the personal aspects now. If she lived through this, there would be plenty of time to nurse her broken heart.

She wheeled into her driveway and brought the car to a jarring halt. Shoving open the door, she barreled out and dashed to the house. When she reached the porch steps, she stumbled against someone sitting on the top one. She cried out in alarm.

Her unexpected guest surged to his feet and grabbed her arms.

"Cat! Where have you been?"

She almost collapsed, first from fright, then with relief.

"Jeff, thank God!" Clutching the sleeves of his jacket, she leaned against him and tried to catch her breath. "You've got to help me."

"Good God, Cat, you're virtually . . . Where are your clothes?" he stammered.

"It's a long story." She unlocked her front door and disengaged the alarm. He followed her inside. "I've got to call the police," she told him. "Alex Pierce is the one who's been terrorizing me."

"What?"

"Because of a woman he loved. She died giving birth to their son. He consented for her heart to be harvested."

. While explaining Alex's motivation, she pillaged the contents of her handbag, looking for Lieutenant Hunsaker's business card. "Where is that damn thing? I know it's in here somewhere. I've got to call him right away. Today's the anniversary—"

"I know. I realized it at midnight. I got worried because I hadn't heard from you all day. I came over to see if you were okay and to stay with you if you were alone."

"He'll come after me, Jeff. If for no other reason than to shut me up about the other three murders. He's incredibly resourceful. And relentless. You wouldn't believe how methodically he's carried out his plan."

The doorbell rang, followed by a hard knocking. "Cat!"

They froze. Then Jeff stepped in front of her and faced the door, using his body to shield her. At any other time, Cat would have laughed at his heroic but comic attempt to protect her.

"The police are on their way," Jeff shouted.

"Cat? It's Bill."

She moved Jeff aside and rushed to open the door.

Bill Webster strode in. "What the hell is going on? What are you doing here, Doyle? Cat, why're you dressed like that?"

"Alex Pierce is the one who sent her those clippings," Jeff told him. "He killed those other transplantees and now he's after Cat."

Bill was as astonished by this development as Jeff had been. "How do you know it's Pierce? Where is he now?"

"I just left him." Both men took uneasy glances at her bare legs. She didn't have time to be embarrassed. "I'm calling Lieutenant Hunsaker."

She quickly described to them Alex's locked room, the files she'd discovered, the vast amount of information he had collected. "It all makes sense now," she said. "He must have been gloating on the inside when I pleaded with him to help me find my stalker. He fed me the clues about Sparky. He 'discovered' Paul Reyes and needlessly put that poor man and his family through a terrible ordeal today."

"Who's Reyes?" Bill asked.

She gave them a thumbnail sketch of the trip to Fort Worth. They were as astounded as she by the lengths to which Alex had gone to throw her off track.

"Here it is." She held up Hunsaker's card and reached for the telephone.

"I'll do that while you change," Jeff suggested.

"Thanks." She headed for her bedroom, but Bill detained her.

"Cat, are we still friends? Can you forgive me for Melia?" he asked in an undertone.

It was strange how quickly a life-threatening experience snapped everything into a new perspective. Priorities came into sharper focus. "I was angry and disappointed in you. But it's not my place to forgive you, Bill. And of course we're still friends."

It suddenly struck her as curious that he was there. "What brought you to my door at this hour?"

Before he could answer, Jeff told them that Hunsaker was on his way. "He said he'll be here asap."

"Will you stay with me until he arrives?"

In unison, the two men agreed to. Cat thanked them and retreated to the privacy of her bedroom.

Dr. Dean Spicer laid the plastic key on the dresser and left his hotel room.

It was early. The corridors were deserted. He was alone in the elevator. As he made his way across the lobby, he noticed only one sleepy clerk at the reception desk. The clerk didn't see him.

He'd arrived in San Antonio just after midnight on a flight from LAX that had stopped for an hour layover in Dallas. He had tried to call Cat from D-FW Airport, then again upon his arrival in San Antonio. She hadn't answered either time.

He had considered leaving messages on her answering machine, but decided against it. On the chance that Pierce was there with her, he didn't want to appear a fool and have his voice broadcast into the bedroom where they were making love.

Besides, he was uncertain of the welcome he'd receive from her. The last time they spoke, she'd hung up on him. He'd told her about the fatal shooting of a Houston undercover police officer that was attributed to Pierce. Where Pierce was concerned, she was thinking with her heart rather than her head.

But what woman didn't?

Upon reflection, maybe it was better that he hadn't reached her by telephone. His visit would come as a complete surprise. Although it shouldn't. Today was the anniversary of her transplant.

The street was dark and quiet.

Cyc parked his bike in the deep shadows of a live oak tree at the opposite end of the block and squinted his good eye into focus on Cat Delaney's house.

He recognized the car in the driveway—it belonged to Pierce. There was another car parked at the curb. The lights were on in the front rooms.

"Shit."

Things just weren't working out for him these days. Obviously it would be stupid to barge in while her cop friend was with her.

He was considering his next move, when a man he'd never seen before opened her front door. He said something over his shoulder, then came out onto the porch, closing the door behind him.

He glanced around furtively. Cyclops held his breath, but he went unnoticed in his shadowy hiding place. The man walked quickly to Pierce's car and drove it into the garage. He came out moments later and manually lowered the heavy door. He then hurried to the car at the curb, and, after juggling a set of keys, got in and drove away in the opposite direction from where Cyclops was hiding.

He ruminated on the peculiar activity. He didn't know for certain that the car in the driveway belonged to Pierce, did he? He'd only seen Pierce driving it. It might, in fact, belong to her.

And maybe she had something going with someone besides Pierce. Why else would the dude be leaving her house at this time of morning, real sneaky-like? Now that he'd left, was she alone?

Cyc left his bike beneath the live oak and started up the street on foot.

Cat felt the need to cleanse herself of Alex's touch, his smell, all essence of him. She could spare a few minutes in the tub before Hunsaker arrived. What would happen after that was anybody's guess.

With a heavy sigh, she sank into the hot bubble bath and laid her head against the rim of the tub. She longed to immerse herself just as completely in her despair, to cry until she was hollow. But she couldn't allow her emotions to surface now. She had to be pragmatic, cold, hard, as ruthless as he had been.

Heartless, she thought cynically.

She closed her eyes in an effort to blot out images of Alex, but still she envisioned his face in all its various modes—while making love, while talking intently about his work, while speaking of his devotion to Amanda.

Rising emotion caused a catch in her throat. She cleared it away, impatiently, aggressively. That's probably why she didn't hear the bathroom door open. In fact, if it hadn't been for a faint draft, she probably wouldn't have opened her eyes.

When she did, she jerked erect, sloshing water over the rim of the tub. "What are you doing?"

"Surprised?"

She was stunned. Too stunned even to scream. Bewildered, she watched as her hair dryer was plugged into the wall socket above her dressing table. When the switch was flicked, it began to whir softly.

"I'm sorry, Cat." The sad-sweet smile caused her blood to turn cold. "You're about to become the victim of a tragic accident."

Chapter Fifty-five

*S*hit!"

Alex banged his fist against the BMW's steering wheel. These sons of bitches weren't supposed to run out of gas! Of all the damn luck—to steal a car with an empty gas tank.

He twisted the wheel hard enough to get the car onto the shoulder of the freeway, flung the door open, and took off at a full run. It would serve his yuppie neighbor right if the goddamn thing got stolen and stripped. Out of gas, for crissake!

There was little traffic. He raised his thumb to several passing vehicles, but he doubted that anyone would stop for him. He didn't look very trustworthy—hair uncombed, unshaven, shirttail flapping.

He took the exit ramp, his feet pounding the pavement while he mentally counted the number of blocks he had to cover before reaching Cat's street.

He was afraid to think about what he might find when he got there.

He'd awakened that morning with the solution to the mystery. While he was asleep, his subconscious had worked it out. A key piece to this complicated chessboard had been missing all along. That empty space seemed so glaring to him now. Why hadn't he noticed it before three innocent people were killed? He cursed his stupidity. Everyone in this tangle of intertwined lives was present and accounted for except one.

Unfortunately, it was the lethal one.

Legs pumping, arms churning, he turned a corner and would have maimed himself on a fireplug if he hadn't seen it in the nick of time. He hurdled it, barely breaking stride.

"Live, Cat. Don't die on me. Not you, too."

Cat's teeth were chattering. "Why are you doing this? I don't understand."

"Of course you do. Your death by electrocution will be just like the others. A lamentable accident."

"Well, you couldn't make your intention any plainer than that, could you?"

"Cat Delaney. Ever the joker."

"You won't get away with it this time. Lieutenant Hunsaker is on his way here."

Jeff Doyle merely smiled. "I called time and temperature, not the police."

"Bill—"

"I sent him out on an errand. His unexpected arrival was a glitch, but I devised a way to get rid of him. I suggested that he move his car away from the house, so that when Pierce shows up to do you in, he won't be warned off."

"Very clever."

"Oh yes. I've learned to cover my tracks well. When Bill gets back, he'll find me on the phone demanding to know why Hunsaker isn't here yet. We'll eventually get worried about you and come looking. We'll discover your body.

"I'll get hysterical, as gay men are wont to do in times of stress," he said with a short laugh. "I'll berate myself for not urging you to update the wiring in this old house. You should have had a ground fault interrupter installed to prevent this kind of catastrophe.

"I'll theorize that you were so upset over Pierce's treachery, you weren't thinking straight and reached for your hair dryer. Webster will back my story. He saw how shaken you were to discover that your lover was planning to kill you."

"Which Alex will deny."

"No doubt. But he'll also be implicated in the other deaths when the authorities see that incriminating evidence in his apartment. Thank you for telling me about his secret room, Cat. Apparently he kept extensive files of those interviews."

"Interviews?"

"His interviews with the heart transplantees. He makes quite an impression on people, you know. Each of them mentioned him to me. All were flattered that he'd interviewed them for his book. Mr. Pierce is very clever and extremely charming. None realized that he was actually searching for Amanda's heart.

"Even I fell for his ruse and believed he was researching a book. That is, until I began doing research for you and discovered that his lady love had been a heart donor.

"Once the police find those files, he'll have some fancy explaining to do, won't he?" He gave a high-pitched giggle. "I must admit I was quite taken aback when he suddenly appeared on the scene. I was afraid he'd ruin everything by catching on to me. He obviously began to smell a rat when the heart transplantees he'd interviewed began turning up dead. Granted, a year apart. But to a former crime-solver the pattern would be too curious to ignore.

"Besides wanting to find his Amanda in you, the dear man probably wanted to save you from the same fate as the others. His desire to protect you was really quite noble.

"I even suspected that he was the one who sent you those articles. They threw me for a loop. It made me nervous to learn that someone had figured out my plan. Not that that would have stopped me.

"Pierce did, however, add some excitement. He made the situation more complex and therefore more interesting. The other disposals were almost too easily accomplished. I came to regard him as a challenge. And now he'll make an excellent scapegoat that I hadn't planned on."

He shook his head and smacked his lips with regret. "It doesn't bode well for our bestselling author, does it? Especially considering all those files that he keeps under lock and key. It sounds as though the man is positively obsessed, doesn't it?"

Striking a pensive posture, he added, "Actually, Pierce and I are similarly motivated."

"You mean to find Amanda's heart? You knew her, too?"

"Cat," he said in a chastising tone. "Where's your imagination? Haven't you figured it out yet? Shame on you."

His calm articulation terrified her. If he'd been ranting and raving and frothing at the mouth, she would have feared him less. Instead, his cool logic and soft voice clearly indicated to her his level of madness. He was totally detached from reality.

"As usual, no one will suspect me of wrongdoing," he said. "You blamed Melia for everything that went wrong, never suspecting me. I leaked the O'Connor story to Ron Truitt. I also called him, identified myself as Cyclops, and fed him that malarkey about child molestation. I was afraid he'd recognize my voice during that meeting in Webster's office. But he was too intent on attacking you to pay any attention to me.

"It was tricky to rig the light, but I did that, too. The

damned thing nearly killed you ahead of schedule. It was only supposed to scare you."

His lips formed a moue of remorse. "After suffering so many setbacks, both personal and professional, it will be understandable that you became overwrought, even suicidal, on the anniversary of your transplant.

"I'll move to another part of the country, get a job, and blend into the woodwork again. I can play almost any role, pass myself off as anything. I'm very adaptable. Very average. Very forgettable. People rarely notice me." His eyes turned wistful. "Only Judy thought I was special."

"Judy? Judy Reyes? You're her lover!"

"Ah! You finally figured it out. That's me, the nameless man who escaped that cretin."

In a dramatic mood shift, his eyes suddenly filled with tears. "He brained her with a baseball bat."

"How'd you manage to get away?"

"He stood over her, looking down at what he'd done. He seemed to be fascinated by the amount of blood that pooled beneath her head. He was sort of in a trance and paid no attention to me. I grabbed my clothes and ran. I knew I couldn't do Judy any good. I knew she was dead. I felt her death as keenly as if I'd died myself."

His chest rose and fell with pent-up rage as he recalled that sultry afternoon in Fort Worth. "Judy was very religious, and steeped in the Hispanic culture. Her husband knew how she would feel about her body being butchered."

"She wouldn't have approved of organ donation," Cat said.

She had to keep him talking, in order to give Bill time to return. Her eyes darted around the room, looking for a means of escape or a weapon with which to defend herself. But as long as he held the humming hair dryer over the tub just beyond her grasp, she was afraid even to move. The second she did, he'd drop the dryer and she would be history.

"She would have been mortified by the mere suggestion of it," he was saying. "She would have wanted her body to be buried intact. Reyes knew that. Donating her organs was his way of punishing us for loving each other. He had her dismembered to torture us throughout eternity. The only way I can release us from this curse is to stop her heart."

"By killing the recipient."

"Yes," he said flatly. "As long as her heart goes on beating, her soul will be in torment. I vowed over her grave that I would give her the rest and peace she deserves. So I had to kill that boy."

"The young man in Memphis. How'd you locate him?"

He shrugged as though that had been the easiest part. "I got a job with an organ procurement agency. Soon, I had the ONUS number assigned to Judy's heart and tracked it to him."

"Then, if you'd done what you promised Judy, why the others? Why were they killed? Why kill me?"

"Computers are fallible because people operate them. What if the numbers had been accidentally scrambled?" He shook his head as though that were unthinkable. "I couldn't take a chance on there being a mistake."

"So you decided to eliminate any patient who received a heart that day."

"That's the only way I could guarantee the completion of my mission."

Cat shivered, but tried not to show her mounting terror. "Why'd you wait until the anniversary each year?"

"Otherwise, it would have been an ordinary killing spree. I'm not psychotic. Keeping to the anniversary lends the killings a ceremonious aspect that Judy would've liked. She attended only formal masses. She liked ritual, order, traditional rites. This is the way she would want it."

"You actually believe that she'd be proud of you for murdering three people?"

"She would want me to reunite her with her heart. That's what I'm going to do. Then her soul can cease its search." He wiped the tears from his eyes with the back of his hand.

"I love her too much to let her spirit remain in torment. I'm sorry that you have to die, Cat. I like you very much. But there's simply no other way."

He kissed his fingertips, then pressed them against Cat's chest. "Rest well, Judy, my love. I'll love you forever."

Cat grabbed his hand just as the other one released the hair dryer. She screamed.

The lights went out.

The hair dryer fell into the water but did no more damage than cause a splash.

Jeff cried out in dismay and frustration.

Cat surged up out of the water, but he knocked her back down. She heard his kneecaps crack against the tile floor as he dropped beside the tub. His hands landed hard on the top of her head and pushed it beneath the surface of the water.

He held her down. She struggled, flailing her arms and legs, twisting her head from side to side, clawing his arms. But he didn't let go. Reflexively, she opened her mouth to scream. It filled with bath water.

As if from a distance, she heard footsteps pounding down the hall. The bathroom door crashed open, and suddenly she was free. She raised her head out of the water and gasped for air, choking on the water in her throat and nasal passages. Her hair clung to her face, obscuring her vision, although it was so dark in the bathroom that she couldn't have seen much anyway.

"*Cat?*" It was Alex.

"I'm here."

"Stay out of the way," he shouted.

He had wrestled Jeff to the floor. It would be no contest. Alex was by far the stronger. "You son of a bitch, if you've hurt her—" His threat ended in a grunt of surprise and pain.

"Is she all right?" It was Bill, standing in the open door.

A tongue of flame shot from the barrel of Alex's pistol. The roar ricocheted off the bathroom walls.

Bill went down without a sound.

Alex bellowed in fury.

By now Cat's eyes had adjusted to the darkness. She was able to see that Jeff had somehow managed to get his hands around Alex's pistol. They were struggling for possession.

The side of the porcelain tub was slippery and wet, but Cat scrambled over it. She attacked Jeff's face with her bare hands, pummeling it with her fists, scratching it with her nails, pulling his hair.

He screamed in pain and let go of the pistol, which Alex shoved against the back of his ear as he flipped him over and straddled the small of his back.

"Move," he said, heaving to regain his breath. "Please. I'd enjoy nothing better than to blow your fucking head off."

"Go ahead and shoot me," Jeff sobbed. "I've failed Judy. I want to die."

"Don't tempt me."

Cat picked her way around them, stumbled through the doorway, and tripped over Webster's feet. "Bill?" In the meager light, she saw him sprawled on his back. The stain spreading across the front of his shirt looked as black as ink. "Oh, God, no. No," she whimpered.

Too weak to stand, she crawled to the nightstand and dragged the phone to the floor. She punched out 911.

Then she crawled back to Bill, grasped his hand tightly, and whispered for him to hold on. "Help's on the way," she called to Alex, and was startled by the faintness of her voice.

"How's Webster?" he asked.

"He hasn't moved."

"Christ," she heard him say. "You might have another murder chalked up to you, Mr. Doyle."

Jeff was babbling incoherently.

Cat's teeth were chattering. She grabbed a corner of the bedspread and pulled it toward her. But instead of wrapping herself in it, she spread it over Bill, tucking it around him.

The wail of approaching sirens was the sweetest sound she'd ever heard. She bent over Bill and said urgently, "Hang on, Bill. Help's here. Can you hear me? You'll be all right. You will!" He didn't respond, but she hoped he sensed her presence.

Lieutenant Hunsaker was the first one into the house. "What's wrong with the lights?"

"Fuse box in the kitchen pantry," Alex shouted from the bathroom. "Hit the main breaker switch."

"I need help in the bedroom," Cat called out. "A man's been shot in the chest."

Within seconds the lights came back on. Cat squinted against the sudden brightness. When she reopened her eyes, two paramedics and Hunsaker were squeezing through the bedroom door.

Hunsaker had drawn his pistol. "Okay, Pierce. You're surrounded. Come out with your hands up."

"What the hell are you talking about?" Alex shouted.

'Not Alex. He's apprehended . . ." Unable to say more, Cat gestured toward the open bathroom door.

One of the paramedics nudged her shoulder. "Your friend's in bad shape, ma'am. Move aside and let us help him."

"Will he be all right?"

"We'll do what we can."

In a cautious, crouching position, Hunsaker approached the bathroom door. He held his pistol out in front of him with both hands. "Throw down your gun, Pierce."

"Gladly, you dumb bastard. If you'll cover him."

"Who's that on the floor?"

"Jeff Doyle."

"Is that the sumbitch who called time and temperature and pretended he was talking to me?"

"The surveillance on her phone wasn't canceled yet, right?" Alex asked.

"That's right. Damn good thing, too. Who is this little shit, anyway?"

"It's a long story. Cuff him and read him his rights."

"Just a goddamn minute, Pierce. Don't be telling me who to arrest. I was coming after you."

"Do it," Alex said tightly, pushing Hunsaker out of his way.

He stepped around the paramedics who were bent over Webster, working feverishly to save his life. Cat stood rigid, watching. Alex snatched her robe off the chair and wrapped her in it.

He held her tightly, one strong hand palming her head and holding it against his chest. "Are you all right?" She nodded. "Sure?"

"Yes. Scared. Is Bill—"

"Still alive, I think."

Placing his hand beneath her chin, he turned her face up to his. "That was a damned brave thing you did. He could have shot me, too. Thanks."

Now that it was over, her knees were weak and she was trembling all over. "I'm not brave."

"The hell you're not." He pulled her close again, almost squeezing the breath out of her. "If anything had happened to you . . ." He placed a fervent kiss at her hair line. "I love you, Cat."

"Do you, Alex?" she murmured against his chest. "Is it really *me* you love?"

Chapter Fifty-six

W hat did he say?'' Dean asked. He nodded thanks to the flight attendant who'd brought him a second scotch and water.

"Nothing," Cat replied. "That's when you arrived. It was chaos. Alex and I didn't have another opportunity to speak alone."

"I was planning to surprise you with a bottle of champagne to toast the fourth year of your second life," he said. "Instead, when I reached your house, it was surrounded by police cars, and a body was being loaded into an ambulance. Scared the hell out of me."

She patted his hand, then rested her head against the first-class seat. "I'm so tired. I don't want to talk about it anymore. But I have to. I need to talk it out and then let it go."

After a moment of introspection, she added, "I've learned that it's not good to keep bad memories bottled up. It's better to let them out, air them, analyze them, deal with them, and then bury them for good.''

"Who dispensed those pearls of wisdom?" he asked in a snide tone. "Or need I ask?"

"You promised, Dean," she said, wearily closing her eyes. "No Pierce-bashing."

"Right. But I conceded grudgingly." He sipped his drink. "We've pieced together most of it. But there are several points I'm still unclear on. You said that Bill returned to your house on foot after moving his car. He got there the same time Alex did."

"Yes. Bill saw him racing up the walk and threw a body tackle. He warned Alex that we were on to him and that he and Jeff were there to protect me. Alex told Bill that he was protecting mc from the wrong guy and explained that Jeff had been Judy Reyes's lover.''

"He must have been convincing."

"He's talented that way," she said softly. "Anyhow, Alex called Bill's attention to the absence of Jeff's car. Obviously he'd hidden it so no one would know that he was at my house. Even I wouldn't know until he was inside and it was too late.

"That convinced Bill. He asked what he could do to help. They sneaked around the house, peeping in the windows, trying to see what was going on inside. They wanted it to be a surprise attack."

The cardiologist joined in the telling. "And when Alex saw Jeff holding the hair dryer over your bathtub, he ran to the back of the house, entered through the kitchen window, located the fuse box, and hit the breaker switch. Quick thinking on his part."

"Luckily, he'd noticed the breaker box before that night, so he knew where to find it." She didn't tell him under what circumstances Alex had sneaked into her house twice before.

"Thank God. Another second or two and—''

"Don't remind me," she said, shuddering. "Poor Bill. They finally allowed me to see him this morning before we left. He's still in ICU and very weak, but he'll be fine. Nancy hasn't left his side."

"What brought him to your house at that time of morning?"

"A brainstorm for *Cat's Kids*." She told the white lie to protect the privacy of the Websters.

Miraculously, the stray bullet had gone straight through Bill without hitting any vital organs. He'd suffered shock, loss of blood, entry and exit wounds, but he would recover completely.

That morning, he had asked the ICU nurse for a moment alone with Cat. He thanked her for shaming him into ending his affair with Melia.

"I love Nancy. Without her love and support . . ." He paused, as if speaking drained his energy.

"Until Carla's death, we'd led charmed lives. It was as though we were exempt from the suffering other people experienced. When she was killed, we learned differently.

"I was distraught. I couldn't get over it. I went looking for something that would alleviate the pain. Stupidly, I ended up in a sordid affair with a woman who is the antithesis of my beautiful, gracious wife. I figured I deserved no better. I was punishing myself for not being able to protect Carla from death.

"Melia pestered me until I hired her. Then she insisted on working on *Cat's Kids*. You know the rest. That night you caught us together, you said some things that brought me to my senses. Last night, I realized it had to end. Once I'd made up my mind, I couldn't get out of there fast enough."

He reached for her hand. "I immediately drove to your house to tell you that you'd saved the most important thing in the world to me—my family. Thank you."

"Thank me by getting well. You and I still have a lot of work to do." She kissed his forehead.

Out in the corridor, she met Nancy, who hugged her. "Thank you, Cat."

"For what? If it weren't for me, Bill wouldn't have been shot."

Nancy looked at her, communicating a deeper understanding. "He told me everything. I've forgiven him, but can you forgive me? I . . . I did you a grave disservice for suspecting—"

"It doesn't matter," Cat interrupted. "I value your friendship. And I admire your talent for fund-raising. Can I depend on you to continue working on *Cat's Kids*?"

"As soon as I get Bill up and around."

Dean pulled Cat away from her recollections and back to the present. "Webster and Pierce seem to have formed a mutual admiration society."

She laughed. "Which is odd since they didn't like each other when they first met. Alex felt terrible about letting Jeff get hold of his gun during their struggle. Bill dismissed his apologies. If he'd remained in the kitchen, as Alex had instructed him to do, he wouldn't have been in the line of fire."

"What's to become of this Doyle character?"

She'd watched as Jeff was dragged away in handcuffs and stuffed into the backseat of a squad car. She still had difficulty connecting the sensitive young man who'd worked so diligently on *Cat's Kids*, with a cold-blooded killer.

"When police searched his apartment, they found scrapbooks and old newspapers that made Alex's research look paltry. Obviously he has been obsessed since Judy Reyes's death. Alex says he'll eventually face three counts of murder and two counts of attempted murder. But four states are involved. Extradition. Postponements. It's a legal spaghetti bowl. No matter how it's eventually resolved, he'll spend the rest of his life behind bars." She thought for a minute. "That's three."

"Three what?"

"Three people who're behind bars. Jeff, Paul Reyes, and George Murphy."

"Cyclops. I can't believe he was apprehended just a few blocks from your house. Wonder what his intentions were?"

"They couldn't have been good," she said. "He violently resisted arrest and injured a policeman in the process. The future doesn't look good for George Baby."

She smiled happily. "Thank God Patricia and Michael won't have him haunting their lives anymore. You know, Patricia is already working as an apprentice in a jewelry-making firm. She'll be able to earn a living and hone her skills at the same time. A child psychologist is working with Michael. Now that he no longer lives in fear of Cyclops, he's coming out of his shell like a baby chick."

"And what about Reyes?"

Her smile dimmed. "I feel sorry for him and his family. His sister was pathetically grateful when I called to tell her that he hadn't killed the other transplantees.

"When we were at the psychiatric hospital, he wasn't threatening me. He was *warning* me. According to Jeff's statement to the police, he'd sent Reyes the clippings about the transplantees' deaths. He wanted to let Reyes know that he'd found an ingenious way around his diabolical punishment scheme. Jeff never imagined that those clippings would wind up in my mailbox as a warning.

"In spite of his mental instability, Reyes caught on to their meaning. Somewhere along the way, he'd reached the conclusion that the soap opera actress Cat Delaney had received his wife's heart. Once he recognized the pattern of the killings, he figured that I was next in line, just as Alex did.

"Alex was stalking me, too—in the hope of saving my life. Reyes was more or less of the same mind. He came to San Antonio to keep an eye on me. I guess he learned my home address by following me home from the TV station."

"Why didn't he just call you up, introduce himself, and tell you what he suspected?"

"Even though he was acquitted on a technicality, he brutally killed his wife in a fit of jealous rage. He has a history of mental illness. Would I, or anyone else, have believed him?"

"Valid point."

"As the anniversary date drew near, he grew so stressed out that he returned to the scene of the crime, so to speak. At least that's what his sister hypothesized. Yesterday, I wrote him a letter explaining all that had happened. I thanked him for trying to warn me. I'm not sure he'll understand all of it, but writing to him made me feel better."

She bobbed the ice cubes in her soda, which had remained untouched. "So much tragedy resulted from that single day four years ago."

"And so much good," he said gently, taking her hand.

"Those people died for no reason, Dean."

"But they also lived with their new hearts. Their transplants were worthwhile. If they had it to do over, they'd make the same choice. Their lives were extended. That's all we try to do—give the patient more time. Then destiny takes control. None of us can foresee it or alter it."

"All that's true. I know it up here," she said, pointing to her temple. "I've got to assimilate it here." She touched her breast.

"And where better to do that than on your private beach." He stroked the back of her hand with his thumb. "I'm so glad you'll be close again. I've missed you."

"I'm going back, Dean. *Cat's Kids* has been put on hiatus until I can regroup and hire a new staff, but it's not a closed issue. Not by a long shot. We're discussing the possibility of syndicating to other cities. It would be an enormous undertaking. But think of the number of kids we could help," she said excitedly. "I'm only going to rest in Malibu for a few weeks, then I'm going back."

"What about him? Where does he figure in?"

"Alex." His name slipped from her lips without her even being aware of it. A pang of yearning shot through her. He'd risked his life to save hers, and she would never forget that.

But she would also never forget his deception.

Their entire relationship was founded on a lie of omission. When he told her he loved her, had that been a lie, too? There was only one way to banish all doubt.

"There's something you must do for me, Dean."

"Your wish is my command," he said, salaaming.

"Don't joke. You're not going to like it."

She drew a shaky breath, wondering if, in spite of her resolve, she had the nerve to follow through on this request.

"I want to know if I have Amanda's heart."

He was stunned.

"I know I've always said I didn't want to know anything about my donor. And I don't. Unless it was Amanda. Then I must know."

"Cat—"

She held up both hands, staving off his arguments. "I don't care how you go about finding out. Call in favors, play dirty politics, breach every medical ethic, lie, beg, bribe, steal. You've got the contacts and the know-how to root out the answer."

His eyes bored into hers. "You do realize that it would be in my best interest to refuse?"

"But you won't."

"I could also lie about my findings to protect you from further heartache. That would also be self-serving."

"But you won't do that either. You'll tell me the truth."

"How can you be so sure?"

"Because four years ago, you had the guts to look me

straight in the eye and tell me I might not last very long.''
His image was blurred by her tears. She laid her hand against
his cheek. ''You never hedged on the truth, no matter how
unpleasant or painful it was. I need you to be that kind of
friend again, Dean. I need you to be as brutally honest with
me now as you were when you told me I was dying.''

''And you compare living without him to dying?''

''The only thing worse would be living with him and
always wondering if he loved me for being me, or for being
someone else.''

She reached for his hand and squeezed it hard. ''Find out
if I've got Amanda's heart. Please.''

Chapter Fifty-seven

Something compelled Cat to glance up at the house at the precise moment that Dean stepped to the balcony railing and waved down at her. She waved back and was about to return her gaze to the low tide when another figure appeared beside him.

The wind was flapping the wide brim of her hat. She anchored it more securely to her head with one hand and held the brim with the other so it wouldn't obstruct her view.

Even though he was silhouetted against the sky, she recognized his lean, rangy body, the shape of his head, his stance. He turned and said something to Dean; the two of them shook hands.

Dean looked down at her and waved once again, then disappeared into the house.

She had an impulse to run to him, but she stood her ground, following his progress down the steep incline. When he stepped off the last step into the sand, his cowboy boots sank to the ankles, but he appeared not to notice. His attention was fixed on her, just as she couldn't take her eyes off him.

"Hi."

"Hi."

"I like the hat."

"Thank you."

Hungrily they gazed at each other for what seemed an endless span of time. She finally worked up the wherewithal to say, "This neighborhood is restricted to residents. How'd you get in?"

"I used my powers of persuasion."

"They worked."

"Like a charm."

"And here you are."

"Here I am. And sorely pissed because Spicer answered your door."

"He's been staying here with me. Only as a friend."

"So he said." He rolled his shoulders and said with an air of arrogance, "He's a good sport."

"Did he lose something?"

"Yeah. His sleep-over privileges. He's spent his last night with you—even as a friend. Tonight, I start sleeping over. It'll be the first night of thousands."

"Oh really?"

"Really. I won't take no for an answer, Cat. I gave you time to sort things out. I've held out for three long weeks, and each of those twenty-one days has been pure hell."

"Were you able to write?"

"I wrote like a son of a bitch. 'Round the clock. Nonstop. Until I finished."

"You finished the whole book?"

"All six hundred thirty-two pages. I sent the manuscript to Arnie overnight. He called yesterday and said it was brilliant, the best work I've done. Has 'bestseller' stamped all over it."

He reached out and caught a blowing strand of hair that had escaped her hat. He studied it intently as he rubbed it between his fingers. "Arnie was curious to know why I changed the outline to incorporate a love story."

"To which you said . . . ?"

"That I'd had inspiration." His eyes moved to hers. "I couldn't have written a love story before meeting you, Cat. I thought that part of me had died with Amanda. I was wrong."

He slid his hands around her neck, linking his fingers together at her nape. "I'll hound you until you give in from sheer exhaustion, if that's what it comes to.

"I want to be with Cat Delaney today, tomorrow, forty years from now. I don't care if you've got the heart of a goddamn chimpanzee. I want to see your red hair on the pillow next to mine every morning of my life. I love you."

"And about what I did . . ." He turned his head and gazed out to sea for a long moment before coming back to her. "There was never any closure to my life with Amanda. I never got to apologize for being such a selfish bastard and not marrying her. Never got to say thanks for all the times she listened to me bitch about my troubles. Never got to grieve with her over the loss of our son."

He closed his eyes as though willing her to understand. Then he looked at her bleakly, all cockiness and self-assurance gone. "I never got to say goodbye, Cat. I wanted to tell her goodbye."

"I understand," she said huskily. "In fact, I think I'm very lucky to be loved by a man who has loved so well before."

He folded her hands between his and raised them to his lips. "Can you forgive me?"

"I love you."

He bent his head to kiss her, but caught movement out of the corner of his eye and turned to see a young woman approaching.

"Oh, Sarah, you're back," Cat said. "Did you enjoy your walk?"

"Very much. It's beautiful here."

The slender woman gazed at Alex tentatively from beneath the wide brim of her hat. She had on jeans and sneakers and a Bruins sweatshirt. The sleeves covered her arms to her wrists. Her hair was straight and dark. She had large, coffee-colored eyes.

"Sarah Choate," Cat said, taking her arm and drawing her forward. "This is Alex Pierce. Alex, Sarah's a devoted fan of yours."

"I always enjoy meeting a fan. Hello, Sarah. It's a pleasure."

"Likewise," she replied breathlessly.

He indicated her sweatshirt. "Are you a student at UCLA?"

"Yes, sir. I'm an English major."

"Terrific. What year?"

"Sophomore."

"Sarah's too modest to tell you that she's a genius," Cat said. "She's written several award-winning stories and has had them published."

"I'm impressed," he said. "Congratulations."

She blushed to the roots of her hair. "Thank you. But I'll never be as good as you."

"Do you write fiction?"

"Nonfiction mostly."

Cat said, "Actually, she's written several critically acclaimed articles on her experiences as a heart transplantee."

Alex, who'd obviously been basking in the girl's hero worship, suddenly tensed. His gaze swung from Sarah to Cat, then back to Sarah, who was now looking up at him through a veil of tears.

"Thank you so much." The rushing sounds of surf and

wind muffled her words, but Cat and Alex could easily read her lips, as well as her expressive eyes.

She grabbed Alex's hand and clasped it tightly. "I'm sorry about Amanda and your baby son. Cat told me the hell you went through when you lost them.

"But thank you for making the decision you did. I mean, I know that Amanda had specified on her driver's license that she wished to be an organ donor, but you made good her intentions. Without her heart, I would have died. I owe you my life and can never thank you enough. Never."

Cat held her breath, uncertain what his response would be.

He searched the girl's eyes for a moment, then laid his wide hand over the center of her chest. She didn't recoil. Instead, she smiled.

When she did, he pulled her into his arms. They embraced for several long minutes, rocking back and forth while the wind whipped around them. When at last he released her, his voice was gruff, his eyes suspiciously wet. "Amanda would be very pleased with you. Extremely pleased."

"Thank you," she replied, licking tears off her lips. "For a long time, I didn't want to know anything about my donor or the family. I felt the same as Cat about it. She still doesn't know, and doesn't want to.

"But, not too long ago, I changed my mind. I can't explain why. All of a sudden I felt very strongly that I should look up the person responsible for my new heart and say thank you. So I asked the organ bank for information. I was awaiting word when Dr. Spicer contacted me.

"He explained that the situation was rather unusual, but asked if I would speak with Cat before meeting my donor family. Of course I knew who she was, I said, sure, I'd love to meet her!

"I was really astonished when they told me that my favorite fiction writer was . . . well . . . you know. Cat asked me to stay a few days with her. We've had long talks. She explained everything that happened. She said she didn't think you'd mind if she told me the story about you and Amanda.''

"No," he said. "I don't mind. In fact, I'm very glad we found you, Sarah. It has more significance than you know."

He looked at Cat in a way that made her breath catch in her throat. He slipped his arm around her shoulders and pulled her close to his side.

Sarah must have sensed that she was now a fifth wheel. "Well, I think it's time I left," she said with a knowing smile. "Dr. Spicer promised to drive me back to campus before he's due at the hospital."

She looked at Alex shyly. "I think it was intended that we meet, don't you?"

"Yes, I do."

"Would you mind if I wrote to you every now and then? I won't bug you or anything, I promise. I just thought—"

"If you don't stay in touch, I'll be terribly disappointed. Amanda would be, too. She'd want us to be friends."

Sarah's radiant smile came straight from her heart.

They watched as she made her way up the steps to the deck, where she paused to wave before entering the house.

"She's wonderful," he said.

"I thought you'd like her."

"It sounds crazy, but I wish Amanda could meet her."

"It doesn't sound crazy at all."

He turned to face her and clasped her shoulders. "Thank you."

"I did it for me, too, Alex. I had to know who you really love."

"You know who I love," he whispered.

He kissed her, his mouth open and warm, receiving and giving, full of promise and expectation.

When at last they pulled apart, and before they began another kiss, she took a moment to adore him—the angles of his face, the unruliness of his dark hair, the irregular shape of his eyebrow. And in his eyes she saw love.

"Amanda has my gratitude," she said.

He cocked his head in puzzlement. "She didn't have anything to do with your heart."

"But she had quite a lot to do with yours."

More
Sandra Brown!

**Please turn this page
for a
bonus excerpt from**

The Witness

**a new
Warner Books hardcover
available at
bookstores everywhere**

Prologue

The infant's mouth sucked at his mother's breast.

"He seems like a real happy baby," the nurse observed. "Somehow you can just tell whether or not a baby's contented. I'd say that one is."

Kendall managed only a weak smile. She could barely form a coherent thought, much less engage in conversation. Her mind was still trying to absorb the fact that she and her child had survived the accident.

In the examination room of the hospital's emergency wing, a sheer yellow curtain provided patients with a minimum of privacy from the corridor. Next to the white metal cabinets that stored bandages, syringes, and splints was a stainless steel sink. Kendall sat on a padded table in the center of the cubicle cradling her baby son in her arms.

"How old is he?" the nurse asked.

"Three months."

"Only three months? He's a big one!"

"He's very healthy."

"What'd you say his name is?"

"Kevin."

The nurse smiled down at them, then shook her head in wonder and awe. "It's a miracle that you two walked away from that wreck. Must've been awful for you, honey. Weren't you scared half out of your wits?"

The accident had happened too quickly for fear to register in Kendall's brain. The car was practically on top of the felled tree before it became visible through the downpour. The passenger in the front seat had shouted a warning, and the driver had sharply cut the steering wheel and stomped on the brake, but it had been too late.

Once the tires lost traction on the wet pavement, the car went into a 180-degree spin that propelled it off the road and across the soft, narrow shoulder. It leveled the inadequate barricade. From there, it was a matter of physics and gravity.

Kendall recalled the sounds as the car plunged down the heavily vegetated ravine. Tree limbs scraped off paint, peeled away the rubber nick guards, and knocked off hubcaps. Windows shattered. The car's chassis was brutalized by boulders and tree stumps. Oddly, no one inside the car uttered a sound. She supposed resignation had rendered them silent.

Although she'd anticipated the inevitable final crash, the impact of the car hitting the massive pine tree that blocked its path was incredible.

Inertia forced the rear wheels off the ground. When the car crashed down again, it landed with the graceless, solid thud of a mortally wounded buffalo, then seemed to emit a wheezing death rattle.

In the backseat, strapped in by a seat belt and shoulder harness, Kendall had survived. And even though the car was precariously perched on the steep slope, she had managed to get out of the wreckage with Kevin in her arms.

4

"That's rugged country out there," the nurse observed. "How in the world did you climb out of that ravine?"

It hadn't been easy.

She'd known that the climb back up to the road would be difficult, but she'd underestimated the physical effort it required. Protecting Kevin in the process had made it doubly tough.

The terrain wasn't sympathetic; the weather was downright hostile. The ground was a mush of humus and mud. Covering it was a tangled blanket of undergrowth interspersed with jutting rocks. The wind-driven rain was falling almost horizontally, and in minutes she was soaked to the skin.

The muscles of her arms, legs, and back began to burn with fatigue and strain before she had covered a third of the distance. Her exposed skin had been gouged, scraped, cut, bruised, and lashed. At several points she had thought it was futile and longed to surrender, to stop and sleep until the elements claimed their lives.

But her survival instinct was stronger than that lulling temptation, so she kept going. Using vines and boulders for handgrips and footholds, she had pulled herself up until she finally reached the road, where she began walking to seek help.

She had been on the verge of delirium when a pair of headlights appeared through the rain. Relief and exhaustion overcame her. Rather than run toward the car, she had collapsed to her knees on the center stripe of the narrow country road, waiting for the car to reach her.

Her rescuer was a garrulous woman on her way to a Wednesday night prayer meeting. She drove Kendall to the nearest house and notified the authorities of the accident. It amazed Kendall to learn later that she had walked only a mile from the site of the accident. It had seemed like ten.

She and Kevin had been transported by ambulance to

the nearest community hospital, where they were given thorough examinations. Kevin was uninjured. He had been nursing when the car plunged over the cliff. Acting on instinct, Kendall had clutched him to her breast and bent forward before the shoulder harness caught and held. Her body had protected him.

Her numerous cuts and scrapes were painful but superficial. Splinters of glass had been picked out of her arms individually, an uncomfortable and time-consuming process but insignificant when compared to what she might have suffered. Her wounds were treated with a local antiseptic; she had declined a painkiller because she was breast-feeding.

Besides, now that they had been rescued and medically treated, she had to figure out how to sneak away. Sedated, she would be unable to think straight. In order to plan another disappearance, she needed a clear head.

"Is it okay if the deputy sheriff comes in now?"

"Sheriff?" Kendall repeated. The nurse's question had jarred her from her musings.

"He's been waiting to talk to you ever since they brought you in. He's got to go over the official stuff with you."

"Oh. Of course. Ask him to come in."

Having nursed his fill, Kevin was now sleeping peacefully. Kendall pulled together the hospital tunic that she had been given after stripping off her wet, dirty, bloody clothes and taking a hot shower.

At a signal from the nurse, the local lawman stepped through the curtain and nodded in greeting. "How're you doin', ma'am? Y'all okay?" He politely removed his hat and looked at her with concern.

"We're fine, I think." She cleared her throat and tried for more conviction. "We're fine."

"I'd say y'all're real lucky to be alive and all in one piece, ma'am."

"I agree."

"Easy to see how it happened, what with that felled tree lying across the road and all. Lightning got it. Broke it clean off at ground level. Been storming 'round here for days. Seems like the rain ain't never gonna quit. Floodin' all over the region. Ain't no wonder to me that Bingham Creek sucked your car clean out of sight."

The creek had been no more than ten yards in front of the battered car. Once she had climbed out of the wreckage, she had crouched in the mud and stared at the creek with fascination and fear. The muddy water had crested far above flood level, carrying with it all manner of debris. It roiled around trees that lined its normally placid banks.

She shuddered to think what would have been their fate if the car had skidded a few more yards following its collision with the tree. She had watched in horror as the car slid down the incline and was claimed by the raging creek.

For several moments the car had remained buoyant, bobbing its way to the middle of the swift stream before dipping into a nose dive. Within seconds it had disappeared beneath the churning surface. Besides the cars left on the trunk of the felled pine tree and the deep, parallel furrows plowed by the tires, the accident had left the landscape unscathed.

"Miracle y'all got out in time and didn't drown when it went down," the deputy was saying.

"Not all of us got out," Kendall corrected him in an emotion-husky voice. "There was a passenger in the front seat. She went down with the car."

At the mention of a fatality, the deputy's routine interrogation suddenly became anything but routine. He frowned. "What? A passenger?"

As though watching from outside herself, Kendall saw her face crumple as she began to cry, a delayed reaction to the trauma. "I'm sorry."

The nurse passed her a box of Kleenex and patted her

7

shoulder. "It's okay, honey. After the brave thing you did, you just go right ahead and bawl all you want to."

"Didn't know there was anybody else in the car 'cept you, your baby, and the driver," the deputy said quietly, in deference to her emotional state.

Kendall blotted her nose. "She was in the passenger seat and was already dead when the car went into the creek. She probably died instantly, upon impact."

After making certain that Kevin was unharmed, and noting how quickly the creek was rising, Kendall had approached the passenger side of the car with trepidation almost certain of what she would find. This side had sustained the brunt of the collision. The door was caved in and the window had been broken out.

At a glance, Kendall had known the woman inside was dead. Her pleasant features were no longer recognizable from the facial bones and tissue that had been ravaged. The dashboard and a mishmash of engine parts had been driven into her chest cavity. Her head lolled against the headrest at an unnatural angle.

Ignoring the blood and gore, Kendall had reached in and pressed her fingers against the woman's neck in the vicinity of the carotid artery. She felt no pulse.

"I thought I should try and save the rest of us," she explained to the deputy after describing the scene. "I wish I could have gotten her out, too, but, knowing that she was already dead—"

"Under the circumstances you did what you had to do little lady. You saved the living. Nobody can fault you for the choice you made." He nodded down at the sleeping infant. "You did a damn sight more than anybody could ask of you. How'd you go about getting the driver out?"

After determining that the passenger was dead, Kendall had laid Kevin on the ground and covered his face with a corner of his blanket. Although he would uncomfortable, he would be safe for the moment. The

8

she stumbled around to the other side of the car. The driver's head way slumped over the steering wheel. Swallowing her dread, Kendall had called his name and pressed his shoulder.

She remembered giving it a slight shake, and how startled she'd been when this caused him to flop backward against the seat. She had recoiled as blood trickled from the corner of his slack lips. There was a deep gash on his right temple; otherwise his face was intact. His eyes were closed and still, but at that point she wasn't certain that he was dead. She reached in and placed her hand on his chest.

He had a heartbeat.

Then, without warning, the car had shifted on the uneven ground and slid several feet down the slope, dragging her along with it. Her arm, still inside the car, was nearly wrenched from its socket.

The auto came to a rocking, unsteady rest, but she'd known it was only a matter of time before it would be swallowed by the floodwaters, which were already lapping at the tires. Saturated ground was giving way beneath the weight of the car. There had been no time to contemplate the situation, or to carefully weigh her options, or to consider how badly she wanted to be rid of him.

She had every reason to fear and despise him. But she didn't wish him dead. She would never want that. A life, any life, was worth saving.

So, with a surge of adrenaline, she used her bare hands to scoop aside mud and tear at tenacious vines that prevented her from opening the driver's door.

Finally, she managed to wedge it open, and when she did, his torso slumped into her waiting arms. His bloody head fell onto her shoulder. Beneath his dead weight, she collapsed to her knees.

Wrapping her arms around his chest, she pulled him from beneath the steering wheel. It was a struggle. Several times she lost her footing in the slippery mud and landed hard on her backside. But each time she clambered to her feet, dug her heels in, and put forth enormous effort into pulling him free of the wreckage. His heels had barely cleared the door when the car snapped free of its temporary moorings and slid into the creek.

Kendall related her story, omitting her private thoughts. When she finished, the deputy was practically standing at attention, looking as though he might salute her. "Lady, you'll prob'ly get a medal or something."

"I seriously doubt that," she murmured.

He removed a small spiral notebook and a ballpoint pen from the breast pocket of his shirt. "Name?"

Buying time, she pretended not to understand. "Pardon?"

"Your name?"

The small hospital staff had been kind enough to admit them without first thrusting forms and questionnaires at her. That kind of trusting, informal procedure would be unheard of in a large city hospital. But in rural Georgia, compassion superseded collecting insurance cards.

Now, however, Kendall was faced with the grim realities of her situation, and she wasn't ready to deal with them. She hadn't yet decided what to do, how much to tell, where to go from here.

She had no compunctions about stretching the truth. She had done it before. All her life. Many times. Extensively and elaborately. But lying to the police was serious business. She had never gone quite that far before.

Bowing her head, she massaged her temples and reconsidered asking for a painkiller to muffle her drumming headache. "My name?" she repeated, stalling, praying that a brilliant idea would suddenly occur to her. "Or the name of the woman who died?"

"Let's start with you."

She held her breath for a moment, then said softly, "Kendall."

"That'd be K-e-n-d-a-l-l?" he asked as he wrote it in his notebook.

She nodded.

"Okay, Mrs. Kendall. Was that also the name of the fatality?"

"No, it's Kendall—"

Before she could correct the deputy's mistake, the curtain was whisked aside with a screech of metal rings on an unoiled track. The doctor on call strode in.

Kendall's heart skipped a beat. Breathlessly, she asked, "How is he?"

The doctor grinned. "Alive, thanks to you."

"Has he regained consciousness? Has he said anything? What has he told you?"

"Want to take a look-see for yourself?"

"I . . . I suppose."

"Hey, Doc, hold on a sec. I have some questions to ask her," the deputy complained. "Lots of important paperwork, don'cha know."

"Can't that wait? She's upset, and I can't give her anything to calm her down because she's nursing."

The deputy glanced at the baby, then at Kendall's chest. His face turned the color of a ripe tomato. "Well, I reckon it'll keep for a spell. But it's got to be done."

"Sure, sure," the doctor said.

The nurse lifted Kevin from Kendall's arms. He remained asleep. "I'll find this little precious one a crib in the nursery. Don't worry about him. You go with the doctor."

The deputy fiddled with the brim of his hat while shifting his weight from one foot to the other. "I'll just sit out here. Then, whenever you're ready, ma'am, to, uh, you know, finish up here . . ."

"Have a cup of coffee, why don't you?" the doctor suggested, humoring the officer.

The doctor was young and brash and, in Kendall's estimation, very full of himself. She doubted that the ink on his medical diploma was dry yet, but he obviously enjoyed asserting his limited authority. Without a backward glance at the deputy, he ushered her down the corridor.

"He has a tibial shaft fracture, or your basic broken shinbone," he explained. "There was no displacement, so he won't require surgery, or a rod, etcetera. In that respect, he was extremely lucky. From the way you described the car—"

"The hood was pleated like a paper fan. I don't know why the steering wheel didn't crush his chest."

"Right. I was afraid he'd have busted ribs, internal bleeding, organ damage, but I see no evidence of any. His vital signs have stabilized. That's the good news.

"The bad news is that he took quite a knock on the head. X rays show only a hairline fracture on the skull, but I had to take several dozen stitches to close the wound. It isn't too pretty right now, but eventually his hair'll grow back over it. Won't spoil his good looks too much," he said, smiling down at her.

"He bled quite a lot."

"We've given him a unit of blood just to be on the safe side. He sustained a concussion, but if he's quiet for several days, he'll be okay. With his leg broken like it is, he'll be on crutches for at least a month. He won't have much choice but to lie around, be lazy, and let himself heal. Here we are." He steered her toward a room. "He just regained consciousness a few minutes ago, so he's still groggy."

The doctor went into the dimly lighted room ahead of her. She hesitated on the threshold and surveyed the room. On one wall was an atrocious paint-by-number picture of Jesus ascending into the clouds; an AIDS awareness poster hung on the opposite wall. It was a semiprivate room with two beds, but he was the only patient.

His lower leg, secured in a cast, was propped up on a pillow. He'd been dressed in a hospital gown that reached only to the middle of his thighs. They looked strong and tan against the white sheets, out of keeping with an infirmary.

A nurse was taking his blood pressure. His dark eyebrows were drawn into a frown beneath the wide gauze bandage encircling his head. His hair was matted with dried blood and an antispetic solution. A ghastly number of bruises discolored his arms. The features of his face had been distorted by swelling, contusions, and bruises, but he was recognizable by the vertical cleft in his chin and the hard slant of his mouth, from which protruded a thermometer.

Briskly, the doctor moved to the bedside and consulted the blood pressure reading the nurse had noted on the patient's chart. "Looking better all the time." He also murmured approval when the nurse showed him the patient's current body temperature.

Although Kendall still hesitated just outside the door, the patient's eyes instantly homed in on her. They penetrated the shadowed depths of his eyes, which were sunken and dark from blood loss and pain. But his unflinching stare was as incisive as ever.

The first time she had looked directly into his eyes, she had sensed and respected their keen perception. She had even feared it a little. She still did. He seemed to possess an uncanny ability to see straight into her in a way that was most unsettling.

He had her pegged from their first meeting. He knew a liar when he saw one.

She hoped that his talent for reading her thoughts would serve now to let him know how genuinely sorry she was that he'd been injured. If not for her, the wreck never would have occurred. He had been driving, but it was she who was accountable for the pain and discomfort he was suffering. Realizing this, she was filled with remorse. She was the last person he would want hovering over his hospital bed.

Misreading the cause of her hesitation, the nurse smiled and motioned her forward. "He's decent. You can come in now."

Battling her apprehension, Kendall stepped into the room and gave the patient a faltering smile. "Hi. How do you feel?"

He fixed an unblinking stare on her that lasted for several moments. Finally, he glanced up at the doctor, then at the nurse, before his gaze moved back to Kendall. Then in a weak, hoarse voice, he asked, "Who are you?"

The doctor bent over his patient. "You mean you don't recognize her?"

"No. Am I supposed to? Where am I? *Who* am I?"

The doctor just gaped at his patient. The nurse stood dumbfounded, the hose of the blood pressure gauge dangling from her hand. Kendall appeared stunned, although she felt her emotions rioting. Her mind scurried to assimilate this shocking twist and how she might use it to her advantage.

The doctor was the first to recover. With a bravado belied by his weak smile, he said, "Well, it seems that the concussion has left our patient with amnesia. This frequently happens. It's temporary, I'm sure. Nothing to worry about. You'll laugh over it in a day or two."

He turned to Kendall. "For now, you're our only source of information. Guess you'd better tell us—and tell him—who he is."

She hesitated so long that the moment stretched taut. The doctor and nurse looked at her expectantly. The man in the hospital bed seemed both interested in and wary of her answer. His eyes narrowed suspiciously, but Kendall could tell that, miraculously, he genuinely remembered nothing. *Nothing!*

This was a blessing unforeseen, an incredibly generous gift of fate. It was almost too good, almost overwhelming, too intricate to handle without having time to prepare. But she knew one thing for certain: She would be a fool not to seize it with both hands.

with remarkable calm, she declared, "he's my husband."

14